Rudyard Kipling

A DIVERSITY OF
CREATURES

EDITED
BY PAUL DRIVER

PENGUIN BOOKS

PENGUIN BOOKS

Published by the Penguin Group
Penguin Books Ltd, 27 Wrights Lane, London W8 5TZ, England
Penguin Books USA Inc., 375 Hudson Street, New York, New York 10014, USA
Penguin Books Australia Ltd, Ringwood, Victoria, Australia
Penguin Books Canada Ltd, 10 Alcorn Avenue, Toronto, Ontario, Canada M4V 3B2
Penguin Books (NZ) Ltd, 182–190 Wairau Road, Auckland 10, New Zealand

Penguin Books Ltd, Registered Offices: Harmondsworth, Middlesex, England

Published in Penguin Classics 1987
Reprinted in Penguin Books 1994
1 3 5 7 9 10 8 6 4 2

Introduction and Notes Copyright © Paul Driver, 1987
All rights reserved

Printed in England by Clays Ltd, St Ives plc
Typeset in 10/11 pt Monophoto Ehrhardt 453

A DIVERSITY OF CREATURES

Rudyard Joseph Kipling was born in Bombay in 1865. His father, John Lockwood Kipling, was the author and illustrator of *Beast and Man in India* and his mother, Alice, was the sister of Lady Burne-Jones. In 1871 Kipling was brought home from India and spent five unhappy years with a foster family in Southsea, an experience he later drew on in *The Light That Failed* (1890). The years he spent at the United Services College, a school for officers' children, are depicted in *Stalky and Co.* (1899) and the character of Beetle is something of a self-portrait. It was during his time at the college that he began writing poetry and *Schoolboy Lyrics* was published privately in 1881. In the following year he started work as a journalist in India, and while there produced a body of work, stories, sketches and poems – notably *Plain Tales from the Hills* (1888) – which made him an instant literary celebrity when he returned to England in 1889. *Barrack Room Ballads* (1892) contains some of his most popular pieces, including 'Mandalay', 'Gunga Din' and 'Danny Deever'. In this collection Kipling experimented with form and dialect, notably the cockney accent of the soldier poems, but the influence of hymns, music-hall songs, ballads and public poetry can be found throughout his verse.

In 1892 he married an American, Caroline Balestier, and from 1892 to 1896 they lived in Vermont where Kipling wrote *The Jungle Book*, published in 1894. In 1901 came *Kim* and in 1902 the *Just So Stories*. Tales of every kind – including historical and science fiction – continued to flow from his pen, but *Kim* is generally thought to be his greatest long work, putting him high among the chroniclers of British expansion.

From 1902 Kipling made his home in Sussex, but he continued to travel widely and caught his first glimpse of warfare in South Africa, where he wrote some excellent reportage on the Boer War. However, many of the views he expressed were rejected by anti-imperialists who accused him of jingoism and love of violence. Though rich and successful, he never again enjoyed the literary esteem of his early years. With the onset of the Great War his work became a great deal more sombre. The stories he subsequently wrote, *A Diversity of Creatures* (1917), *Debits and Credits* (1926) and *Limits and Renewals* (1932) are now thought by many to contain some of his finest writing. The death of his only son in 1915 also contributed to a new inwardness of vision.

Kipling refused to accept the role of Poet Laureate and other civil honours, but he was the first English writer to be awarded the Nobel Prize, in 1907. He died in 1936 and his autobiographical fragment *Something of Myself* was published the following year.

•

Paul Driver was born in Manchester in 1954. He read English at Oxford from 1972 to 1979. Subsequently he has worked as a music critic and freelance writer in London and, during 1983–4, Boston, Massachusetts.

Contents

Introduction

The creatures depicted within are diverse indeed – sky patrollers of the future, Sussex peasants, neurotic society-folk, Stalky & Co. forty years on, American parvenus, elderly women incongruously exposed to the horrors of the First World War, the members of two English village casts, and a cock-eyed dog. 'I was quite free to return thanks yet once more to Allah for the diversity of His creatures in His adorable world,' says the narrator of 'The Honours of War', ironically; and the indefinite article of the book's title is perhaps slightly wilful – here is not so much the marvellous panoply of existence as a selection of its peculiarities. The modern reader, unfamiliar with the contexts of many of the stories, may find his literary abilities sorely tested by so much strangeness suddenly presented. Kipling's *métier* – the short tale – is not, one hears, a currently popular one: the reader of today, used to the blandishments of television and cinema, resents the effort of reacclimatizing himself to a succession of fictional worlds. But far from allowing for this, Kipling's fiction determinedly makes the reader work: he will likely be at once plunged into the middle of things, surrounded by a babble of exactly rendered dialects, daunted by the technicalities of a profession, science or trade, and disoriented by narrative frames and all the finicky precision of an essentially Pre-Raphaelite craft. The symbolic structure of the more ambitious Kipling stories (though none in this book have the complexity and elusiveness of ' "They" ', 'Mrs Bathurst' or 'Dayspring Mishandled') is usually difficult to follow and absorb. His endings are often as perplexing, moreover, as his beginnings – elliptical or blunt, and unfulfilling. Entering and exiting from a Kipling story are, in short, problematic literary activities; while in between are encountered all the interpretive difficulties posed by his wide and curious tonal spectrum, and his oblique yet readily embarrassing authorial presence.

At their worst, his tales may seem to add up precisely to what

Introduction

Tom Paulin, writing on the short-story collection as a form, calls 'a surfeit of chill privacies'. In the present volume, 'The Horse Marines' is a particularly exasperating example of Kipling's most mannered, jargonish style. (In *The Strange Ride of Rudyard Kipling* (Secker and Warburg, 1977) Angus Wilson speaks of the 'empty narrative device' – Pyecroft – as 'an intrusive unfunny "funny" voice in . . . tales of motoring larks on shore', in 'Steam Tactics' and this story.) 'The Vortex' also labours excessively at tone of voice, and is not easy for the reader to assimilate. The deflationary note of the opening pages is wavering; the characterization is over-zealous and cramped; and in spite of one of Kipling's marvellously literate lists, evoking the life of the English road ('one renewed and unreasoned orgy of delight'), the mind's eye of the reader is likely to remain filmed-over until the village farce with bees gets underway and the writing gains focus. Kipling's angle of vision and kind of authorial sympathy so often seem uncertain and offbeam. The reader is seldom carried along from the first sentence of a story in the way he is frequently seduced by the clearly delineated beginnings of tales by James or Conrad – both contemporaries of Kipling. Comparison is instructive. The peculiar terms of the writer-reader exchange in Kipling almost amount to a gentleman's agreement – nothing is too strongly emphasized or too carefully clarified, and in spite of his numerous exegetical problems, the reader is hardly invited to enjoy the sort of single-minded participation in the narrative process appropriate to the relatively conventional, lucidly ironic, tales of Conrad or James. Whereas James teases out his subject into the fullest consciousness (even dramatizing the business of 'knowing' in stories like *The Turn of the Screw*), and Conrad compels his reader with the suspenseful unravelling of a 'yarn', Kipling prefers to assume knowledge, limit suspense, and situate events rather by an urbane itemizing of local detail than the application of a few bold and basic strokes. His stories float on a sea of suggestion, and the reader is expected to be able to swim.

At their best, the stories make refractoriness and soft-focused irony a distinct virtue – they become highly original narratives of a strange, thematically unusual, static, richly scrutinizing, and – to be sure – essentially verbal kind. Most of the time in *A Diversity of Creatures* Kipling comfortably and fascinatingly transcends his apparent limitations. He achieves consummate success with two or three of the stories ('Friendly Brook', '"Swept and Garnished"', 'Mary Postgate'), and in the others, as in virtually all his productions, there is a guaranteed minimum interest deriving from the sheer written-ness of the artefact. Few prose-writers have taken such pains over sentence-construction as Kipling: also a great verse-writer, he applies as much effort to the one medium as to the other. Not even the work of James and Conrad is as *written* as Kipling's, who avoids the excessive periphrasis of the former and the labori-ousness of the latter. Kipling's greatest mastery lies in an inti-mate, fundamental rapport with words, which was for him both an aural and oral familiarity: 'There is no line of my verse or prose which has not been mouthed till the tongue had made all smooth, and memory, after many recitals, has mechanically skipped the grosser superfluities,' he declared in *Something of Myself* (Macmillan, 1937) – in part a *vade-mecum* for writers – having eloquently spoken of his 'experiments in the weights, colours, perfumes, and attributes of words in relation to other words, either as read aloud so that they may hold the ear, or, scattered over the page, draw the eye'. He has been criticized for a *too* scrupulous regard in these matters, as he has for the habit of intense compression, which went with a sifting and savouring of his texts often prolonged over many years; yet such assiduity was the *sine qua non* of his writing. When he talks of working the material of the *Rewards and Fairies* volume, 'in three or four overlaid tints and textures, which might or might not reveal themselves according to the shifting light of sex, youth, and experience', he is doing so rather un-selfconsciously, as a painter-by-other-means, an inheritor of Pre-Raphaelite aesthetic approaches and values. His 'brush-strokes' of composition could be literal ones: he recommends using a camel-hair brush, 'proportionate to the inter-spaces of your lines', with 'as much as suffices' of 'well-ground Indian Ink', when performing the tasks of 'Higher Editing'. Kipling is painterly where Henry James was pictorial-minded; and one of the reasons for his relative failure with longer fiction was no doubt this miniaturizing attention to sentences. The 'built book' for him had to be an elaborate compilation of stories and poems (sometimes illustrations); could not, for reasons of his creative temperament, be a 'novel', with its conceptual rather than exclusively literate structure, although he dreamed for years of 'building a veritable three-decker ... worthy to lie alongside *The Cloister and the Hearth*'. The word itself was all in all for Kipling. He affixed to his Royal Academy address, 'Literature', the epigraph, 'I am Earth, overtaking all things except words. They alone escape me. Therefore, I lie heavy on their makers.' The collection containing this speech is called *A Book of Words* (Macmillan, 1928).

The absolute infatuation with words reflects Kipling's dual nature as both a sort of literary plumber – an eminently practical man of the imagination – and one for whom the mystical 'rightness' of artistic detail was achieved at the promptings of what he called 'It' or his 'Daemon'. (Note the coincidence of these writing metaphors when, in *Something of Myself*, Kipling knows that his Daemon was with him 'because when [the *Jungle Books*, *Kim* and both Puck books] were finished they said so themselves with, almost, the water-hammer click of a tap turned off'.) This infatuation is a state of affairs to which all critical questions about Kipling's poems and fiction should perhaps be referred. When characters behave in a way where moral or psychological or logical endorsement is not forthcoming, where a certain hollowness or end-stopped quality appears in the narrative – whose *personae* by no means step out confidently into the real world of experience – we might take into account the purely verbal satisfaction on offer, satisfaction of phrase-, sentence- and paragraph-structure, and that more impalpable satisfaction – the author's and ours alike – of sensing that a given subject has been tricked out in words, neatly parcelled and tied; that a body of material has been used up. All artistic practice remembers the childish pleasure of making mud-pies, and Kipling's art is more atavistic than most.

Written-ness is what gives unity to Kipling's career: the *Plain Tales from the Hills*, with their irresistible journalistic freshness, are linked thereby to complex and problematic later tales like 'Dayspring Mishandled', apropos of which John Bayley is led to comment (in *The Uses of Division*, Chatto and Windus, 1976) that 'characteristically [Kipling] prefers to present himself as a technician rather than a creator'. And written-ness — sheer directed verbal energy, a vector of style, not merely 'fine writing' — brings together the popular and specialist images of Kipling the author; for the verses which, travelling around the globe, in and out of languages, made Kipling the most quoted English poet since Shakespeare, are not firmer of facture than the symbolical stories, nor are the latter always more abstruse in matters of syntax, tonality and mood: '"If"' and '"They"' are in closer proximity than at first appears. There was, and still lingers, Edmund Wilson's 'Kipling that Nobody Read' (*The Wound and the Bow*, 1929), paralleling the one whom everybody read but who had 'in a sense been dropped out of modern literature'; yet Kipling the Daemon-driven virtuoso with words is a true description of him at all stages, in all aspects. If there is a real enough division between the man given to political exhortation in public and the writer secluded in Sussex under the dire aegis of a wife, there is hardly any essential distinction between Kipling's occasions for literary expression and the different forms (poem, ballad, tale, children's piece) they take. It is time to discard the 'other' Kipling, and to recognize that a brilliant deployment of words — in poems often as dense as they are felicitous — certainly needn't be at the expense of popular appeal. Shakespeare provides an example and Elgar — whom Kipling resembles in so many ways — an analogy: for a long time there appeared the public, popular Elgar of *Pomp and Circumstance* and beside him the private, recherché composer of works like the Cello Concerto; but the two figures were actually one, and the works closely allied in craft (Kipling's popular and private work is more unified still). Audiences to-day can respond with equal alacrity to both musical styles, and accept Elgar whole.

Kipling's development may then be accurately seen as a succession of affiliations for subjects and methods — a sequence of fresh appetites — rather than as the standard, unitary progression through early, middle and late spiritual stations: distinctions should be chiefly of compositional kind rather than spiritual degree. As T. S. Eliot (commenting on the later verse in his introduction to *A Choice of Kipling's Verse*, Faber, 1941) confesses: 'just as, with Kipling, the term 'development' does not seem quite right, so neither does the term 'experimentation'. There is great variety, and there are some very remarkable innovations indeed ... But there were equally original inventions earlier ... and there are too, among the later poems, some very fine ones cast in more conventional form ...' He reiterates: 'in Kipling as a poet there is no development, but mutation ... for development we must look to changes in the environment and in the man himself.' One can generally guess the date of Kipling's stories, but here again his 'development' is, properly speaking, a stylistic mutation: the later stories develop the earlier primarily, one might say, by the application of 'overlaid tints and textures', which varyingly reveal themselves to the reader.

Kipling's very presumption to write both verse and prose, and to print it side by side (a device apparently learned from Peacock) has caused critical worry: T. S. Eliot contorts himself searching for a formula to define the writer of 'verse' (ballads) as opposed to 'poems', and of prose that is inseparable from his verse. (George Orwell, in 'Rudyard Kipling', *Horizon*, February 1942, who in trying to refute Eliot ends up equivocating just as much, arrives at the absurd formula of the 'good bad poet', and tells us that a 'good bad poem' is 'a graceful monument to the obvious' – not a very happy tribute to Kipling.) Eliot's conclusion, that Kipling was 'completely ambidextrous ... completely able to express himself in verse or prose', but whose 'necessity for often expressing the same thing in a story and in a poem is a much deeper necessity than that merely to exhibit skill' is, I think, a completely true one. His Daemon brought about that necessity; and the resulting volumes in 'mixed form' are complexly and fascinatingly inwrought. *A Diversity of Creatures* is no exception.

The poems here interleaved between stories include half a dozen of Kipling's (deservedly) most famous; and reading them in context can show them in a markedly unfamiliar light. The anti-democratic ironies of 'MacDonough's Song' are lost without the foregoing tale, 'As Easy as A.B.C.', which literally would not make sense without the poem (in this case it is part of the story's action). 'The Land', with its celebrated last line, 'For whoever pays the taxes old Mus' Hobden owns the land', comes more profoundly after 'Friendly Brook', whose account of Sussex rural life is as hard-headed and convincing as any, than it would have come, say, after the rather sentimental story 'An Habitation Enforced' (in *Actions and Reactions*), to which it might seem more logically applicable. The juxtaposition of 'The Honours of War' – an emotionally disengaged farce – and the poem 'The Children' – an intensely felt, sardonic World War threnody – is intriguing to ponder. 'Rebirth' follows 'The Edge of Evening', as the metaphysical hard on the heels of the physical: the poem is a Hardyesque vision of life before things went wrong, cast in poignant stanzas, the story a queer, semi-farcical business of rich Americans staying in an English country house which is visited in the evening by a German biplane; the connection seems to be an arbitrary lexical one, both poem and story exploring the word 'edge'. '"My Son's Wife"' is followed by two poems: 'The Floods', which connects with it straightforwardly, and 'The Fabulists', which has no obvious connection, but is impressive enough (as elaborate as a rondel; and a poet's profound complaint) for Eliot to have singled out and fully quoted it in his essay. The placement of 'The Beginnings' after 'Mary Postgate' (and at the end of the book, like an ominous farewell) has been criticized: the poem's message, it is claimed, too bluntly asserts the story's meaning; and indeed, there would seem to be a collision here between Kipling's extreme subtlety and his monumental obviousness. Yet the juxtaposition involves some fluctuations of irony (as with 'MacDonough's Song' and 'As Easy as A.B.C.'): the exercise of practical hatred has, after all, brought Mary Postgate a sort of sexual satisfaction; and while there is a repugnant hint of Kitchener and poster-art about the poem, it also has a balladic note which is soothing after the story, and it contains the striking line, 'They were icy willing to wait'.

Kipling published *A Diversity of Creatures* in 1917; all the stories except 'The Village that Voted the Earth was Flat' and '"My Son's Wife"' had appeared earlier in magazines; in composition some date back to 1908 ('Regulus'). It is one of his best books, arguably the most distinguished example of his 'mixed form'. His antepenultimate book of stories and poems, it combines directness and obliquity in mostly satisfying and engaging ways. Two outstanding stories, '"Swept and Garnished"' and 'Mary Postgate', achieve a notable lucidity of utterance, and although a group of the stories, as I have mentioned, is less than ideally clear of focus, and 'In the Presence' exceedingly slight (it doesn't get a mention in Angus Wilson's comprehensive study), many of them are happily poised between Kipling's mature and later compositional manners.

The volume opens with what an anonymous reviewer (in the *Athenaeum*, May 1917) thought was 'perhaps the finest short story of the future ever written': 'As Easy as A.B.C.'. It is a follow-up to 'With the Night Mail' from the *Actions and Reactions* collection. The A.B.C., or Aerial Board of Control, is the controlling body of an international, somewhat Shavian utopia – though a rather listless and complacent one – whose chief priority is the maintenance of interplanetary traffic ('Transportation is Civilization. Democracy is Disease') and the limiting, thereby, of crowds. A resurgence of crowd-behaviour in the undemocratic bastion of Chicago brings the multi-racial, chatty and picturesquely-named (De Forest, Dragomiroff, Takahira, Pirolo) representatives of the Board into action. With their immobilizing, benign 'ray' they rapidly control the situation and dispatch the insurgents to a London seen as 'an untouched primitive community, with all the old ideas', where their preaching will pass unnoticed because 'Londoners talk for hours – like you.' The science-fiction apparatus – airship, ray, 'ground-circuiting', and so on – is skilfully wielded. The ray used by the A.B.C. ('a thin thread of almost intolerable light, let down from heaven at an immense distance – one vertical hairsbreadth of frozen lightning') can be associated both with enlightened attitudes in the Punjab of Kipling's cub-reporter days, when 'killing in Civil Administration was ... reckoned confession of failure' (*Something of Myself*), and with the imagery of extreme psychological states often appearing in his stories (cf. 'In the Same Boat') and discussed in the marvellous Royal Geographical Society address in February 1914, 'Some Aspects of Travel' (*A Book of Words*) – a speech almost as future-prophesying (travel in a real, existential sense is doomed by the coming, clearly envisioned, of commercial aircraft) as the story in question. The satirical touch in 'As Easy as A.B.C.' is not too heavy, its comic tone discreet if a little peculiar, its welter of talk not too discouraging. The tale has a written perfection, and its indirect theme – the vitalizing nature of the very democratic forces which it, and its author, want to subdue – is wryly satisfactory.

If 'As Easy as A.B.C.' is a group-life story typical of Kipling, 'In the Same Boat' is a rarer example of focus on individual consciousness – albeit pathologically disturbed consciousness that is selected for an examination which is notably breezy and outward-looking, not at all introspective. The protagonists – a most unhappy, well-to-do young man and a beautiful, rich, Northern young woman, who have not previously met – share repeated night train-journeys in a mutual effort to stave off, without resorting to drugs, the spasms of black despair which regularly and simultaneously afflict them. These extreme states are memorably described: '"Well," said Conroy, twisting in the chair, "I'm no musician, but suppose you were a violin-string – vibrating – and someone put his finger on you? As if a finger were put on the naked soul! Awful!"' The therapeutic journeys (in the company of the slightly comic Nurse Blaber) are evoked with surprising charm and all the romance of trains. The other, inevitable romance theme is merely a contrapuntal thread in a narrative devoted to much more unusual matter. The outcome is implausible and ingenious: the mothers of both man and woman experienced physical trauma while pregnant with them. This knowledge neatly ensures the characters' immediate recovery; they do not marry, as the appended poem, 'Helen all Alone' goes on to explain.

Kipling's tales of depression and its cure are valuable for their literary rarity and the searing conviction with which they make disturbance vivid. The Shared agony of 'In the Same Boat' is rendered with tight drama:

Presently her soul came back and stood behind her eyes – only thing that had life in all that place – stood and looked for Conroy's soul. He too was fettered in every limb, but somewhere at an immense distance he heard his heart going about its work as the engine-room carries on through and beneath the all but overwhelming wave.

and a dazzling stroke of bathos:

The rest was darkness through which some distant planet spun while cymbals clashed. (Beyond Farnborough the 10.8 rolls out many empty milk-cans at every halt.) Then a body came to life with intolerable pricklings. Limb by limb, after agonies of terror, that body returned to him . . .

The descent of general depression ('like a light of blackness turned on us') upon the inhabitants of Holmescroft in the superb Sherlockian story, 'The House Surgeon', from *Actions and Reactions*, is even more alarmingly real. Here, as in 'In the Same Boat' and the present volume's 'The Dog Hervey', story-telling finds an intriguing niche on the border of the super-natural and psychological: ghosts are laid (by means of a certain amount of detective work), and neuroses are seen to be cured. It has been remarked that the deductive practices of Sherlock Holmes and Sigmund Freud were not altogether dissimilar (cf. *Sherlock Holmes and the Case of Dr Freud*, by Michael Shepherd, Tavistock, 1985); in such tales as these Kipling has unwittingly made the likeness clear and brought the two into happy textual partnership. It is an achievement quite distinct from Henry James's in his ghost stories: less deep, though more urgent.

Kipling's personal experience of mental torment is amply proven. Who but a chronic sufferer would have devised a 'Hymn to Physical Pain' (*Limits and Renewals*):

> Wherefore we praise Thee in the deep,
> And on our beds we pray
> For Thy return that Thou mays't keep
> The Pains of Hell at bay!

and who else could have written that morbid, ingrown, tor-mented story of 'The Dog Hervey', the inscrutable, inescapable dog, diabolic version of the friendly Four-Feet 'trotting behind' from *Limits and Renewals*? 'Where I sat, he sat and stared; where I walked, he walked beside, head stiffly slewed over one shoulder in single-barrelled contemplation of me.' The blurred spaces of the unconscious, where Holmes found clues and Freud looked for them, are nicely annexed by this story:

Miss Sichliffe, her hands joined across her long knees, drawled, 'You ought always to verify your quotations.'

It was not a kindly thrust, but something in the word 'quotation' set the automatic side of my brain at work on some shadow of a word or phrase that kept itself out of memory's reach as a cat sits just beyond a dog's jump.

The plot turns out to hinge on a remark of Dr Johnson's ('If you call a dog Hervey, I shall love him') and, as it were, on the discrepancy of spelling between the story's title (Hervey) and the story's dog (Harvey) – a stratagem worthy of Raymond Roussel.

'"My Son's Wife"' has connections with Kipling's neurotic and healing stories, and also with his investigations of rural life –'An Habitation Enforced' and 'Friendly Brook'. Frankwell Midmore, suffering from 'the disease of the century' – i.e. leisured and Bloomsburyish intellectual posturing – is cured by a literal immersion in the all too sympathetically observed ways of Sussex and The Land. What the characters in 'Friendly Brook' would call his 'Lunnon ways' are washed out of him by a splendidly dramatized flood (the succeeding poem takes up the theme). He ends up marrying a huntin' lady and turning his back on the London life, which nonetheless remains for the reader scarcely to be despised in the manner prescribed. There are some excellent vignettes in the story – the 'thirty joyous young voices' rehearsing the local 'winter cantata', breaking in on Midmore's meeting with his lawyer; the feisty, unpredictable farmer, Mr Sidney, who withstands all attempts to patronize him – and there are items of verbal interest such as the re-markable list, which Randall Jarrell admired, of Midmore's newly inherited possessions, or the description, with its bizarrely insistent epithet, of Midmore's aunt's funeral – a fine sentence:

There he faced the bracing ritual of the British funeral, and was wept at across the raw grave by an elderly coffin-shaped female with a long nose, who called him 'Master Frankie'; and there he was congratulated behind an echoing top-hat by a man he mistook for a mute, who turned out to be his aunt's lawyer.

But the satire is heavy-handed, too partial; and we will probably concur with T. S. Eliot's Johnsonian verdict:

The contrast between a bucolic world in which the second rate still participates in the good, and an intellectual world in which the second rate is usually sham and always tiresome, is not quite fair. The animus which [Kipling] displays against the latter suggests that he did not have his eye on the object: for we can judge only what we understand, and must constantly dine with the opposition.

'Friendly Brook', on the other hand, is consummately done – there is nothing merely picturesque about the portrayal of the Sussex peasants and their speech: Kipling combines a fellow-countryman's accurate observation and sympathy with an artist's true impersonality. His design is highly effective: the details of the story – the blackmailing attempt by a sottish London father to reclaim his long-abandoned daughter from a farmer and the latter's fierce, mute old mother; the father's eventual demise when, reeling from the whisky poured into him by the old woman, he drowns in the brook which is flooding but friendly to the farmer – are passed from one hedger to another, and the frame not only distances and mellows the turbulent (quite recent) events, but provides for satisfying moral judgement ('he had the law with him – no gettin' over that,' said Jesse. 'But he had the drink with him, too, an' that was where he failed, like'), and reduces the risk of quaintness in the rural observation. The old mother with a writing-slate tied to her waist-string and a quite real manslaughtering impulse, her son with his pagan superstitions ('The Brook's been a good friend to me . . . an' if she's minded to have a snatch at my hay, *I* ain't settin' out to withstand her') are seen in their strangeness; their adopted daughter, though absent from the picture, is a felt presence with her modern ways (studying to become a schoolteacher). The serio-comic tone is perfectly sustained, the construction is faultless, and the dialogue – the story is all dialogue – flows on as luckily and gently as the Friendly Brook itself, always 'mumbling something soft'.

This tale, together with 'The Wish House' (*Debits and Credits*), is perhaps Kipling's best work in the low-life (semi-supernatural) genre (cf. also 'Wireless', *Traffics and Discoveries*), whose converse is exemplified by a couple of stories in *A Diversity of Creatures* – 'Regulus' and 'The Honours of War' – which are about the upper-class, prosaic, hard, militaristic world of *Stalky & Co.* The first is actually a school-story, though written nine years later than *Stalky*, and centring not on the original Stalky trio (who have supporting roles) but another kind of boy, 'Pater' Winton, a paragon ('practically a member of the First Fifteen') who knowingly lets himself in for humiliating punishment – after the fashion of the Roman general of the title and of the Horace ode which is being translated in class. The story is superbly inlaid with detail, and the school atmosphere is more sympathetically conjured up than in the original *Stalky* chapters: the little underlying drama is more pointed and widely relevant than anything there. 'The Honours of War' is one of several stories where Kipling continues the lives of Stalky & Co. into late middle age and unappealing crusty jocularity. The practical jokiness has become silly, sentimental and tiresome, though Kipling succeeds in making the character of priggish, Oxonian subaltern, Mr Wontner, every bit as repugnant to us as to the other characters. Angus Wilson's criticism of *Stalky & Co.* – 'in its language and in its failure to suggest any further dimension to the exploits on the page, it is never poetic, lacks all verbal overtones' – remains true of these later stories, where, as before, Marx Brothers antics take place in the kind of narrative vacuum associated with, of all things, pornography.

High jinks come with more arresting artistic purpose in that most richly and skilfully orchestrated of farces, 'The Village that Voted the Earth was Flat'. The practical jokes, although revenge-ploys not without their streak of sadism, are preposterous and excessive enough, and complemented by a sufficiently absurd object of attack in Sir Thomas Ingell, Bart., M P, magistrate, bigwig, and general personification (he seems strangely familiar) of the 'Model Village' of Huckley, to ensure that their cumulative effect leans to the artistically sublime. The concluding mad euphoria in the House of Commons is worthy of comparison with the end of Gilbert and Sullivan's *Iolanthe*, when the Peers sprout wings and flit to Fairyland. What is difficult to accept in the story is the author's paranoia, which makes Sir Thomas and the entire village 'Rads' – radicals, or 'radical tinkers'.

'The Village that Voted' has a headlong energy of narration and relative clarity of detail matching its clearly defined – farcical and disruptive – purpose. Kipling's most remarkable achievements are by no means always his clearest of enunciation, but there is some correlation between the clarity of stories and their excellence – a fact indicated by the *Plain Tales* or *Kim*, or that early Indian tale, 'The Strange Ride of Morrowbie Jukes', which has the lucid horror of something by Beckett. The last two tales in *A Diversity of Creatures*, '"Swept and Garnished"' and 'Mary Postgate', both written during and about World War I, are remorseless in their clarity – far easier for the reader to follow than anything preceding them in the volume: simple and deadly.

They are also short; but the dozen pages of '"Swept and Garnished"' are the concise articulation of a nightmare. Frau Ebermann's sufferings from influenza are realistically sketched – her obsession when feverish with the precise position of the 'imitation-lace cover' on the 'imitation-marble top of the radiator' in her room is immediately plausible; and the mysterious entry of a small girl, who is besought to straighten the cover, follows with hallucinatory logic. The girl, and four other children who join her in a second visitation, are representative victims of German atrocities in Belgium; and Frau Ebermann's *gemütlich* concern that her comfortable Berlin flat and belongings should be properly 'swept and garnished' turns into a frantic attempt at blood-cleansing and expiation. The ghosts, albeit explained as delirious visions, have an exact presence and are slipped into their places in the story with quiet finesse: here, as rarely, Kipling draws close in method to Henry James. The degree of inwardness in the portrayal of Frau Ebermann is unusual for Kipling: like Mary Postgate she is adamantly real and individual and 'there' – not merely a function of some group-life. The reticence and brevity of the tale convey mental anguish and primal horror all the more forcibly: Angus Wilson supplies a valuable, desperate gloss on a detail of the ending when he remembers being 'told again and again as a small child, that the Germans had cut off the little Belgian boys' right arms so that they could never serve their country': '"Oh, but look, lady!" said the elder girl. Frau Ebermann looked and saw.'

'Mary Postgate', Kipling's most famous and controversial story, exceeds '"Swept and Garnished"' in explicit horror: little Edna Gerritt is 'ripped and shredded' before our eyes as a bomb drops on her; the German – he is surely German – aviator responsible, who crashes into shrubbery, is allowed to expire in agony as the 'thoroughly conscientious, tidy, companionable, and ladylike' Miss Postgate gloats. I am not convinced that there is any fundamental divergence between the aesthetic superiority of this tale and its supposed ethical repulsiveness: the force of the final pages is indivisible and tragic – it is as beside the point to impose strictly humanistic criteria here (though it isn't in other Kipling war-revenge stories such as 'Sea-Constables', from *Debits and Credits*) as upon extreme passages in Shakespeare, Dostoyevsky and Hardy. Aesthetic superiority is plainly apparent, nevertheless. The story doesn't waste a single word – not even in the long list of childish possessions, which Mary is about to incinerate, of her employer's nephew, Wynn, killed in a trial flight: the insistent accumulation and fierce accuracy are unbearably poignant. Kipling is always the master of the inventory – rarely does he infuse it with such desolate feeling as, later, in this climactic sentence:

[Mary] would stay where she was till she was entirely satisfied that It was dead – dead as dear papa in the late 'eighties; aunt Mary in 'eighty-nine; mamma in 'ninety-one; cousin Dick in 'ninety-five; Lady McCausland's housemaid in 'ninety-nine; Lady McCausland's sister in nineteen hundred and one; Wynn buried five days ago; and Edna Gerritt still waiting for decent earth to hide her.

Verbal nuances, modulations of tone, have exceptional power in 'Mary Postgate'. Kipling's words for the actuality of death are few and simple and startling: when Mary brings the letter announcing Wynn's death to her employer:

'I never expected anything else,' said Miss Fowler; 'but I'm sorry it happened before he had done anything.'
The room was whirling round Mary Postgate, but she found herself quite steady in the midst of it.
'Yes,' she said. 'It's a great pity he didn't die in action after he had killed somebody.'

Edmund Wilson has demonstrated the moving effect of that clash in the sentence – 'As she lit the match that would burn her heart to ashes, she heard a groan or a grunt behind the dense Portugal laurels' – between the characteristic specificity of detail in 'Portugal laurels', where another writer would simply have had 'shrubbery', and the emotiveness, unique in the story, of the first twelve words; but did not draw attention to the extraordinary pun, perhaps involuntary, perhaps not, in the sentence which follows: '"Cheape?" she called impatiently, but Cheape, with his ancient lumbago, in his comfortable cottage would be the last man to profane the sanctuary. "Sheep," she concluded, and threw in the fusee.' (Another sheep reference occurs earlier, when Wynn says to Mary, 'A sheep would know more than you do, Postey.') Gratuitousness of this verbal kind is found elsewhere in Kipling – for example, the 'coffin-shaped female' of the funeral in '"My Son's Wife's"'. The dubious pun in 'Mary Postgate', positioned, deliberately or not, at the head of Kipling's most terrifying pages, acts as a strategic release of tension – an emotional hiccup – and complicates the tone of the story by its momentary suggestion of a sort of Dostoyevskian voice of controlled hysteria, a voice which obliviously laughs in all the wrong places.

'Mary Postgate' is not just arguably Kipling's greatest tale, but outstanding among his works for flawless simplicity of structure combined with success in articulating an evident depth of private feeling. Most of his stories – the best along with the worst – conform to the kinds of dicta embedded in such late tales as 'Teem' (1935), with its 'Outside of his art, an artist must never dream', and 'The Bull that Thought' (1924), where '[Apis the bull] raged enormously; he feigned defeat; he despaired in statuesque abandon, and thence flashed into fresh paroxysms of wrath – but always with the detachment of the true artist who knows he is but the vessel of an emotion whence others, not he, must drink.' 'Mary Postgate' was written some months before Kipling's only son was killed at Loos in 1915, and can be seen as having, like Mahler's *Kindertötenlieder* (composed when his infants were alive and well), a ghastly proleptic power. Neither it, nor Kipling's other tales of war-loss (notably 'The Gardener' in *Debits and Credits*) exactly typify his ideal (Angus Wilson's phrase) of a 'purely externally orientated art', and they communicate no less forcefully for that. Still, it is the 'outward' story, the non-introspective, vir-

Introduction

tuosic working-out in words of an unusual *donnée*, the complex aesthetic dreaming of the late tales – the ornately realized 'Dayspring Mishandled' (1929), that quasi-Flaubertian *conte*, 'The Church that was at Antioch' (1929) – which must account in large part for Kipling's enduring fascination and the currently huge esteem in which he is held. His new reputation is among a generation of readers who value the written pleasure of his texts, the unpredictability and compactness of his treatments, the bewildering diversity of his themes, his creatures. Kipling the imperialist is dead and gone; it is Kipling the verbal prophet who commands attention now.

Paul Driver

Note on the Text

Kipling's work declared itself in an unusually large number of collected editions during his lifetime. Three at least deserve attention: the Sussex Edition of the Complete Works in Prose and Verse (only 520 copies printed), 1937–1939 (Macmillan), the American 'Outward Bound' Scribner's Edition (1897–1937), and Macmillan's Pocket Edition (1907–1937), which became Macmillan's Centenary Edition (1965). There are few, if any, textual discrepancies between these editions, as indeed between the original magazine versions of the stories and their collected versions. The original publication of 'The Dog Hervey' in *Century Magazine* was, for instance, entitled 'The Dog Harvey': an error. The Sussex Edition of *A Diversity of Creatures* (volume IX) omits 'Regulus' and replaces it with the Pyecroft story, 'A Tour of Inspection' (1904). The order of the stories here varies slightly, too, from Scribner's and the Pocket Edition: in the Sussex volume ' "My Son's Wife" ' is followed by the poem 'The Floods', which is followed by the story 'The Vortex', which gives place to two poems – 'The Fabulists' then 'The Song of Seven Cities'.

The text used here is that of the Pocket Edition. Emendments are minute. Kipling's sparse footnotes (all of them references to his previous stories) are incorporated into the notes at the end.

Original magazine publication of the stories was as follows:
'As Easy as ABC': *London Magazine*, March and April 1912
'Friendly Brook': *Metropolitan Magazine*, March 1914
'In the Same Boat': *Harper's*, December 1911
'The Honours of War': *Family Magazine* (USA), May 1911
    (under the title 'Honours Even')
'The Dog Hervey': *Century Magazine*, April 1914
'The Village that Voted the Earth was Flat': first published
    in *A Diversity of Creatures*, 1917

Note on the Text

'In the Presence': *Pearson's Magazine* and *Everybody's Magazine*, March 1912

'Regulus': *Nash's Pall Mall Magazine*, April 1917

'The Edge of the Evening': *Nash's Pall Mall Magazine* and *Metropolitan Magazine*, December 1913

'The Horse Marines': *Pearson's Magazine*, October 1910

'"My Son's Wife"': first published in *A Diversity of Creatures*, 1917

'The Vortex': *Scribner's Magazine*, August 1914

'"Swept and Garnished"': *Century Magazine* and *Nash's Pall Mall Magazine*, January 1915

'Mary Postgate': *Century Magazine* and *Nash's Pall Mall Magazine*, September 1915 (in both under the title, 'How Does Your Garden Grow')

Preface

With three exceptions, the dates at the head of these stories show when they were published in magazine form. 'The Village that Voted the Earth was Flat', 'Regulus', and '"My Son's Wife"' carry the dates when they were written.

Rudyard Kipling

AS EASY AS A.B.C.

As Easy as A.B.C.

(1912)

> The A.B.C., that semi-elected, semi-nominated body of a few score persons, controls the Planet. Transportation is Civilization, our motto runs. Theoretically we do what we please, so long as we do not interfere with the traffic *and all it implies*. Practically, the A.B.C. confirms or annuls all international arrangements, and, to judge from its last report, finds our tolerant, humorous, lazy little Planet only too ready to shift the whole burden of public administration on its shoulders.
>
> *'With the Night Mail'* [1]

Isn't it almost time that our Planet took some interest in the proceedings of the Aerial Board of Control? One knows that easy communications nowadays, and lack of privacy in the past, have killed all curiosity among mankind, but as the Board's Official Reporter I am bound to tell my tale.

At 9.30 a.m., August 26, A.D. 2065, the Board, sitting in London, was informed by De Forest that the District of Northern Illinois had riotously cut itself out of all systems and would remain disconnected till the Board should take over and administer it direct.

Every Northern Illinois freight and passenger tower was, he reported, out of action; all District main, local, and guiding lights had been extinguished; all General Communications were dumb, and through traffic had been diverted. No reason had been given, but he gathered unofficially from the Mayor of Chicago that the District complained of 'crowd-making and invasion of privacy.'

As a matter of fact, it is of no importance whether Northern Illinois stay in or out of planetary circuit; as a matter of policy, any complaint of invasion of privacy needs immediate investigation, lest worse follow.

29

By 9.45 a.m. De Forest, Dragomiroff (Russia), Takahira (Japan), and Pirolo (Italy) were empowered to visit Illinois and 'to take such steps as might be necessary for the resumption of traffic and *all that that implies*.' By 10 a.m. the Hall was empty, and the four Members and I were aboard what Pirolo insisted on calling 'my leetle godchild' – that is to say, the new *Victor Pirolo*. Our Planet prefers to know Victor Pirolo as a gentle, grey-haired enthusiast who spends his time near Foggia,[2] inventing or creating new breeds of Spanish-Italian olive-trees, but there is another side to his nature – the manufacture of quaint inventions, of which the *Victor Pirolo* is, perhaps, not the least surprising. She and a few score sister-craft of the same type embody his latest ideas. But she is not comfortable. An A.B.C. boat does not take the air with the level-keeled lift of a liner, but shoots up rocket-fashion like the 'aeroplane' of our ancestors, and makes her height at top-speed from the first. That is why I found myself sitting suddenly on the large lap of Eustace Arnott, who commands the A.B.C. Fleet. One knows vaguely that there is such a thing as a Fleet somewhere on the Planet, and that, theoretically, it exists for the purposes of what used to be known as 'war'. Only a week before, while visiting a glacier sanatorium behind Gothaven,[3] I had seen some squadrons making false auroras far to the north while they manoeuvred round the Pole; but, naturally, it had never occurred to me that the things could be used in earnest.

Said Arnott to De Forest as I staggered to a seat on the chart-room divan: 'We're tremendously grateful to 'em in Illinois. We've never had a chance of exercising all the Fleet together. I've turned in a General Call, and I expect we'll have at least two hundred keels aloft this evening.'

'Well aloft?' De Forest asked.

'Of course, sir. Out of sight till they're called for.'

Arnott laughed as he lolled over the transparent chart-table where the map of the summer-blue Atlantic slid along, degree by degree, in exact answer to our progress. Our dial already showed 320 m.p.h. and we were two thousand feet above the uppermost traffic lines.

'Now, where is this Illinois District of yours?' said Dragomiroff. 'One travels so much, one sees so little. Oh, I remember! It is in North America.'

As Easy as A.B.C.

De Forest, whose business it is to know the out districts, told us that it lay at the foot of Lake Michigan, on a road to nowhere in particular, was about half an hour's run from end to end, and, except in one corner, as flat as the sea. Like most flat countries nowadays, it was heavily guarded against invasion of privacy by forced timber – fifty-foot spruce and tamarack, grown in five years. The population was close on two millions, largely migratory between Florida and California, with a backbone of small farms (they call a thousand acres a farm in Illinois) whose owners come into Chicago for amusements and society during the winter. They were, he said, noticeably kind, quiet folk, but a little exacting, as all flat countries must be, in their notions of privacy. There had, for instance, been no printed news-sheet in Illinois for twenty-seven years. Chicago argued that engines for printed news sooner or later developed into engines for invasion of privacy, which in turn might bring the old terror of Crowds and blackmail back to the Planet. So news-sheets were not.

'And that's Illinois,' De Forest concluded. 'You see, in the Old Days, she was in the forefront of what they used to call "progress", and Chicago –'

'Chicago?' said Takahira. 'That's the little place where there is Salati's Statue of the Nigger in Flames? A fine bit of old work.'

'When did you see it?' asked De Forest quickly. 'They only unveil it once a year.'

'I know. At Thanksgiving. It was then,' said Takahira, with a shudder. 'And they sang MacDonough's Song, too.'

'Whew!' De Forest whistled. 'I did not know that! I wish you'd told me before. MacDonough's Song may have had its uses when it was composed, but it was an infernal legacy for any man to leave behind.'

'It's protective instinct, my dear fellows,' said Pirolo, rolling a cigarette. 'The Planet, she has had her dose of popular government. She suffers from inherited agoraphobia. She has no – ah – use for crowds.'

Dragomiroff leaned forward to give him a light. 'Certainly,' said the white-bearded Russian, 'the Planet has taken all precautions against crowds for the past hundred years. What is our total population today? Six hundred million, we hope; five hundred, we think; but – but if next year's census shows more than four hundred and fifty, I myself will eat all the extra little babies. We have cut the birth-rate out – right out! For a long time we have said to Almighty God, "Thank You, Sir, but we do not much like Your game of life, so we will not play."'

'Anyhow,' said Arnott defiantly, 'men live a century apiece on the average now.'

'Oh, that is quite well! I am rich – you are rich – we are all rich and happy because we are so few and we live so long. Only *I* think Almighty God He will remember what the Planet was like in the time of Crowds and the Plague. Perhaps He will send us nerves. Eh, Pirolo?'

The Italian blinked into space. 'Perhaps,' he said, 'He has sent them already. Anyhow, you cannot argue with the Planet. She does not forget the Old Days, and – what can you do?'

'For sure we can't remake the world.' De Forest glanced at the map flowing smoothly across the table from west to east. 'We ought to be over our ground by nine tonight. There won't be much sleep afterwards.'

On which hint we dispersed, and I slept till Takahira waked me for dinner. Our ancestors thought nine hours' sleep ample for their little lives. We, living thirty years longer, feel ourselves defrauded with less than eleven out of the twenty-four.

By ten o'clock we were over Lake Michigan. The west shore was lightless, except for a dull ground-glare at Chicago, and a single traffic-directing light – its leading beam pointing north – at Waukegan on our starboard bow. None of the Lake villages gave any sign of life; and inland, westward, so far as we could see, blackness lay unbroken on the level earth. We swooped down and skimmed low across the dark, throwing calls county by county. Now and again we picked up the faint glimmer of a house-light, or heard the rasp and rend of a cultivator being played across the fields, but Northern Illinois as a whole was one inky, apparently uninhabited, waste of high, forced woods. Only our illuminated map, with its little pointer switching from county to county, as we wheeled and twisted, gave us any idea of our position. Our calls, urgent, pleading, coaxing or commanding, through the General Communicator brought no answer. Illinois strictly maintained her own privacy in the timber which she grew for that purpose.

'Oh, this is absurd!' said De Forest. 'We're like an owl trying to work a wheat-field. Is this Bureau Creek?[4] Let's land, Arnott, and get hold of someone.'

We brushed over a belt of forced woodland – fifteen-year-old maple sixty feet high – grounded on a private meadow-dock, none too big, where we moored to our own grapnels, and hurried out through the warm dark night towards a light in a verandah. As we neared the garden gate I could have sworn we had stepped knee-deep in quicksand, for we could scarcely drag our feet against the prickling currents that clogged them. After five paces we stopped, wiping our foreheads, as hopelessly stuck on dry smooth turf as so many cows in a bog.

'Pest!' cried Pirolo angrily. 'We are ground-circuited. And it is my own system of ground-circuits too! I know the pull.'

'Good evening,' said a girl's voice from the verandah. 'Oh, I'm sorry! We've locked up. Wait a minute.'

We heard the click of a switch, and almost fell forward as the currents round our knees were withdrawn.

The girl laughed, and laid aside her knitting. An old-fashioned Controller stood at her elbow, which she reversed from time to time, and we could hear the snort and clank of the obedient cultivator half a mile away, behind the guardian woods.

'Come in and sit down,' she said. 'I'm only playing a plough. Dad's gone to Chicago to – Ah! Then it was *your* call I heard just now!'

She had caught sight of Arnott's Board uniform, leaped to the switch, and turned it full on.

We were checked, gasping, waist-deep in current this time, three yards from the verandah.

'We only want to know what's the matter with Illinois,' said De Forest placidly.

'Then hadn't you better go to Chicago and find out?' she answered. 'There's nothing wrong here. We own ourselves.'

'How can we go anywhere if you won't loose us?' De Forest went on, while Arnott scowled. Admirals of Fleets are still quite human when their dignity is touched.

'Stop a minute – you don't know how funny you look!' She put her hands on her hips and laughed mercilessly.

'Don't worry about that,' said Arnott, and whistled. A voice answered from the *Victor Pirolo* in the meadow.

'Only a single-fuse ground-circuit!' Arnott called. 'Sort it out gently, please.'

We heard the ping of a breaking lamp; a fuse blew out somewhere in the verandah roof, frightening a nest full of birds. The ground-circuit was open. We stooped and rubbed our tingling ankles.

'How rude – how very rude of you!' the maiden cried.

''Sorry, but we haven't time to look funny,' said Arnott. 'We've got to go to Chicago; and if I were you, young lady, I'd go into the cellars for the next two hours, and take mother with me.'

Off he strode, with us at his heels, muttering indignantly, till the humour of the thing struck and doubled him up with laughter at the foot of the gangway ladder.

'The Board hasn't shown what you might call a fat spark on this occasion,' said De Forest, wiping his eyes. 'I hope I didn't look as big a fool as you did, Arnott! Hullo! What on earth is that? Dad coming home from Chicago?'

There was a rattle and a rush, and a five-plough cultivator, blades in air like so many teeth, trundled itself at us round the edge of the timber, fuming and sparking furiously.

'Jump!' said Arnott, as we bundled ourselves through the none-too-wide door. 'Never mind about shutting it. Up!'

The *Victor Pirolo* lifted like a bubble, and the vicious machine shot just underneath us, clawing high as it passed.

'There's a nice little spit-kitten for you!' said Arnott, dusting his knees. 'We ask her a civil question. First she circuits us and then she plays a cultivator at us.'

'And then we fly,' said Dragomiroff. 'If I were forty years more young, I would go back and kiss her. Ho! Ho!'

'I,' said Pirolo, 'would smack her! My pet ship has been chased by a dirty plough; a – how do you say? – agricultural implement.'

'Oh, that is Illinois all over,' said De Forest. 'They don't content themselves with talking about privacy. They arrange to have it. And now, where's your alleged fleet, Arnott? We must assert ourselves against this wench.'

Arnott pointed to the black heavens.

'Waiting on – up there,' said he. 'Shall I give them the whole installation, sir?'

'Oh, I don't think the young lady is quite worth that,' said De Forest. 'Get over Chicago, and perhaps we'll see something.'

In a few minutes we were hanging at two thousand feet over an oblong block of incandescence in the centre of the little town.

'That looks like the old City Hall. Yes, there's Salati's Statue in front of it,' said Takahira. 'But what on earth are they doing to the place? I thought they used it for a market nowadays! Drop a little, please.'

We could hear the sputter and crackle of road-surfacing machines – the cheap Western type which fuse stone and rubbish into lava-like ribbed glass for their rough country roads. Three or four surfacers worked on each side of a square of ruins. The brick and stone wreckage crumbled, slid forward, and presently spread out into white-hot pools of sticky slag, which the levelling-rods smoothed more or less flat. Already a third of the big block had been so treated, and was cooling to dull red before our astonished eyes.

'It is the Old Market,' said De Forest. 'Well, there's nothing to prevent Illinois from making a road through a market. It doesn't interfere with traffic, that I can see.'

'Hsh!' said Arnott, gripping me by the shoulder. 'Listen! They're singing. Why on the earth are they singing?'

We dropped again till we could see the black fringe of people at the edge of that glowing square.

At first they only roared against the roar of the surfacers and levellers. Then the words came up clearly – the words of the Forbidden Song that all men knew, and none let pass their lips – poor Pat MacDonough's Song, made in the days of the Crowds and the Plague – every silly word of it loaded to sparking-point with the Planet's inherited memories of horror, panic, fear and cruelty. And Chicago – innocent, contented little Chicago – was singing it aloud to the infernal tune that carried riot, pestilence and lunacy round our Planet a few generations ago!

> 'Once there was The People – Terror gave it birth;
> Once there was The People, and it made a hell of earth!'

(Then the stamp and pause):

> 'Earth arose and crushed it. Listen, oh, ye slain!
> Once there was The People – it shall never be again!'

The levellers thrust in savagely against the ruins as the song renewed itself again, again and again, louder than the crash of the melting walls.

De Forest frowned.

'I don't like that,' he said. 'They've broken back to the Old Days! They'll be killing somebody soon. I think we'd better divert 'em, Arnott.'

'Ay, ay, sir.' Arnott's hand went to his cap, and we heard the hull of the *Victor Pirolo* ring to the command: 'Lamps! Both watches stand by! Lamps! Lamps! Lamps!'

'Keep still!' Takahira whispered to me. 'Blinkers, please, quartermaster.'

'It's all right – all right!' said Pirolo from behind, and to my horror slipped over my head some sort of rubber helmet that locked with a snap. I could feel thick colloid bosses before my eyes, but I stood in absolute darkness.

'To save the sight,' he explained, and pushed me on to the chart-room divan. 'You will see in a minute.'

As he spoke I became aware of a thin thread of almost intolerable light, let down from heaven at an immense distance – one vertical hairsbreadth of frozen lightning.

'Those are our flanking ships,' said Arnott at my elbow. 'That one is over Galena. Look south – that other one's over Keithburg. Vincennes is behind us, and north yonder is Winthrop Woods. The Fleet's in position, sir' – this to De Forest. 'As soon as you give the word.'

'Ah no! No!' cried Dragomiroff at my side. I could feel the old man tremble. 'I do not know all that you can do, but be kind! I ask you to be a little kind to them below! This is horrible – horrible!'

'When a Woman kills a Chicken,
Dynasties and Empires sicken,' [5]

Takahira quoted. 'It is too late to be gentle now.'

'Then take off my helmet! Take off my helmet!' Dragomiroff began hysterically.

Pirolo must have put his arm round him.

'Hush,' he said, 'I am here. It is all right, Ivan, my dear
fellow.'

'I'll just send our little girl in Bureau County a warning,' said
Arnott. 'She don't deserve it, but we'll allow her a minute or
two to take mamma to the cellar.'

In the utter hush that followed the growling spark after
Arnott had linked up his Service Communicator with the in-
visible Fleet, we heard MacDonough's Song from the city
beneath us grow fainter as we rose to position. Then I clapped
my hand before my mask lenses, for it was as though the floor
of Heaven had been riddled and all the inconceivable blaze of
suns in the making was poured through the manholes.

'You needn't count,' said Arnott. I had had no thought of
such a thing. 'There are two hundred and fifty keels up there,
five miles apart. Full power, please, for another twelve
seconds.'

The firmament, as far as eye could reach, stood on pillars of
white fire. One fell on the glowing square at Chicago, and
turned it black.

'Oh! Oh! Oh! Can men be allowed to do such things?'
Dragomiroff cried, and fell across our knees.

'Glass of water, please,' said Takahira to a helmeted shape
that leaped forward. 'He is a little faint.'

The lights switched off, and the darkness stunned like an
avalanche. We could hear Dragomiroff's teeth on the glass
edge.

Pirolo was comforting him.

'All right, all ra–ight,' he repeated. 'Come and lie down.
Come below and take off your mask. I give you my word, old
friend, it is all right. They are my siege-lights. Little Victor
Pirolo's leetle lights. You know *me*! I do not hurt people.'

'Pardon!' Dragomiroff moaned. 'I have never seen Death. I

have never seen the Board take action. Shall we go down and burn them alive, or is that already done?'

'Oh, hush,' said Pirolo, and I think he rocked him in his arms.

'Do we repeat, sir?' Arnott asked De Forest.

'Give 'em a minute's break,' De Forest replied. 'They may need it.'

We waited a minute, and then MacDonough's Song, broken but defiant, rose from undefeated Chicago.

'They seem fond of that tune,' said De Forest. 'I should let 'em have it, Arnott.'

'Very good, sir,' said Arnott, and felt his way to the Communicator keys.

No lights broke forth, but the hollow of the skies made herself the mouth for one note that touched the raw fibre of the brain. Men hear such sounds in delirium, advancing like tides from horizons beyond the ruled foreshores of space.

'That's our pitch-pipe,' said Arnott. 'We may be a bit ragged. I've never conducted two hundred and fifty performers before.' He pulled out the couplers, and struck a full chord on the Service Communicators.

The beams of light leaped down again, and danced, solemnly and awfully, a stilt-dance, sweeping thirty or forty miles left and right at each stiff-legged kick, while the darkness delivered itself – there is no scale to measure against that utterance – of the tune to which they kept time. Certain notes – one learnt to expect them with terror – cut through one's marrow, but, after three minutes, thought and emotion passed in indescribable agony.

We saw, we heard, but I think we were in some sort swooning. The two hundred and fifty beams shifted; re-formed, straddled and split, narrowed, widened, rippled in ribbons, broke into a thousand white-hot parallel lines, melted and revolved in interwoven rings like old-fashioned engine-turning, flung up to the zenith, made as if to descend and renew the torment, halted at the last instant, twizzled insanely round the horizon, and vanished, to bring back for the hundredth time darkness more shattering than their instantly renewed light over all Illinois. Then the tune and lights ceased together, and we heard one single devastating wail that shook all the horizon as a rubbed wet finger shakes the rim of a bowl.

'Ah, that is my new siren,' said Pirolo. 'You can break an iceberg in half, if you find the proper pitch. They will whistle by squadrons now. It is the wind through pierced shutters in the bows.'

I had collapsed beside Dragomiroff, broken and snivelling feebly, because I had been delivered before my time to all the terrors of Judgment Day, and the Archangels of the Resurrection were hailing me naked across the Universe to the sound of the music of the spheres.

Then I saw De Forest smacking Arnott's helmet with his open hand. The wailing died down in a long shriek as a black shadow swooped past us, and returned to her place above the lower clouds.

'I hate to interrupt a specialist when he's enjoying himself,' said De Forest. 'But, as a matter of fact, all Illinois has been asking us to stop for these last fifteen seconds.'

'What a pity.' Arnott slipped off his mask. 'I wanted you to hear us really hum. Our lower C can lift street-paving.'

'It is Hell – Hell!' cried Dragomiroff, and sobbed aloud.

Arnott looked away as he answered:

'It's a few thousand volts ahead of the old shoot-'em-and-sink-'em game, but I should scarcely call it *that*. What shall I tell the Fleet, sir?'

'Tell 'em we're very pleased and impressed. I don't think they need wait on any longer. There isn't a spark left down there.' De Forest pointed. 'They'll be deaf and blind.'

'Oh, I think not, sir. The demonstration lasted less than ten minutes.'

'Marvellous!' Takahira sighed. 'I should have said it was half a night. Now, shall we go down and pick up the pieces?'

'But first a small drink,' said Pirolo. 'The Board must not arrive weeping at its own works.'

'I am an old fool – an old fool!' Dragomiroff began piteously. 'I did not know what would happen. It is all new to me. We reason with them in Little Russia.'

Chicago North landing-tower was unlighted, and Arnott worked his ship into the clips by her own lights. As soon as these broke out we heard groanings of horror and appeal from many people below.

'All right,' shouted Arnott into the darkness. 'We aren't beginning again!' We descended by the stairs, to find ourselves knee-deep in a grovelling crowd, some crying that they were blind, others beseeching us not to make any more noises, but the greater part writhing face downward, their hands or their caps before their eyes.

It was Pirolo who came to our rescue. He climbed the side of a surfacing-machine, and there, gesticulating as though they could see, made oration to those afflicted people of Illinois.

'You stchewpids!' he began. 'There is nothing to fuss for. Of course, your eyes will smart and be red tomorrow. You will look as if you and your wives had drunk too much, but in a little while you will see again as well as before. I tell you this, and I – *I* am Pirolo. Victor Pirolo!'

The crowd with one accord shuddered, for many legends attach to Victor Pirolo of Foggia, deep in the secrets of God.

'Pirolo?' An unsteady voice lifted itself. 'Then tell us was there anything except light in those lights of yours just now?'

The question was repeated from every corner of the darkness.

Pirolo laughed.

'No!' he thundered. (Why have small men such large voices?) 'I give you my word and the Board's word that there was nothing except light – just light! You stchewpids! Your birthrate is too low already as it is. Some day I must invent something to send it up, but send it down – never!'

'Is that true? – We thought – somebody said –'

One could feel the tension relax all round.

'You *too* big fools,' Pirolo cried. 'You could have sent us a call and we would have told you.'

'Send you a call!' a deep voice shouted. 'I wish you had been at our end of the wire.'

'I'm glad I wasn't,' said De Forest. 'It was bad enough from behind the lamps. Never mind! It's over now. Is there any one here I can talk business with? I'm De Forest – for the Board.'

'You might begin with me, for one – I'm Mayor,' the bass voice replied.

A big man rose unsteadily from the street, and staggered towards us where we sat on the broad turf-edging, in front of the garden fences.

'I ought to be the first on my feet. Am I?' said he.

'Yes,' said De Forest, and steadied him as he dropped down beside us.

'Hello, Andy. Is that you?' a voice called.

'Excuse me,' said the Mayor; 'that sounds like my Chief of Police, Bluthner!'

'Bluthner it is; and here's Mulligan and Keefe – on their feet.'

'Bring 'em up please, Blut. We're supposed to be the Four in charge of this hamlet. What we says, goes. And, De Forest, what do you say?'

'Nothing – yet,' De Forest answered, as we made room for the panting, reeling men. '*You*'ve cut out of system. Well?'

'Tell the steward to send down drinks, please,' Arnott whispered to an orderly at his side.

'Good!' said the Mayor, smacking his dry lips. 'Now I suppose we can take it, De Forest, that henceforward the Board will administer us direct?'

'Not if the Board can avoid it,' De Forest laughed. 'The A.B.C. is responsible for the planetary traffic only.'

'*And all that that implies.*' The big Four who ran Chicago chanted their Magna Charta like children at school.

'Well, get on,' said De Forest wearily. 'What is your silly trouble anyway?'

'Too much dam' Democracy,' said the Mayor, laying his hand on De Forest's knee.

'So? I thought Illinois had had her dose of that.'

'She has. That's why. Blut, what did you do with our prisoners last night?'

'Locked 'em in the water-tower to prevent the women killing 'em,' the Chief of Police replied. 'I'm too blind to move just yet, but –'

'Arnott, send some of your people, please, and fetch 'em along,' said De Forest.

'They're triple-circuited,' the Mayor called. 'You'll have to blow out three fuses.' He turned to De Forest, his large outline just visible in the paling darkness. 'I hate to throw any more work on the Board. I'm an administrator myself, but we've had a little fuss with our Serviles. What? In a big city there's bound to be a few men and women who can't live without listening to themselves, and who prefer drinking out of pipes they don't own both ends of. They inhabit flats and hotels all the year round. They say it saves 'em trouble. Anyway, it gives 'em more time to make trouble for their neighbours. We call 'em Serviles locally. And they are apt to be tuberculous.'

'Just so!' said the man called Mulligan. 'Transportation is Civilization. Democracy is Disease. I've proved it by the blood-test, every time.'

'Mulligan's our Health Officer, and a one-idea man,' said the Mayor, laughing. 'But it's true that most Serviles haven't much control. They *will* talk; and when people take to talking as a business, anything may arrive – mayn't it, De Forest?'

'Anything – except the facts of the case,' said De Forest, laughing.

'I'll give you those in a minute,' said the Mayor. 'Our Serviles got to talking – first in their houses and then on the streets, telling men and women how to manage their own affairs. (You can't teach a Servile not to finger his neighbour's soul.) That's invasion of privacy, of course, but in Chicago we'll suffer anything sooner than make crowds. Nobody took much notice, and so I let 'em alone. My fault! I was warned there would be trouble, but there hasn't been a crowd or murder in Illinois for nineteen years.'

'Twenty-two,' said his Chief of Police.

'Likely. Anyway, we'd forgot such things. So, from talking in the houses and on the streets, our Serviles go to calling a meeting at the Old Market yonder.' He nodded across the square where the wrecked buildings heaved up grey in the dawn-glimmer behind the square-cased statue of The Negro in Flames. 'There's nothing to prevent any one calling meetings except that it's against human nature to stand in a crowd, besides being bad for the health. I ought to have known by the way our men and women attended that first meeting that trouble was brewing. There were as many as a thousand in the market-place, touching each other. Touching! Then the Serviles turned in all tongue-switches and talked, and we –'

'What did they talk about?' said Takahira.

'First, how badly things were managed in the city. That pleased us Four – we were on the platform – because we hoped to catch one or two good men for City work. You know how rare executive capacity is. Even if we didn't it's – it's refreshing to find any one interested enough in our job to damn our eyes. You don't know what it means to work, year in, year out, without a spark of difference with a living soul.'

'Oh, don't we!' said De Forest. 'There are times on the Board when we'd give our positions if any one would kick us out and take hold of things themselves.'

'But they won't,' said the Mayor ruefully. 'I assure you, sir, we Four have done things in Chicago, in the hope of rousing people, that would have discredited Nero. But what do they say? "Very good, Andy. Have it your own way. Anything's better than a crowd. I'll go back to my land." You *can't* do anything with folk who can go where they please, and don't want anything on God's earth except their own way. There isn't a kick or a kicker left on the Planet.'

'Then I suppose that little shed yonder fell down by itself?' said De Forest. We could see the bare and still smoking ruins, and hear the slag-pools crackle as they hardened and set.

'Oh, that's only amusement. 'Tell you later. As I was saying, our Serviles held the meeting, and pretty soon we had to ground-circuit the platform to save 'em from being killed. And that didn't make our people any more pacific.'

'How d'you mean?' I ventured to ask.

'If you've ever been ground-circuited,' said the Mayor, 'you'll know it don't improve any man's temper to be held up straining against nothing. No, sir! Eight or nine hundred folk kept pawing and buzzing like flies in treacle for two hours, while a pack of perfectly safe Serviles invades their mental and spiritual privacy, may be amusing to watch, but they are not pleasant to handle afterwards.'

Pirolo chuckled.

'Our folk own themselves. They were of opinion things were going too far and too fiery. I warned the Serviles; but they're born house-dwellers. Unless a fact hits 'em on the head, they cannot see it. Would you believe me, they went on to talk of what they called "popular government"? They did! They wanted us to go back to the old Voodoo-business of voting with papers and wooden boxes, and word-drunk people and printed formulas, and news-sheets! They said they practised it among themselves about what they'd have to eat in their flats and hotels. Yes, sir! They stood up behind Bluthner's doubled ground-circuits, and they said that, in this present year of grace, *to* self-owning men and women, *on* that very spot! Then they finished' – he lowered his voice cautiously – 'by talking about "The People". And then Bluthner he had to sit up all night in charge of the circuits because he couldn't trust his men to keep 'em shut.'

'It was trying 'em too high,' the Chief of Police broke in. 'But we couldn't hold the crowd ground-circuited for ever. I gathered in all the Serviles on charge of crowd-making, and put 'em in the water-tower, and then I let things cut loose. I had to! The District lit like a sparked gas-tank!'

'The news was out over seven degrees of country,' the Mayor continued; 'and when once it's a question of invasion of privacy, goodbye to right and reason in Illinois! They began turning out traffic-lights and locking up landing-towers on Thursday night. Friday, they stopped all traffic and asked for the Board to take over. Then they wanted to clean Chicago off the side of the Lake and rebuild elsewhere – just for a souvenir of "The People" that the Serviles talked about. I suggested that they should slag the Old Market where the meeting was held, while I turned in a call to you all on the Board. That kept 'em quiet till you came along. And – and now *you* can take hold of the situation.'

''Any chance of their quieting down?' De Forest asked.

'You can try,' said the Mayor.

De Forest raised his voice in the face of the reviving crowd that had edged in towards us. Day was come.

'Don't you think this business can be arranged?' he began. But there was a roar of angry voices:

'We've finished with Crowds! We aren't going back to the Old Days! Take us over! Take the Serviles away! Administer direct or we'll kill 'em! Down with The People!'

An attempt was made to begin MacDonough's Song. It got no further than the first line, for the *Victor Pirolo* sent down a warning drone on one stopped horn. A wrecked side-wall of the Old Market tottered and fell inwards on the slag-pools. None spoke or moved till the last of the dust had settled down again, turning the steel case of Salati's Statue ashy grey.

'You see you'll just *have* to take us over,' the Mayor whispered.

De Forest shrugged his shoulders.

'You talk as if executive capacity could be snatched out of the air like so much horse-power. Can't you manage yourselves on any terms?' he said.

'We can, if you say so. It will only cost those few lives to begin with.'

The Mayor pointed across the square, where Arnott's men guided a stumbling group of ten or twelve men and women to the lake front and halted them under the Statue.

'Now I think,' said Takahira under his breath, 'there will be trouble.'

The mass in front of us growled like beasts.

At that moment the sun rose clear, and revealed the blinking assembly to itself. As soon as it realized that it was a crowd we saw the shiver of horror and mutual repulsion shoot across it precisely as the steely flaws shot across the lake outside. Nothing was said, and, being half blind, of course it moved slowly. Yet in less than fifteen minutes most of that vast multitude – three thousand at the lowest count – melted away like frost on south eaves. The remnant stretched themselves on the grass, where a crowd feels and looks less like a crowd.

'These mean business, 'the Mayor whispered to Takahira. 'There are a goodish few women there who've borne children. I don't like it.'

The morning draught off the lake stirred the trees round us with promise of a hot day; the sun reflected itself dazzlingly on the canister-shaped covering of Salati's Statue; cocks crew in the gardens, and we could hear gate-latches clicking in the distance as people stumblingly resought their homes.

'I'm afraid there won't be any morning deliveries,' said De Forest. 'We rather upset things in the country last night.'

'That makes no odds,' the Mayor returned. 'We're all provisioned for six months. *We* take no chances.'

Nor, when you come to think of it, does any one else. It must be three-quarters of a generation since any house or city faced a food shortage. Yet is there house or city on the Planet today that has not half a year's provisions laid in? We are like the shipwrecked seamen in the old books, who, having once nearly starved to death, ever afterwards hide away bits of food and biscuit. Truly we trust no Crowds, nor system based on Crowds!

De Forest waited till the last footstep had died away. Meantime the prisoners at the base of the Statue shuffled, posed and fidgeted, with the shamelessness of quite little children. None of them were more than six feet high, and many of them were as grey-haired as the ravaged, harassed heads of old pictures. They huddled together in actual touch, while the crowd, spaced at large intervals, looked at them with congested eyes.

Suddenly a man among them began to talk. The Mayor had not in the least exaggerated. It appeared that our Planet lay sunk in slavery beneath the heel of the Aerial Board of Control. The orator urged us to arise in our might, burst our prison doors and break our fetters (all his metaphors, by the way, were of the most mediaeval). Next he demanded that every matter of daily life, including most of the physical functions, should be submitted for decision at any time of the week, month, or year to, I gathered, anybody who happened to be passing by or residing within a certain radius, and that everybody should forthwith abandon his concerns to settle the matter, first by crowd-making, next by talking to the crowds made, and lastly by describing crosses on pieces of paper, which rubbish should later be counted with certain mystic ceremonies and oaths. Out of this amazing play, he assured us, would automatically arise a higher, nobler, and kinder world, based – he demonstrated this with the awful lucidity of the insane – based on the sanctity of the Crowd and the villainy of the single person. In conclusion, he called loudly upon God to testify to his personal merits and integrity. When the flow ceased, I turned bewildered to Takahira, who was nodding solemnly.

'Quite correct,' said he. 'It is all in the old books. He has left nothing out, not even the war-talk.'

'But I don't see how this stuff can upset a child, much less a district,' I replied.

'Ah, you are too young,' said Dragomiroff. 'For another thing, you are not a mamma. Please look at the mammas.'

Ten or fifteen women who remained had separated themselves from the silent men, and were drawing in towards the prisoners. It reminded one of the stealthy encircling, before the rush in at the quarry, of wolves round musk-oxen in the North. The prisoners saw, and drew together more closely. The Mayor covered his face with his hands for an instant. De Forest, bareheaded, stepped forward between the prisoners and the slowly, stiffly moving line.

'That's all very interesting,' he said to the dry-lipped orator. 'But the point seems that you've been making crowds and invading privacy.'

A woman stepped forward, and would have spoken, but there was a quick assenting murmur from the men, who realized that De Forest was trying to pull the situation down to ground-line.

'Yes! Yes!' they cried. 'We cut out because they made crowds and invaded privacy! Stick to that! Keep on that switch! Lift the Serviles out of this! The Board's in charge! Hsh!'

'Yes, the Board's in charge,' said De Forest. 'I'll take formal evidence of crowd-making if you like, but the Members of the Board can testify to it. Will that do?'

The women had closed in another pace, with hands that clenched and unclenched at their sides.

'Good! Good enough!' the men cried. 'We're content. Only take them away quickly.'

'Come along up!' said De Forest to the captives. 'Breakfast is quite ready.'

It appeared, however, that they did not wish to go. They intended to remain in Chicago and make crowds. They pointed out that De Forest's proposal was gross invasion of privacy.

'My dear fellow,' said Pirolo to the most voluble of the leaders, 'you hurry, or your crowd that can't be wrong will kill you!'

'But that would be murder,' answered the believer in crowds; and there was a roar of laughter from all sides that seemed to show the crisis had broken.

A woman stepped forward from the line of women, laughing, I protest, as merrily as any of the company. One hand, of course, shaded her eyes, the other was at her throat.

'Oh, they needn't be afraid of being killed!' she called.

'Not in the least,' said De Forest. 'But don't you think that, now the Board's in charge, you might go home while we get these people away?'

'I shall be home long before that. It – it has been rather a trying day.'

She stood up to her full height, dwarfing even De Forest's six-foot-eight, and smiled, with eyes closed against the fierce light.

'Yes, rather,' said De Forest. 'I'm afraid you feel the glare a little. We'll have the ship down.'

He motioned to the *Pirolo* to drop between us and the sun, and at the same time to loop-circuit the prisoners, who were a trifle unsteady. We saw them stiffen to the current where they stood. The woman's voice went on, sweet and deep and unshaken:

'I don't suppose you men realize how much this – this sort of thing means to a woman. I've borne three. We women don't want our children given to Crowds. It must be an inherited instinct. Crowds make trouble. They bring back the Old Days. Hate, fear, blackmail, publicity, "The People" – *That! That! That!*' She pointed to the Statue, and the crowd growled once more.

'Yes, if they are allowed to go on,' said De Forest. 'But this little affair –'

'It means so much to us women that this – this little affair should never happen again. Of course, never's a big word, but one feels so strongly that it is important to stop crowds at the very beginning. Those creatures' – she pointed with her left hand at the prisoners swaying like seaweed in a tideway as the circuit pulled them – 'those people have friends and wives and children in the city and elsewhere. One doesn't want anything done to *them*, you know. It's terrible to force a human being out of fifty or sixty years of good life. I'm only forty myself. *I* know. But, at the same time, one feels that an example should be made, because no price is too heavy to pay if — if these people and *all that they imply* can be put an end to. Do you quite understand, or would you be kind enough to tell your men to take the casing off the Statue? It's worth looking at.'

'I understand perfectly. But I don't think anybody here wants to see the Statue on an empty stomach. Excuse me one moment.' De Forest called up to the ship. 'A flying loop ready on the port side, if you please.' Then to the woman he said with some crispness, 'You might leave us a little discretion in the matter.'

'Oh, of course. Thank you for being so patient. I know my arguments are silly, but —' She half turned away and went on in a changed voice, 'Perhaps this will help you to decide.'

She threw out her right arm with a knife in it. Before the blade could be returned to her throat or her bosom it was twitched from her grip, sparked as it flew out of the shadow of the ship above, and fell flashing in the sunshine at the foot of the Statue fifty yards away. The outflung arm was arrested, rigid as a bar for an instant, till the releasing circuit permitted her to bring it slowly to her side. The other women shrank back silent among the men.

Pirolo rubbed his hands, and Takahira nodded.

'That was clever of you, De Forest,' said he.

'What a glorious pose!' Dragomiroff murmured, for the frightened woman was on the edge of tears.

'Why did you stop me? I would have done it!' she cried.

'I have no doubt you would,' said De Forest. 'But we can't waste a life like yours on these people. I hope the arrest didn't sprain your wrist; it's so hard to regulate a flying loop. But I think you are quite right about those persons' women and children. We'll take them all away with us if you promise not to do anything stupid to yourself.'

'I promise — I promise.' She controlled herself with an effort. 'But it is so important to us women. We know what it means; and I thought if you saw I was in earnest —'

'I saw you were, and you've gained your point. I shall take all your Serviles away with me at once. The Mayor will make lists of their friends and families in the city and the district, and he'll ship them after us this afternoon.'

'Sure,' said the Mayor, rising to his feet. 'Keefe, if you can see, hadn't you better finish levelling off the Old Market? It don't look sightly the way it is now, and we shan't use it for crowds any more.'

'I think you had better wipe out that Statue as well, Mr Mayor,' said De Forest. 'I don't question its merits as a work of art, but I believe it's a shade morbid.'

'Certainly, sir. Oh, Keefe! Slag the Nigger before you go on to fuse the Market. I'll get to the Communicators and tell the District that the Board is in charge. Are you making any special appointments, sir?'

'None. We haven't men to waste on these backwoods. Carry on as before, but under the Board. Arnott, run your Serviles aboard, please. Ground ship and pass them through the bilge-doors.⁶ We'll wait till we've finished with this work of art.'

The prisoners trailed past him, talking fluently, but unable to gesticulate in the drag of the current. Then the surfacers rolled up, two on each side of the Statue. With one accord the spectators looked elsewhere, but there was no need. Keefe turned on full power, and the thing simply melted within its case. All I saw was a surge of white-hot metal pouring over the plinth, a glimpse of Salati's inscription, 'To the Eternal Memory of the Justice of the People,' ere the stone base itself cracked and powdered into finest lime. The crowd cheered.

'Thank you,' said De Forest; 'but we want our breakfasts, and I expect you do too. Goodbye, Mr Mayor! Delighted to see you at any time, but I hope I shan't have to, officially, for the next thirty years. Goodbye, madam. Yes. We're all given to nerves nowadays. I suffer from them myself. Goodbye, gentlemen all! You're under the tyrannous heel of the Board from this moment, but if ever you feel like breaking your fetters you've only to let us know. This is no treat to us. Good luck!'

We embarked amid shouts, and did not check our lift till they had dwindled into whispers. Then De Forest flung himself on the chartroom divan and mopped his forehead.

'I don't mind men,' he panted, 'but women are the devil!'

'Still the devil,' said Pirolo cheerfully. 'That one would have suicided.'

'I know it. That was why I signalled for the flying loop to be clapped on her. I owe you an apology for that, Arnott. I hadn't time to catch your eye, and you were busy with our caitiffs. By the way, who actually answered my signal? It was a smart piece of work.'

'Ilroy,' said Arnott; 'but he overloaded the wave. It may be pretty gallery-work to knock a knife out of a lady's hand, but didn't you notice how she rubbed 'em? He scorched her fingers. Slovenly, I call it.'

'Far be it from me to interfere with Fleet discipline, but don't be too hard on the boy. If that woman had killed herself they would have killed every Servile and everything related to a Servile throughout the district by nightfall.'

'That was what she was playing for,' Takahira said. 'And with our Fleet gone we could have done nothing to hold them.'

'I may be ass enough to walk into a ground-circuit,' said Arnott, 'but I don't dismiss my Fleet till I'm reasonably sure that trouble is over. They're in position still, and I intend to keep 'em there till the Serviles are shipped out of the district. That last little crowd meant murder, my friends.'

'Nerves! All nerves!' said Pirolo. 'You cannot argue with agoraphobia.'

'And it is not as if they had seen much dead – or *is* it?' said Takahira.

'In all my ninety years I have never seen death.' Dragomiroff spoke as one who would excuse himself. 'Perhaps that was why – last night –'

Then it came out as we sat over breakfast, that, with the exception of Arnott and Pirolo, none of us had ever seen a corpse, or knew in what manner the spirit passes.

'We're a nice lot to flap about governing the Planet,' De Forest laughed. 'I confess, now it's all over, that my main fear was I mightn't be able to pull it off without losing a life.'

'I thought of that too,' said Arnott; 'but there's no death reported, and I've inquired everywhere. What are we supposed to do with our passengers? I've fed 'em.'

'We're between two switches,' De Forest drawled. 'If we drop them in any place that isn't under the Board, the natives will make their presence an excuse for cutting out, same as Illinois did, and forcing the Board to take over. If we drop them in any place under the Board's control they'll be killed as soon as our backs are turned.'

'If you say so,' said Pirolo thoughtfully, 'I can guarantee that they will become extinct in process of time, quite happily. What is their birth-rate now?'

'Go down and ask 'em,' said De Forest.

'I think they might become nervous and tear me to bits,' the philosopher of Foggia replied.

'Not really? Well?'

'Open the bilge-doors,' said Takahira with a downward jerk of the thumb.

'Scarcely – after all the trouble we've taken to save 'em,' said De Forest.

'Try London,' Arnott suggested. 'You could turn Satan himself loose there, and they'd only ask him to dinner.'

'Good man! You've given me an idea. Vincent! Oh, Vincent!' He threw the General Communicator open so that we could all hear, and in a few minutes the chartroom filled with the rich, fruity voice of Leopold Vincent, who has purveyed all London her choicest amusements for the last thirty years. We answered with expectant grins, as though we were actually in the stalls of, say, the Combination on a first night.

'We've picked up something in your line,' De Forest began.

'That's good, dear man. If it's old enough. There's nothing to beat the old things for business purposes. Have you seen *London, Chatham, and Dover* at Earl's Court? No? I thought I missed you there. Im-mense! I've had the real steam locomotive engines built from the old designs and the iron rails cast specially by hand. Cloth cushions in the carriages, too! Im-mense! And paper railway tickets. And Polly Milton.'

'Polly Milton back again!' said Arnott rapturously. 'Book me two stalls for tomorrow night. What's she singing now, bless her?'

'The old songs. Nothing comes up to the old touch. Listen to this, dear men.' Vincent carolled with flourishes:

> 'Oh, cruel lamps of London,
> If tears your light could drown,
> Your victims' eyes would weep them,
> Oh, lights of London Town!⁷

52

'Then they weep.'

'You see?' Pirolo waved his hands at us. 'The old world always weeped when it saw crowds together. It did not know why, but it weeped. We know why, but we do not weep; except when we pay to be made to by fat, wicked old Vincent.'

'Old, yourself!' Vincent laughed. 'I'm a public benefactor, I keep the world soft and united.'

'And I'm De Forest of the Board,' said De Forest acidly, 'trying to get a little business done. As I was saying, I've picked up a few people in Chicago.'

'I cut out. Chicago is –'

'Do listen! They're perfectly unique.'

'Do they build houses of baked mudblocks while you wait – eh? That's an old contact.'

'They're an untouched primitive community, with all the old ideas.'

'Sewing-machines and maypole-dances? Cooking on coal-gas stoves, lighting pipes with matches, and driving horses? Gerolstein tried that last year. An absolute blow-out!'

De Forest plugged him wrathfully, and poured out the story of our doings for the last twenty-four hours on the top-note.

'And they do it *all* in public,' he concluded. 'You can't stop 'em. The more public, the better they are pleased. They'll talk for hours – like you! Now you can come in again!'

'Do you really mean they know how to vote?' said Vincent. 'Can they act it?'

'Act? It's their life to 'em! And you never saw such faces! Scarred like volcanoes. Envy, hatred, and malice in plain sight. Wonderfully flexible voices. They weep, too.'

'Aloud? In public?'

'I guarantee. Not a spark of shame or reticence in the entire installation. It's the chance of your career.'

'D'you say you've brought their voting props along – those papers and ballot-box things?'

'No, confound you! I'm not a luggage-lifter. Apply direct to the Mayor of Chicago. He'll forward you everything. Well?'

'Wait a minute. Did Chicago want to kill 'em? That 'ud look well on the Communicators.'

'Yes! They were only rescued with difficulty from a howling mob – if you know what that is.'

'But I don't,' answered the Great Vincent simply.

'Well then, they'll tell you themselves. They can make speeches hours long.'

'How many are there?'

'By the time we ship 'em all over they'll be perhaps a hundred, counting children. An old world in miniature. Can't you see it?'

'M-yes; but I've got to pay for it if it's a blow-out, dear man.'

'They can sing the old war songs in the streets. They can get word-drunk, and make crowds, and invade privacy in the genuine old-fashioned way; and they'll do the voting trick as often as you ask 'em a question.'

'Too good!' said Vincent.

'You unbelieving Jew! I've got a dozen head aboard here. I'll put you through direct. Sample 'em yourself.'

He lifted the switch and we listened. Our passengers on the lower deck at once, but not less than five at a time, explained themselves to Vincent. They had been taken from the bosom of their families, stripped of their possessions, given food without finger-bowls, and cast into captivity in a noisome dungeon.

'But look here,' said Arnott aghast; 'they're saying what isn't true. My lower deck isn't noisome, and I saw to the finger-bowls myself.'

'My people talk like that sometimes in Little Russia,' said Dragomiroff. 'We reason with them. We never kill. No!'

'But it's not true,' Arnott insisted. 'What can you do with people who don't tell facts? They're mad!'

'Hsh!' said Pirolo, his hand to his ear. 'It is such a little time since all the Planet told lies.'

We heard Vincent silkily sympathetic. Would they, he asked, repeat their assertions in public – before a vast public? Only let Vincent give them a chance, and the Planet, they vowed, should ring with their wrongs. Their aim in life – two women and a man explained it together – was to reform the world. Oddly enough, this also had been Vincent's life-dream. He offered them an arena in which to explain, and by their living example to raise the Planet to loftier levels. He was eloquent on the moral uplift of a simple, old-world life presented in its entirety to a deboshed civilization.

Could they – would they – for three months certain, devote themselves under his auspices, as missionaries, to the elevation of mankind at a place called Earl's Court, which he said, with some truth, was one of the intellectual centres of the Planet? They thanked him, and demanded (we could hear his chuckle of delight) time to discuss and to vote on the matter. The vote, solemnly managed by counting heads – one head, one vote – was favourable. His offer, therefore, was accepted, and they moved a vote of thanks to him in two speeches – one by what they called the 'proposer' and the other by the 'seconder'.

Vincent threw over to us, his voice shaking with gratitude:

'I've got 'em! Did you hear those speeches? That's Nature, dear men. Art can't teach *that*. And they voted as easily as lying. I've never had a troupe of natural liars before. Bless you, dear men! Remember, you're on my free lists for ever, anywhere – all of you. Oh, Gerolstein will be sick – sick!'

'Then you think they'll do?' said De Forest.

'Do? The Little Village'll go crazy![8] I'll knock up a series of old-world plays for 'em. Their voices will make you laugh and cry. My God, dear men, where *do* you suppose they picked up all their misery from, on this sweet earth? I'll have a pageant of the world's beginnings, and Mosenthal shall do the music. I'll –'

'Go and knock up a village for 'em by tonight. We'll meet you at No. 15 West Landing Tower,' said De Forest. 'Remember the rest will be coming along tomorrow.'

'Let 'em all come!' said Vincent. 'You don't know how hard it is nowadays even for me, to find something that really gets under the public's damned iridium-plated hide. But I've got it at last. Goodbye!'

'Well,' said De Forest when we had finished laughing, 'if any one understood corruption in London I might have played off Vincent against Gerolstein, and sold my captives at enormous prices. As it is, I shall have to be their legal adviser tonight when the contracts are signed. And they won't exactly press any commission on me, either.'

'Meanwhile,' said Takahira, 'we cannot, of course, confine

members of Leopold Vincent's last-engaged company. Chairs for the ladies, please, Arnott.'

'Then I go to bed,' said De Forest. 'I can't face any more women!' And he vanished.

When our passengers were released and given another meal (finger-bowls came first this time) they told us what they thought of us and the Board; and, like Vincent, we all marvelled how they had contrived to extract and secrete so much bitter poison and unrest out of the good life God gives us. They raged, they stormed, they palpitated, flushed and exhausted their poor, torn nerves, panted themselves into silence, and renewed the senseless, shameless attacks.

'But can't you understand,' said Pirolo pathetically to a shrieking woman, 'that if we'd left you in Chicago you'd have been killed?'

'No, we shouldn't. You were bound to save us from being murdered.'

'Then we should have had to kill a lot of other people.'

'That doesn't matter. We were preaching the Truth. You can't stop us. We shall go on preaching in London; and *then* you'll see!'

'You can see now,' said Pirolo, and opened a lower shutter.

We were closing on the Little Village, with her three million people spread out at ease inside her ring of girdling Main-Traffic lights – those eight fixed beams at Chatham, Tonbridge, Redhill, Dorking, Woking, St Albans, Chipping Ongar, and Southend.

Leopold Vincent's new company looked, with small pale faces, at the silence, the size, and the separated houses.

Then some began to weep aloud, shamelessly – always without shame.

MacDonough's Song

Whether the State can loose and bind
    In Heaven as well as on Earth:
If it be wiser to kill mankind
    Before or after the birth —
These are matters of high concern
    Where State-kept schoolmen are;
But Holy State (we have lived to learn)
    Endeth in Holy War.

Whether The People be led by the Lord,
    Or lured by the loudest throat:
If it be quicker to die by the sword
    Or cheaper to die by vote —
These are the things we have dealt with once,
    (And they will not rise from their grave)
For Holy People, however it runs,
    Endeth in wholly Slave.

Whatsoever, for any cause,
Seeketh to take or give,
Power above or beyond the Laws,
    Suffer it not to live!
Holy State or Holy King —
    Or Holy People's Will —
Have no truck with the senseless thing.
    Order the guns and kill!
    Saying — after — me: —

Once there was The People — Terror gave it birth;
Once there was The People and it made a Hell of Earth.
Earth arose and crushed it. Listen, O ye slain!
Once there was The People — it shall never be again!

FRIENDLY BROOK

⟮ Friendly Brook ⟯

(March 1914)

The valley was so choked with fog that one could scarcely see a cow's length across a field. Every blade, twig, bracken-frond, and hoof-print carried water, and the air was filled with the noise of rushing ditches and field-drains, all delivering to the brook below. A week's November rain on water-logged land had gorged her to full flood, and she proclaimed it aloud.

Two men in sackcloth aprons were considering an untrimmed hedge that ran down the hillside and disappeared into mist beside those roarings. They stood back and took stock of the neglected growth, tapped an elbow of hedge-oak here, a mossed beech-stub there, swayed a stooled ash back and forth, and looked at each other.

'I reckon she's about two rod thick,' [1] said Jabez the younger, 'an' she hasn't felt iron since – when has she, Jesse?'

'Call it twenty-five year, Jabez, an' you won't be far out.'

'Umm!' Jabez rubbed his wet handbill [2] on his wetter coat-sleeve. 'She ain't a hedge. She's all manner o' trees. We'll just about have to –' He paused, as professional etiquette required.

'Just about have to side her up an' see what she'll bear. But hadn't we best –?' Jesse paused in his turn, both men being artists and equals.

'Get some kind o' line to go by.' Jabez ranged up and down till he found a thinner place, and with clean snicks of the handbill revealed the original face of the fence. Jesse took over the dripping stuff as it fell forward, and, with a grasp and a kick, made it to lie orderly on the bank till it should be faggoted.

By noon a length of unclean jungle had turned itself into a cattle-proof barrier, tufted here and there with little plumes of the sacred holly which no woodman touches without orders.

'Now we've a witness-board [3] to go by!' said Jesse at last.

'She won't be as easy as this all along,' Jabez answered. 'She'll need plenty stakes and binders when we come to the brook.'

'Well, ain't we plenty?' Jesse pointed to the ragged perspective ahead of them that plunged downhill into the fog. 'I lay there's a cord an' a half⁴ o' firewood, let alone faggots, 'fore we get anywheres anigh the brook.'

'The brook's got up a piece since morning,' said Jabez. 'Sounds like's if she was over Wickenden's door-stones.'

Jesse listened, too. There was a growl in the brook's roar as though she worried something hard.

'Yes. She's over Wickenden's door-stones,' he replied. 'Now she'll flood acrost Alder Bay an' that'll ease her.'

'She won't ease Jim Wickenden's hay none if she do,' Jabez grunted. 'I told Jim he'd set that liddle hay-stack o' his too low down in the medder. I *told* him so when he was drawin' the bottom for it.'

'I told him so, too,' said Jesse. 'I told him 'fore ever you did. I told him when the County Council tarred the roads up along.' He pointed up-hill, where unseen automobiles and road-engines droned past continually. 'A tarred road, she shoots every drop o' water into a valley same's a slate roof. 'Tisn't as 'twas in the old days, when the waters soaked in and soaked out in the way o' nature. It rooshes off they tarred roads all of a lump, and naturally every drop is bound to descend into the valley. And there's tar roads both two sides this valley for ten mile. That's what I told Jim Wickenden when they tarred the roads last year. But he's a valley-man. He don't hardly ever journey up-hill.'

'What did he say when you told him that?' Jabez demanded, with a little change of voice.

'Why? What did he say to you when *you* told him?' was the answer.

'What he said to you, I reckon, Jesse.'

'Then, you don't need me to say it over again, Jabez.'

'Well, let be how 'twill, what was he gettin' *after* when he said what he said to me?' Jabez insisted.

'*I* dunno; unless you tell me what manner o' words he said to *you*.'

Jabez drew back from the hedge – all hedges are nests of treachery and eavesdropping – and moved to an open cattle-lodge in the centre of the field.

'No need to go ferretin' around,' said Jesse. 'None can't see us here 'fore we see them.'

'What was Jim Wickenden gettin' at when I said he'd set his stack too near anigh the brook?' Jabez dropped his voice. 'He was in his mind.'

'He ain't never been out of it yet to my knowledge,' Jesse drawled, and uncorked his tea-bottle.

'But then Jim says: "I ain't goin' to shift my stack a yard," he says. "The Brook's been good friends to me, and if she be minded," he says, "to take a snatch at my hay, *I* ain't settin' out to withstand her." That's what Jim Wickenden says to me last – last June-end 'twas,' said Jabez.

'Nor he hasn't shifted his stack, neither,' Jesse replied. 'An' if there's more rain, the brook she'll shift it for him.'

'No need tell *me*! But I want to know what Jim was gettin' *at*?'

Jabez opened his clasp-knife very deliberately; Jesse as carefully opened his. They unfolded the newspapers that wrapped their dinners, coiled away and pocketed the string that bound the packages, and sat down on the edge of the lodge manger. The rain began to fall again through the fog, and the brook's voice rose.

'But I always allowed Mary was his lawful child, like,' said Jabez, after Jesse had spoken for a while.

''Tain't so ... Jim Wickenden's woman she never made nothing. She come out o' Lewes with her stockin's round her heels, an' she never made nor mended aught till she died. *He* had to light fire an' get breakfast every mornin' except Sundays, while she sowed it abed.[5] Then she took an' died, sixteen, seventeen, year back; but she never had no childern.'

'They was valley-folk,' said Jabez apologetically. 'I'd no call to go in among 'em, but I always allowed Mary –'

'No. Mary come out o' one o' those Lunnon Childern Societies. After his woman died, Jim got his mother back from his sister over to Peasmarsh, which she'd gone to house with when Jim married. His mother kept house for Jim after his woman died. They do say 'twas his mother led him on toward adoptin' of Mary – to furnish out the house with a child, like, and to keep him off of gettin' a noo woman. He mostly done what his mother contrived. 'Cardenly,[6] twixt 'em, they asked for a child from one o' those Lunnon societies – same as it might ha' been these Barnardo children – an' Mary was sent down to 'em, in a candle-box, I've heard.'

'Then Mary is chance-born.[7] I never knowed that,' said Jabez. 'Yet I must ha' heard it some time or other . . .'

'No. She ain't. 'Twould ha' been better for some folk if she had been. She come to Jim in a candle-box with all the proper papers – lawful child o' some couple in Lunnon somewheres – mother dead, father drinkin'. *And* there was that Lunnon society's five shillin's a week for her. Jim's mother she wouldn't despise week-end money, but I never heard Jim was much of a muck-grubber.[8] Let be how 'twill, they two mothered up Mary no bounds, till it looked at last like they'd forgot she wasn't their own flesh an' blood. Yes, I reckon they forgot Mary wasn't their'n by rights.'

'That's no new thing,' said Jabez. 'There's more'n one or two in this parish wouldn't surrender back their Bernarders. You ask Mark Copley an' his woman an' that Bernarder cripple-babe o' theirs.'

'Maybe they need the five shillin',' Jesse suggested.

'It's handy,' said Jabez. 'But the child's more. "Dada" he says, an' "Mumma" he says, with his great rollin' head-piece all hurdled up in that iron collar. *He* won't live long – his backbone's rotten, like. But they Copleys do just about set store by him – five bob or no five bob.'

'Same way with Jim an' his mother,' Jesse went on. 'There was talk betwixt 'em after a few years o' not takin' any more week-end money for Mary; but let alone *she* never passed a farden in the mire[9] 'thout longin's, Jim didn't care, like, to push himself forward into the Society's remembrance. So naun came of it. The week-end money would ha' made no odds to Jim – not after his uncle willed him they four cottages at Eastbourne *an'* money in the bank.'

'That was true, too, then? I heard something in a scadderin'[10] word-o'-mouth way,' said Jabez.

'I'll answer for the house property, because Jim he reequested my signed name at the foot o' some papers concernin' it. Regardin' the money in the bank, he nature-ally wouldn't like such things talked about all round the parish, so he took strangers for witnesses.'

'Then 'twill make Mary worth seekin' after?'

'She'll need it. Her Maker ain't done much for her outside nor yet in.'

'That ain't no odds.' Jabez shook his head till the water showered off his hat-brim. 'If Mary has money, she'll be wed before any likely pore maid. She's cause to be grateful to Jim.'

'She hides it middlin' close, then,' said Jesse. 'It don't sometimes look to me as if Mary has her natural rightful feelin's. She don't put on an apron o' Mondays 'thout being druv to it – in the kitchen *or* the hen-house. She's studyin' to be a schoolteacher. She'll make a beauty! I never knowed her show any sort o' kindness to nobody – not even when Jim's mother was took dumb. No! 'Twadn't no stroke. It stifled the old lady in the throat here. First she couldn't shape her words no shape; then she clucked, like, an' lastly she couldn't more than suck down spoon-meat an' hold her peace. Jim took her to Doctor Harding, an' Harding he bundled her off to Brighton Hospital on a ticket, but they couldn't make no stay to her afflictions there; and she was bundled off to Lunnon, an' they lit a great old lamp inside her, and Jim told me they couldn't make out nothing in no sort there; and, along o' one thing an' another, an' all their spyin's and pryin's, she come back a hem[11] sight worse than when she started. Jim said he'd have no more hospitalizin', so he give her a slate, which she tied to her waist-string, and what she was minded to say she writ on it.'

'Now, I never knowed that! But they're valley-folk,' Jabez repeated.

''Twadn't particular noticeable, for she wasn't a talkin' woman any time o' her days. Mary had all three's tongue ... Well, then, two years this summer, come what I'm tellin' you. Mary's Lunnon father, which they'd put clean out o' their minds, arrived down from Lunnon with the law on his side, sayin' he'd take his daughter back to Lunnon, after all. I was working for Mus' Dockett at Pounds Farm that summer, but I was obligin' Jim that evenin' muckin' out his pig-pen. I seed a stranger come traipsin' over the bridge agin' Wickenden's door-stones. 'Twadn't the new County Council bridge with the hand-rail. They hadn't given it in for a public right o' way then. 'Twas just a bit o' lathy old plank which Jim had throwed acrost the brook for his own conveniences. The man wasn't drunk – only a little concerned in liquor,[12] like – an' his back was a mask[13] where he'd slipped in the muck comin' along. He went up the bricks past Jim's mother, which was feedin' the ducks, an' set himself down at the table inside – Jim was just changin' his socks – an' the man let Jim know all his rights and aims regardin' Mary. Then there just about *was* a hurly-bulloo? Jim's fust mind was to pitch him forth, but he'd done that once in his young days, and got six months up to Lewes jail along o' the man fallin' on his head. So he swallowed his spittle an' let him talk. The law about Mary *was* on the man's side from fust to last, for he showed us all the papers. Then Mary come downstairs – she'd been studyin' for an examination – an' the man tells her who he was, an' she says he had ought to have took proper care of his own flesh and blood while he had it by him, an' not to think he could ree-claim it when it suited. He says somethin' or other, but she looks him up an' down, front an' backwent,[14] an' she just tongues him scadderin' out o' doors, and he went away stuffin' all the papers back into his hat, talkin' most abusefully. Then she come back an' freed her mind against Jim an' his mother for not havin' warned her of her upbringin's, which it come out she hadn't ever been told. They didn't say naun[15] to her. They never did. *I*'d ha' packed her off with any man that would ha' took her – an' God's pity on him!'

'Umm!' said Jabez, and sucked his pipe.

'So then, that was the beginnin'. The man come back again next week or so, an' he catched Jim alone, 'thout his mother this time, an' he fair beazled[16] him with his papers an' his talk – for the law *was* on his side – till Jim went down into his money-purse an' give him ten shillings hush-money – he told me – to withdraw away for a bit an' leave Mary with 'em.'

'But that's no way to get rid o' man or woman,' Jabez said.

'No more 'tis. I told Jim so. "What can I do?" Jim says.
"The law's *with* the man, I walk about daytimes thinkin' o' it
till I sweats my underclothes wringin', an' I lie abed nights
thinkin' o' it till I sweats my sheets all of a sop. 'Tisn't as if I
was a young man," he says, "nor yet as if I was a pore man.
Maybe he'll drink hisself to death." I e'en a'most told him
outright what foolishness he was enterin' into, but he knowed it
—he knowed it – because he said next time the man come
'twould be fifteen shillin's. An' next time 'twas. Just fifteen
shillin's!'

'An' *was* the man her father?' asked Jabez.

'He had the proofs an' the papers. Jim showed me what that
Lunnon Childern's Society had answered when Mary writ up
to 'em an' taxed 'em with it. I lay she hadn't been proper polite
in her letters to 'em, for they answered middlin' short. They
said the matter was out o' their hands, but – let's see if I
remember – oh, yes – they ree-gretted there had been an over-
sight. I reckon they had sent Mary out in the candle-box as a
orphan instead o' havin' a father. Terrible awkward! Then,
when he'd drinked up the money, the man come again – in his
usuals[17] – an' he kept hammerin' on and hammerin' on
about his duty to his pore dear wife, an' what he'd do for his
dear daughter in Lunnon, till the tears runned down his two
dirty cheeks an' he come away with more money. Jim used to
slip it into his hand behind the door; but his mother she heard
the chink. She didn't hold with hush-money. She'd write out
all her feelin's on the slate, an' Jim 'ud be settin' up half the
night answerin' back an showing that the man had the law with
him.'

'Hadn't that man no trade nor business, then?'

'He told me he was a printer. I reckon, though, he lived on
the rates like the rest of 'em up there in Lunnon.'

'An' how did Mary take it?'

'She said she'd sooner go into service than go with the man. I
reckon a mistress 'ud be middlin' put to it for a maid 'fore she
put Mary into cap an' gown. She was studyin' to be a school-
teacher. A beauty she'll make! . . . Well, that was how things
went that fall. Mary's Lunnon father kep' comin' an' comin'
'carden as he'd drinked out the money Jim gave him; an' each

time he'd put up his price for not takin' Mary away. Jim's mother, she didn't like partin' with no money, an' bein' obliged to write her feelin's on the slate instead o' givin' 'em vent by mouth, she was just about mad. Just about she *was* mad!

'Come November, I lodged with Jim in the outside room over 'gainst his hen-house. I paid *her* my rent. I was workin' for Dockett at Pounds – gettin' chestnut-bats[18] out o' Perry Shaw. Just such weather as this be – rain atop o' rain after a wet October. (An' I remember it ended in dry frostes right away up to Christmas.) Dockett he'd sent up to Perry Shaw for me – no, he comes puffin' up to me himself – because a big corner-piece o' the bank had slipped into the brook where she makes that elber[19] at the bottom o' the Seventeen Acre, an' all the rubbishy alders an' sallies[20] which he ought to have cut out when he took the farm, they'd slipped with the slip, an' the brook was comin' rooshin' down atop of 'em, an' they'd just about back an' spill the waters over his winter wheat. The water was lyin' in the flats already. "Gor a-mighty, Jesse!" he bellers out at me, "get that rubbish away all manners you can. Don't stop for no fagottin', but give the brook play or my wheat's past salvation. I can't lend you no help," he says, "but work an' I'll pay ye."'

'You had him there,' Jabez chuckled.

'Yes. I reckon I had ought to have drove my bargain, but the brook was backin' up on good bread-corn. So 'cardenly, I laid into the mess of it, workin' off the bank where the trees was drownin' themselves head-down in the roosh – just such weather as this – an' the brook creepin' up on me all the time. 'Long toward noon, Jim comes mowchin' along with his toppin' axe over his shoulder.

'"Be you minded for an extra hand at your job?" he says.

'"Be you minded to turn to?" I ses, an' – no more talk to it – Jim laid in alongside o' me. He's no bunger with a toppin' axe.'

'Maybe, but I've seed him at a job o' throwin' in the woods, an' he didn't seem to make out no shape,' said Jabez. 'He haven't got the shoulders, nor yet the judgment – *my* opinion – when he's dealin' with full-girt timber. He don't rightly make up his mind where he's goin' to throw her.'

'We wasn't throwin' nothin'. We was cuttin' out they soft

alders, an' haulin' 'em up the bank 'fore they could back the waters on the wheat. Jim didn't say much, 'less it was that he'd had a post-card from Mary's Lunnon father, night before, sayin' he was comin' down that mornin'. Jim, he'd sweated all night, an' he didn't reckon hisself equal to the talkin' an' the swearin' an' the cryin', an' his mother blamin' him afterwards on the slate. "It spiled my day to think of it," he ses, when we was eatin' our pieces.[21] "So I've fair cried dunghill an' run.[22] Mother'll have to tackle him by herself. I lay *she* won't give him no hush-money," he ses. "I lay he'll be surprised by the time he's done with *her*," he ses. An' that was e'en a'most all the talk we had concernin' it. But he's no bunger with the toppin' axe.

'The brook she'd crep' up an' up on us, an' she kep' creepin' upon us till we was workin' knee-deep in the shallers, cuttin' an' pookin' an' pullin' what we could get to o' the rubbish. There was a middlin' lot comin' down-stream, too — cattle-bars an' hop-poles and odds-ends bats, all poltin'[23] down together; but they rooshed round the elber good shape by the time we'd backed out they drowned trees. Come four o'clock we reckoned we'd done a proper day's work, an' she'd take no harm if we left her. We couldn't puddle about there in the dark an' wet to no more advantage. Jim he was pourin' the water out of his boots — no, I was doin' that. Jim was kneelin' to unlace his'n. "Damn it all, Jesse," he ses, standin' up; "the flood must be over my doorsteps at home, for here comes my old white-top bee-skep!"'[24]

'Yes. I allus heard he paints his bee-skeps,' Jabez put in. 'I dunno paint don't tarrify bees more'n it keeps 'em dry.'

'"I'll have a pook at it," he ses, an' he pooks at it as it comes round the elber. The roosh nigh jerked the pooker out of his hand-grips, an' he calls to me, an' I come runnin' barefoot. Then we pulled on the pooker, an' it reared up on eend in the roosh, an' we guessed what 'twas. 'Cardenly we pulled it in into a shaller, an' it rolled a piece, an' a great old stiff man's arm nigh hit me in the face. Then we was sure. "'Tis a man," ses Jim. But the face was all a mask. "I reckon it's Mary's Lunnon father," he ses presently. "Lend me a match and I'll make sure." He never used baccy. We lit three matches one by another, well's we could in the rain, an' he cleaned off some o' the slob with a tussick o' grass. "Yes," he ses. "It's Mary's Lunnon father. He won't tarrify us no more. D'you want him, Jesse?" he ses.

'"No," I ses. "If this was Eastbourne beach like, he'd be half-a-crown apiece to us' fore the coroner; but now we'd only lose a day havin' to 'tend the inquest. I lay he fell into the brook."

'"I lay he did," ses Jim. "I wonder if he saw mother." He turns him over, an' opens his coat and puts his fingers in the waistcoat pocket an' starts laughin'. "He's seen mother, right enough," he ses. "An' he's got the best of her, too. *She* won't be able to crow no more over *me* 'bout givin' him money. *I* never give him more than a sovereign. She's give him two!" an' he trousers 'em, laughin' all the time. "An' now we'll pook him back again, for I've done with him," he ses.

'So we pooked him back into the middle of the brook, an' we saw he went round the elber 'thout balkin', an' we walked quite a piece beside of him to set him on his ways. When we couldn't see no more, we went home by the high road, because we knowed the brook 'u'd be out acrost the medders, an' we wasn't goin' to hunt for Jim's little rotten old bridge in that dark — an' rainin' Heavens' hard, too. I was middlin' pleased to see light an' vittles again when we got home. Jim he pressed me to come insides for a drink. He don't drink in a generality, but he was rid of all his troubles that evenin', d'ye see? "Mother," he ses so soon as the door ope'd, "have you see him?" She whips out her slate an' writes down —"No." "Oh, no," ses Jim. "You don't get out of it that way, mother. I lay you *have* seen him, an' I lay he's bested you for all your talk, same as he bested me. Make a clean breast of it, mother," he ses. "He got round you too." She was goin' for the slate again, but he stops her. "It's all right, mother," he ses. "I've seen him sense you have, an' he won't trouble us no more." The old lady looks up quick as a robin, an' she writes, "Did he say so?" "No," ses Jim, laughin'. "He didn't say so. That's how I know. But he bested *you*, mother. You can't have it in at *me* for bein' soft-hearted. You're twice as tender-hearted as what I be. Look!" he ses, an' he shows her the two sovereigns. "Put 'em away where they belong," he ses. "He won't never come for no more; an' now we'll have our drink," he ses, "for we've earned it."

'Nature-ally they weren't goin' to let me see where they kep' their monies. She went upstairs with it – for the whisky.'

'I never knowed Jim was a drinkin' man – in his own house, like,' said Jabez.

'No more he isn't; but what he takes he likes good. He won't tech no publican's hogwash acrost the bar. Four shillin's he paid for that bottle o' whisky. I know, because when the old lady brought it down there wasn't more'n jest a liddle few dreenin's an' dregs in it. Nothin' to set before neighbours, I do assure you.'

'"Why, 'twas half full last week, mother," he ses. "You don't mean," he ses, "you've given him all that as well? It's two shillin's worth," he ses. (That's how I knowed he paid four.) "Well, well, mother, you be too tender-'earted to live. But I don't grudge it to him," he ses. "I don't grudge him nothin' he can keep." So, 'cardenly, we drinked up what little sup was left.'

'An' what come to Mary's Lunnon father?' said Jabez, after a full minute's silence.

'I be too tired to go readin' papers of evenin's; but Dockett he told me, that very week, I think, that they'd inquested on a man down at Robertsbridge which had polted and polted up agin' so many bridges an' banks, like they couldn't make naun out of him.'

'An' what did Mary say to all these doin's?'

'The old lady bundled her off to the village 'fore her Lunnon father come, to buy week-end stuff (an' she forgot the half o' it). When we come in she was upstairs studyin' to be a school-teacher. None told her naun about it. 'Twadn't girls' affairs.'

''Reckon *she* knowed?' Jabez went on.

'She? She must have guessed it middlin' close when she saw her money come back. But she never mentioned it in writing so far's I know. She were more worritted that night on account of two-three her chickens bein' drowned, for the flood had skewed their old hen-house round on her postes. I cobbled her up next mornin' when the brook shrinked.'

'An' where did you find the bridge? Some fur down-stream, didn't ye?'

'Just where she allus was. She hadn't shifted but very little. The brook had gulled out the bank a piece under one eend o' the plank, so's she was liable to tilt ye sideways if you wasn't careful. But I pooked three-four bricks under her, an' she was all plumb again.'

'Well, I dunno how it *looks* like, but let be how 'twill,' said Jabez, 'he hadn't no business to come down from Lunnon tarrifyin' people, an' threatenin' to take away children which they'd hobbed²⁵ up for their lawful own – even if 'twas Mary Wickenden.'

'He had the business right enough, an' he had the law with him – no gettin' over that,' said Jesse. 'But he had the drink with him, too, an' that was where he failed, like.'

'Well, well! Let be how 'twill, the brook was a good friend to Jim. I see it now. I allus *did* wonder what he was gettin' at when he said that, when I talked to him about shiftin' the stack. "You dunno everythin'," he ses. "The Brook's been a good friend to me," he ses, "an' if she's minded to have a snatch at my hay, *I* ain't settin' out to withstand her."'

'I reckon she's about shifted it, too, by now,' Jesse chuckled. 'Hark! That ain't any slip off the bank which she's got hold of.'

The Brook had changed her note again. It sounded as though she were mumbling something soft.

The Land

When Julius Fabricius, Sub-Prefect of the Weald,
In the days of Diocletian owned our Lower River-field,
He called to him Hobdenius – a Briton of the Clay,
Saying: 'What about that River-piece for layin' in to hay?'

And the aged Hobden [1] answered: 'I remember as a lad
My father told your father that she wanted dreenin' bad.
An' the more that you neeglect her the less you'll get her clean.
Have it jest *as* you've a mind to, but, if I was you, I'd dreen.'

So they drained it long and crossways in the lavish Roman style.
Still we find among the river-drift their flakes of ancient tile,
And in drouthy middle August, when the bones of meadows show,
We can trace the lines they followed sixteen hundred years ago.

Then Julius Fabricius died as even Prefects do,
And after certain centuries, Imperial Rome died too.
Then did robbers enter Britain from across the Northern main
And our Lower River-field was won by Ogier the Dane.

Well could Ogier work his war-boat – well could Ogier wield
his brand
Much he knew of foaming waters – not so much of farming land.
So he called to him a Hobden of the old unaltered blood,
Saying: 'What about that River-bit, she doesn't look no good?'

And that aged Hobden answered: ''Tain't for *me* to interfere,
But I've known that bit o' meadow now for five and fifty year.
Have it *jest* as you've a mind to, but I've proved it time on time,
If you want to change her nature you have *got* to give her lime!'

Ogier sent his wains to Lewes, twenty hours' solemn walk,
And drew back great abundance of the cool, grey, healing chalk.
And old Hobden spread it broadcast, never heeding what was in't;
Which is why in cleaning ditches, now and then we find a flint.

Ogier died. His sons grew English. Anglo-Saxon was their name,
Till out of blossomed Normandy another pirate came;
For Duke William conquered England and divided with his men,
And our Lower River-field he gave to William of Warenne.

But the Brook (you know her habit) rose one rainy Autumn night
And tore down sodden flitches of the bank to left and right.
So, said William to his Bailiff as they rode their dripping rounds:
'Hob, what about that River-bit – the Brook's got up no bounds?'

And that aged Hobden answered: ''Tain't my business to advise,
But ye might ha' known 'twould happen from the way the valley lies
When ye can't hold back the water you must try and save the sile.
Hev it jest as you've a *mind* to, but, if I was you, I'd spile!'

They spiled along the water-course with trunks of willow-trees
And planks of elms behind 'em and immortal oaken knees.
And when the spates of Autumn whirl the gravel-beds away
You can see their faithful fragments iron-hard in iron clay.

Georgii Quinti Anno Sexto, I, who own the River-field,
Am fortified with title-deeds, attested, signed and sealed,
Guaranteeing me, my assigns, my executors and heirs
All sorts of powers and profits which – are neither mine nor theirs

I have rights of chase and warren, as my dignity requires.
I can fish – but Hobden tickles. I can shoot – but Hobden wires.
I repair, but he reopens, certain gaps which, men allege,
Have been used by every Hobden since a Hobden swapped a hedge

Shall I dog his morning progress o'er the track-betraying dew?
Demand his dinner-basket into which my pheasant flew?
Confiscate his evening faggot into which the conies ran,
And summons him to judgment? I would sooner summons Pan.

His dead are in the churchyard – thirty generations laid.
Their names went down in Domesday Book when Domesday Book
was made.
And the passion and the piety and prowess of his line
Have seeded, rooted, fruited in some land the Law calls mine.

Not for any beast that burrows, not for any bird that flies,
Would I lose his large sound council, miss his keen amending eyes.
He is bailiff, woodman, wheelwright, field-surveyor, engineer,
And if flagrantly a poacher – 'tain't for me to interfere.

'Hob, what about that River-bit?' I turn to him again
With Fabricius and Ogier and William of Warenne.
'Hev it jest as you've a mind to, *but*' – and so he takes command.
For whoever pays the taxes old Mus' Hobden owns the land.

IN THE SAME BOAT

{ In the Same Boat }

(1911)

'A throbbing vein,' said Dr Gilbert soothingly, 'is the mother of delusion.'

'Then how do you account for my knowing when the thing is due?' Conroy's voice rose almost to a break.

'Of course, but you should have consulted a doctor before using – palliatives.'

'It was driving me mad. And now I can't give them up.'

'Not so bad as that! One doesn't form fatal habits at twenty-five. Think again. Were you ever frightened as a child?'

'I don't remember. It began when I was a boy.'

'With or without the spasm? By the way, do you mind describing the spasm again?'

'Well,' said Conroy, twisting in the chair, 'I'm no musician, but suppose you were a violin-string – vibrating – and someone put his finger on you? As if a finger were put on the naked soul! Awful!'

'So's indigestion – so's nightmare – while it lasts.'

'But the horror afterwards knocks me out for days. And the waiting for it . . . and then this drug habit! It can't go on!' He shook as he spoke, and the chair creaked.

'My dear fellow,' said the doctor, 'when you're older you'll know what burdens the best of us carry. A fox to every Spartan.'[1]

'That doesn't help *me*. I can't! I can't!' cried Conroy, and burst into tears.

'Don't apologize,' said Gilbert, when the paroxysm ended. 'I'm used to people coming a little – unstuck in this room.'

'It's those tabloids!' Conroy stamped his foot feebly as he blew his nose. 'They've knocked me out. I used to be fit once. Oh, I've tried exercise and everything. But – if one sits down for a minute when it's due – even at four in the morning – it runs up behind one.'

'Ye-es. Many things come in the quiet of the morning. You always know when the visitation is due?'

'What would I give not to be sure!' he sobbed.

'We'll put that aside for the moment. I'm thinking of a case where what we'll call anaemia of the brain was masked (I don't say cured) by vibration. He couldn't sleep, or thought he couldn't, but a steamer voyage and the thump of the screw –'

'A steamer? After what I've told you!' Conroy almost shrieked. 'I'd sooner . . .'

'Of course *not* a steamer in your case, but a long railway journey the next time you think it will trouble you. It sounds absurd, but –'

'I'd try anything. I nearly have,' Conroy sighed.

'Nonsense! I've given you a tonic that will clear *that* notion from your head. Give the train a chance, and don't begin the journey by bucking yourself up with tabloids. Take them along, but hold them in reserve – in reserve.'

'D'you think I've self-control enough, after what you've heard?' said Conroy.

Dr Gilbert smiled. 'Yes. After what I've seen,' he glanced round the room, 'I have no hesitation in saying you have quite as much self-control as many other people. I'll write you later about your journey. Meantime, the tonic,' and he gave some general directions before Conroy left.

An hour later Dr Gilbert hurried to the links, where the others of his regular week-end game awaited him. It was a rigid round, played as usual at the trot, for the tension of the week lay as heavy on the two King's Counsels and Sir John Chartres as on Gilbert. The lawyers were old enemies of the Admiralty Court, and Sir John of the frosty eyebrows and Abernethy[2] manner was bracketed with, but before, Rutherford Gilbert among nerve-specialists.

At the Club-house afterwards the lawyers renewed their squabble over a tangled collision case, and the doctors as naturally compared professional matters.

'Lies – all lies,' said Sir John, when Gilbert had told him Conroy's trouble. '*Post hoc, propter hoc.*[3] The man or woman who drugs is *ipso facto*[4] a liar. You've no imagination.'

' 'Pity you haven't a little – occasionally.'

'I have believed a certain type of patient in my time. It's always the same. For reasons not given in the consulting-room they take to the drug. Certain symptoms follow. They will swear to you, and believe it, that they took the drug to mask the symptoms. What does your man use? Najdolene? I thought so. I had practically the duplicate of your case last Thursday. Same old Najdolene – same old lie.'

'Tell me the symptoms, and I'll draw my own inferences, Johnnie.'

'Symptoms! The girl was rank poisoned with Najdolene. Ramping, stamping possession. Gad, I thought she'd have the chandelier down.'

'Mine came unstuck too, and he has the physique of a bull,' said Gilbert. 'What delusions had yours?'

'Faces – faces with mildew on them. In any other walk of life we'd call it the Horrors. She told me, of course, she took the drugs to mask the faces. *Post hoc, propter hoc* again. All liars!'

'What's that?' said the senior K.C. quickly. ''Sounds professional.'

'Go away! Not for you, Sandy.' Sir John turned a shoulder against him and walked with Gilbert in the chill evening.

To Conroy in his chambers came, one week later, this letter:

DEAR MR CONROY–
If your plan of a night's trip on the 17th still holds good, and you have no particular destination in view, you could do me a kindness. A Miss Henschil, in whom I am interested, goes down to the West by the 10.8 from Waterloo (Number 3 platform) on that night. She is not exactly an invalid, but, like so many of us, a little shaken in her nerves. Her maid, of course, accompanies her, but if I knew you were in the same train it would be an additional source of strength. Will you please write and let me know whether the 10.8 from Waterloo, Number 3 platform, on the 17th, suits you, and I will meet you there? Don't forget my caution, and keep up the tonic.

Yours sincerely,
L. RUTHERFORD GILBERT

'He knows I'm scarcely fit to look after myself,' was Conroy's thought. 'And he wants me to look after a woman!'

Yet, at the end of half an hour's irresolution, he accepted.

Now Conroy's trouble, which had lasted for years, was this: On a certain night, while he lay between sleep and wake, he would be overtaken by a long shuddering sigh, which he learned to know was the sign that his brain had once more conceived its horror, and in time – in due time – would bring it forth.

Drugs could so well veil that horror that it shuffled along no worse than as a freezing dream in a procession of disorderly dreams; but over the return of the event drugs had no control. Once that sigh had passed his lips the thing was inevitable, and through the days granted before its rebirth he walked in torment. For the first two years he had striven to fend it off by distractions, but neither exercise nor drink availed. Then he had come to the tabloids of the excellent M. Najdol. These guarantee, on the label, 'Refreshing and absolutely natural sleep to the soul-weary.' They are carried in a case with a spring which presses one scented tabloid to the end of the tube, whence it can be lipped off in stroking the moustache or adjusting the veil.

Three years of M. Najdol's preparations do not fit a man for many careers. His friends, who knew he did not drink, assumed that Conroy had strained his heart through valiant outdoor exercises, and Conroy had with some care invented an imaginary doctor, symptoms, and regimen, which he discussed with them and with his mother in Hereford. She maintained that he would grow out of it, and recommended nux vomica.[5]

When at last Conroy faced a real doctor, it was, he hoped, to be saved from suicide by a strait-waistcoat. Yet Dr Gilbert had but given him more drugs – a tonic, for instance, that would couple railway carriages – and had advised a night in the train. Not alone the horrors of a railway journey (for which a man who dare keep no servant must e'en pack, label, and address his own bag), but the necessity for holding himself in hand before a stranger 'a little shaken in her nerves'.

He spent a long forenoon packing, because when he assembled and counted things his mind slid off to the hours that remained of the day before his night, and he found himself counting minutes aloud. At such times the injustice of his fate would drive him to revolts which no servant should witness, but on this evening Dr Gilbert's tonic held him fairly calm while he put up his patent razors.

Waterloo Station shook him into real life. The change for his ticket needed concentration, if only to prevent shillings and pence turning into minutes at the booking-office; and he spoke quickly to a porter about the disposition of his bag. The old 10.8 from Waterloo to the West was an all-night caravan that halted, in the interests of the milk traffic, at almost every station.

Dr Gilbert stood by the door of the one composite corridor-coach; an older and stouter man behind him. 'So glad you're here!' he cried. 'Let me get your ticket.'

'Certainly not,' Conroy answered. 'I got it myself – long ago. My bag's in too,' he added proudly.

'I beg your pardon. Miss Henschil's here. I'll introduce you.'

'But – but,' he stammered – 'think of the state I'm in. If anything happens I shall collapse.'

'Not you. You'd rise to the occasion like a bird. And as for the self-control you were talking of the other day' – Gilbert swung him round – 'look!'

A young man in an ulster over a silk-faced frock-coat stood by the carriage window, weeping shamelessly.

'Oh, but that's only drink,' Conroy said, 'I haven't had one of my – my things since lunch.'

'Excellent!' said Gilbert. 'I knew I could depend on you. Come along. Wait for a minute, Chartres.'

A tall woman, veiled, sat by the far window. She bowed her head as the doctor murmured Conroy knew not what. Then he disappeared and the inspector came for tickets.

'My maid – next compartment,' she said slowly.

Conroy showed his ticket, but in returning it to the sleeve-pocket of his ulster the little silver Najdolene case slipped from his glove and fell to the floor. He snatched it up as the moving train flung him into his seat.

'How nice!' said the woman. She leisurely lifted her veil, unbuttoned the first button of her left glove, and pressed out from its palm a Najdolene-case.

'Don't!' said Conroy, not realizing he had spoken.

'I beg your pardon.' The deep voice was measured, even, and low. Conroy knew what made it so.

'I said "don't"! He wouldn't like you to do it!'

'No,' he would not.' She held the tube with its ever-presented tabloid between finger and thumb. 'But aren't you one of the – ah – "soul-weary" too?'

'That's why. Oh, please don't! Not at first. I – I haven't had one since morning. You – you'll set me off!'

'You? Are you so far gone as that?'

He nodded, pressing his palms together. The train jolted through Vauxhall points, and was welcomed with the clang of empty milk-cans for the West.

After long silence she lifted her great eyes, and, with an innocence that would have deceived any sound man, asked Conroy to call her maid to bring her a forgotten book.

Conroy shook his head. 'No. Our sort can't read. Don't!'

'Were you sent to watch me?' The voice never changed.

'Me? I need a keeper myself much more – *this* night of all.'

'This night? Have you a night, then? They disbelieved *me* when I told them of mine.' She leaned back and laughed, always slowly. 'Aren't doctors stu-upid? They don't know.'

She leaned her elbow on her knee, lifted her veil that had fallen, and, chin in hand, stared at him. He looked at her – till his eyes were blurred with tears.

'Have *I* been there, think you?' she said.

'Surely – surely,' Conroy answered, for he had well seen the fear and the horror that lived behind the heavy-lidded eyes, the fine tracing on the broad forehead, and the guard set about the desirable mouth.

'Then – suppose we have one – just one apiece? I've gone without since this afternoon.'

He put up his hand, and would have shouted, but his voice broke.

'Don't! Can't you see that it helps me to help you to keep it off? Don't let's both go down together.'

'But I want one. It's a poor heart that never rejoices. Just one. It's my night.'

'It's mine – too. My sixty-fourth, fifth, sixth, seventh.' He shut his lips firmly against the tide of visualized numbers that threatened to carry him along.

'Ah, it's only my thirty-ninth.' She paused as he had done. 'I wonder if I shall last into the sixties . . . Talk to me or I shall go crazy. You're a man. You're the stronger vessel. Tell me when you went to pieces.'

'One, two, three, four, five, six, seven – eight – I beg your pardon.'

'Not in the least. I always pretend I've dropped a stitch of my knitting. I count the days till the last day, then the hours, then the minutes. Do you?'

'I don't think I've done very much else for the last –' said Conroy, shivering, for the night was cold, with a chill he recognized.

'Oh, how comforting to find some one who can talk sense! It's not always the same date, is it?'

'What difference would that make?' He unbuttoned his ulster with a jerk. 'You're a sane woman. Can't you see the wicked – wicked – wicked' (dust flew from the padded arm-rest as he struck it) 'unfairness of it? What have *I* done?'

She laid her large hand on his shoulder very firmly.

'If you begin to think over that,' she said, 'you'll go to pieces and be ashamed. Tell me yours, and I'll tell you mine. Only be quiet – be quiet, lad, or you'll set me off!' She made shift to soothe him, though her chin trembled.

'Well,' said he at last, picking at the arm-rest between them, 'mine's nothing much, of course.'

'Don't be a fool! That's for doctors – and mothers.'

'It's Hell,' Conroy muttered. 'It begins on a steamer – on a stifling hot night. I come out of my cabin. I pass through the saloon where the stewards have rolled up the carpets, and the boards are bare and hot and soapy.'

'I've travelled too,' she said.

'Ah! I come on deck. I walk down a covered alleyway. Butcher's meat, bananas, oil, that sort of smell.'

Again she nodded.

'It's a lead-coloured steamer, and the sea's lead-coloured. Perfectly smooth sea – perfectly still ship, except for the engines running, and her waves going off in lines and lines and lines – dull grey. All this time I know something's going to happen.'

'*I* know. Something going to happen,' she whispered.

'Then I hear a thud in the engine-room. Then the noise of machinery falling down – like fire-irons – and then two most awful yells. They're more like hoots, and I know – I know while I listen – that it means that two men have died as they hooted. It was their last breath hooting out of them – in most awful pain. Do you understand?'

'I ought to. Go on.'

'That's the first part. Then I hear bare feet running along the alleyway. One of the scalded men comes up behind me and says quite distinctly, "My friend! All is lost!" Then he taps me on the shoulder and I hear him drop down dead.' He panted and wiped his forehead.

'So that is your night?' she said.

'That is my night. It comes every few weeks – so many days after I get what I call sentence. Then I begin to count.'

'Get sentence? D'you mean *this*?' She half closed her eyes, drew a deep breath, and shuddered. '"Notice" I call it. Sir John thought it was all lies.'

She had unpinned her hat and thrown it on the seat opposite, showing the immense mass of her black hair, rolled low in the nape of the columnar neck and looped over the left ear. But Conroy had no eyes except for her grave eyes.

'Listen now!' said she. 'I walk down a road, a white sandy road near the sea. There are broken fences on either side, and Men come and look at me over them.'

'Just men? Do they speak?'

'They try to. Their faces are all mildewy – eaten away,' and she hid her face for an instant with her left hand. 'It's the Faces – the Faces!'

'Yes. Like my two hoots. *I* know.'

'Ah! But the place itself – the bareness – and the glitter and the salt smells, and the wind blowing the sand! The Men run after me and I run ... I know what's coming too. One of them touches me.'

'Yes! What comes then? We've both shirked that.'

'One awful shock – not palpitation, but shock, shock, shock!'

'As though your soul were being stopped – as you'd stop a finger-bowl humming?' he said.

'Just that,' she answered. 'One's very soul – the soul that one lives by – stopped. So!'

She drove her thumb deep into the arm-rest. 'And now,' she

whined to him, 'now that we've stirred each other up this way, mightn't we have just one?'

'No,' said Conroy, shaking. 'Let's hold on. We're past' – he peered out of the black windows – 'Woking. There's the Necropolis.[6] How long till dawn?'

'Oh, cruel long yet. If one dozes for a minute, it catches one.'

'And how d'you find that this' – he tapped the palm of his glove – 'helps you?'

'It covers up the thing from being too real – if one takes enough – you know. Only – only – one loses everything else. I've been no more than a bogie-girl for two years. What would you give to be real again? This lying's such a nuisance.'

'One must protect oneself – and there's one's mother to think of,' he answered.

'True. I hope allowances are made for us somewhere. Our burden – can you hear? – our burden is heavy enough.'

She rose, towering into the roof of the carriage. Conroy's ungentle grip pulled her back.

'Now *you* are foolish. Sit down,' said he.

'But the cruelty of it! Can't you see it? Don't you feel it. Let's take one now – before I –'

'Sit down!' cried Conroy, and the sweat stood again on his forehead. He had fought through a few nights, and had been defeated on more, and he knew the rebellion that flares beyond control to exhaustion.

She smoothed her hair and dropped back, but for a while her head and throat moved with the sickening motion of a captured wry-neck.[7]

'Once,' she said, spreading out her hands, 'I ripped my counterpane from end to end. That takes strength. I had it then. I've little now. "All dorn,"[8] as my little niece says. And you, lad?'

'"All dorn"! Let me keep your case for you till the morning.'

'But the cold feeling is beginning.'

'Lend it me, then.'

'And the drag down my right side. I shan't be able to move in a minute.'

'I can scarcely lift my arm myself,' said Conroy. 'We're in for it.'

'Then why are you so foolish? You know it'll be easier if we have only one – only one apiece.'

She was lifting the case to her mouth. With tremendous effort Conroy caught it. The two moved like jointed dolls, and when their hands met it was as wood on wood.

'You must – not!' said Conroy. His jaws stiffened, and the cold climbed from his feet up.

'Why – must – I – not?' She repeated the words idiotically.

Conroy could only shake his head, while he bore down on the hand and the case in it.

Her speech went from her altogether. The wonderful lips rested half over the even teeth, the breath was in the nostrils only, the eyes dulled, the face set grey, and through the glove the hand struck like ice.

Presently her soul came back and stood behind her eyes – only thing that had life in all that place – stood and looked for Conroy's soul. He too was fettered in every limb, but somewhere at an immense distance he heard his heart going about its work as the engine-room carries on through and beneath the all but overwhelming wave. His one hope, he knew, was not to lose the eyes that clung to his, because there was an Evil abroad which would possess him if he looked aside by a hairbreadth.

The rest was darkness through which some distant planet spun while cymbals clashed. (Beyond Farnborough the 10.8 rolls out many empty milk-cans at every halt.) Then a body came to life with intolerable pricklings. Limb by limb, after agonies of terror, that body returned to him, steeped in most perfect physical weariness such as follows a long day's rowing. He saw the heavy lids droop over her eyes – the watcher behind them departed – and, his soul sinking into assured peace, Conroy slept.

Light on his eyes and a salt breath roused him without shock. Her hand still held his. She slept, forehead down upon it, but the movement of his waking waked her too, and she sneezed like a child.

'I – I think it's morning,' said Conroy.

'And nothing has happened! Did you see your Men? I didn't see my Faces. Does it mean we've escaped? Did – did you take any after I went to sleep? I'll swear *I* didn't,' she stammered.

'No, there wasn't any need. We've slept through it.'

'No need! Thank God! There was no need! Oh, look!'

The train was running under red cliffs along a sea-wall washed by waves that were colourless in the early light. Southward the sun rose mistily upon the Channel.

She leaned out of the window and breathed to the bottom of her lungs, while the wind wrenched down her dishevelled hair and blew it below her waist.

'Well!' she said with splendid eyes. 'Aren't you still waiting for something to happen?'

'No. Not till next time. We've been let off,' Conroy answered, breathing as deeply as she.

'Then we ought to say our prayers.'

'What nonsense! Some one will see us.'

'We needn't kneel. Stand up and say "Our Father". We *must*!'

It was the first time since childhood that Conroy had prayed. They laughed hysterically when a curve threw them against an arm-rest.

'Now for breakfast!' she cried. 'My maid — Nurse Blaber — has the basket and things. It'll be ready in twenty minutes. Oh! Look at my hair!' and she went out laughing.

Conroy's first discovery, made without fumbling or counting letters on taps, was that the London and South Western's allowance of washing-water is inadequate. He used every drop, rioting in the cold tingle on neck and arms. To shave in a moving train balked him, but the next halt gave him a chance, which, to his own surprise, he took. As he stared at himself in the mirror he smiled and nodded. There were points about this person with the clear, if sunken, eye and the almost uncompressed mouth. But when he bore his bag back to his compartment, the weight of it on a limp arm humbled that new pride.

'My friend,' he said, half aloud, 'you go into training. You're putty.'

She met him in the spare compartment, where her maid had laid breakfast.

'By Jove!' he said, halting at the doorway, 'I hadn't realized how beautiful you were!'

'The same to you, lad. Sit down. I could eat a horse.'

'I shouldn't,' said the maid quietly. 'The less you eat the better.' She was a small, freckled woman, with light fluffy hair and pale-blue eyes that looked through all veils.

'This is Miss Blaber,' said Miss Henschil. 'He's one of the soul-weary too, Nursey.'

'I know it. But when one has just given it up a full meal doesn't agree. That's why I've only brought you bread and butter.'

She went out quietly, and Conroy reddened.

'We're still children, you see,' said Miss Henschil. 'But I'm well enough to feel some shame of it. D'you take sugar?'

They starved together heroically, and Nurse Blaber was good enough to signify approval when she came to clear away.

'Nursey?' Miss Henschil insinuated, and flushed.

'Do you smoke?' said the nurse coolly to Conroy.

'I haven't in years. Now you mention it, I think I'd like a cigarette – or something.'

'I used to. D'you think it would keep me quiet?' Miss Henschil said.

'Perhaps. Try these.' The nurse handed them her cigarette-case.

'Don't take anything else,' she commanded, and went away with the tea-basket.

'Good!' grunted Conroy, between mouthfuls of tobacco.

''Better than nothing,' said Miss Henschil; but for a while théy felt ashamed, yet with the comfort of children punished together.

'Now,' she whispered, 'who were you when you were a man?'

Conroy told her, and in return she gave him her history. It delighted them both to deal once more in worldly concerns – families, names, places, and dates – with a person of understanding.

She came, she said, of Lancashire folk – wealthy cotton-spinners, who still kept the broadened *a* and slurred aspirate of the old stock. She lived with an old masterful mother in an opulent world north of Lancaster Gate, where people in Society gave parties at a Mecca called the Langham Hotel.

She herself had been launched into Society there, and the flowers at the ball had cost eighty-seven pounds; but, being reckoned peculiar, she had made few friends among her own sex. She had attracted many men, for she was a beauty – *the* beauty, in fact, of Society, she said.

She spoke utterly without shame or reticence, as a life-prisoner tells his past to a fellow-prisoner; and Conroy nodded across the smoke-rings.

'Do you remember when you got into the carriage?' she asked. '(Oh, I wish I had some knitting!) Did you notice aught, lad?'

Conroy thought back. It was ages since. 'Wasn't there some one outside the door – crying?' he asked.

'He's – he's the little man I was engaged to,' she said. 'But I made him break it off. I told him 'twas no good. But he won't, yo' see.'

'*That* fellow? Why, he doesn't come up to your shoulder.'

'That's naught to do with it. I think all the world of him. I'm a foolish wench' – her speech wandered as she settled herself cosily, one elbow on the arm-rest. 'We'd been engaged – I couldn't help that – and he worships the ground I tread on. But it's no use. I'm not responsible, you see. His two sisters are against it, though I've the money. They're right, but they think it's the dri–ink,' she drawled. 'They're Methody [9] –the Skinners. You see, their grandfather that started the Patton Mills, he died o' the dri–ink.'

'I see,' said Conroy. The grave face before him under the lifted veil was troubled.

'George Skinner.' She breathed it softly. 'I'd make him a good wife, by God's gra-ace – if I could. But it's no use. I'm not responsible. But he'll not take "No" for an answer. I used to call him "Toots". He's of no consequence, yo' see.'

'That's in Dickens,' said Conroy, quite quickly. 'I haven't thought of Toots for years. He was at Doctor Blimber's.' [10]

'And so – that's my trouble,' she concluded, ever so slightly wringing her hands. 'But I – don't you think – there's hope now?'

'Eh?' said Conroy. 'Oh yes! This is the first time I've turned my corner without help. With your help, I should say.'

'It'll come back, though.'

'Then shall we meet it in the same way? Here's my card. Write me your train, and we'll go together.'

'Yes. We must do that. But between times – when we want –'
She looked at her palm, the four fingers working on it. 'It's
hard to give 'em up.'

'But think what we have gained already, and let me have the
case to keep.'

She shook her head, and threw her cigarette out of the
window. 'Not yet.'

'Then let's lend our cases to Nurse, and we'll get through
today on cigarettes. I'll call her while we feel strong.'

She hesitated, but yielded at last, and Nurse accepted the
offerings with a smile.

'*You'll* be all right,' she said to Miss Henschil. 'But if I were
you' – to Conroy – 'I'd take strong exercise.'

When they reached their destination Conroy set himself to
obey Nurse Blaber. He had no remembrance of that day, except
one streak of blue sea to his left, gorse-bushes to his right, and,
before him, a coast-guard's track marked with white-washed
stones that he counted up to the far thousands. As he returned
to the little town he saw Miss Henschil on the beach below the
cliffs. She kneeled at Nurse Blaber's feet, weeping and
pleading.

Twenty-five days later a telegram came to Conroy's rooms:
'*Notice given. Waterloo again. Twenty-fourth.*' That same
evening he was wakened by the shudder and the sigh that told
him his sentence had gone forth. Yet he reflected on his pillow
that he had, in spite of lapses, snatched something like three
weeks of life, which included several rides on a horse before
breakfast – the hour one most craves Najdolene; five con-
secutive evenings on the river at Hammersmith in a tub where
he had well stretched the white arms that passing crews mocked
at; a game of rackets at his club; three dinners, one small dance,
and one human flirtation with a human woman. More notable
still, he had settled his month's accounts, only once confusing
petty cash with the days of grace allowed him. Next morning he
rode his hired beast in the park victoriously. He saw Miss
Henschil on horseback near Lancaster Gate, talking to a young
man at the railings.

She wheeled and cantered toward him.

'By Jove! How well you look!' he cried, without salutation. 'I didn't know you rode.'

'I used to once,' she replied. 'I'm all soft now.'

They swept off together down the ride.

'Your beast pulls,' he said.

'Wa-ant him to. Gi-gives me something to think of. How've you been?' she panted. 'I wish chemists' shops hadn't red lights.'

'Have you slipped out and bought some, then?'

'You don't know Nursey. Eh, but it's good to be on a horse again! This chap cost me two hundred.'

'Then you've been swindled,' said Conroy.

'I know it, but it's no odds. I must go back to Toots and send him away. He's neglecting his work for me.'

She swung her heavy-topped animal on his none too sound hocks. ' 'Sentence come, lad?'

'Yes. But I'm not minding it so much this time.'

'Waterloo, then – and God help us!' She thundered back to the little frock-coated figure that waited faithfully near the gate.

Conroy felt the spring sun on his shoulders and trotted home. That evening he went out with a man in a pair oar, and was rowed to a standstill. But the other man owned he could not have kept the pace five minutes longer.

He carried his bag all down Number 3 platform at Waterloo, and hove it with one hand into the rack.

'Well done!' said Nurse Blaber, in the corridor. 'We've improved too.'

Dr Gilbert and an older man came out of the next compartment.

'Hallo!' said Gilbert. 'Why haven't you been to see me, Mr Conroy? Come under the lamp. Take off your hat. No – no. Sit, you young giant. Ve-ry good. Look here a minute, Johnnie.'

A little, round-bellied, hawk-faced person glared at him.

'Gilbert was right about the beauty of the beast,' he muttered. 'D'you keep it in your glove now?' he went on, and punched Conroy in the short ribs.

'No,' said Conroy meekly, but without coughing. 'Nowhere – on my honour! I've chucked it for good.'

'Wait till you are a sound man before you say *that*, Mr Conroy.' Sir John Chartres stumped out, saying to Gilbert in the corridor, 'It's all very fine, but the question is shall I or we "Sir Pandarus of Troy become",[11] eh? We're bound to think of the children.'

'Have you been vetted?' said Miss Henschil, a few minutes after the train started. 'May I sit with you? I – I don't trust myself yet. I can't give up as easily as you can, seemingly.'

'Can't you? I never saw any one so improved in a month.'

'Look here!' She reached across to the rack, single-handed lifted Conroy's bag, and held it at arm's length. 'I counted ten slowly. And I didn't think of hours or minutes,' she boasted.

'Don't remind me,' he cried.

'Ah! Now I've reminded myself. I wish I hadn't. Do you think it'll be easier for us tonight?'

'Oh, don't.' The smell of the carriage had brought back all his last trip to him, and Conroy moved uneasily.

'I'm sorry. I've brought some games,' she went on. 'Draughts and cards – but they all mean counting. I wish I'd brought chess, but I can't play chess. What can we do? Talk about something.'

'Well, how's Toots, to begin with?' said Conroy.

'Why? Did you see him on the platform?'

'No. Was he there? I didn't notice.'

'Oh yes. He doesn't understand. He's desperately jealous. I told him it doesn't matter. Will you please let me hold your hand? I believe I'm beginning to get the chill.'

'Toots ought to envy me,' said Conroy.

'He does. He paid you a high compliment the other night. He's taken to calling again – in spite of all they say.'

Conroy inclined his head. He felt cold, and knew surely he would be colder.

'He said,' she yawned. '(Beg your pardon.) He said he couldn't see how I could help falling in love with a man like you; and he called himself a damned little rat, and he beat his head on the piano last night.'

'The piano? You play, then?'

'Only to him. He thinks the world of my accomplishments. Then I told him I wouldn't have you if you were the last man on earth instead of only the best-looking – not with a million in each stocking.'

'No, not with a million in each stocking,' said Conroy vehemently. 'Isn't that odd?'

'I suppose so – to any one who doesn't know. Well, where was I? Oh, George as good as told me I was deceiving him, and he wanted to go away without saying goodnight. He hates standing a-tiptoe, but he must if I won't sit down.'

Conroy would have smiled, but the chill that foreran the coming of the Lier-in-Wait was upon him, and his hand closed warningly on hers.

'And – and so –' she was trying to say, when her hour also overtook her, leaving alive only the fear-dilated eyes that turned to Conroy. Hand froze on hand and the body with it as they waited for the horror in the blackness that heralded it. Yet through the worst Conroy saw, at an uncountable distance, one minute glint of light in his night. Thither would he go and escape his fear; and behold, that light was the light in the watch-tower of her eyes, where her locked soul signalled to his soul: 'Look at me!'

In time, from him and from her, the Thing sheered aside, that each soul might step down and resume its own concerns. He thought confusedly of people on the skirts of a thunderstorm, withdrawing from windows where the torn night is, to their known and furnished beds. Then he dozed, till in some drowsy turn his hand fell from her warmed hand.

'That's all. The Faces haven't come,' he heard her say. 'All – thank God! I don't feel even I need what Nursey promised me. Do you?'

'No.' He rubbed his eyes. 'But don't make too sure.'

'Certainly not. We shall have to try again next month. I'm afraid it will be an awful nuisance for you.'

'Not for me, I assure you,' said Conroy, and they leaned back and laughed at the flatness of the words, after the hells through which they had just risen.

'And now,' she said, strict eyes on Conroy, '*why* wouldn't you take me – not with a million in each stocking?'

'I don't know. That's what I've been puzzling over.'

'So have I. We're as handsome a couple as I've ever seen. Are you well off, lad?'

'They call me so,' said Conroy, smiling.

'That's North country.' She laughed again. 'Setting aside my good looks and yours, I've four thousand a year of my own, and the rents should make it six. That's a match some old cats would lap tea all night to fettle up.'[12]

'It is. Lucky Toots!' said Conroy.

'Ay,' she answered, 'he'll be the luckiest lad in London if I win through. Who's yours?'

'No – no one, dear. I've been in Hell for years. I only want to get out and be alive and – so on. Isn't that reason enough?'

'Maybe, for a man. But I never minded things much till George came. I was all stu-upid like.'

'So was I, but now I think I can live. It ought to be less next month, oughtn't it?' he said.

'I hope so. Ye-es. There's nothing much for a maid except to be married, and *I* ask no more. Whoever yours is, when you've found her, she shall have a wedding present from Mrs George Skinner that –'

'But she wouldn't understand it any more than Toots.'

'He doesn't matter – except to me. I can't keep my eyes open, thank God! Goodnight, lad.'

Conroy followed her with his eyes. Beauty there was, grace there was, strength, and enough of the rest to drive better men than George Skinner to beat their heads on piano-tops – but for the new-found life of him Conroy could not feel one flutter of instinct or emotion that turned to herward. He put up his feet and fell asleep, dreaming of a joyous, normal world recovered – with interest on arrears. There were many things in it, but no one face of any one woman.

Thrice afterward they took the same train, and each time their trouble shrank and weakened. Miss Henschil talked of Toots, his multiplied calls, the things he had said to his sisters, the much worse things his sisters had replied; of the late (he seemed very dead to them) M. Najdol's gifts for the soul-weary; of shopping, of house rents, and the cost of really artistic furniture and linen.

Conroy explained the exercises in which he delighted – mighty labours of play undertaken against other mighty men, till he sweated and, having bathed, slept. He had visited his mother, too, in Hereford, and he talked something of her and of the home-life, which his body, cut out of all clean life for five years, innocently and deeply enjoyed. Nurse Blaber was a little interested in Conroy's mother, but, as a rule, she smoked her cigarette and read her paper-backed novels in her own compartment.

On their last trip she volunteered to sit with them, and buried herself in *The Cloister and the Hearth* [13] while they whispered together. On that occasion (it was near Salisbury) at two in the morning, when the Lier-in-Wait brushed them with his wing, it meant no more than that they should cease talk for the instant, and for the instant hold hands, as even utter strangers on the deep may do when their ship rolls underfoot.

'But still,' said Nurse Blaber, not looking up, 'I think your Mr Skinner might feel jealous of all this.'

'It would be difficult to explain,' said Conroy.

'Then you'd better not be at my wedding,' Miss Henschil laughed.

'After all we've gone through, too. But I suppose you ought to leave me out. Is the day fixed?' he cried.

'Twenty-second of September – in spite of both his sisters. I can risk it now.' Her face was glorious as she flushed.

'My dear chap!' He shook hands unreservedly, and she gave back his grip without flinching. 'I can't tell you how pleased I am!'

'Gracious Heavens!' said Nurse Blaber, in a new voice. 'Oh, I beg your pardon. I forgot I wasn't paid to be surprised.'

'What at? Oh, I see!' Miss Henschil explained to Conroy. 'She expected you were going to kiss me, or I was going to kiss you, or something.'

'After all you've gone through, as Mr Conroy said.'

'But I couldn't, could you?' said Miss Henschil, with a disgust as frank as that on Conroy's face. 'It would be horrible – horrible. And yet, of course, you're wonderfully handsome. How d'you account for it, Nursey?'

Nurse Blaber shook her head. 'I was hired to cure you of a

habit, dear. When you're cured I shall go on to the next case – that senile-decay one at Bournemouth I told you about.'

'And I shall be left alone with George! But suppose it isn't cured,' said Miss Henschil of a sudden. 'Suppose it comes back again. What can I do? I can't send for *him* in this way when I'm a married woman!' She pointed like an infant.

'I'd come, of course,' Conroy answered. 'But, seriously, that is a consideration.'

They looked at each other, alarmed and anxious, and then toward Nurse Blaber, who closed her book, marked the place, and turned to face them.

'Have you ever talked to your mother as you have to me?' she said.

'No. I might have spoken to dad – but mother's different. What d'you mean?'

'And you've never talked to your mother either, Mr Conroy?'

'Not till I took Najdolene. Then I told her it was my heart. There's no need to say anything, now that I'm practically over it, is there?'

'Not if it doesn't come back, but–' She beckoned with a stumpy, triumphant finger that drew their heads close together. 'You know I always go in and read a chapter to mother at tea, child.'

'I know you do. You're an angel.' Miss Henschil patted the blue shoulder next her. 'Mother's Church of England now,' she explained. 'But she'll have her Bible with her pikelets [14] at tea every night like the Skinners.'

'It was Naaman and Gehazi [15] last Tuesday that gave me a clue. I said I'd never seen a case of leprosy, and your mother said she'd seen too many.'

'Where? She never told me,' Miss Henschil began.

'A few months before you were born – on her trip to Australia – at Mola or Molo [16] something or other. It took me three evenings to get it all out.'

'Ay – mother's suspicious of questions,' said Miss Henschil to Conroy. 'She'll lock the door of every room she's in, if it's but for five minutes. She was a Tackberry from Jarrow [17] way, yo' see.'

'She described your men to the life – men with faces all

eaten away, staring at her over the fence of a lepers' hospital in this Molo Island. They begged from her, and she ran, she told me, all down the street, back to the pier. One touched her and she nearly fainted. She's ashamed of that still.'

'My men? The sand and the fences?' Miss Henschil muttered.

'Yes. You know how tidy she is and how she hates wind. She remembered that the fences were broken – she remembered the wind blowing. Sand – sun – salt wind – fences – faces – I got it all out of her, bit by bit. You don't know what I know! And it all happened three or four months before you were born. There!' Nurse Blaber slapped her knee with her little hand triumphantly.

'Would that account for it?' Miss Henschil shook from head to foot.

'Absolutely. I don't care who you ask! You never imagined the thing. It was *laid* on you. It happened on earth to *you*! Quick, Mr Conroy, she's too heavy for me! I'll get the flask.'

Miss Henschil leaned forward and collapsed, as Conroy told her afterwards, like a factory chimney. She came out of her swoon with teeth that chattered on the cup.

'No – no,' she said, gulping. 'It's not hysterics. Yo' see I've no call to hev 'em any more. No call – no reason whatever. God be praised! Can't yo' *feel* I'm a right woman now?'

'Stop hugging me!' said Nurse Blaber. 'You don't know your strength. Finish the brandy and water. It's perfectly reasonable, and I'll lay long odds Mr Conroy's case is something of the same. I've been thinking –'

'I wonder –' said Conroy, and pushed the girl back as she swayed again.

Nurse Blaber smoothed her pale hair. 'Yes. Your trouble, or something like it, happened somewhere on earth or sea to the mother who bore you. Ask her, child. Ask her and be done with it once for all.'

'I will,' said Conroy . . . 'There ought to be –' He opened his bag and hunted breathlessly.

'Bless you! Oh, God bless you, Nursey!' Miss Henschil was sobbing. 'You don't know what this means to me. It takes it all off – from the beginning.'

'But doesn't it make any difference to you now?' the nurse asked curiously. 'Now that you're rightfully a woman?'

Conroy, busy with his bag, had not heard. Miss Henschil stared across, and her beauty, freed from the shadow of any fear, blazed up within her. 'I see what you mean,' she said. 'But it hasn't changed anything. I want Toots. *He* has never been out of his mind in his life – except over silly me.'

'It's all right,' said Conroy, stooping under the lamp, Bradshaw [18] in hand. 'If I change at Templecombe – for Bristol (Bristol – Hereford – yes) – I can be with mother for breakfast in her room and find out.'

'Quick, then,' said Nurse Blaber. 'We've passed Gillingham quite a while. You'd better take some of our sandwiches.' She went out to get them. Conroy and Miss Henschil would have danced, but there is no room for giants in a South-Western compartment.

'Goodbye, good luck, lad. Eh, but you've changed already – like me. Send a wire to our hotel as soon as you're sure,' said Miss Henschil. 'What should I have done without you?'

'Or I?' said Conroy. 'But it's Nurse that's saving us really.'

'Then thank her,' said Miss Henschil, looking straight at him. 'Yes, I would. She'd like it.'

When Nurse Blaber came back after the parting at Templecombe her nose and her eyelids were red, but for all that, her face reflected a great light even while she sniffed over *The Cloister and the Hearth.*

Miss Henschil, deep in a house furnisher's catalogue, did not speak for twenty minutes. Then she said, between adding totals of best, guest, and servants' sheets, 'But why should our times have been the same, Nursey?'

'Because a child is born somewhere every second of the clock,' Nurse Blaber answered. 'And besides that, you probably set each other off by talking and thinking about it. You shouldn't, you know.'

'Ay, but you've never been in Hell,' said Miss Henschil.

The telegram handed in at Hereford at 12:46 and delivered to Miss Henschil on the beach of a certain village at 2.7 ran thus:

'"*Absolutely confirmed. She says she remembers hearing noise of accident in engine-room returning from India eighty-five.*"' [19]

'He means the year, not the thermometer,' said Nurse Blaber, throwing pebbles at the cold sea.

'"*And two men scalded thus explaining my hoots.*" (The idea of telling me that!) '*Subsequently silly clergyman passenger ran up behind her calling for joke, "Friend, all is lost," thus accounting very words.*"'

Nurse Blaber purred audibly.

'"*She says only remembers being upset minute or two. Unspeakable relief. Best love Nursey, who is jewel. Get out of her what she would like best.*" Oh, I oughtn't to have read that,' said Miss Henschil.

'It doesn't matter. I don't want anything,' said Nurse Blaber, 'and if I did I shouldn't get it.'

'Helen all Alone'

There was darkness under Heaven
  For an hour's space —
Darkness that we knew was given
  Us for special grace.
Sun and moon and stars were hid,
  God had left His Throne,
When Helen came to me, she did,
  Helen all alone!

Side by side (because our fate
  Damned us ere our birth)
We stole out of Limbo Gate
  Looking for the Earth.
Hand in pulling hand amid
  Fear no dreams have known,
Helen ran with me, she did,
  Helen all alone!

When the Horror passing speech
  Hunted us along,
Each laid hold on each, and each
  Found the other strong.
In the teeth of things forbid
  And Reason overthrown,
Helen stood by me, she did,
  Helen all alone!

When, at last, we heard the Fires
  Dull and die away,
When, at last, our linked desires
  Dragged us up to day,
When, at last, our souls were rid
  Of what that Night had shown,
Helen passed from me, she did,
  Helen all alone!

Let her go and find a mate,
  As I will find a bride,
Knowing naught of Limbo Gate

In the Same Boat

Or Who are penned inside.
There is knowledge God forbid
  More than one should own.
So Helen went from me, she did,
Oh my soul, be glad she did!
  Helen all alone!

THE HONOURS OF WAR

The Honours of War

(1911)

A hooded motor had followed mine from the Guildford Road up the drive to The Infant's ancestral hall, and had turned off to the stables.

'We're having a quiet evening together. Stalky's upstairs changing. Dinner's at 7.15 sharp, because we're hungry. His room's next to yours,' said The Infant, nursing a cobwebbed bottle of Burgundy.

Then I found Lieutenant-Colonel A. L. Corkran, I.A., who borrowed a collar-stud and told me about the East and his Sikh regiment.

'And are your subalterns as good as ever?' I asked.

'Amazin' – simply amazin'! All I've got to do is to find 'em jobs. They keep touchin' their caps to me and askin' for more work. 'Come at me with their tongues hangin' out. *I* used to run the other way at their age.'

'And when they err?' said I. 'I suppose they do sometimes?'

'Then they run to me again to weep with remorse over their virgin peccadilloes. I never cuddled my Colonel when I was in trouble. Lambs – positive lambs!'

'And what do you say to 'em?'

'Talk to 'em like a papa. Tell 'em how I can't understand it, an' how shocked I am, and how grieved their parents 'll be; and throw in a little about the Army Regulations and the Ten Commandments. 'Makes one feel rather a sweep when one thinks of what one used to do at their age. D'you remember –'

We remembered together till close on seven o'clock. As we went out into the gallery that runs round the big hall, we saw The Infant, below, talking to two deferential well-set-up lads whom I had known, on and off, in the holidays, any time for the last ten years. One of them had a bruised cheek, and the other a weeping left eye.

'Yes, that's the style,' said Stalky below his breath. 'They're brought up on lemon-squash and mobilization text-books. I say, the girls we knew must have been much better than they pretended they were; for I'll swear it isn't the fathers.'

'But why on earth did you do it?' The Infant was shouting. 'You know what it means nowadays.'

'Well, sir,' said Bobby Trivett, the taller of the two, 'Wontner talks too much, for one thing. He didn't join till he was twenty-three, and, besides that, he used to lecture on tactics in the ante-room. He said Clausewitz [1] was the only tactician, and he illustrated his theories with cigar-ends. He was that sort of chap, sir.'

'And he didn't much care whose cigar-ends they were,' said Eames, who was shorter and pinker.

'And then he *would* talk about the 'Varsity,' said Bobby. 'He got a degree there. And he told us we weren't intellectual. He told the Adjutant so, sir. He was just that kind of chap, sir, if you understand.'

Stalky and I backed behind a tall Japanese jar of chrysanthemums and listened more intently.

'Was all the Mess in it, or only you two?' The Infant demanded, chewing his moustache.

'The Adjutant went to bed, of course, sir, and the Senior Subaltern said he wasn't going to risk his commission — they're awfully down on ragging nowadays in the Service — but the rest of us — er — attended to him,' said Bobby.

'Much?' The Infant asked. The boys smiled deprecatingly.

'Not in the ante-room, sir,' said Eames. 'Then he called us silly children, and went to bed, and we sat up discussin', and I suppose we got a bit above ourselves, and we — er —'

'Went to his quarters and drew him?' The Infant suggested.

'Well, we only asked him to get out of bed, and we put his helmet and sword-belt on for him, and we sung him bits out of the Blue Fairy Book [2] — the cram-book on Army organization. Oh yes, and then we asked him to drink old Clausewitz's health, as a brother-tactician, in milk punch and Worcester sauce, and so on. We had to help him a little there. He bites. There wasn't much else that time; but, you know, the War Office is severe on ragging these days.' Bobby stopped with a lop-sided smile.

'And then,' Eames went on, 'then Wontner said we'd done several pounds' worth of damage to his furniture.'

'Oh,' said The Infant, 'he's that kind of man, is he? Does he brush his teeth?'

'Oh yes, he's quite clean all over!' said Trivett; 'but his father's a wealthy barrister.'

'Solicitor,' Eames corrected, 'and so this Mister Wontner is out for our blood. He's going to make a first-class row about it – appeal to the War Office – court of inquiry – spicy bits in the papers, and songs in the music-halls. He told us so.'

'That's the sort of chap he is,' said Trivett. 'And that means old Dhurrah-bags, our Colonel, 'll be put on half-pay, same as that case in the Scarifungers' Mess; and our Adjutant 'll have to exchange, like it was with that fellow in the 73rd Dragoons, and there'll be misery all round. He means making it too hot for us, and his papa 'll back him.'

'Yes, that's all very fine,' said The Infant; 'but I left the Service about the time you were born, Bobby. What's it got to do with me?'

'Father told me I was always to go to you when I was in trouble, and you've been awfully good to me since he . . .'

'Better stay to dinner.' The Infant mopped his forehead.

'Thank you very much, but the fact is –' Trivett halted.

'This afternoon, about four, to be exact –' Eames broke in.

'We went over to Wontner's quarters to talk things over. The row only happened last night, and we found him writing letters as hard as he could to his father – getting up his case for the War Office, you know. He read us some of 'em, but I'm not a good judge of style. We tried to ride him off quietly – apologies and so forth – but it was the milk-punch and mayonnaise that defeated us.'

'Yes, he wasn't taking anything except pure revenge,' said Eames.

'He said he'd make an example of the regiment, and he was particularly glad that he'd landed our Colonel. He told us so. Old Dhurrah-bags don't sympathize with Wontner's tactical lectures. He says Wontner ought to learn manners first, but we thought –' Trivett turned to Eames, who was less a son of the house than himself, Eames' father being still alive.

'Then,' Eames went on, 'he became rather noisome, and we thought we might as well impound the correspondence' – he wrinkled his swelled left eye – 'and after that, we got him to take a seat in my car.'

'He was in a sack, you know,' Trivett explained. 'He wouldn't go any other way. But we didn't hurt him.'

'Oh no! His head's sticking out quite clear, and' – Eames rushed the fence – 'we've put him in your garage – er *pendente lite.*' [3]

'My garage!' Infant's voice nearly broke with horror.

'Well, father always told me if I was in trouble, Uncle George –'

Bobby's sentence died away as The Infant collapsed on a divan and said no more than, 'Your commissions!' There was a long, long silence.

'What price your latter-day lime-juice subaltern?' I whispered to Stalky behind my hand. His nostrils expanded, and he drummed on the edge of the Japanese jar with his knuckles.

'Confound your father, Bobby!' The Infant groaned. 'Raggin's a criminal offence these days. It isn't as if –'

'Come on,' said Stalky. 'That was my old Line battalion in Egypt. They nearly slung old Dhurrah-bags and me out of the Service in '85 for ragging.' He descended the stairs and The Infant rolled appealing eyes on him.

'I heard what you youngsters have confessed,' he began; and in his orderly-room voice, which is almost as musical as his singing one, he tongue-lashed those lads in such sort as was a privilege and a revelation to listen to. Till then they had known him almost as a relative – we were all brevet, deputy, or acting uncles to The Infant's friends' brood – a sympathetic elder brother, sound on finance. They had never met Colonel A. L. Corkran in the Chair of Justice. And while he flayed and rent and blistered, and wiped the floor with them, and while they looked for hiding-places and found none on that floor, I remembered (1) the up-ending of 'Dolly' Macshane at Dalhousie, which came perilously near a court-martial on Second-Lieutenant Corkran; (2) the burning of Captain Parmilee's mosquito-curtains on a hot Indian dawn, when the captain slept in his garden, and Lieutenant Corkran, smoking, rode by after a successful whist night at the club; (3) the introduction of an ekka [4] pony, with ekka attached, into a brother captain's tent on a frosty night in Peshawur, and the removal of tent, pole, cot, and captain all wrapped in chilly canvas; (4) the bath that was given to Elliot-Hacker on his own verandah – his lady-love saw it and broke off the engagement, which was what the Mess intended, she being an Eurasian – and the powdering all over of Elliot-Hacker with flour and turmeric from the bazaar.

When he took breath I realized how only Satan can rebuke sin. The good don't know enough.

'Now,' said Stalky, 'get out! No, not out of the house. Go to your rooms.'

'I'll send your dinner, Bobby,' said The Infant. 'Ipps!'

Nothing had ever been known to astonish Ipps, the butler. He entered and withdrew with his charges. After all, he had suffered from Bobby since Bobby's twelfth year.

'They've done everything they could, short of murder,' said The Infant. 'You know what this'll mean for the regiment. It isn't as if we were dealing with Sahibs nowadays.'

'Quite so.' Stalky turned on me. 'Go and release the bagman,' he said.

' 'Tisn't my garage,' I pleaded. 'I'm company. Besides, he'll probably slay me. He's been in the sack for hours.'

'Look here,' Stalky thundered – the years had fallen from us both – 'is your – am I commandin' or are you? We've got to pull this thing off somehow or other. Cut over to the garage, make much of him, and bring him over. He's dining with us. Be quick, you dithering ass!'

I was quick enough; but as I ran through the shrubbery I wondered how one extricates the subaltern of the present day from a sack without hurting his feelings. Anciently, one slit the end open, taking off his boots first, and then fled.

Imagine a sumptuously-equipped garage, half-filled by The Infant's cobalt-blue, grey-corded silk limousine and a mud-splashed, cheap, hooded four-seater. In the back-seat of this last, conceive a fiery chestnut head emerging from a long oat-sack; an implacable white face, with blazing eyes and jaws that worked ceaselessly at the loop of the string that was drawn round its neck. The effect, under the electrics, was that of a demon caterpillar wrathfully spinning its own cocoon.

'Good evening!' I said genially. 'Let me help you out of that.' The head glared. 'We've got 'em,' I went on. 'They came to quite the wrong shop for this sort of game – quite the wrong shop.'

'Game!' said the head. 'We'll see about that. Let me out.'

It was not a promising voice for one so young, and, as usual, I had no knife.

'You've chewed the string so I can't find the knot,' I said as I worked with trembling fingers at the caterpillar's throat. Something untied itself, and Mr Wontner wriggled out, collarless, tieless, his coat split half down his back, his waistcoat unbuttoned, his watch-chain snapped, his trousers rucked well above the knees.

'Where,' he said grimly, as he pulled them down, 'are Master Trivett and Master Eames?'

'Both arrested, of course,' I replied. 'Sir George' – I gave The Infant's full title as a baronet – 'is a Justice of the Peace. He'd be very pleased if you dined with us. There's a room ready for you.' I picked up the sack.

'D'you know,' said Mr Wontner through his teeth – but the car's bonnet was between us, 'that this looks to me like – I won't say conspiracy *yet*, but uncommonly like a confederacy.'

When injured souls begin to distinguish and qualify, danger is over. So I grew bold.

''Sorry you take it that way,' I said. 'You come here in trouble –'

'My good fool,' he interrupted, with a half-hysterical snort, 'let me assure you that the trouble will recoil on the other men!'

'As you please,' I went on. 'Anyhow, the chaps who got you into trouble are arrested, and the magistrate who arrested 'em asks you to dinner. Shall I tell him you're walking back to Aldershot?'

He picked some fluff off his waistcoat.

'I'm in no position to dictate terms yet,' he said. 'That will come later. I must probe into this a little further. In the meantime, I accept your invitation without prejudice – if you understand what that means.'

I understood and began to be happy again. Subalterns without prejudices were quite new to me. 'All right,' I replied; 'if you'll go up to the house, I'll turn out the lights.'

He walked off stiffly, while I searched the sack and the car for the impounded correspondence that Bobby had talked of. I found nothing except, as the police reports say, the trace of a struggle. He had kicked half the varnish off the back of the front seat, and had bitten the leather padding where he could reach it. Evidently a purposeful and hard-mouthed young gentleman.

'Well done!' said Stalky at the door. 'So he didn't slay you. Stop laughing. He's talking to The Infant now about depositions. Look here, you're nearest his size. Cut up to your rooms and give Ipps your dinner things and a clean shirt for him.'

'But I haven't got another suit,' I said.

'You! I'm not thinking of you! We've got to conciliate *him*. He's in filthy rags and a filthy temper, and he won't feel decent till he's dressed. You're the sacrifice. Be quick! And clean socks, remember!'

Once more I trotted up to my room, changed into unseasonable unbrushed grey tweeds, put studs into a clean shirt, dug out fresh socks, handed the whole garniture over to Ipps, and returned to the hall just in time to hear Stalky say, 'I'm a stockbroker, but I have the honour to hold His Majesty's commission in a Territorial battalion.' Then I felt as though I might be beginning to be repaid.

'I have a very high opinion of the Territorials myself,' said Mr Wontner above a glass of sherry. (Infant never lets us put bitters into anything above twenty years old.) 'But if you had any experience of the Service, you would find that the Average Army Man –'

Here The Infant suggested changing, and Ipps, before whom no human passion can assert itself, led Mr Wontner away.

'Why the devil did you tell him I was on the Bench?' said Infant wrathfully to me. 'You know I ain't now. Why didn't he stay in his father's office? He's a raging blight!'

'Not a bit of it,' said Stalky cheerfully. 'He's a little shaken and excited. Probably Beetle annoyed him in the garage, but we must overlook that. We've contained him so far, and I'm going to nibble round his outposts at dinner. All you've got to do, Infant, is to remember you're a gentleman in your own house. Don't hop! You'll find it pretty difficult before dinner's over. I don't want to hear anything at all from you, Beetle.'

'But I'm just beginning to like him,' I said. 'Do let me play!'

'Not till I ask you. You'll overdo it. Poor old Dhurrah-bags! A scandal 'ud break him up!'

'But as long as a regiment has no say as to who joins it, it's bound to rag,' Infant began. 'Why – why, they varnished me when I joined!' He squirmed at the thought of it.

'Don't be owls! We ain't discussing principles! We've got to save the court of inquiry if we can,' said Stalky.

Five minutes later – at 7.45 to be precise – we four sat down to such a dinner as, I hold, only The Infant's cook can produce, with wines worthy of pontifical banquets. A man in the extremity of rage and injured dignity is precisely like a typhoid patient. He asks no questions, accepts what is put before him, and babbles in one key – very often of trifles. But food and drink are the very best of drugs. I think it was Heidsieck [5] Dry Monopole '92 – Stalky as usual stuck to Burgundy – that began to unlock Mr Wontner's heart behind my shirt-front. Me he snubbed throughout, after the Oxford manner, because I had seen him in the sack, and he did not intend me to presume; but to Stalky and The Infant, while I admired the set of my dinner-jacket across his shoulders, he made his plans of revenge very clear indeed. He had even sketched out some of the paragraphs that were to appear in the papers, and if Stalky had allowed me to speak, I would have told him that they were rather neatly phrased.

'You ought to be able to get whackin' damages out of 'em, into the bargain,' said Stalky, after Mr Wontner had outlined his position legally.

'My de-ah sir,' Mr Wontner applied himself to his glass, 'it isn't a matter that gentlemen usually discuss, but, I assure you, we Wontners' – he waved a well-kept hand – 'do not stand in any need of filthy lucre.' In the next three minutes, we learned exactly what his father was worth, which, as he pointed out, was a trifle no man of the world dwelt on. Stalky envied aloud, and I delivered my first kick at The Infant's ankle. Thence we drifted to education, and the Average Army Man, and the desolating vacuity – I remember these words – of Army Society, notably among its womenkind. It appeared there was some sort of narrow convention in the Army against mentioning a woman's name at Mess. We were much surprised at this – Stalky would not let me express my surprise – but we took it from Mr Wontner, who said we might, that it was so. Next he touched on Colonels of the old school, and their cognizance of tactics. Not that he himself pretended to any skill in tactics, but after three years at the 'Varsity – none of us had had a 'Varsity education – a man insensibly contracted the habit of clear thinking. At least, he could automatically co-ordinate his ideas, and the jealousy of these muddle-headed Colonels was inconceivable. We would understand that it was his duty to force on the retirement of his Colonel, who had been in the conspiracy against him; to make his Adjutant resign or exchange; and to give the half-dozen childish subalterns who had vexed his dignity a chance to retrieve themselves in other corps – West African ones, he hoped. For himself, after the case was decided, he proposed to go on living in the regiment, just to prove – for he bore no malice – that times had changed, *nosque mutamur in illis*[6] – if we knew what that meant. Infant had curled his legs out of reach, so I was quite free to return thanks yet once more to Allah for the diversity of His creatures in His adorable world.

And so, by way of an eighty-year-old liqueur brandy, to tactics and the great General Clausewitz, unknown to the Average Army Man. Here The Infant, at a whisper from Ipps – whose face had darkened like a mulberry while he waited – excused himself and went away, but Stalky, Colonel of Territorials, wanted some tips on tactics. He got them unbrokenly for ten minutes – Wontner and Clausewitz mixed, but Wontner in a film of priceless cognac distinctly on top. When The Infant came back, he renewed his clear-spoken demand that Infant should take his depositions. I supposed this to be a family trait of the Wontners, whom I had been visualizing for some time past even to the third generation.

'But, hang it all, they're both asleep!' said Infant, scowling at me. 'Ipps let 'em have the '81 port.'

'Asleep!' said Stalky, rising at once. 'I don't see that makes any difference. As a matter of form, you'd better identify them. I'll show you the way.'

We followed up the white stone side-staircase that leads to the bachelors' wing. Mr Wontner seemed surprised that the boys were not in the coal-cellar.

'Oh, a chap's assumed to be innocent until he's proved guilty,' said Stalky, mounting step by step. 'How did they get you into the sack, Mr Wontner?'

'Jumped on me from behind – two to one,' said Mr Wontner briefly. 'I think I handed each of them something first, but they roped my arms and legs.'

'And did they photograph you in the sack?'

'Good Heavens, no!' Mr Wontner shuddered.

'That's lucky. Awful thing to live down – a photograph, isn't it?' said Stalky to me as we reached the landing. 'I'm thinking of the newspapers, of course.'

'Oh, but you can easily have sketches in the illustrated papers from accounts supplied by eye-witnesses,' I said.

Mr Wontner turned him round. It was the first time he had honoured me by his notice since our talk in the garage.

'Ah,' said he, 'do you pretend to any special knowledge in these matters?'

'I'm a journalist by profession,' I answered simply but nobly. 'As soon as you're at liberty, I'd like to have your account of the affair.'

Now I thought he would have loved me for this, but he only replied in an uncomfortable, uncoming-on voice, 'Oh, you would, would you?'

'Not if it's any trouble, of course,' I said. 'I can always get their version from the defendants. Do either of 'em draw or sketch at all, Mr Wontner? Or perhaps your father might –'

Then he said quite hotly, 'I wish you to understand very clearly, my good man, that a gentleman's name can't be dragged through the gutter to bolster up the circulation of your wretched sheet, whatever it may be.'

'It is —' I named a journal of enormous sales which specializes in scholastic, military, and other scandals. 'I don't know yet what it can't do, Mr Wontner.'

'I didn't know that I was dealing with a reporter,' said Mr Wontner.

We were all halted outside a shut door. Ipps had followed us.

'But surely you want it in the papers, don't you?' I urged. 'With a scandal like this, one couldn't, in justice to the democracy, be exclusive. We'd syndicate it here and in the United States. I helped you out of the sack, if you remember.'

'I wish to goodness you'd stop talking!' he snapped, and sat down on a chair. Stalky's hand on my shoulder quietly signalled me out of action, but I felt that my fire had not been misdirected.

'I'll answer for him,' said Stalky to Wontner, in an undertone that dropped to a whisper. I caught – 'Not without my leave – dependent on me for market-tips,' and other gratifying tributes to my integrity.

Still Mr Wontner sat in his chair, and still we waited on him. The Infant's face showed worry and heavy grief; Stalky's, a bright and bird-like interest; mine was hidden behind his shoulders, but on the face of Ipps were written emotions that no butler should cherish towards any guest. Contempt and wrath were the least of them. And Mr Wontner was looking full at Ipps, as Ipps was looking at him. Mr Wontner's father, I understood, kept a butler and two footmen.

'D'you suppose they're shamming, in order to get off?' he said at last. Ipps shook his head and noiselessly threw the door open. The boys had finished their dinner and were fast asleep – one on a sofa, one in a long chair – their faces fallen back to the lines of their childhood. They had had a wildish night, a hard day, that ended with a telling-off from an artist, and the assurance they had wrecked their prospects for life. What else should youth do, then, but eat, and drink '81 port, and remember their sorrows no more?

Mr Wontner looked at them severely, Ipps within easy reach, his hands quite ready. 'Childish,' said Mr Wontner at last. 'Childish but necessary. Er – have you such a thing as a rope on the premises, and a sack – two sacks and two ropes? I'm afraid I can't resist the temptation. That man understands, doesn't he, that this is a private matter?'

'That man,' who was me, was off to the basement like one of

Infant's own fallow-deer. The stables gave me what I wanted, and coming back with it through a dark passage, I ran squarely into Ipps. 'Go on!' he grunted. 'The minute he lays hands on Master Bobby, Master Bobby's saved. But that person ought to be told how near he came to being assaulted. It was touch-and-go with me all the time from the soup down, I assure you.'

I arrived breathless with the sacks and the ropes. 'They were two to one with me,' said Mr Wontner, as he took them. 'If they wake –'

'We'll stand by,' Stalky replied. 'Two to one is quite fair.'

But the boys hardly grunted as Mr Wontner roped first one and then the other. Even when they were slid into the sacks they only mumbled, with rolling heads, through sticky lips and snored on.

'Port?' said Mr Wontner virtuously.

'Nervous exhaustion. They aren't much more than kids, after all. What's next?' said Stalky.

'I want to take 'em away with me, please.'

Stalky looked at him with respect.

'I'll have my car round in five minutes,' said The Infant. 'Ipps'll help carry 'em downstairs,' and he shook Mr Wontner by the hand.

We were all perfectly serious till the two bundles were dumped on a divan in the hall, and the boys waked and began to realize what had happened.

'Yah!' said Mr Wontner, with the simplicity of twelve years old. 'Who's scored now?' And he sat upon them. The tension broke in a storm of laughter, led, I think, by Ipps.

'Asinine – absolutely asinine!' said Mr Wontner, with folded arms from his lively chair. But he drank in the flattery and the fellowship of it all with quite a brainless grin, as we rolled and stamped round him, and wiped the tears from our cheeks.

'Hang it!' said Bobby Trivett. 'We're defeated!'

'By tactics, too,' said Eames. 'I didn't think you knew 'em, Clausewitz. It's a fair score. What are you going to do with us?'

'Take you back to Mess,' said Mr Wontner.

'Not like this?'

'Oh no. Worse – much worse! I haven't begun with you yet. And you thought you'd scored! Yah!'

They had scored beyond their wildest dream. The man in whose hands it lay to shame them, their Colonel, their Adjutant, their Regiment, and their Service, had cast away all shadow of his legal rights for the sake of a common or bear-garden rag — such a rag as if it came to the ears of the authorities, would cost him his commission. They were saved, and their saviour was their equal and their brother. So they chaffed and reviled him as such till he again squashed the breath out of them, and we others laughed louder than they.

'Fall in!' said Stalky when the limousine came round. 'This is the score of the century. I wouldn't miss it for a brigade! We shan't be long, Infant!'

I hurried into a coat.

'Is there any necessity for that reporter-chap to come too?' said Mr Wontner in an unguarded whisper. 'He isn't dressed for one thing.'

Bobby and Eames wriggled round to look at the reporter, began a joyous bellow, and suddenly stopped.

'What's the matter?' said Wontner with suspicion.

'Nothing,' said Bobby. 'I die happy, Clausewitz. Take me up tenderly.'

We packed into the car, bearing our sheaves with us, and for half an hour, as the cool night-air fanned his thoughtful brow, Mr Wontner was quite abreast of himself. Though he said nothing unworthy, he triumphed and trumpeted a little loudly over the sacks. I sat between them on the back seat, and applauded him servilely till he reminded me that what I had seen and what he had said was not for publication. I hinted, while the boys plunged with joy inside their trappings, that this might be a matter for arrangement. 'Then a sovereign shan't part us,' said Mr Wontner cheerily, and both boys fell into lively hysterics. 'I don't see where the joke comes in for you,' said Mr Wontner. 'I thought it was my little jokelet tonight.'

'No, Clausewitz,' gasped Bobby. 'Some is, but not all. I'll be good now. I'll give you my parole till we get to Mess. I wouldn't be out of this for a fiver.'

'Nor me,' said Eames, and he gave his parole to attempt no escape or evasion.

'Now, I suppose,' said Mr Wontner largely to Stalky, as we

neared the suburbs of Ash, 'you have a good deal of practical joking on the Stock Exchange, haven't you?'

'And when were you on the Stock Exchange, Uncle Leonard?' piped Bobby, while Eames laid his sobbing head on my shoulder.

'I'm sorry,' said Stalky, 'but the fact is, I command a regiment myself when I'm at home. Your Colonel knows me, I think.' He gave his name. Mr Wontner seemed to have heard of it. We had to pick Eames off the floor, where he had cast himself from excess of delight.

'Oh, Heavens!' said Mr Wontner after a long pause. 'What have I done? What haven't I done?' We felt the temperature in the car rise as he blushed.

'You didn't talk tactics, Clausewitz?' said Bobby. 'Oh, say it wasn't tactics, darling!'

'It was,' said Wontner.

Eames was all among our feet again, crying, 'If you don't let me get my arms up, I'll be sick. Let's hear what you said. Tell us.'

But Mr Wonter turned to Stalky. 'It's no good my begging your pardon, sir, I suppose,' he said.

'Don't you notice 'em,' said Stalky. 'It was a fair rag all round, and anyhow you two youngsters haven't any right to talk tactics. You've been rolled up, horse, foot, and guns.'

'I'll make a treaty. If you'll let us go and change presently,' said Bobby, 'I'll promise we won't tell about you, Clausewitz. *You* talked tactics to Uncle Len? Old Dhurrah-bags will like that. He don't love you, Claus.'

'If I've made one ass of myself, I shall take extra care to make asses of you!' said Wontner. 'I want to stop, please, at the next milliner's shop on the right. It ought to be close here.'

He evidently knew the country even in the dark, for the car stopped at a brilliantly-lighted millinery establishment, where – it was Saturday evening – a young lady was clearing up the counter. I followed him, as a good reporter should.

'Have you got –' he began. 'Ah, those'll do!' He pointed to two hairy plush beehive bonnets, one magenta, the other a conscientious electric blue. 'How much, please? I'll take them both, and that bunch of peacock feathers, and that red feather thing.' It was a brilliant crimson-dyed pigeon's wing.

'Now I want some yards of muslin with a nice, fierce pattern, please.' He got it — yellow with black tulips — and returned heavily laden.

'Sorry to have kept you,' said he. 'Now we'll go to my quarters to change and beautify.'

We came to them — opposite a dun waste of parade-ground that might have been Mian Mir — and bugles as they blew and drums as they rolled set heart-strings echoing.

We hoisted the boys out and arranged them on chairs, while Wontner changed into uniform, but stopped when he saw me taking off my jacket.

'What on earth's that for?' said he.

'Because you've been wearing my evening things,' I said. 'I want to get into 'em again, if you don't mind.'

'Then you aren't a reporter?' he said.

'No,' I said, 'but that shan't part us.'

'Oh, hurry!' cried Eames in desperate convulsions. 'We can't stand this much longer. 'Tisn't fair on the young.'

'I'll attend to you in good time,' said Wontner; and when he had made careful toilet, he unwrapped the bonnets, put the peacock's feather into the magenta one, pinned the crimson wing on the blue one, set them daintily on the boys' heads, and bade them admire the effect in his shaving-glass while he ripped the muslin into lengths, bound it first, and draped it artistically afterwards a little below their knees. He finished off with a gigantic sash-bow, obi fashion. 'Hobble skirts,' he explained to Stalky, who nodded approval.

Next he split open the bottom of each sack so that they could walk, but with very short steps. 'I ought to have got you white satin slippers,' he murmured, 'and I'm sorry there's no rouge.'

'Don't worry on our account, old man — you're doing us proud,' said Bobby from under his hat. 'This beats milk-punch and mayonnaise.'

'Oh, why didn't we think of these things when we had him at our mercy?' Eames wailed. 'Never mind — we'll try it on the next chap. You've a mind, Claus.'

'Now we'll call on 'em at Mess,' said Wontner, as they minced towards the door.

'I think I'll call on your Colonel,' said Stalky. 'He oughtn't to miss this. Your first attempt? I assure you I couldn't have done it better myself. Thank you!' He held out his hand.

'Thank *you*, sir!' said Wontner, shaking it. 'I'm more grateful to you than I can say, and – and I'd like you to believe some time that I'm not quite as big a –'

'Not in the least,' Stalky interrupted. 'If I were writing a confidential report on you, I should put you down as rather adequate. Look after your geishas, or they'll fall!'

We watched the three cross the road and disappear into the shadow of the mess verandah. There was a noise. Then telephone bells rang, a sergeant and a mess waiter charged out, and the noise grew, till at last the Mess was a little noisy.

We came back, ten minutes later, with Colonel Dalziell, who had been taking his sorrows to bed with him. The ante-room was quite full and visitors were still arriving, but it was possible to hear oneself speak occasionally. Trivett and Eames, in sack and sash, sat side by side on a table, their hats at a ravishing angle, coquettishly twiddling their tied feet. In the intervals of singing 'Put Me Among the Girls,'[7] they sipped whisky-and-soda held to their lips by, I regret to say, a Major. Public opinion seemed to be against allowing them to change their costume till they should have danced in it. Wontner, lying more or less gracefully at the level of the chandelier in the arms of six subalterns, was lecturing on tactics and imploring to be let down, which he was with a run when they realized that the Colonel was there. Then he picked himself up from the sofa and said: 'I want to apologize, sir, to you and the Mess for having been such an ass ever since I joined!'

This was when the noise began.

Seeing the night promised to be wet, Stalky and I went home again in The Infant's car. It was some time since we had tasted the hot air that lies between the cornice and the ceiling of crowded rooms.

After half an hour's silence, Stalky said to me: 'I don't know what you've been doing, but I believe I've been weepin'. Would you put that down to Burgundy or senile decay?'

The Children

These were our children who died for our lands: they were dear in
our sight.
We have only the memory left of their home-treasured sayings
and laughter.
The price of our loss shall be paid to our hands, not another's
hereafter.
Neither the Alien nor Priest shall decide on it.
That is our right.
But who shall return us the children?

At the hour the Barbarian chose to disclose his pretences,
And raged against Man, they engaged, on the breasts that they
bared for us,
The first felon-stroke of the sword he had long-time prepared
for us —
Their bodies were all our defence while we wrought our defences.

They bought us anew with their blood, forbearing to blame us,
Those hours which we had not made good when the Judgment
o'ercame us.
They believed us and perished for it. Our statecraft, our learning
Delivered them bound to the Pit and alive to the burning
Whither they mirthfully hastened as jostling for honour.
Not since her birth has our Earth seen such worth loosed upon
her.

Nor was their agony brief, or once only imposed on them.
The wounded, the war-spent, the sick received no exemption:
Being cured they returned and endured and achieved our
redemption,
Hopeless themselves of relief, till Death, marvelling, closed on them.

That flesh we had nursed from the first in all cleanness was given
To corruption unveiled and assailed by the malice of Heaven —
By the heart-shaking jests of Decay where it lolled on the wires —
To be blanched or gay-painted by fumes — to be cindered by fires
To be senselessly tossed and retossed in stale mutilation
From crater to crater. For this we shall take expiation.
But who shall return us our children?

THE DOG HERVEY

The Dog Hervey

(April 1914)

My friend Attley, who would give away his own head if you told him you had lost yours, was giving away a six-months-old litter of Bettina's pups, and half-a-dozen women were in raptures at the show on Mittleham lawn.

We picked by lot. Mrs Godfrey drew first choice; her married daughter, second. I was third, but waived my right because I was already owned by Malachi,[1] Bettina's full brother, whom I had brought over in the car to visit his nephews and nieces, and he would have slain them all if I had taken home one. Milly, Mrs Godfrey's younger daughter, pounced on my rejection with squeals of delight, and Attley turned to a dark, sallow-skinned, slack-mouthed girl, who had come over for tennis, and invited her to pick. She put on a pair of pince-nez that made her look like a camel, knelt clumsily, for she was long from the hip to the knee, breathed hard, and considered the last couple.

'I think I'd like that sandy-pied one,' she said.

'Oh, not him, Miss Sichliffe!' Attley cried. 'He was overlaid or had sunstroke or something. They call him The Looney in the kennels. Besides, he squints.'

'I think that's rather fetching,' she answered. Neither Malachi nor I had ever seen a squinting dog before.

'That's chorea – St Vitus's dance,'[2] Mrs Godfrey put in. 'He ought to have been drowned.'

'But I like his cast of countenance,' the girl persisted.

'He doesn't look a good life,' I said, 'but perhaps he can be patched up.' Miss Sichliffe turned crimson; I saw Mrs Godfrey exchange a glance with her married daughter, and knew I had said something which would have to be lived down.

'Yes,' Miss Sichliffe went on, her voice shaking, 'he isn't a good life, but perhaps I can – patch him up. Come here, sir.' The misshapen beast lurched toward her, squinting down his

125

own nose till he fell over his own toes. Then, luckily, Bettina ran across the lawn and reminded Malachi of their puppyhood. All that family are as queer as Dick's hatband,[3] and fight like man and wife. I had to separate them, and Mrs Godfrey helped me till they retired under the rhododendrons and had it out in silence.

'D'you know what that girl's father was?' Mrs Godfrey asked.

'No,' I replied. 'I loathe her for her own sake. She breathes through her mouth.'

'He was a retired doctor,' she explained. 'He used to pick up stormy young men in the repentant stage, take them home, and patch them up till they were sound enough to be insured. Then he insured them heavily, and let them out into the world again – with an appetite. Of course, no one knew him while he was alive, but he left pots of money to his daughter.'

'Strictly legitimate – highly respectable,' I said. 'But what a life for the daughter!'

'Mustn't it have been! *Now* d'you realize what you said just now?'

'Perfectly; and now you've made me quite happy, shall we go back to the house?'

When we reached it they were all inside, sitting on committee of names.

'What shall you call yours?' I heard Milly ask Miss Sichliffe.

'Harvey,' she replied – 'Harvey's Sauce, you know. He's going to be quite saucy when I've' – she saw Mrs Godfrey and me coming through the French window – 'when he's stronger.'

Attley, the well-meaning man, to make me feel at ease, asked what I thought of the name.

'Oh, splendid,' I said at random. 'H with an A, A with an R, R with a –'

'But that's Little Bingo,'[4] someone said, and they all laughed.

Miss Sichliffe, her hands joined across her long knees, drawled, 'You ought always to verify your quotations.'

It was not a kindly thrust, but something in the word 'quotation' set the automatic side of my brain at work on some shadow of a word or phrase that kept itself out of memory's reach as a cat sits just beyond a dog's jump. When I was going home, Miss Sichliffe came up to me in the twilight, the pup on a leash, swinging her big shoes at the end of her tennis-racket.

''Sorry,' she said in her thick schoolboy-like voice. 'I'm sorry for what I said to you about verifying quotations. I didn't know you well enough and – anyhow, I oughtn't to have.'

'But you were quite right about Little Bingo,' I answered. 'The spelling ought to have reminded me.'

'Yes, of course. It's the spelling,' she said, and slouched off with the pup sliding after her. Once again my brain began to worry after something that would have meant something if it had been properly spelled. I confided my trouble to Malachi on the way home, but Bettina had bitten him in four places, and he was busy.

Weeks later, Attley came over to see me, and before his car stopped Malachi let me know that Bettina was sitting beside the chauffeur. He greeted her by the scruff of the neck as she hopped down; and I greeted Mrs Godfrey, Attley, and a big basket.

'You've got to help me,' said Attley tiredly. We took the basket into the garden, and there staggered out the angular shadow of a sandy-pied, broken-haired terrier, with one imbecile and one delirious ear, and two most hideous squints. Bettina and Malachi, already at grips on the lawn, saw him, let go, and fled in opposite directions.

'Why have you brought that fetid hound here?' I demanded.

'Harvey? For you to take care of,' said Attley. 'He's had distemper, but *I'm* going abroad.'

'Take him with you. I won't have him. He's mentally afflicted.'

'Look here,' Attley almost shouted, 'do I strike you as a fool?'

'Always,' said I.

'Well, then, if you say so, and Ella says so, that proves I ought to go abroad.'

'Will's wrong, quite wrong,' Mrs Godfrey interrupted; 'but you must take the pup.'

'My dear boy, my dear boy, don't you ever give anything to a woman,' Attley snorted.

Bit by bit I got the story out of them in the quiet garden

(never a sign from Bettina and Malachi), while Harvey stared me out of countenance, first with one cuttlefish eye and then with the other.

It appeared that, a month after Miss Sichliffe took him, the dog Harvey developed distemper. Miss Sichliffe had nursed him herself for some time; then she carried him in her arms the two miles to Mittleham, and wept – actually wept – at Attley's feet, saying that Harvey was all she had or expected to have in this world, and Attley must cure him. Attley, being by wealth, position, and temperament guardian to all lame dogs, had put everything aside for this unsavoury job, and, he asserted, Miss Sichliffe had virtually lived with him ever since.

'She went home at night, of course,' he exploded, 'but the rest of the time she simply infested the premises. Goodness knows, I'm not particular, but it was a scandal. Even the servants! . . . Three and four times a day, and notes in between, to know how the beast was. Hang it all, don't laugh! And wanting to send me flowers and goldfish. Do I look as if I wanted goldfish? Can't you two stop for a minute?' (Mrs Godfrey and I were clinging to each other for support.) 'And it isn't as if I was – was so alluring a personality, is it?'

Attley commands more trust, goodwill, and affection than most men, for he is that rare angel, an absolutely unselfish bachelor, content to be run by contending syndicates of zealous friends. His situation seemed desperate, and I told him so.

'Instant flight is your only remedy,' was my verdict. 'I'll take care of both your cars while you're away, and you can send me over all the greenhouse fruit.'

'But why should I be chased out of my house by a she-dromedary?' he wailed.

'Oh, stop! Stop!' Mrs Godfrey sobbed. 'You're both wrong. I admit you're right, but I *know* you're wrong.'

'Three *and* four times a day,' said Attley, with an awful countenance. 'I'm not a vain man, but – look here, Ella, I'm not sensitive, I hope, but if you persist in making a joke of it –'

'Oh, be quiet!' she almost shrieked. 'D'you imagine for one instant that your friends would ever let Mittleham pass out of their hands? I quite agree it is unseemly for a grown girl to come to Mittleham at all hours of the day and night –'

'I told you she went home o' nights,' Attley growled.

'Specially if she goes home o' nights. Oh, but think of the life she must have led, Will!'

'I'm not interfering with it; only she must leave me alone.'

'She may want to patch you up and insure you,' I suggested.

'D'you know what *you* are?' Mrs Godfrey turned on me with the smile I have feared for the last quarter of a century. 'You're the nice, kind, wise, doggy friend. You don't know how wise and nice you are supposed to be. Will has sent Harvey to you to complete the poor angel's convalescence. You know all about dogs, or Will wouldn't have done it. He's written her that. You're too far off for her to make daily calls on you. P'r'aps she'll drop in two or three times a week, and write on other days. But it doesn't matter what she does, because you don't own Mittleham, don't you see?'

I told her I saw most clearly.

'Oh, you'll get over that in a few days,' Mrs Godfrey countered. 'You're the sporting, responsible, doggy friend who –'

'He used to look at me like that at first,' said Attley, with a visible shudder, 'but he gave it up after a bit. It's only because you're new to him.'

'But, confound you! he's a ghoul –' I began.

'And when he gets quite well, you'll send him back to her direct with your love, and she'll give you some pretty four-tailed goldfish,' said Mrs Godfrey, rising. 'That's all settled. Car, please. We're going to Brighton to lunch together.'

They ran before I could get into my stride, so I told the dog Harvey what I thought of them and his mistress. He never shifted his position, but stared at me, an intense, lopsided stare, eye after eye. Malachi came along when he had seen his sister off, and from a distance counselled me to drown the brute and consort with gentlemen again. But the dog Harvey never even cocked his cockable ear.

And so it continued as long as he was with me. Where I sat, he sat and stared; where I walked, he walked beside, head stiffly slewed over one shoulder in single-barrelled contemplation of me. He never gave tongue, never closed in for a caress, seldom let me stir a step alone. And, to my amazement,

Malachi, who suffered no stranger to live within our gates, saw this gaunt, growing, green-eyed devil wipe him out of my service and company without a whimper. Indeed, one would have said the situation interested him, for he would meet us returning from grim walks together, and look alternately at Harvey and at me with the same quivering interest that he showed at the mouth of a rat-hole. Outside these inspections, Malachi withdrew himself as only a dog or a woman can.

Miss Sichliffe came over after a few days (luckily I was out) with some elaborate story of paying calls in the neighbourhood. She sent me a note of thanks next day. I was reading it when Harvey and Malachi entered and disposed themselves as usual, Harvey close up to stare at me, Malachi half under the sofa, watching us both. Out of curiosity I returned Harvey's stare, then pulled his lopsided head on to my knee, and took his eye for several minutes. Now, in Malachi's eye I can see at any hour all that there is of the normal decent dog, flecked here and there with that strained half-soul which man's love and association have added to his nature. But with Harvey the eye was perplexed, as a tortured man's. Only by looking far into its deeps could one make out the spirit of the proper animal, beclouded and cowering beneath some unfair burden.

Leggatt, my chauffeur, came in for orders.

'How d'you think Harvey's coming on?' I said, as I rubbed the brute's gulping neck. The vet had warned me of the possibilities of spinal trouble following distemper.

'He ain't *my* fancy,' was the reply. 'But *I* don't question his comings and goings so long as I 'aven't to sit alone in a room with him.'

'Why? He's as meek as Moses,' I said.

'He fair gives me the creeps. P'r'aps he'll go out in fits.'

But Harvey, as I wrote his mistress from time to time, throve, and when he grew better, would play by himself grisly games of spying, walking up, hailing, and chasing another dog. From these he would break off of a sudden and return to his normal stiff gait, with the air of one who had forgotten some matter of life and death, which could be reached only by staring at me. I left him one evening posturing with the unseen on the lawn, and went inside to finish some letters for the post. I must have been at work nearly an hour, for I was going to turn on the lights, when I felt there was somebody in the room whom, the short hairs at the back of my neck warned me, I was not in the least anxious to face. There was a mirror on the wall. As I lifted my eyes to it I saw the dog Harvey reflected near the shadow by the closed door. He had reared himself full-length on his hind legs, his head a little one side to clear a sofa between us, and he was looking at me. The face, with its knitted brows and drawn lips, was the face of a dog, but the look, for the fraction of time that I caught it, was human — wholly and horribly human. When the blood in my body went forward again he had dropped to the floor, and was merely studying me in his usual one-eyed fashion. Next day I returned him to Miss Sichliffe. I would not have kept him another day for the wealth of Asia, or even, Ella Godfrey's approval.

Miss Sichliffe's house I discovered to be a mid-Victorian mansion of peculiar villainy even for its period, surrounded by gardens of conflicting colours, all dazzling with glass and fresh paint on ironwork. Striped blinds, for it was a blazing autumn morning, covered most of the windows, and a voice sang to the piano an almost forgotten song of Jean Ingelow's —[5]

> Methought that the stars were blinking bright,
>   And the old brig's sails unfurled —

Down came the loud pedal,[6] and the unrestrained cry swelled out across a bed of tritomas consuming in their own fires —

> When I said I will sail to my love this night
>   On the other side of the world.

I have no music, but the voice drew. I waited till the end:

> Oh, maid most dear, I am not here
>   I have no place apart —
> No dwelling more on sea or shore,
>   But only in thy heart.

It seemed to me a poor life that had no more than that to do at eleven o'clock of a Tuesday forenoon. Then Miss Sichliffe suddenly lumbered through a French window in clumsy haste, her brows contracted against the light.

'Well?' she said, delivering the word like a spear-thrust, with the full weight of a body behind it.

'I've brought Harvey back at last,' I replied. 'Here he is.'

But it was at me she looked, not at the dog who had cast himself at her feet – looked as though she would have fished my soul out of my breast on the instant.

'Wha – what did you think of him? What did *you* make of him?' she panted. I was too taken aback for the moment to reply. Her voice broke as she stooped to the dog at her knees. 'O Harvey, Harvey! You utterly worthless old devil!' she cried, and the dog cringed and abased himself in servility that one could scarcely bear to look upon. I made to go.

'Oh, but please, you mustn't!' She tugged at the car's side. 'Wouldn't you like some flowers or some orchids? We've really splendid orchids, and' – she clasped her hands – 'there are Japanese goldfish – real Japanese goldfish, with four tails. If you don't care for 'em, perhaps your friends or somebody – oh, please!'

Harvey had recovered himself, and I realized that this woman beyond the decencies was fawning on me as the dog had fawned on her.

'Certainly,' I said, ashamed to meet her eye. 'I'm lunching at Mittleham, but –'

'There's plenty of time,' she entreated. 'What do *you* think of Harvey?'

'He's a queer beast,' I said, getting out. 'He does nothing but stare at me.'

'Does he stare at you all the time he's with you?'

'Always. He's doing it now. Look!'

We had halted. Harvey had sat down, and was staring from one to the other with a weaving motion of the head.

'He'll do that all day,' I said. 'What is it, Harvey?'

'Yes, what *is* it, Harvey?' she echoed. The dog's throat twitched, his body stiffened and shook as though he were going to have a fit. Then he came back with a visible wrench to his unwinking watch.

''Always so?' she whispered.

'Always,' I replied, and told her something of his life with me. She nodded once or twice, and in the end led me into the house.

There were unaging pitch-pine doors of Gothic design in it; there were inlaid marble mantel-pieces and cut-steel fenders; there were stupendous wall-papers, and octagonal, medallioned Wedgwood what-nots, and black-and-gilt Austrian images holding candelabra, with every other refinement that Art had achieved or wealth had bought between 1851 and 1878. And everything recked of varnish.

'Now!' she opened a baize door, and pointed down a long corridor flanked with more Gothic doors. 'This was where we used to – to patch 'em up. You've heard of us. Mrs Godfrey told you in the garden the day I got Harvey given me. I' – she drew in her breath – 'I live here by myself, and I have a very large income. Come back, Harvey.'

He had tiptoed down the corridor, as rigid as ever, and was sitting outside one of the shut doors. 'Look here!' she said, and planted herself squarely in front of me. 'I tell you this because you – you've patched up Harvey, too. Now, I want you to remember that my name is Moira. Mother calls me Marjorie because it's more refined; but my real name is Moira, and I am in my thirty-fourth year.'

'Very good,' I said. 'I'll remember all that.'

'Thank you.' Then with a sudden swoop into the humility of an abashed boy – ''Sorry if I haven't said the proper things. You see – there's Harvey looking at us again. Oh, I want to say – if ever you want anything in the way of orchids or goldfish or – or anything else that would be useful to you, you've only to come to me for it. Under the will I'm perfectly independent, and we're a long-lived family, worse luck!' She looked at me, and her face worked like glass behind driven flame. 'I may reasonably expect to live another fifty years,' she said.

'Thank you, Miss Sichliffe,' I replied. 'If I want anything, you may be sure I'll come to you for it.' She nodded. 'Now I must get over to Mittleham,' I said.

'Mr Attley will ask you all about this.' For the first time she laughed aloud. 'I'm afraid I frightened him nearly out of the country. I didn't think, of course. But I dare say he knows by this time he was wrong. Say goodbye to Harvey.'

'Goodbye, old man,' I said. 'Give me a farewell stare, so we shall know each other when we meet again.'

The dog looked up, then moved slowly toward me, and stood, head bowed to the floor, shaking in every muscle as I patted him; and when I turned, I saw him crawl back to her feet.

That was not a good preparation for the rampant boy-and-girl-dominated lunch at Mittleham, which, as usual, I found in possession of everybody except the owner.

'But what did the dromedary say when you brought her beast back?' Attley demanded.

'The usual polite things,' I replied. 'I'm posing as the nice doggy friend nowadays.'

'I don't envy you. She's never darkened my doors, thank goodness, since I left Harvey at your place. I suppose she'll run about the county now swearing you cured him. That's a woman's idea of gratitude.' Attley seemed rather hurt, and Mrs Godfrey laughed.

'That proves you were right about Miss Sichliffe, Ella,' I said. 'She had no designs on anybody.'

'I'm always right in these matters. But didn't she even offer you a goldfish?'

'Not a thing,' said I. 'You know what an old maid's like where her precious dog's concerned.' And though I have tried vainly to lie to Ella Godfrey for many years, I believe that in this case I succeeded.

When I turned into our drive that evening, Leggatt observed half aloud:

'I'm glad Zvengali's[7] back where he belongs. It's time our Mike had a look in.'

Sure enough, there was Malachi back again in spirit as well as flesh, but still with that odd air of expectation he had picked up from Harvey.

It was in January that Attley wrote me that Mrs Godfrey, wintering in Madeira with Milly, her unmarried daughter, had been attacked with something like enteric; that the hotel, anxious for its good name, had thrust them both out into a cottage annexe; that he was off with a nurse, and that I was not to leave England till I heard from him again. In a week he wired that Milly was down as well, and that I must bring out two more nurses, with suitable delicacies.

Within seventeen hours I had got them all aboard the Cape boat, and had seen the women safely collapsed into sea-sickness. The next few weeks were for me, as for the invalids, a low delirium, clouded with fantastic memories of Portuguese officials trying to tax calves'-foot jelly; voluble doctors insisting that true typhoid was unknown in the island; nurses who had to be exercised, taken out of themselves, and returned on the tick of change of guard; night slides down glassy, cobbled streets, smelling of sewage and flowers, between walls whose every stone and patch Attley and I knew; vigils in stucco verandahs, watching the curve and descent of great stars or drawing auguries from the break of dawn; insane interludes of gambling at the local Casino, where we won heaps of unconsoling silver; blasts of steamers arriving and departing in the roads; help offered by total strangers, grabbed at or thrust aside; the long nightmare crumbling back into sanity one forenoon under a vine-covered trellis, where Attley sat hugging a nurse, while the others danced a noiseless, neat-footed break-down never learned at the Middlesex Hospital. At last, as the tension came out all over us in aches and tingles that we put down to the country wine, a vision of Mrs Godfrey, her grey hair turned to spun-glass, but her eyes triumphant over the shadow of retreating death beneath them, with Milly, enormously grown, and clutch-ing life back to her young breast, both stretched out on cane chairs, clamouring for food.

In this ungirt hour there imported himself into our life a youngish-looking middle-aged man of the name of Shend, with a blurred face and deprecating eyes. He said he had gambled with me at the Casino, which was no recommendation, and I remember that he twice gave me a basket of champagne and liqueur brandy for the invalids, which a sailor in a red-tasselled cap carried up to the cottage for me at 3 a.m. He turned out to be the son of some merchant prince in the oil and colour line, and the owner of a four-hundred-ton steam yacht, into which, at his gentle insistence, we later shifted our camp, staff, and equipage, Milly weeping with delight to escape from the hor-rible cottage. There we lay off Funchal for weeks, while Shend did miracles of luxury and attendance through deputies, and never once asked how his guests were enjoying themselves.

Indeed, for several days at a time we would see nothing of him. He was, he said, subject to malaria. Giving as they do with both hands, I knew that Attley and Mrs Godfrey could take nobly; but I never met a man who so nobly gave and so nobly received thanks as Shend did.

'Tell us why you have been so unbelievably kind to us gipsies,' Mrs Godfrey said to him one day on deck.

He looked up from a diagram of some Thames-mouth shoals which he was explaining to me, and answered with his gentle smile:

'I will. It's because it makes me happy – it makes me more than happy – to be with you. It makes me comfortable. You know how selfish men are? If a man feels comfortable all over with certain people, he'll bore them to death, just like a dog. You always make me feel as if pleasant things were going to happen to me.'

'Haven't any ever happened before?' Milly asked.

'This is the most pleasant thing that has happened to me in ever so many years,' he replied. 'I feel like the man in the Bible, "It's good for me to be here." [8] Generally, I don't feel that it's good for me to be anywhere in particular.' Then, as one begging a favour. 'You'll let me come home with you – in the same boat, I mean? I'd take you back in this thing of mine, and that would save you packing your trunks, but she's too lively for spring work across the Bay.'

We booked our berths, and when the time came, he wafted us and ours aboard the Southampton mailboat with the pomp of plenipotentiaries and the precision of the Navy. Then he dismissed his yacht, and became an inconspicuous passenger in a cabin opposite to mine, on the port side.

We ran at once into early British spring weather, followed by sou'west gales. Mrs Godfrey, Milly, and the nurses disappeared. Attley stood it out, visibly yellowing, till the next meal, and followed suit, and Shend and I had the little table all to ourselves. I found him even more attractive when the women were away. The natural sweetness of the man, his voice, and bearing all fascinated me, and his knowledge of practical seamanship (he held an extra master's certificate) was a real joy. We sat long in the empty saloon and longer in the smoking-room, making dashes downstairs over slippery decks at the eleventh hour.

It was on Friday night, just as I was going to bed, that he came into my cabin, after cleaning his teeth, which he did half a dozen times a day.

'I say,' he began hurriedly, 'do you mind if I come in here for a little? I'm a bit edgy.' I must have shown surprise. 'I'm ever so much better about liquor than I used to be, but – it's the whisky in the suitcase that throws me. For God's sake, old man, don't go back on me tonight! Look at my hands!'

They were fairly jumping at the wrists. He sat down on a trunk that had slid out with the roll. We had reduced speed, and were surging in confused seas that pounded on the black port-glasses. The night promised to be a pleasant one!

'You understand, of course, don't you?' he chattered.

'Oh yes,' I said cheerily; 'but how about –'

'No, no; on no account the doctor. 'Tell a doctor, tell the whole ship. Besides, I've only got a touch of 'em. You'd never have guessed it, would you? The tooth-wash does the trick. I'll give you the prescription.'

'I'll send a note to the doctor for a prescription, shall I?' I suggested.

'Right! I put myself unreservedly in your hands. 'Fact is, I always did. I said to myself – 'sure I don't bore you? – the minute I saw you, I said, "Thou art the man."'[9] He repeated the phrase as he picked at his knees. 'All the same, you can take it from me that the ewe-lamb business is a rotten bad one. I don't care how unfaithful the shepherd may be. Drunk or sober, 'tisn't cricket.'

A surge of the trunk threw him across the cabin as the steward answered my bell. I wrote my requisition to the doctor while Shend was struggling to his feet.

'What's wrong?' he began. 'Oh, I know. We're slowing for soundings off Ushant. It's about time, too. You'd better ship the dead-lights when you come back, Matchem. It'll save you waking us later. This sea's going to get up when the tide turns. That'll show you,' he said as the man left, 'that I am to be trusted. You – you'll stop me if I say anything I shouldn't, won't you?'

'Talk away,' I replied, 'if it makes you feel better.'

'That's it; you've hit it exactly. You always make me feel better. I can rely on you. It's awkward soundings but you'll see me through it. We'll defeat him yet ... I may be an utterly worthless devil, but I'm not a brawler ... I told him so at breakfast. I said, "Doctor, I detest brawling, but if ever you allow that girl to be insulted again as Clements insulted her, I will break your neck with my own hands." You think I was right?'

'Absolutely,' I agreed.

'Then, we needn't discuss the matter any further. That man was murderer in intention – outside the law, you understand, as it was then. They've changed it since – but he never deceived *me*. I told him so. I said to him at the time, "I don't know what price you're going to put on my head, but if ever you allow Clements to insult her again, you'll never live to claim it."'

'And what did he do?' I asked, to carry on the conversation, for Matchem entered with the bromide.

'Oh, crumpled up at once. 'Lead still going, Matchem?'

'I 'aven't 'eard,' said that faithful servant of the Union-Castle Company.

'Quite right. Never alarm the passengers. Ship the dead-light, will you?' Matchem shipped it, for we were rolling very heavily. There were tramplings and gull-like cries from on deck. Shend looked at me with a mariner's eye.

'That's nothing,' he said protectingly.

'Oh, it's all right for you,' I said, jumping at the idea. '*I* haven't an extra master's certificate. I'm only a passenger. I confess it funks me.'

Instantly his whole bearing changed to answer the appeal.

'My dear fellow, it's as simple as houses. We're hunting for sixty-five fathom water. Anything short of sixty, with a sou'west wind means – but I'll get my Channel Pilot out of my cabin and give you the general idea. I'm only too grateful to do anything to put your mind at ease.'

And so, perhaps, for another hour – he declined the drink – Channel Pilot in hand, he navigated us round Ushant, and at my request up-channel to Southampton, light by light, with explanations and reminiscences. I professed myself soothed at last, and suggested bed.

'In a second,' said he. 'Now, you wouldn't think, would you'
– he glanced off the book toward my wildly swaying dressing-
gown on the door – 'that I've been seeing things for the last
half-hour? 'Fact is, I'm just on the edge of 'em, skating on thin
ice round the corner – nor'east as near as nothing – where that
dog's looking at me.'

'What's the dog like?' I asked.

'Ah, that *is* comforting of you! Most men walk through 'em
to show me they aren't real. As if I didn't know! But *you're*
different. Anybody could see that with half an eye.' He stiffened and pointed. 'Damn it all! The dog sees it too with half
an – Why, he knows you! Knows you perfectly. D'you know
him?'

'How can I tell if he isn't real?' I insisted.

'But you can! *You're* all right. I saw that from the first.
Don't go back on me now or I shall go to pieces like the
Drummond Castle.[10] I beg your pardon, old man; but, you see,
you *do* know the dog. I'll prove it. What's that dog doing?
Come on! *You* know.' A tremor shook him, and he put his hand
on my knee, and whispered with great meaning: 'I'll letter or
halve it with you. There! You begin.'

'S,' said I to humour him, for a dog would most likely be
standing or sitting, or may be scratching or sniffing or staring.

'Q,' he went on, and I could feel the heat of his shaking
hand.

'U,' said I. There was no other letter possible; but I was
shaking too.

'I.'

'N.'

'T-i-n-g,' he ran out. 'There! That proves it. I knew you
knew him. You don't know what a relief that is. Between ourselves, old man, he – he's been turning up lately a – a damn
sight more often than I cared for. And a squinting dog – a dog
that squints! I mean that's a bit *too* much. Eh? What?' He
gulped and half rose, and I thought that the full tide of delirium
would be on him in another sentence.

'Not a bit of it,' I said as a last chance, with my hand over
the bellpush. 'Why, you've just proved that I know him; so
there are two of us in the game, anyhow.'

'By Jove! that *is* an idea! Of course there are. I knew you'd
see me through. We'll defeat them yet. Hi, pup! . . . He's gone.
Absolutely disappeared!' He sighed with relief, and I caught
the lucky moment.

'Good business! I expect he only came to have a look at me,'
I said. 'Now, get this drink down and turn in to the lower
bunk.'

He obeyed, protesting that he could not inconvenience me,
and in the midst of apologies sank into a dead sleep. I expected
a wakeful night, having a certain amount to think over; but no
sooner had I scrambled into the top-bunk than sleep came on
me like a wave from the other side of the world.

In the morning there were apologies, which we got over at
breakfast before our party were about.

'I suppose – after this – well, I don't blame you. I'm rather a
lonely chap, though.' His eyes lifted dog-like across the table.

'Shend,' I replied, 'I'm not running a Sunday school. You're
coming home with me in my car as soon as we land.'

'That is kind of you – kinder than you think.'

'That's because you're a little jumpy still. Now, I don't want
to mix up in your private affairs –'

'But I'd like you to,' he interrupted.

'Then, would you mind telling me the Christian name of a
girl who was insulted by a man called Clements?'

'Moira,' he whispered; and just then Mrs Godfrey and Milly
came to table with their shore-going hats on.

We did not tie up till noon, but the faithful Leggatt had
intrigued his way down to the dock-edge, and beside him sat
Malachi, wearing his collar of gold,[11] or Leggatt makes it look
so, as eloquent as Demosthenes.[12] Shend flinched a little when
he saw him. We packed Mrs Godfrey and Milly into Attley's
car – they were going with him to Mittleham, of course – and
drew clear across the railway lines to find England all lit and
perfumed for spring. Shend sighed with happiness.

'D'you know,' he said, 'if – if you'd chucked me – I should
have gone down to my cabin after breakfast and cut my throat.
And now – it's like a dream – a good dream, you know.'

We lunched with the other three at Romsey. Then I sat in
front for a little while to talk to my Malachi. When I looked

back, Shend was solidly asleep, and stayed so for the next two hours, while Leggatt chased Attley's fat Daimler along the green-speckled hedges. He woke up when we said goodbye at Mittleham, with promises to meet again very soon.

'And I hope,' said Mrs Godfrey, 'that everything pleasant will happen to you.'

'Heaps and heaps – all at once,' cried long, weak Milly, waving her wet handkerchief.

'I've just got to look in at a house near here for a minute to inquire about a dog,' I said, 'and then we will go home.'

'I used to know this part of the world,' he replied, and said no more till Leggatt shot past the lodge at the Sichliffes's gate. Then I heard him gasp.

Miss Sichliffe, in a green waterproof, an orange jersey, and a pinkish leather hat, was working on a bulb-border. She straightened herself as the car stopped, and breathed hard. Shend got out and walked towards her. They shook hands, turned round together, and went into the house. Then the dog Harvey pranced out corkily from under the lee of a bench. Malachi, with one joyous swoop, fell on him as an enemy and an equal. Harvey, for his part, freed from all burden whatsoever except the obvious duty of a man-dog on his own ground, met Malachi without reserves or remorse, and with six months' additional growth to come and go on.

'Don't check 'em!' cried Leggatt, dancing round the flurry. 'They've both been saving up for each other all this time. It'll do 'em worlds of good.'

'Leggatt,' I said, 'will you take Mr Shend's bag and suitcase up to the house and put them down just inside the door? Then we will go on.'

So I enjoyed the finish alone. It was a dead heat, and they licked each other's jaws in amity till Harvey, one imploring eye on me, leaped into the front seat, and Malachi backed his appeal. It was theft, but I took him, and we talked all the way home of r-rats and r-rabbits and bones and baths and the other basic facts of life. That evening after dinner they slept before the fire, with their warm chins across the hollows of my ankles – to each chin an ankle – till I kicked them upstairs to bed.

*

I was not at Mittleham when she came over to announce her engagement, but I heard of it when Mrs Godfrey and Attley came, forty miles an hour, over to me, and Mrs Godfrey called me names of the worst for suppression of information.

'As long as it wasn't me, I don't care,' said Attley.

'I believe you knew it all along,' Mrs Godfrey repeated. 'Else what made you drive that man literally into her arms?'

'To ask after the dog Harvey,' I replied.

'Then, what's the beast doing here?' Attley demanded, for Malachi and the dog Harvey were deep in a council of the family with Bettina, who was being out-argued.

'Oh, Harvey seemed to think himself *de trop* where he was,' I said. 'And she hasn't sent after him. You'd better save Bettina before they kill her.'

'There's been enough lying about that dog,' said Mrs Godfrey to me. 'If he wasn't born in lies, he was baptized in 'em. D'you know why she called him Harvey? It only occurred to me in those dreadful days when I was ill, and one can't keep from thinking, and thinks everything. D'you know your Boswell? What did Johnson say about Hervey – with an e?'

'Oh, *that's* it, is it?' I cried incautiously. 'That was why I ought to have verified my quotations. The spelling defeated me. Wait a moment, and it will come back. Johnson said: "He was a vicious man,"' I began.

'"But very kind to me,"' Mrs Godfrey prompted. Then, both together, '"If you call a dog Hervey, I shall love him."'[13]

'So you *were* mixed up in it. At any rate, you had your suspicions from the first? Tell me,' she said.

'Ella,' I said, 'I don't know anything rational or reasonable about any of it. It was all – all woman-work, and it scared me horribly.'

'Why?' she asked.

That was six years ago. I have written this tale to let her know – wherever she may be.

The Comforters

Until thy feet have trod the Road
  Advise not wayside folk,
Nor till thy back has borne the Load
  Break in upon the Broke.

Chase not with undesired largesse
  Of sympathy the heart
Which, knowing her own bitterness,
  Presumes to dwell apart.

Employ not that glad hand to raise
  The God-forgotten head
To Heaven, and all the neighbours' gaze –
  Cover thy mouth instead.

The quivering chin, the bitten lip,
  The cold and sweating brow,
Later may yearn for fellowship –
  Not now, you ass, not now!

Time, not thy ne'er so timely speech,
  Life, not thy views thereon,
Shall furnish or deny to each
  His consolation.

Or, if impelled to interfere,
  Exhort, uplift, advise,
Lend not a base, betraying ear
  To all the victim's cries.

Only the Lord can understand
  When those first pangs begin,
How much is reflex action and
  How much is really sin.

E'en from good words thyself refrain,
  And tremblingly admit
There is no anodyne for pain
  Except the shock of it.

A Diversity of Creatures

So, when thine own dark hour shall fall,
  Unchallenged canst thou say:
'I never worried *you* at all,
  For God's sake go away!'

THE VILLAGE THAT VOTED THE
EARTH WAS FLAT

The Village that Voted the Earth was Flat

(1913)

Our drive till then had been quite a success. The other men in the car were my friend Woodhouse, young Ollyett, a distant connection of his, and Pallant, the M.P. Woodhouse's business was the treatment and cure of sick journals. He knew by instinct the precise moment in a newspaper's life when the impetus of past good management is exhausted and it fetches up on the dead-centre between slow and expensive collapse and the new start which can be given by gold injections – and genius. He was wisely ignorant of journalism; but when he stooped on a carcase there was sure to be meat. He had that week added a half-dead, halfpenny evening paper to his collection, which consisted of a prosperous London daily, one provincial ditto, and a limp-bodied weekly of commercial leanings. He had also, that very hour, planted me with a large block of the evening paper's common shares, and was explaining the whole art of editorship to Ollyett, a young man three years from Oxford, with coir-matting-coloured hair and a face harshly modelled by harsh experiences, who, I understood, was assisting in the new venture. Pallant, the long, wrinkled M.P., whose voice is more like a crane's than a peacock's, took no shares, but gave us all advice.

'You'll find it rather a knacker's yard,' Woodhouse was saying. 'Yes, I know they call me The Knacker; but it will pay inside a year. All my papers do. I've only one motto: Back your luck and back your staff. It'll come out all right.'

Then the car stopped, and a policeman asked our names and addresses for exceeding the speed-limit. We pointed out that the road ran absolutely straight for half a mile ahead without even a side-lane. 'That's just what we depend on,' said the policeman unpleasantly.

'The usual swindle,' said Woodhouse under his breath. 'What's the name of this place?'

'Huckley,' said the policeman. 'H-u-c-k-l-e-y,' and wrote something in his note-book at which young Ollyett protested. A large red man on a grey horse who had been watching us from the other side of the hedge shouted an order we could not catch. The policeman laid his hand on the rim of the right driving-door (Woodhouse carries his spare tyres aft), and it closed on the button of the electric horn. The grey horse at once bolted, and we could hear the rider swearing all across the landscape.

'Damn it, man, you've got your silly fist on it! Take it off!' Woodhouse shouted.

'Ho!' said the constable, looking carefully at his fingers as though we had trapped them. 'That won't do you any good either,' and he wrote once more in his note-book before he allowed us to go.

This was Woodhouse's first brush with motor law, and since I expected no ill consequences to myself, I pointed out that it was very serious. I took the same view myself when in due time I found that I, too, was summonsed on charges ranging from the use of obscene language to endangering traffic.

Judgment was done in a little pale-yellow market-town with a small, Jubilee clock-tower and a large corn-exchange. Woodhouse drove us there in his car. Pallant, who had not been included in the summons, came with us as moral support. While we waited outside, the fat man on the grey horse rode up and entered into loud talk with his brother magistrates. He said to one of them – for I took the trouble to note it down – 'It falls away from my lodge-gates, dead straight, three-quarters of a mile. I'd defy any one to resist it. We rooked seventy pounds out of 'em last month. No car can resist the temptation. You ought to have one your side the county, Mike. They simply can't resist it.'

'Whew!' said Woodhouse. 'We're in for trouble. Don't you say a word – or Ollyett either! I'll pay the fines and we'll get it over as soon as possible. Where's Pallant?'

'At the back of the court somewhere,' said Ollyett. 'I saw him slip in just now.'

The fat man then took his seat on the Bench, of which he was chairman, and I gathered from a bystander that his name was Sir Thomas Ingell, Bart., M.P., of Ingell Park, Huckley. He began with an allocution pitched in a tone that would have justified revolt throughout empires. Evidence, when the crowded little court did not drown it with applause, was given in the pauses of the address. They were all very proud of their Sir Thomas, and looked from him to us, wondering why we did not applaud too.

Taking its time from the chairman, the Bench rollicked with us for seventeen minutes. Sir Thomas explained that he was sick and tired of processions of cads of our type, who would be better employed breaking stones on the road than in frightening horses worth more than themselves or their ancestors. This was after it had been proved that Woodhouse's man had turned on the horn purposely to annoy Sir Thomas, who 'happened to be riding by'! There were other remarks too – primitive enough – but it was the unspeakable brutality of the tone, even more than the quality of the justice, or the laughter of the audience that stung our souls out of all reason. When we were dismissed – to the tune of twenty-three pounds, twelve shillings and sixpence – we waited for Pallant to join us, while we listened to the next case – one of driving without a licence. Ollyett with an eye to his evening paper, had already taken very full notes of our own, but we did not wish to seem prejudiced.

'It's all right,' said the reporter of the local paper soothingly. 'We never report Sir Thomas *in extenso*. Only the fines and charges.'

'Oh, thank you,' Ollyett replied, and I heard him ask who everyone in court might be. The local reporter was very communicative.

The new victim, a large, flaxen-haired man in somewhat striking clothes, to which Sir Thomas, now thoroughly warmed, drew public attention, said that he had left his licence at home. Sir Thomas asked him if he expected the police to go to his home address at Jerusalem [1] to find it for him; and the court roared. Nor did Sir Thomas approve of the man's name, but insisted on calling him 'Mr Masquerader', and every time he did so, all his people shouted. Evidently this was their established *auto-da-fé*.

'He didn't summons me – because I'm in the House, I

suppose. I think I shall have to ask a Question,' said Pallant, reappearing at the close of the case.

'I think *I* shall have to give it a little publicity too,' said Woodhouse. 'We can't have this kind of thing going on, you know.' His face was set and quite white. Pallant's, on the other hand, was black, and I know that my very stomach had turned with rage. Ollyett was dumb.

'Well, let's have lunch,' Woodhouse said at last. 'Then we can get away before the show breaks up.'

We drew Ollyett from the arms of the local reporter, crossed the Market Square to the Red Lion and found Sir Thomas's 'Mr Masquerader' just sitting down to beer, beef and pickles.

'Ah!' said he, in a large voice. 'Companions in misfortune. Won't you gentlemen join me?'

'Delighted,' said Woodhouse. 'What did you get?'

'I haven't decided. It might make a good turn, but – the public aren't educated up to it yet. It's beyond 'em. If it wasn't, that red dub² on the Bench would be worth fifty a week.'

'Where?' said Woodhouse. The man looked at him with unaffected surprise.

'At any one of My places,' he replied. 'But perhaps you live here?'

'Good heavens!' cried young Ollyett suddenly. 'You *are* Masquerier, then? I thought you were!'

'Bat Masquerier.' He let the words fall with the weight of an international ultimatum. 'Yes, that's all I am. But you have the advantage of me, gentlemen.'

For the moment, while we were introducing ourselves, I was puzzled. Then I recalled prismatic music-hall posters – of enormous acreage – that had been the unnoticed background of my visits to London for years past. Posters of men and women, singers, jongleurs, impersonators and audacities of every draped and undraped brand, all moved on and off in London and the Provinces by Bat Masquerier – with the long wedge-tailed flourish following the final 'r'.

'*I* knew you at once,' said Pallant, the trained M.P., and I promptly backed the lie. Woodhouse mumbled excuses. Bat Masquerier was not moved for or against us any more than the frontage of one of his own palaces.

'I always tell My people there's a limit to the size of the lettering,' he said. 'Overdo that and the ret'na doesn't take it in. Advertisin' is the most delicate of all the sciences.'

'There's one man in the world who is going to get a little of it if I live for the next twenty-four hours,' said Woodhouse, and explained how this would come about.

Masquerier stared at him lengthily with gun-metal-blue eyes.

'You mean it?' he drawled; the voice was as magnetic as the look.

'*I* do,' said Ollyett. 'That business of the horn alone ought to have him off the Bench in three months.' Masquerier looked at him even longer than he had looked at Woodhouse.

'He told *me*,' he said suddenly, 'that my home-address was Jerusalem. You heard that?'

'But it was the tone – the tone,' Ollyett cried.

'You noticed that, too, did you?' said Masquerier. 'That's the artistic temperament. You can do a lot with it. And I'm Bat Masquerier,' he went on. He dropped his chin in his fists and scowled straight in front of him . . . 'I made the Silhouettes – I made the Trefoil and the Jocunda. I made 'Dal Benzaguen.' Here Ollyett sat straight up, for in common with the youth of that year he worshipped Miss Vidal Benzaguen of the Trefoil immensely and unreservedly. '"*Is* that a dressing-gown or an ulster you're supposed to be wearing?" You heard *that*? . . . "And I suppose you hadn't time to brush your hair either?" You heard *that*? . . . Now, you hear *me*!' His voice filled the coffee-room, then dropped to a whisper as dreadful as a surgeon's before an operation. He spoke for several minutes. Pallant muttered 'Hear! hear!' I saw Ollyett's eye flash – it was to Ollyett that Masquerier addressed himself chiefly – and Woodhouse leaned forward with joined hands.

'Are you *with* me?' he went on, gathering us all up in one sweep of the arm. 'When I begin a thing I see it through, gentlemen. What Bat can't break, breaks him! But I haven't struck that thing yet. This is no one-turn turn-it-down show. This is business to the dead finish. Are you with me, gentlemen? Good! Now, we'll pool our assets. One London morning, and one provincial daily, didn't you say? One weekly commercial ditto and one M.P.'

'Not much use, I'm afraid,' Pallant smirked.

'But privileged. *But* privileged,' he returned. 'And we have also my little team – London, Blackburn, Liverpool, Leeds – I'll tell you about Manchester later – and Me! Bat Masquerier.' He breathed the name reverently into his tankard. 'Gentlemen, when our combination has finished with Sir Thomas Ingell, Bart., M.P., and everything else that is his, Sodom and Gomorrah will be a winsome bit of Merrie England beside 'em. I must go back to town now, but I trust you gentlemen will give me the pleasure of your company at dinner tonight at the Chop Suey – the Red Amber Room – and we'll block out the scenario.' He laid his hand on young Ollyett's shoulder and added: 'It's your brains I want.' Then he left, in a good deal of astrachan collar and nickel-plated limousine, and the place felt less crowded.

We ordered our car a few minutes later. As Woodhouse, Ollyett and I were getting in, Sir Thomas Ingell, Bart., M.P., came out of the Hall of Justice across the square and mounted his horse. I have sometime thought that if he had gone in silence he might even then have been saved, but as he settled himself in the saddle he caught sight of us and must needs shout: 'Not off yet? You'd better get away and you'd better be careful.' At that moment Pallant, who had been buying picture-postcards, came out of the inn, took Sir Thomas's eye and very leisurely entered the car. It seemed to me that for one instant there was a shade of uneasiness on the baronet's grey-whiskered face.

'I hope,' said Woodhouse after several miles, 'I hope he's a widower.'

'Yes,' said Pallant. 'For his poor, dear wife's sake I hope that, very much indeed. I suppose he didn't see me in Court. Oh, here's the parish history of Huckley written by the Rector and here's your share of the picture-postcards. Are we all dining with this Mr Masquerier tonight?'

'Yes!' said we all.

If Woodhouse knew nothing of journalism, young Ollyett, who had graduated in a hard school, knew a good deal. Our half-penny evening paper, which we will call *The Bun* to distinguish her from her prosperous morning sister, *The Cake*, was not only diseased but corrupt. We found this out when a man brought us the prospectus of a new oil-field and demanded sub-leaders on its prosperity. Ollyett talked pure Brasenose[3] to him for three minutes. Otherwise he spoke and wrote trade-English – a toothsome amalgam of Americanisms and epigrams. But though the slang changes the game never alters, and Ollyett and I and, in the end, some others enjoyed it immensely. It was weeks ere we could see the wood for the trees, but so soon as the staff realized that they had proprietors who backed them right or wrong, and specially when they were wrong (which is the sole secret of journalism), and that their fate did not hang on any passing owner's passing mood, they did miracles.

But we did not neglect Huckley. As Ollyett said our first care was to create an 'arresting atmosphere' round it. He used to visit the village of week-ends, on a motor-bicycle with a side-car; for which reason I left the actual place alone and dealt with it in the abstract. Yet it was I who drew first blood. Two inhabitants of Huckley wrote to contradict a small, quite solid paragraph in *The Bun* that a hoopoe had been seen at Huckley and had, 'of course, been shot by the local sportsmen'. There was some heat in their letters, both of which we published. Our version of how the hoopoe got his crest from King Solomon was, I grieve to say, so inaccurate that the Rector himself – no sportsman as he pointed out, but a lover of accuracy – wrote to us to correct it. We gave his letter good space and thanked him.

'This priest is going to be useful,' said Ollyett. 'He has the impartial mind. I shall vitalize him.'

Forthwith he created M. L. Sigden, a recluse of refined tastes who in *The Bun* demanded to know whether this Huckley-of-the-Hoopoe was the Hugly of his boyhood and whether, by any chance, the fell change of name had been wrought by collusion between a local magnate and the railway, in the mistaken interests of spurious refinement. 'For I knew it and loved it with the maidens of my day – *eheu ab angulo!*[4] – as Hugly,' wrote M. L. Sigden from Oxford.

Though other papers scoffed, *The Bun* was gravely sympathetic. Several people wrote to deny that Huckley had been changed at birth. Only the Rector – no philosopher as he pointed out, but a lover of accuracy – had his doubts, which he laid publicly before Mr M. L. Sigden, who suggested, through *The Bun*, that the little place might have begun life in Anglo-Saxon days as 'Hogslea' or among the Normans as 'Argilé', on account of its much clay. The Rector had his own ideas too (he said it was mostly gravel), and M. L. Sigden had a fund of reminiscences. Oddly enough – which is seldom the case with free reading-matter – our subscribers rather relished the correspondence, and contemporaries quoted freely.

'The secret of power,' said Ollyett, 'is not the big stick. It's the liftable stick.' (This means the 'arresting' quotation of six or seven lines.) 'Did you see the *Spec*.[5] had a middle on "Rural Tenacities" last week. That was all Huckley. I'm doing a "Mobiquity" on Huckley next week.'

Our 'Mobiquities' were Friday evening accounts of easy motor-bike-*cum*-side-car trips round London, illustrated (we could never get that machine to work properly) by smudgy maps. Ollyett wrote the stuff with a fervour and a delicacy which I always ascribed to the side-car. His account of Epping Forest, for instance, was simply young love with its soul at its lips. But his Huckley 'Mobiquity' would have sickened a soap-boiler. It chemically combined loathsome familiarity, leering suggestion, slimy piety and rancid 'social service' in one fuming compost that fairly lifted me off my feet.

'Yes,' said he, after compliments. 'It's the most vital, arresting and dynamic bit of tump I've done up to date. *Non nobis gloria!*[6] I met Sir Thomas Ingell in his own park. He talked to me again. He inspired most of it.'

'Which? The "glutinous native drawl", or "the neglected adenoids of the village children"?' I demanded.

'Oh, no! That's only to bring in the panel doctor. It's the last flight we – I'm proudest of.'

This dealt with 'the crepuscular penumbra spreading her dim limbs over the boskage';[7] with 'jolly rabbits'; with a herd of 'gravid polled Angus';[8] and with the 'arresting, gipsy-like face of their swart, scholarly owner – as well known at the Royal Agricultural Shows as that of our late King-Emperor.'[9]

'"Swart" is good and so's "gravid",' said I, 'but the panel doctor will be annoyed about the adenoids.'

'Not half as much as Sir Thomas will about his face,' said Ollyett. 'And if you only knew what I've left out!'

He was right. The panel doctor spent his week-end (this is the advantage of Friday articles) in overwhelming us with a professional counterblast of no interest whatever to our subscribers. We told him so, and he, then and there, battered his way with it into the *Lancet* where they are keen on glands, and forgot us altogether. But Sir Thomas Ingell was of sterner stuff. He must have spent a happy week-end too. The letter which we received from him on Monday proved him to be a kinless loon of upright life, for no woman, however remotely interested in a man would have let it pass the home wastepaper-basket. He objected to our references to his own herd, to his own labours in his own village, which he said was a Model Village, and to our infernal insolence; but he objected most to our invoice of his features. We wrote him courteously to ask whether the letter was meant for publication. He, re-membering, I presume, the Duke of Wellington, wrote back, 'publish and be damned.'

'Oh! This is too easy,' Ollyett said as he began heading the letter.

'Stop a minute,' I said. 'The game is getting a little beyond us. Tonight's the Bat dinner.' (I may have forgotten to tell you that our dinner with Bat Masquerier in the Red Amber Room of the Chop Suey had come to be a weekly affair.) 'Hold it over till they've all seen it.'

'Perhaps you're right,' he said. 'You might waste it.'

At dinner, then, Sir Thomas's letter was handed round. Bat seemed to be thinking of other matters, but Pallant was very interested.

'I've got an idea,' he said presently. 'Could you put something into *The Bun* tomorrow about foot-and-mouth disease in that fellow's herd?'

'Oh, plague if you like,' Ollyett replied. 'They're only five measly Shorthorns. I saw one lying down in the park. She'll serve as a substratum of fact.'

'Then, do that; and hold the letter over meanwhile. I think *I* come in here,' said Pallant.

'Why?' said I.

'Because there's something coming up in the House about foot-and-mouth, and because he wrote me a letter after that little affair when he fined you. 'Took ten days to think it over. Here you are,' said Pallant. 'House of Commons paper, you see.'

We read:

DEAR PALLANT –

Although in the past our paths have not lain much together, I am sure you will agree with me that on the floor of the House all members are on a footing of equality. I make bold, therefore, to approach you in a matter which I think capable of a very different interpretation from that which perhaps was put upon it by your friends. Will you let them know that that was the case and that I was in no way swayed by animus in the exercise of my magisterial duties, which you, as a brother magistrate, can imagine are frequently very distasteful to –

Yours very sincerely,
T. INGELL

P.S. – I have seen to it that the motor vigilance to which your friends took exception has been considerably relaxed in my district.

'What did you answer?' said Ollyett, when all our opinions had been expressed.

'I told him I couldn't do anything in the matter. And I couldn't – then. But you'll remember to put in that foot-and-mouth paragraph. I want something to work upon.'

'It seems to me *The Bun* has done all the work up to date,' I suggested. 'When does *The Cake* come in?'

'*The Cake*,' said Woodhouse, and I remembered afterwards that he spoke like a Cabinet Minister on the eve of a Budget, 'reserves to itself the fullest right to deal with situations as they arise.'

'Ye-eh!' Bat Masquerier shook himself out of his thoughts. '"Situations as they arise." I ain't idle either. But there's no use fishing till the swim's baited. You' – he turned to Ollyett – 'manufacture very good ground-bait . . . I always tell My people – What the deuce is that?'

There was a burst of song from another private dining-room across the landing. 'It ees some ladies from the Trefoil,' the waiter began.

'Oh, I know that. What are they singing, though?'

He rose and went out, to be greeted by shouts of applause

from that merry company. Then there was silence, such as one hears in the form-room after a master's entry. Then a voice that we loved began again: 'Here we go gathering nuts in May – nuts in May – nuts in May!'

'It's only 'Dal – and some nuts,'[10] he explained when he returned. 'She says she's coming in to dessert.' He sat down, humming the old tune to himself, and till Miss Vidal Benzaguen entered, he held us speechless with tales of the artistic temperament.

We obeyed Pallant to the extent of slipping into *The Bun* a wary paragraph about cows lying down and dripping at the mouth, which might be read either as an unkind libel or, in the hands of a capable lawyer, as a piece of faithful nature-study.

'And besides,' said Ollyett, 'we allude to "gravid polled Angus". I am advised that no action can lie in respect of virgin Shorthorns. Pallant wants us to come to the House tonight. He's got us places for the Strangers' Gallery. I'm beginning to like Pallant.'

'Masquerier seems to like you,' I said.

'Yes, but I'm afraid of him,' Ollyett answered with perfect sincerity. 'I am. He's the Absolutely Amoral Soul. I've never met one yet.'

We went to the House together. It happened to be an Irish afternoon, and as soon as I had got the cries and the faces a little sorted out, I gathered there were grievances in the air, but how many of them was beyond me.

'It's all right,' said Ollyett of the trained ear. 'They've shut their ports against – oh yes – export of Irish cattle! Foot-and-mouth disease at Ballyhellion. *I* see Pallant's idea!'

The House was certainly all mouth for the moment, but, as I could feel, quite in earnest. A Minister with a piece of type-written paper seemed to be fending off volleys of insults. He reminded me somehow of a nervous huntsman breaking up a fox in the face of rabid hounds.

'It's question-time. They're asking questions,' said Ollyett. 'Look! Pallant's up.'

There was no mistaking it. His voice, which his enemies said was his one parliamentary asset, silenced the hubbub as tooth-ache silences mere singing in the ears. He said:

157

'Arising out of that, may I ask if any special consideration has recently been shown in regard to any suspected outbreak of this disease on *this* side of the Channel?'

He raised his hand; it held a noon edition of *The Bun*. We had thought it best to drop the paragraph out of the later ones. He would have continued, but something in a grey frock-coat roared and bounded on a bench opposite, and waved another *Bun*. It was Sir Thomas Ingell.

'As the owner of the herd so dastardly implicated –' His voice was drowned in shouts of 'Order!' – the Irish leading.

'What's wrong?' I asked Ollyett. 'He's got his hat on his head, hasn't he?'

'Yes, but his wrath should have been put as a question.'

'Arising out of that, Mr Speaker, Sirrr!' Sir Thomas bellowed through a lull, 'are you aware that – that all this is a conspiracy – part of a dastardly conspiracy to make Huckley ridiculous – to make *us* ridiculous? Part of a deep-laid plot to make *me* ridiculous, Mr Speaker, Sir!'

The man's face showed almost black against his white whiskers, and he struck out swimmingly with his arms. His vehemence puzzled and held the House for an instant, and the Speaker took advantage of it to lift his pack from Ireland to a new scent. He addressed Sir Thomas Ingell in tones of measured rebuke, meant also, I imagine, for the whole House, which lowered its hackles at the word. Then Pallant, shocked and pained: 'I can only express my profound surprise that in response to my simple question the honourable member should have thought fit to indulge in a personal attack. If I have in any way offended – '

Again the Speaker intervened, for it appeared that he regulated these matters.

He, too, expressed surprise, and Sir Thomas sat back in a hush of reprobation that seemed to have the chill of the centuries behind it. The Empire's work was resumed.

'Beautiful!' said I, and I felt hot and cold up my back.

'And now we'll publish his letter,' said Ollyett.

We did – on the heels of his carefully reported outburst. We made no comment. With that rare instinct for grasping the heart of a situation which is the mark of the Anglo-Saxon, all our contemporaries and, I should say, two-thirds of our correspondents demanded how such a person could be made more ridiculous than he had already proved himself to be. But beyond spelling his name 'Injle', we alone refused to hit a man when he was down.

'There's no need,' said Ollyett. 'The whole press is on the huckle from end to end.'

Even Woodhouse was a little astonished at the ease with which it had come about, and said as much.

'Rot!' said Ollyett. 'We haven't really begun. Huckley isn't news yet.'

'What do you mean?' said Woodhouse, who had grown to have great respect for his young but by no means distant connection.

'Mean? By the grace of God, Master Ridley,[11] I mean to have it so that when Huckley turns over in its sleep, Reuters and the Press Association jump out of bed to cable.' Then he went off at score about certain restorations in Huckley Church which, he said – and he seemed to spend his every week-end there – had been perpetrated by the Rector's predecessor, who had abolished a 'leper-window' or a 'squinch-hole' (whatever these may be) to institute a lavatory in the vestry. It did not strike me as stuff for which Reuters or the Press Association would lose much sleep, and I left him declaiming to Woodhouse about a fourteenth-century font which, he said, he had unearthed in the sexton's tool-shed.

My methods were more on the lines of peaceful penetration. An odd copy, in *The Bun's* rag-and-bone library, of Hone's *Every-Day Book*[12] had revealed to me the existence of a village dance founded, like all village dances, on Druidical mysteries connected with the Solar Solstice (which is always unchallengeable) and Midsummer Morning, which is dewy and refreshing to the London eye. For this I take no credit – Hone being a mine any one can work – but that I rechristened that dance, after I had revised it, 'The Gubby' is my title to immortal fame. It was still to be witnessed, I wrote, 'in all its poignant purity at Huckley, that last home of significant medieval survivals'; and I fell so in love with my creation that I kept it back for days, enamelling and burnishing.

'You'd better put it in,' said Ollyett at last. 'It's time we asserted ourselves again. The other fellows are beginning to poach. You saw that thing in the *Pinnacle* about Sir Thomas's Model Village? He must have got one of their chaps down to do it.'

''Nothing like the wounds of a friend,' I said. 'That account of the non-alcoholic pub alone was – '

'I liked the bit best about the white-tiled laundry and the Fallen Virgins who wash Sir Thomas's dress shirts. Our side couldn't come within a mile of that, you know. We haven't the proper flair for sexual slobber.'

'That's what I'm always saying,' I retorted. 'Leave 'em alone. The other fellows are doing our work for us now. Besides I want to touch up my "Gubby Dance" a little more.'

'No. You'll spoil it. Let's shove it in today. For one thing it's Literature. I don't go in for compliments as you know, but, etc. etc.'

I had a healthy suspicion of young Ollyett in every aspect, but though I knew that I should have to pay for it, I fell to his flattery, and my priceless article on the 'Gubby Dance' appeared. Next Saturday he asked me to bring out *The Bun* in his absence, which I naturally assumed would be connected with the little maroon side-car. I was wrong.

On the following Monday I glanced at *The Cake* at breakfast-time to make sure, as usual, of her inferiority to my beloved but unremunerative *Bun*. I opened on a heading: 'The Village that Voted the Earth was Flat'. I read ... I read that the Geo-planarian Society – a society devoted to the proposition that the earth is flat – had held its Annual Banquet and Exercises at Huckley on Saturday, when after convincing addresses, amid scenes of the greatest enthusiasm, Huckley village had decided by an unanimous vote of 438 that the earth was flat. I do not remember that I breathed again till I had finished the two columns of description that followed. Only one man could have written them. They were flawless – crisp, nervous, austere yet human, poignant, vital, arresting – most distinctly arresting – dynamic enough to shift a city – and quotable by whole sticks at a time. And there was a leader, a grave and poised leader, which tore me in two with mirth, until I remembered that I had been left out — infamously and unjustifiably dropped. I went to Ollyett's rooms. He was breakfasting, and, to do him justice, looked conscience-stricken.

'It wasn't my fault,' he began. 'It was Bat Masquerier. I swear *I* would have asked you to come if — '

'Never mind that,' I said. 'It's the best bit of work you've ever done or will do. Did any of it happen?'

'Happen? Heavens! D'you think even *I* could have invented it?'

'Is it exclusive to *The Cake*?' I cried.

'It cost Bat Masquerier two thousand,' Ollyett replied. 'D'you think he'd let anyone else in on that? But I give you my sacred word I knew nothing about it till he asked me to come down and cover it. He had Huckley posted in three colours, "The Geoplanarians' Annual Banquet and Exercises". Yes, he invented "Geoplanarians". He wanted Huckley to think it meant aeroplanes. Yes, I know that there is a real Society that thinks the world's flat — they ought to be grateful for the lift — but Bat made his own. He did! He created the whole show, I tell you. He swept out half his Halls for the job. Think of that — on a Saturday! They — we went down in motor char-à-bancs — three of 'em — one pink, one primrose, and one forget-me-not blue — twenty people in each one and "The Earth *is* Flat" on each side and across the back. I went with Teddy Rickets and Lafone from the Trefoil, and both the Silhouette Sisters, and — wait a minute! — the Crossleigh Trio. You know the Every-Day Dramas Trio at the Jocunda — Ada Crossleigh, "Bunt" Crossleigh, and little Victorine? Them. And there was Hoke Ramsden, the lightning-change chap in *Morgiana and Drexel* — and there was Billy Turpeen. Yes, you know him! The North London Star. "I'm the Referee that got himself disliked at Blackheath." *That* chap! And there was Mackaye — that one-eyed Scotch fellow that all Glasgow is crazy about. Talk of subordinating yourself for Art's sake! Mackaye was the earnest inquirer who got converted at the end of the meeting. And there was quite a lot of girls I didn't know, and — oh, yes — there was 'Dal! 'Dal Benzaguen herself! We sat together, going and coming. She's all the darling there ever was. She sent you her love, and she told me to tell you that she won't forget about

Nellie Farren.[13] She says you've given her an ideal to work for. She? Oh, she was the Lady Secretary to the Geoplanarians, of course. I forget who were in the other brakes – provincial stars mostly – but they played up gorgeously. The art of the music-hall's changed since your day. They didn't overdo it a bit. You see, people who believe the earth is flat don't dress quite like other people. You may have noticed that I hinted at that in my account. It's a rather flat-fronted Ionic style – neo-Victorian, except for the bustles, 'Dal told me – but 'Dal looked heavenly in it! So did little Victorine. And there was a girl in the blue brake – she's a provincial – but she's coming to town this winter and she'll knock 'em – Winnie Deans. Remember that! She told Huckley how she had suffered for the Cause as a governess in a rich family where they believed that the world is round, and how she threw up her job sooner than teach immoral geography. That was at the overflow meeting outside the Baptist chapel. She knocked 'em to sawdust! We must look out for Winnie ... But Lafone! Lafone was beyond everything. Impact, personality – conviction – the whole bag o' tricks! He sweated conviction. Gad, he convinced *me* while he was speaking! (Him? He was President of the Geoplanarians, of course. Haven't you read my account?) It *is* an infernally plausible theory. After all, no one has actually proved the earth is round, have they?'

'Never mind the earth. What about Huckley?'

'Oh, Huckley got tight. That's the worst of these model villages if you let 'em smell fire-water. There's one alcoholic pub in the place that Sir Thomas can't get rid of. Bat made it his base. He sent down the banquet in two motor lorries – dinner for five hundred and drinks for ten thousand. Huckley voted all right. Don't you make any mistake about that. No vote, no dinner. A unanimous vote – exactly as I've said. At least, the Rector and the Doctor were the only dissentients. We didn't count them. Oh yes, Sir Thomas was there. He came and grinned at us through his park gates. He'll grin worse today. There's an aniline dye that you rub through a stencil-plate that eats about a foot into any stone and wears good to the last. Bat had both the lodge-gates stencilled "The Earth *is* flat!" and all the barns and walls they could get at ... Oh Lord, but Huckley

162

was drunk! We had to fill 'em up to make 'em forgive us for not being aeroplanes. Unthankful yokels! D'you realize that Emperors couldn't have commanded the talent Bat decanted on 'em? Why, 'Dal alone was . . . And by eight o'clock not even a bit of paper left! The whole show packed up and gone, and Huckley hoo-raying for the earth being flat.'

'Very good,' I began. 'I am, as you know, a one-third proprietor of *The Bun*.'

'I didn't forget that,' Ollyett interrupted. 'That was uppermost in my mind all the time. I've got a special account for *The Bun* today – it's an idyll – and just to show how I thought of you, I told 'Dal, coming home, about your Gubby Dance, and she told Winnie. Winnie came back in our char-à-banc. After a bit we had to get out and dance it in a field. It's quite a dance the way we did it – and Lafone invented a sort of gorilla lockstep procession at the end. Bat had sent down a film-chap on the chance of getting something. He was the son of a clergyman – a most dynamic personality. He said there isn't anything for the cinema in meetings *qua* meetings – they lack action. Films are a branch of art by themselves. But he went wild over the Gubby. He said it was like Peter's vision at Joppa.[14] He took about a million feet of it. Then I photoed it exclusive for *The Bun*. I've sent 'em in already, only remember we must eliminate Winnie's left leg in the first figure. It's too arresting . . . And there you are! But I tell you I'm afraid of Bat. That man's the Personal Devil. He did it all. He didn't even come down himself. He said he'd distract his people.'

'Why didn't he ask me to come?' I persisted.

'Because he said you'd distract me. He said he wanted my brains on ice. He got 'em. I believe it's the best thing I've ever done.' He reached for *The Cake* and re-read it luxuriously. 'Yes, out and away the best – supremely quotable,' he concluded, and – after another survey – 'By God, what a genius I was yesterday!'[15]

I would have been angry, but I had not the time. That morning, Press agencies grovelled to me in *The Bun* office for leave to use certain photos, which, they understood, I controlled, of a certain village dance. When I had sent the fifth man away on the edge of tears, my self-respect came back a little. Then there was *The Bun*'s poster to get out. Art being elimination, I fined it down to two words (one too many, as it proved) – 'The Gubby!' in red, at which our manager protested; but by five o'clock he told me that I was *the* Napoleon of Fleet Street. Ollyett's account in *The Bun* of the Geoplanarians' Exercises and Love Feast lacked the supreme shock of his version in *The Cake*, but it bruised more; while the photos of 'The Gubby' (which, with Winnie's left leg, was why I had set the doubtful press to work so early) were beyond praise and, next day, beyond price. But even then I did not understand.

A week later, I think it was, Bat Masquerier telephoned to me to come to the Trefoil.

'It's your turn now,' he said. 'I'm not asking Ollyett. Come to the stage-box.'

I went, and, as Bat's guest, was received as Royalty is not. We sat well back and looked out on the packed thousands. It was *Morgiana and Drexel*, that fluid and electric review which Bat – though he gave Lafone the credit – really created.

'Ye-es,' said Bat dreamily, after Morgiana had given 'the nasty jar' to the Forty Thieves in their forty oil 'combinations'. 'As you say, I've got 'em and I can hold 'em. What a man does doesn't matter much; and how he does it don't matter either. It's the *when* – the psychological moment. 'Press can't make up for it; money can't; brains can't. A lot's luck, but all the rest is genius. I'm not speaking about My people now. I'm talking of Myself.'

Then 'Dal – she was the only one who dared – knocked at the door and stood behind us all alive and panting as Morgiana. Lafone was carrying the police-court scene, and the house was ripped up crossways with laughter.

'Ah! Tell a fellow now,' she asked me for the twentieth time, 'did you love Nellie Farren when you were young?'

'Did we love her?' I answered. '"If the earth and the sky and the sea" – There were three million of us, 'Dal, and we worshipped her.'

'How did she get it across?' 'Dal went on.

'She was Nellie. The houses used to coo over her when she came on.'

'I've had a good deal, but I've never been cooed over yet,' said 'Dal wistfully.

'It isn't the how, it's the when,' Bat repeated. 'Ah!'

He leaned forward as the house began to rock and peal full-throatedly. 'Dal fled. A sinuous and silent procession was filing into the police-court to a scarcely audible accompaniment. It was dressed – but the world and all its picture-palaces know how it was dressed. It danced and it danced, and it danced the dance which bit all humanity in the leg for half a year, and it wound up with the lockstep finale that mowed the house down in swathes, sobbing and aching. Somebody in the gallery moaned, 'Oh Gord, the Gubby!' and we heard the word run like a shudder, for they had not a full breath left among them. Then 'Dal came on, an electric star in her dark hair, the diamonds flashing in her three-inch heels – a vision that made no sign for thirty counted seconds while the police-court scene dissolved behind her into Morgiana's Manicure Palace, and they recovered themselves. The star on her forehead went out, and a soft light bathed her as she took – slowly, slowly to the croon of adoring strings – the eighteen paces forward. We saw her first as a queen alone; next as a queen for the first time conscious of her subjects, and at the end, when her hands fluttered, as a woman delighted, awed not a little, but transfigured and illuminated with sheer, compelling affection and goodwill. I caught the broken mutter of welcome – the coo which is more than tornadoes of applause. It died and rose and died again lovingly.'

'She's got it across,' Bat whispered. 'I've never seen her like this. I told her to light up the star, but I was wrong, and she knew it. She's an artist.'

' 'Dal, you darling!' someone spoke, not loudly but it carried through the house.

'Thank *you*!' 'Dal answered, and in that broken tone one heard the last fetter riveted. 'Good evening, boys! I've just come from – now – where the dooce was it I have come from?' She turned to the impassive files of the Gubby dancers, and went on: 'Ah, so good of you to remind me, you dear, bun-faced things. I've just come from the village – The Village that Voted the Earth was Flat.'

She swept into that song with the full orchestra. It devastated the habitable earth for the next six months. Imagine, then, what its rage and pulse must have been at the incandescent hour of its birth! She only gave the chorus once. At the end of the second verse, 'Are you *with* me, boys?' she cried, and the house tore it clean away from her – '*Earth* was flat – *Earth* was flat. Flat as my hat – Flatter than that' – drowning all but the bassoons and double-basses that marked the word.

'Wonderful,' I said to Bat. 'And it's only "Nuts in May" with variations.'

'Yes – but *I* did the variations,' he replied.

At the last verse she gestured to Carlini the conductor, who threw her up his baton. She caught it with a boy's ease. 'Are you *with* me?' she cried once more, and – the maddened house behind her – abolished all the instruments except the guttural belch of the double-basses on '*Earth*' – 'The Village that voted the *Earth* was flat – *Earth* was flat!' It was delirium. Then she picked up the Gubby dancers and led them in a clattering improvised lockstep thrice round the stage till her last kick sent her diamond-hilted shoe catherine-wheeling to the electrolier.

I saw the forest of hands raised to catch it, heard the roaring and stamping pass through hurricanes to full typhoon; heard the song, pinned down by the faithful double-basses as the bull-dog pins down the bellowing bull, overbear even those; till at last the curtain fell and Bat took me round to her dressing-room, where she lay spent after her seventh call. Still the song, through all those white-washed walls, shook the reinforced concrete of the Trefoil as steam pile-drivers shake the flanks of a dock.

'I'm all out – first time in my life. Ah! Tell a fellow now, did I get it across?' she whispered huskily.

'You know you did,' I replied as she dipped her nose deep in a beaker of barley-water. 'They cooed over you.'

Bat nodded. 'And poor Nellie's dead – in Africa, ain't it?'

'I hope I'll die before they stop cooing,' said 'Dal.

'"*Earth* was flat – *Earth* was flat!"' Now it was more like mine-pumps in flood.

'They'll have the house down if you don't take another,' someone called.

'Bless 'em!' said 'Dal, and went out for her eighth, when in the face of that cataract she said yawning, 'I don't know how *you* feel, children, but *I'm* dead. You be quiet.'

'Hold a minute,' said Bat to me. 'I've got to hear how it went in the provinces. Winnie Deans had it in Manchester, and Ramsden at Glasgow – and there are all the films too. I had rather a heavy week-end.'

The telephones presently reassured him.

'It'll do,' said he. 'And *he* said my home address was Jerusalem.' He left me humming the refrain of 'The Holy City.'[16] Like Ollyett I found myself afraid of that man.

When I got out into the street and met the disgorging picture-palaces capering on the pavements and humming it (for he had put the gramophones on with the films), and when I saw far to the south the red electrics flash 'Gubby' across the Thames, I feared more than ever.

A few days passed which were like nothing except, perhaps, a suspense of fever in which the sick man perceives the search-lights of the world's assembled navies in act to converge on one minute fragment of wreckage – one only in all the black and agony-strewn sea. Then those beams focused themselves. Earth as we knew it – the full circuit of our orb – laid the weight of its impersonal and searing curiosity on this Huckley which had voted that it was flat. It asked for news about Huckley – where and what it might be, and how it talked – it knew how it danced – and how it thought in its wonderful soul. And then, in all the zealous, merciless press, Huckley was laid out for it to look at, as a drop of pond water is exposed on the sheet of a magic-lantern show. But Huckley's sheet was only coterminous with the use of type among mankind. For the precise moment that was necessary, Fate ruled it that there should be nothing of first importance in the world's idle eye. One atrocious murder, a political crisis, an incautious or heady continental statesman, the mere catarrh of a king, would have wiped out the significance of our message, as a passing cloud annuls the urgent helio. But it was halcyon weather in every respect. Ollyett and I did not need to lift our little fingers any more than the Alpine climber whose last sentence has unkeyed the arch of the avalanche. The thing roared and pulverized and swept beyond eyesight all by itself – all by itself. And once well away, the fall of kingdoms could not have diverted it.

Ours is, after all, a kindly earth. While The Song ran and raped it with the cataleptic kick of 'Ta-ra-ra-boom-de-ay,'[17] multiplied by the West African significance of 'Everybody's doing it,'[18] plus twice the infernal elementality of a certain tune in *Dona et Gamma*; when for all practical purposes, literary, dramatic, artistic, social, municipal, political, commercial, and administrative, the Earth *was* flat, the Rector of Huckley wrote to us – again as a lover of accuracy – to point out that the Huckley vote on 'the alleged flatness of this scene of our labours here below' was *not* unanimous; he and the doctor having voted against it. And the great Baron Reuter himself (I am sure it could have been none other) flashed that letter in full to the front, back, and both wings of this scene of our labours. For Huckley was News. *The Bun* also contributed a photograph which cost me some trouble to fake.

'We are a vital nation,' said Ollyett while we were discussing affairs at a Bat dinner. 'Only an Englishman could have written that letter at this present juncture.'

'It reminded me of a tourist in the Cave of the Winds under Niagara. Just one figure in a mackintosh. But perhaps you saw our photo?' I said proudly.

'Yes,' Bat replied. 'I've been to Niagara, too. And how's Huckley taking it?'

'They don't quite understand, of course,' said Ollyett. 'But it's bringing pots of money into the place. Ever since the motor-bus excursions were started –'

'I didn't know they had been,' said Pallant.

'Oh yes. Motor char-à-bancs – uniformed guides and key-bugles[19] included. They're getting a bit fed up with the tune there nowadays,' Ollyett added.

'They play it under his windows, don't they?' Bat asked. 'He can't stop the right of way across his park.'

'He cannot,' Ollyett answered. 'By the way, Woodhouse, I've bought that font for you from the sexton. I paid fifteen pounds for it.'

'What am I supposed to do with it?' asked Woodhouse.

'You give it to the Victoria and Albert Museum. It is fourteenth-century work all right. You can trust me.'

'Is it worth it — now?' said Pallant. 'Not that I'm weakening, but merely as a matter of tactics?'

'But this is true,' said Ollyett. 'Besides, it is my hobby, I always wanted to be an architect. I'll attend to it myself. It's too serious for *The Bun* and miles too good for *The Cake*.'

He broke ground in a ponderous architectural weekly, which had never heard of Huckley. There was no passion in his statement, but mere fact backed by a wide range of authorities. He established beyond doubt that the old font at Huckley had been thrown out, on Sir Thomas's instigation, twenty years ago, to make room for a new one of Bath stone adorned with Limoges enamels; and that it had lain ever since in a corner of the sexton's shed. He proved, with learned men to support him, that there was only one other font in all England to compare with it. So Woodhouse bought it and presented it to a grateful South Kensington[20] which said it would see the earth still flatter before it returned the treasure to purblind Huckley. Bishops by the benchful and most of the Royal Academy, not to mention 'Margaritas ante Porcos',[21] wrote fervently to the papers. *Punch* based a political cartoon on it; the *Times* a third leader, 'The Lust of Newness'; and the *Spectator* a scholarly and delightful middle, 'Village Hausmania.'[22] The vast amused outside world said in all its tongues and types: 'Of course! This is just what Huckley would do!' And neither Sir Thomas nor the Rector nor the sexton nor any one else wrote to deny it.

'You see,' said Ollyett, 'this is much more of a blow to Huckley than it looks — because every word of it's true. Your Gubby dance was inspiration, I admit, but it hadn't its roots in—'

'Two hemispheres and four continents so far,' I pointed out.

'Its roots in the hearts of Huckley was what I was going to say. Why don't you ever come down and look at the place? You've never seen it since we were stopped there.'

'I've only my week-ends free,' I said, 'and you seem to spend yours there pretty regularly — with the side-car. I was afraid—'

'Oh, *that's* all right,' he said cheerily. 'We're quite an old engaged couple now. As a matter of fact, it happened after "the gravid polled Angus" business. Come along this Saturday. Woodhouse says he'll run us down after lunch. He wants to see Huckley too.'

Pallant could not accompany us, but Bat took his place.

'It's odd,' said Bat, 'that none of us except Ollyett has ever set eyes on Huckley since that time. That's what I always tell My people. Local colour is all right after you've got your idea. Before that, it's a mere nuisance.' He regaled us on the way down with panoramic views of the success – geographical and financial – of 'The Gubby' and The Song.

'By the way,' said he, 'I've assigned 'Dal all the gramophone rights of "The Earth". She's a born artist. 'Hadn't sense enough to hit me for triple-dubs [23] the morning after. She'd have taken it out in coos.'

'Bless her! And what'll she make out of the gramophone rights?' I asked.

'Lord knows!' he replied. 'I've made fifty-four thousand my little end of the business, and it's only just beginning. Hear *that*!'

A shell-pink motor-brake roared up behind us to the music on a key-bugle of 'The Village that Voted the Earth was Flat'. In a few minutes we overtook another, in natural wood, whose occupants were singing it through their noses.

'I don't know that agency. It must be Cook's,' said Ollyett. 'They *do* suffer.' We were never out of ear-shot of the tune the rest of the way to Huckley.

Though I knew it would be so, I was disappointed with the actual aspect of the spot we had – it is not too much to say – created in the face of the nations. The alcoholic pub; the village green; the Baptist chapel; the church; the sexton's shed; the Rectory whence the so-wonderful letters had come; Sir Thomas's park gate-pillars still violently declaring 'The Earth *is* flat', were as mean, as average, as ordinary as the photograph of a room where a murder has been committed. Ollyett, who, of course, knew the place specially well, made the most of it to us. Bat, who had employed it as a back-cloth to one of his own dramas, dismissed it as a thing used and emptied, but Woodhouse expressed my feelings when he said: 'Is that all – after all we've done?'

'*I* know,' said Ollyett soothingly. '"Like that strange song I heard Apollo sing: When Ilion like a mist rose into towers."[24] I've felt the same sometimes, though it has been Paradise for me. But they *do* suffer.'

The fourth brake in thirty minutes had just turned into Sir Thomas's park to tell the Hall that 'The *Earth* was flat'; a knot of obviously American tourists were kodaking his lodge gates; while the tea-shop opposite the lych-gate was full of people buying postcards of the old font as it had lain twenty years in the sexton's shed. We went to the alcoholic pub and congratulated the proprietor.

'It's bringin' money to the place,' said he. 'But in a sense you can buy money too dear. It isn't doin' us any good. People are laughin' at us. That's what they're doin' . . . Now, with regard to that Vote of ours you may have heard talk about . . .'

'For Gorze sake, chuck that votin' business,' cried an elderly man at the door. 'Money-gettin' or no money-gettin', we're fed up with it.'

'Well, I do think,' said the publican, shifting his ground, 'I do think Sir Thomas might ha' managed better in some things.'

'He tole me,' – the elderly man shouldered his way to the bar – 'he tole me twenty years ago to take an' lay that font in my tool-shed. He *tole* me so himself. An' now, after twenty years, me own wife makin' me out little better than the common 'angman!'

'That's the sexton,' the publican explained. 'His good lady sells the postcards – if you 'aven't got some. But we feel Sir Thomas might ha' done better.'

'What's he got to do with it?' said Woodhouse.

'There's nothin' we can trace 'ome to 'im in so many words, but we think he might 'ave saved us the font business. Now, in regard to that votin' business –'

'Chuck it! Oh, chuck it!' the sexton roared, 'or you'll 'ave me cuttin' my throat at cock-crow. 'Ere's another parcel of fun-makers!'

A motor-brake had pulled up at the door and a multitude of men and women immediately descended. We went out to look. They bore rolled banners, a reading-desk in three pieces, and, I specially noticed, a collapsible harmonium, such as is used on ships at sea.

'Salvation Army?' I said, though I saw no uniforms.

Two of them unfurled a banner between poles which bore the legend: 'The Earth *is* flat'. Woodhouse and I turned to Bat. He shook his head. 'No, no! Not me . . . If I had only seen their costumes in advance!'

'Good Lord!' said Ollyett. 'It's the genuine Society!'

The company advanced on the green with the precision of people well broke to these movements. Scene-shifters could not have been quicker with the three-piece rostrum, nor stewards with the harmonium. Almost before its cross-legs had been kicked into their catches, certainly before the tourists by the lodge-gates had begun to move over, a woman sat down to it and struck up a hymn:

> Hear ther truth our tongues are telling,
>   Spread ther light from shore to shore,
> God hath given man a dwelling
>   Flat and flat for evermore.

> When ther Primal Dark retreated,
>   When ther deeps were undesigned,
> He with rule and level meted
>   Habitation for mankind!

I saw sick envy on Bat's face. 'Curse Nature,' he muttered. 'She gets ahead of you every time. To think *I* forgot hymns and a harmonium!'

Then came the chorus:

> Hear ther truth our tongues are telling,
>   Spread ther light from shore to shore –
> Oh, be faithful! Oh, be truthful!
>   Earth is flat for evermore.

They sang several verses with the fervour of Christians awaiting their lions. Then there were growlings in the air. The sexton, embraced by the landlord, two-stepped out of the pub-door. Each was trying to outroar the other. 'Apologizing in advarnce for what he says,' the landlord shouted: 'You'd better go away' (here the sexton began to speak words). 'This isn't the time nor yet the place for – for any more o' this chat.'

The crowd thickened. I saw the village police-sergeant come out of his cottage buckling his belt.

'But surely,' said the woman at the harmonium, 'there must be some mistake. We are not suffragettes.'

'Damn it! They'd be a change,' cried the sexton. 'You get out of this! Don't talk! *I* can't stand it for one! Get right out, or we'll font you!'

The crowd which was being recruited from every house in sight echoed the invitation. The sergeant pushed forward. A man beside the reading-desk said: 'But surely we are among dear friends and sympathizers. Listen to me for a moment.'

It was the moment that a passing char-à-banc chose to strike into The Song. The effect was instantaneous. Bat, Ollyett, and I, who by divers roads have learned the psychology of crowds, retreated towards the tavern door. Woodhouse, the newspaper proprietor, anxious, I presume, to keep touch with the public, dived into the thick of it. Every one else told the Society to go away at once. When the lady at the harmonium (I began to understand why it is sometimes necessary to kill women) pointed at the stencilled park pillars and called them 'the cromlechs of our common faith', there was a snarl and a rush. The police-sergeant checked it, but advised the Society to keep on going. The Society withdrew into the brake fighting, as it were, a rearguard action of oratory up each step. The collapsed harmonium was hauled in last, and with the perfect unreason of crowds, they cheered it loudly, till the chauffeur slipped in his clutch and sped away. Then the crowd broke up, congratulating all concerned except the sexton, who was held to have disgraced his office by having sworn at ladies. We strolled across the green towards Woodhouse, who was talking to the police-sergeant near the park-gates. We were not twenty yards from him when we saw Sir Thomas Ingell emerge from the lodge and rush furiously at Woodhouse with an uplifted stick, at the same time shrieking: 'I'll teach you to laugh, you –' but Ollyett has the record of the language. By the time we reached them, Sir Thomas was on the ground; Woodhouse, very white, held the walking-stick and was saying to the sergeant:

'I give this person in charge for assault.'

'But, good Lord!' said the sergeant, whiter than Woodhouse. 'It's Sir Thomas.'

'Whoever it is, it isn't fit to be at large,' said Woodhouse. The crowd suspecting something wrong began to reassemble, and all the English horror of a row in public moved us, headed by the sergeant, inside the lodge. We shut both park-gates and lodge-door.

'You saw the assault, sergeant,' Woodhouse went on. 'You can testify I used no more force than was necessary to protect myself. You can testify that I have not even damaged this person's property. (Here! take your stick, you!) You heard the filthy language he used.'

'I – I can't say I did,' the sergeant stammered.

'Oh, but *we* did!' said Ollyett, and repeated it, to the apron-veiled horror of the lodge-keeper's wife.

Sir Thomas on a hard kitchen chair began to talk. He said he had 'stood enough of being photographed like a wild beast', and expressed loud regret that he had not killed 'that man', who was 'conspiring with the sergeant to laugh at him'.

'*'*Ad you ever seen 'im before, Sir Thomas?' the sergeant asked.

'No! But it's time an example was made here. I've never seen the sweep in my life.'

I think it was Bat Masquerier's magnetic eye that recalled the past to him, for his face changed and his jaw dropped. 'But I have!' he groaned. 'I remember now.'

Here a writhing man entered by the back door. He was, he said, the village solicitor. I do not assert that he licked Woodhouse's boots, but we should have respected him more if he had and been done with it. His notion was that the matter could be accommodated, arranged and compromised for gold, and yet more gold. The sergeant thought so too. Woodhouse undeceived them both. To the sergeant he said, 'Will you or will you not enter the charge!' To the village solicitor he gave the name of his lawyers, at which the man wrung his hands and cried, 'Oh, Sir T., Sir T.!' in a miserable falsetto, for it was a Bat Masquerier of a firm. They conferred together in tragic whispers.

'I don't dive after Dickens,' said Ollyett to Bat and me by the window, 'but every time *I* get into a row I notice the police-court always fills up with his characters.'

'I've noticed that too,' said Bat. 'But the odd thing is you mustn't give the public straight Dickens – not in My business. I wonder why that is.'

Then Sir Thomas got his second wind and cursed the day that he, or it may have been we, were born. I feared that though he was a Radical he might apologize and, since he was an M.P., might lie his way out of the difficulty. But he was utterly and truthfully beside himself. He asked foolish questions – such as what we were doing in the village at all, and how much blackmail Woodhouse expected to make out of him. But neither Woodhouse nor the sergeant nor the writhing solicitor listened. The upshot of their talk, in the chimney-corner, was that Sir Thomas stood engaged to appear next Monday before his brother magistrates on charges of assault, disorderly conduct, and language calculated, etc. Ollyett was specially careful about the language.

Then we left. The village looked very pretty in the late light – pretty and tuneful as a nest of nightingales.

'You'll turn up on Monday, I hope,' said Woodhouse, when we reached town. That was his only allusion to the affair.

So we turned up – through a world still singing that the Earth was flat – at the little clay-coloured market-town with the large Corn Exchange and the small Jubilee memorial. We had some difficulty in getting seats in the court. Woodhouse's imported London lawyer was a man of commanding personality, with a voice trained to convey blasting imputations by tone. When the case was called, he rose and stated his client's intention not to proceed with the charge. His client, he went on to say, had not entertained, and, of course, in the circumstances could not have entertained, any suggestion of accepting on behalf of public charities any moneys that might have been offered to him on the part of Sir Thomas's estate. At the same time, no one acknowledged more sincerely than his client the spirit in which those offers had been made by those entitled to make them. But, as a matter of fact – here he became the man of the world colloguing with his equals – certain – er – details had come to his client's knowledge *since* the lamentable outburst, which . . . He shrugged his shoulders. Nothing was served by going into them, but he ventured to say that, had those painful circumstances only been known earlier, his client would – again 'of course' – never have dreamed – A gesture concluded the sentence, and the ensnared Bench looked at Sir Thomas with new and withdrawing eyes. Frankly, as they could see, it would be nothing less than cruelty to proceed further with this – er – unfortunate affair. He asked leave, therefore, to withdraw the charge *in toto*, and at the same time to express his client's deepest sympathy with all who had been in any way distressed, as his client had been, by the fact and the publicity of proceedings which he could, of course, again assure them that his client would never have dreamed of instituting if, as he hoped he had made plain, certain facts had been before his client at the time when ... But he had said enough. For his fee it seemed to me that he had.

Heaven inspired Sir Thomas's lawyer – all of a sweat lest his client's language should come out – to rise up and thank him. Then, Sir Thomas – not yet aware what leprosy had been laid upon him, but grateful to escape on any terms – followed suit. He was heard in interested silence, and people drew back a pace as Gehazi [25] passed forth.

'You hit hard,' said Bat to Woodhouse afterwards. 'His own people think he's mad.'

'You don't say so? I'll show you some of his letters tonight at dinner,' he replied.

He brought them to the Red Amber Room of the Chop Suey. We forgot to be amazed, as till then we had been amazed, over the Song or 'The Gubby', or the full tide of Fate that seemed to run only for our sakes. It did not even interest Ollyett that the verb 'to huckle' had passed into the English leader-writers' language. We were studying the interior of a soul, flash-lighted to its grimiest corners by the dread of 'losing its position'.

'And then it thanked you, didn't it, for dropping the case?' said Pallant.

'Yes, and it sent me a telegram to confirm.' Woodhouse turned to Bat. 'Now d'you think I hit too hard?' he asked.

'No–o!' said Bat. 'After all – I'm talking of every one's business now – one can't ever do anything in Art that comes up to Nature in any game in life. Just think how this thing has –'

'Just let me run through that little case of yours again,' said Pallant, and picked up *The Bun* which had it set out in full.

'Any chance of 'Dal looking in on us tonight?' Ollyett began.

'She's occupied with her Art too,' Bat answered bitterly. 'What's the use of Art! Tell me, some one!' A barrel-organ outside promptly pointed out that the *Earth* was flat. 'The gramophone's killing street organs, but I let loose a hundred-and-seventy-four of those hurdygurdys twelve hours after The Song,' said Bat. 'Not counting the Provinces.' His face brightened a little.

'Look here!' said Pallant over the paper. 'I don't suppose you or those asinine J.P.'s knew it – but your lawyer ought to have known that you've all put your foot in it most confoundedly over this assault case.'

'What's the matter?' said Woodhouse.

'It's ludicrous. It's insane. There isn't two penn'orth of legality in the whole thing. Of course, you could have withdrawn the charge, but the way you went about it is childish – besides being illegal. What on earth was the Chief Constable thinking of?'

'Oh, he was a friend of Sir Thomas's. They all were for that matter,' I replied.

'He ought to be hanged. So ought the Chairman of the Bench. I'm talking as a lawyer now.'

'Why, what have we been guilty of? Misprision of treason or compounding a felony – or what?' said Ollyett.

'I'll tell you later.' Pallant went back to the paper with knitted brows, smiling unpleasantly from time to time. At last he laughed.

'Thank you!' he said to Woodhouse. 'It ought to be pretty useful – for us.'

'What d'you mean?' said Ollyett.

'For our side. They are all Rads who are mixed up in this – from the Chief Constable down. There must be a Question. There must be a Question.'

'Yes, but I wanted the charge withdrawn in my own way,' Woodhouse insisted.

'That's nothing to do with the case. It's the legality of your silly methods. You wouldn't understand if I talked till morning.'

He began to pace the room, his hands behind him. 'I wonder if I can get it through our Whip's thick head that it's a chance . . . That comes of stuffing the Bench with radical tinkers,' he muttered.

'Oh, sit down!' said Woodhouse.

'Where's your lawyer to be found now?' he jerked out.

'At the Trefoil,' said Bat promptly. 'I gave him the stage-box for tonight. He's an artist too.'

'Then I'm going to see him,' said Pallant. 'Properly handled this ought to be a godsend for our side.' He withdrew without apology.

'Certainly, this thing keeps on opening up, and up,' I remarked inanely.

'It's beyond me!' said Bat. 'I don't think if I'd known I'd have ever . . . Yes, I would, though. He said my home address was –'

'It was his tone – his tone!' Ollyett almost shouted. Woodhouse said nothing, but his face whitened as he brooded.

'Well, any way,' Bat went on, 'I'm glad I always believed in God and Providence and all those things. Else I should lose my nerve. We've put it over the whole world – the full extent of the geographical globe. We couldn't stop it if we wanted to now. It's got to burn itself out. I'm not in charge any more. What d'you expect'll happen next. Angels?'

I expected nothing. Nothing that I expected approached what I got. Politics are not my concern, but, for the moment, since it seemed that they were going to 'huckle' with the rest, I took an interest in them. They impressed me as a dog's life without a dog's decencies, and I was confirmed in this when an unshaven and unwashen Pallant called on me at ten o'clock one morning, begging for a bath and a couch.

'Bail too?' I asked. He was in evening dress and his eyes were sunk feet in his head.

'No,' he said hoarsely. 'All night sitting. Fifteen divisions. 'Nother tonight. Your place was nearer than mine, so –' He began to undress in the hall.

When he awoke at one o'clock he gave me lurid accounts of what he said was history, but which was obviously collective hysteria. There had been a political crisis. He and his fellow

M.P.s had 'done things' – I never quite got at the things – for eighteen hours on end, and the pitiless Whips were even then at the telephones to herd 'em up to another dog-fight. So he snorted and grew hot all over again while he might have been resting.

'I'm going to pitch in my question about that miscarriage of justice at Huckley this afternoon, if you care to listen to it,' he said. 'It'll be absolutely thrown away – in our present state. I told 'em so; but it's my only chance for weeks. P'raps Woodhouse would like to come.'

'I'm sure he would. Anything to do with Huckley interests us,' I said.

'It'll miss fire, I'm afraid. Both sides are absolutely cooked. The present situation has been working up for some time. You see the row was bound to come, etc. etc.,' and he flew off the handle once more.

I telephoned to Woodhouse; and we went to the House together. It was a dull, sticky afternoon with thunder in the air. For some reason or other, each side was determined to prove its virtue and endurance to the utmost. I heard men snarling about it all round me. 'If they won't spare us, we'll show 'em no mercy.' 'Break the brutes up from the start. They can't stand late hours.' 'Come on! No shirking! I know *you*'ve had a Turkish bath,' were some of the sentences I caught on our way. The House was packed already, and one could feel the negative electricity of a jaded crowd wrenching at one's own nerves, and depressing the afternoon soul.

'This is bad!' Woodhouse whispered. 'There'll be a row before they've finished. Look at the Front Benches!' And he pointed out little personal signs by which I was to know that each man was on edge. He might have spared himself. The House was ready to snap before a bone had been thrown. A sullen minister rose to reply to a staccato question. His supporters cheered defiantly. 'None o' that! None o' that!' came from the Back Benches. I saw the Speaker's face stiffen like the face of a helmsman as he humours a hard-mouthed yacht after a sudden following sea. The trouble was barely met in time. There came a fresh, apparently causeless gust a few minutes later – savage, threatening, but futile. It died out – one could hear the sigh – in sudden wrathful realization of the dreary hours ahead, and the ship of state drifted on.

Then Pallant – and the raw House winced at the torture of his voice – rose. It was a twenty-line question, studded with legal technicalities. The gist of it was that he wished to know whether the appropriate Minister was aware that there had been a grave miscarriage of justice on such and such a date, at such and such a place, before such and such justices of the peace, in regard to a case which arose –

I heard one desperate, weary 'damn!' float up from the pit of that torment. Pallant sawed on – 'out of certain events which occurred at the village of Huckley.'

The House came to attention with a parting of the lips like a hiccough, and it flashed through my mind . . . Pallant repeated, 'Huckley. The village –'

'That voted the *Earth* was flat.' A single voice from a back Bench sang it once like a lone frog in a far pool.

'*Earth* was flat,' croaked another voice opposite.

'*Earth* was flat.' There were several. Then several more.

It was, you understand, the collective, over-strained nerve of the House, snapping, strand by strand to various notes, as the hawser parts from its moorings.

'The Village that voted the *Earth* was flat.' The tune was beginning to shape itself. More voices were raised and feet began to beat time. Even so it did not occur to me that the thing would –

'The Village that voted the *Earth* was flat!' It was easier now to see who were not singing. There were still a few. Of a sudden (and this proves the fundamental instability of the cross-bench mind) a cross-bencher leaped on his seat and there played an imaginary double-bass with tremendous maestro-like wagglings of the elbow.

The last strand parted. The ship of state drifted out helpless on the rocking tide of melody.

'The Village that voted the *Earth* was flat!
The Village that voted the *Earth* was flat!'

The Irish first conceived the idea of using their order-papers as funnels wherewith to reach the correct '*vroom – vroom*' on

'*Earth*.' Labour, always conservative and respectable at a crisis, stood out longer than any other section, but when it came in it was howling syndicalism. Then, without distinction of Party, fear of constituents, desire for office, or hope of emolument, the House sang at the tops and at the bottoms of their voices, swaying their stale bodies and epileptically beating with their swelled feet. They sang 'The Village that voted the *Earth* was flat': first, because they wanted to, and secondly – which is the terror of that song – because they could not stop. For no consideration could they stop.

Pallant was still standing up. Someone pointed at him and they laughed. Others began to point, lunging, as it were, in time with the tune. At this moment two persons came in practically abreast from behind the Speaker's chair, and halted appalled. One happened to be the Prime Minister and the other a messenger. The House, with tears running down their cheeks, transferred their attention to the paralysed couple. They pointed six hundred forefingers at them. They rocked, they waved, and they rolled while they pointed, but still they sang. When they weakened for an instant, Ireland would yell: 'Are ye *with* me, bhoys?' and they all renewed their strength like Antaeus.[26] No man could say afterwards what happened in the Press or the Strangers' Gallery. It was the House, the hysterical and abandoned House of Commons that held all eyes, as it deafened all ears. I saw both Front Benches bend forward, some with their foreheads on their dispatch-boxes, the rest with their faces in their hands; and their moving shoulders jolted the House out of its last rag of decency. Only the Speaker remained unmoved. The entire press of Great Britain bore witness next day that he had not even bowed his head. The Angel of the Constitution, for vain was the help of man,[27] foretold him the exact moment at which the House would have broken into 'The Gubby'. He is reported to have said: 'I heard the Irish beginning to shuffle it. So I adjourned.' Pallant's version is that he added: 'And I was never so grateful to a private member in all my life as I was to Mr Pallant.'

He made no explanation. He did not refer to orders or disorders. He simply adjourned the House till six that evening. And the House adjourned – some of it nearly on all fours.

I was not correct when I said that the Speaker was the only man who did not laugh. Woodhouse was beside me all the time. His face was set and quite white — as white, they told me, as Sir Thomas Ingell's when he went, by request, to a private interview with his Chief Whip.

The Press

The Soldier may forget his sword,
    The Sailorman the sea,
The Mason may forget the Word
    And the Priest his litany:
The maid may forget both jewel and gem,
    And the bride her wedding-dress —
But the Jew shall forget Jerusalem
    Ere we forget the Press!

Who once hath stood through the loaded hour
    Ere, roaring like the gale,
The Harrild and the Hoe devour
    Their league-long paper bale,
And has lit his pipe in the morning calm
    That follows the midnight stress —
He hath sold his heart to the old Black Art
    We call the daily Press.

Who once hath dealt in the widest game
    That all of a man can play,
No later love, no larger frame
    Will lure him long away.
As the war-horse smelleth the battle afar,
    The entered Soul, no less,
He saith: 'Ha! Ha!' where the trumpets are
    And the thunders of the Press.

Canst thou number the days that we fulfil,
    Or the *Times* that we bring forth?
Canst thou send the lightnings to do thy will,
    And cause them reign on earth?
Hast thou given a peacock goodly wings
    To please his foolishness?
Sit down at the heart of men and things,
    Companion of the Press!

The Pope may launch his Interdict,
    The Union its decree,
But the bubble is blown and the bubble is pricked

The Press

By Us and such as We.
Remember the battle and stand aside
  While Thrones and Powers confess
That King over all the children of pride
  Is the Press – the Press – the Press!

IN THE PRESENCE

In the Presence

(1912)

'So the matter,' the Regimental Chaplain concluded, 'was correct; in every way correct. I am well pleased with Rutton Singh and Attar Singh. They have gathered the fruit of their lives.'

He folded his arms and sat down on the verandah. The hot day had ended, and there was a pleasant smell of cooking along the regimental lines, where half-clad men went back and forth with leaf platters and water-goblets. The Subadar-Major, in extreme undress, sat on a chair, as befitted his rank; the Havildar-Major, his nephew, leaning respectfully against the wall. The Regiment was at home and at ease in its own quarters in its own district [1] which takes its name from the great Muhammadan saint Mian Mir, revered by Jehangir and beloved by Guru Har Gobind, sixth of the great Sikh Gurus.

'Quite correct,' the Regimental Chaplain repeated.

No Sikh contradicts his Regimental Chaplain who expounds to him the Holy Book of the Grunth Sahib and who knows the lives and legends of all the Gurus.

The Subadar-Major bowed his grey head. The Havildar-Major coughed respectfully to attract attention and to ask leave to speak. Though he was the Subadar-Major's nephew, and though his father held twice as much land as his uncle, he knew his place in the scheme of things. The Subadar-Major shifted one hand with an iron bracelet on the wrist.

'Was there by any chance any woman at the back of it?' the Havildar-Major murmured. 'I was not here when the thing happened.'

'Yes! Yes! Yes! We all know that thou wast in England eating and drinking with the Sahibs. We are all surprised that thou canst still speak Punjabi.' The Subadar-Major's carefully-tended beard bristled.

'There was no woman,' the Regimental Chaplain growled. 'It was land. Hear, you! Rutton Singh and Attar Singh were the elder of four brothers. These four held land in – what was the village's name? – oh, Pishapur, near Thori, in the Banalu Tehsil of Patiala State, where men can still recognize right behaviour when they see it. The two younger brothers tilled the land, while Rutton Singh and Attar Singh took service with the Regiment, according to the custom of the family.'

'True, true,' said the Havildar-Major. 'There is the same arrangement in all good families.'

'Then, listen again,' the Regimental Chaplain went on. 'Their kin on their mother's side put great oppression and injustice upon the two younger brothers who stayed with the land in Patiala State. Their mother's kin loosened beasts into the four brothers' crops when the crops were green; they cut the corn by force when it was ripe; they broke down the water-courses; they defiled the wells; and they brought false charges in the law-courts against all four brothers. They did not spare even the cotton-seed, as the saying is.

'Their mother's kin trusted that the young men would thus be forced by weight of trouble, and further trouble and perpetual trouble, to quit their lands in Pishapur village in Banalu Tehsil in Patiala State. If the young men ran away, the land would come whole to their mother's kin. I am not a regimental schoolmaster, but is it understood, child?'

'Understood,' said the Havildar-Major grimly. 'Pishapur is not the only place where the fence eats the field instead of protecting it. But perhaps there was a woman among their mother's kin?'

'God knows!' said the Regimental Chaplain. 'Woman, or man, or law-courts, the young men would *not* be driven off the land which was their own by inheritance. They made appeal to Rutton Singh and Attar Singh, their brethren who had taken service with *us* in the Regiment, and so knew the world, to help them in their long war against their mother's kin in Pishapur. For that reason, because their own land and the honour of their house was dear to them, Rutton Singh and Attar Singh needs must very often ask for leave to go to Patiala and attend to the lawsuits and cattle-poundings there.

'It was not, look you, as though they went back to their own village and sat, garlanded with jasmine, in honour, upon chairs before the elders under the trees. They went back always to perpetual trouble, either of lawsuits, or theft, or strayed cattle; and they sat on thorns.'

'I knew it,' said the Subadar-Major. 'Life was bitter for them both. But they were well-conducted men. It was not hard to get them their leave from the Colonel Sahib.'

'They spoke to me also,' said the Chaplain. '"*Let him who desires the four great gifts apply himself to the words of holy men.*" That is written. Often they showed me the papers of the false lawsuits brought against them. Often they wept on account of the persecution put upon them by their mother's kin. Men thought it was drugs when their eyes showed red.'

'They wept in my presence too,' said the Subadar-Major. 'Well-conducted men of nine years' service apiece. Rutton Singh was drill-Naik,[2] too.'

'They did all things correctly as Sikhs should,' said the Regimental Chaplain. 'When the persecution had endured seven years, Attar Singh took leave to Pishapur once again (that was the fourth time in that year only) and he called his persecutors together before the village elders, and he cast his turban at their feet and besought them by his mother's blood to cease from their persecutions. For he told them earnestly that he had marched to the boundaries of his patience, and that there could be but one end to the matter.

'They gave him abuse. They mocked him and his tears, which was the same as though they had mocked the Regiment. Then Attar Singh returned to the Regiment, and laid this last trouble before Rutton Singh, the eldest brother. But Rutton Singh could not get leave all at once.'

'Because he was drill-Naik and the recruits were to be drilled. I myself told him so,' said the Subadar-Major. 'He was a well-conducted man. He said he could wait.'

'But when permission was granted, those two took four days' leave,' the Chaplain went on.

'I do not think Attar Singh should have taken Baynes Sahib's revolver. He was Baynes Sahib's orderly, and all that Sahib's things were open to him. It was, therefore, as I count it, shame to Attar Singh,' said the Subadar-Major.

'All the words had been said. There was need of arms, and how could soldiers use Government rifles upon mere cultivators in the fields?' the Regimental Chaplain replied. 'Moreover, the revolver was sent back, together with a money-order for the cartridges expended. "*Borrow not; but if thou borrowest, pay back soon!*" That is written in the Hymns. Rutton Singh took a sword, and he and Attar Singh went to Pishapur and, after word given, the four brethren fell upon their persecutors in Pishapur village and slew seventeen, wounding ten. A revolver is better than a lawsuit. I say that these four brethren, the two with *us*, and the two mere cultivators, slew and wounded twenty-seven – all their mother's kin, male and female.

'Then the four mounted to their housetop, and Attar Singh, who was always one of the impetuous, said "My work is done," and he made *shinan* (purification) in all men's sight, and he lent Rutton Singh Baynes Sahib's revolver, and Rutton Singh shot him in the head.

'So Attar Singh abandoned his body, as an insect abandons a blade of grass. But Rutton Singh, having more work to do, went down from the housetop and sought an enemy whom he had forgotten – a Patiala man of this regiment who had sided with the persecutors. When he overtook the man, Rutton Singh hit him twice with bullets and once with the sword.'

'But the man escaped and is now in the hospital here,' said the Subadar-Major. 'The doctor says he will live in spite of all.'

'Not Rutton Singh's fault. Rutton Singh left him for dead. Then Rutton Singh returned to the housetop, and the three brothers together, Attar Singh being dead, sent word by a lad to the police station for an army to be dispatched against them that they might die with honours. But none came. And yet Patiala State is not under English law and they should know virtue there when they see it!

'So, on the third day, Rutton Singh also made *shinan*, and the youngest of the brethren shot him also in the head, and *he* abandoned his body.

'Thus was all correct. There was neither heat, nor haste, nor abuse in the matter from end to end. There remained alive not one man or woman of their mother's kin which had oppressed them. Of the other villagers of Pishapur, who had taken no part in the persecutions, not one was slain. Indeed, the villagers sent them food on the housetop for those three days while they waited for the police who would not dispatch that army.

'Listen again! I know that Attar Singh and Rutton Singh omitted no ceremony of the purifications, and when all was done Baynes Sahib's revolver was thrown down from the housetop, together with three rupees twelve annas; and order was given for its return by post.'

'And what befell the two younger brethren who were not in the service?' the Havildar-Major asked.

'Doubtless they too are dead, but since they were not in the Regiment their honour concerns themselves only. So far as *we* were touched, see how correctly we came out of the matter! I think the King should be told; for where could you match such a tale except among us Sikhs? *Sri wah guru ji ki Khalsa! Sri wah guru ji ki futteh!*'[3] said the Regimental Chaplain.

'Would three rupees twelve annas pay for the used cartridges?' said the Havildar-Major.

'Attar Singh knew the just price. All Baynes Sahib's gear was in his charge. They expended one tin box of fifty cartouches,[4] lacking two which were returned. As I said – as I say – the arrangement was made not with heat nor blasphemies as a Mussulman would have made it; not with cries nor caperings as an idolater would have made it; but comfortably to the ritual and doctrine of the Sikhs. Hear you! "*Though hundreds of amusements are offered to a child it cannot live without milk. If a man be divorced from his soul and his soul's desire he certainly will not stop to play upon the road, but he will make haste with his pilgrimage.*" That is written. I rejoice in my disciples.'

'True! True! Correct! Correct!' said the Subadar-Major. There was a long, easy silence. One heard a water-wheel creaking somewhere and the nearer sound of meal being ground in a quern.

'But he –' the Chaplain pointed a scornful chin at the Havildar-Major – '*he* has been so long in England that –'

'Let the lad alone,' said his uncle. 'He was but two months there, and he was chosen for good cause.'

Theoretically, all Sikhs are equal. Practically, there are differences, as none know better than well-born, land-owning folk, or long-descended chaplains from Amritsar.

'Hast thou heard anything in England to match my tale?' the Chaplain sneered.

'I saw more than I could understand, so I have locked up my stories in my own mouth,' the Havildar-Major replied meekly.

'Stories? What stories? I know all the stories about England,' said the Chaplain. 'I know that *terains* run underneath their bazaars there, and as for their streets stinking with *mota-kahars*, only this morning I was nearly killed by Duggan Sahib's *mota-kahar*. That young man is a devil.'

'I expect Grunthi-jee,' said the Subadar-Major, 'you and I grow too old to care for the Kahar-ki-nautch – the Bearer's dance.' He named one of the sauciest of the old-time nautches,[5] and smiled at his own pun. Then he turned to his nephew. 'When I was a lad and came back to my village on leave, I waited the convenient hour, and, the elders giving permission, I spoke of what I had seen elsewhere.'

'Ay, my father,' said the Havildar-Major, softly and affectionately. He sat himself down with respect, as behoved a mere lad of thirty with a bare half-dozen campaigns to his credit.

'There were four men in this affair also,' he began, 'and it was an affair that touched the honour, not of one regiment, nor two, but of all the Army in Hind. Some part of it I saw; some I heard; but *all* the tale is true. My father's brother knows, and my priest knows, that I was in England on business with my Colonel, when the King[6] – the Great Queen's son – completed his life.

'First, there was a rumour that sickness was upon him. Next, we knew that he lay sick in the Palace. A very great multitude stood outside the Palace by night and by day, in the rain as well as the sun, waiting for news.

'Then came out one with a written paper, and set it upon a gate-side – the word of the King's death – and they read, and groaned. This I saw with my own eyes, because the office where my Colonel Sahib went daily to talk with Colonel Forsyth Sahib was at the east end of the very gardens where the Palace stood. They are larger gardens than Shalimar here' – he pointed with his chin up the lines – 'or Shahdera across the river.

'Next day there was a darkness in the streets, because all the city's multitude were clad in black garments, and they spoke as a man speaks in the presence of his dead – all those multitudes. In the eyes, in the air, and in the heart, there was blackness. I saw it. But that is not my tale.

'After ceremonies had been accomplished, and word had gone out to the Kings of the Earth that they should come and mourn, the new King – the dead King's son – gave commandment that his father's body should be laid, coffined, in a certain Temple [7] which is near the river. There are no idols in that Temple; neither any carvings, nor paintings, nor gildings. It is all grey stone, of one colour as though it were cut out of the live rock. It is larger than – yes, than the Durbar Sahib [8] at Amritsar, even though the Akal Bunga and the Baba-Atal were added. How old it may be God knows. It is the Sahibs' most sacred Temple.

'In that place, by the new King's commandment, they made, as it were, a shrine for a saint, with lighted candles at the head and the feet of the Dead, and duly appointed watchers for every hour of the day and the night, until the dead King should be taken to the place of his fathers, which is at Wanidza. [9]

'When all was in order, the new King said, "Give entrance to all people," and the doors were opened, and O my uncle! O my teacher! all the world entered, walking through that Temple to take farewell of the Dead. There was neither distinction, nor price, nor ranking in the host, except an order that they should walk by fours.

'As they gathered in the streets without – very, very far off – so they entered the Temple, walking by fours: the child, the old man; mother, virgin, harlot, trader, priest; of all colours and faiths and customs under the firmament of God, from dawn till late at night. I saw it. My Colonel gave me leave to go. I stood in the line, many hours, one *koss*, [10] two *koss*, distant from the temple.'

'Then why did the multitude not sit down under the trees?' asked the priest.

'Because we were still between houses. The city is many *koss* wide,' the Havildar-Major resumed. 'I submitted myself to that slow-moving river and thus – thus – a pace at a time – I made pilgrimage. There were in my rank a woman, a cripple, and a lascar from the ships.

'When we entered the Temple, the coffin itself was as a shoal in the Ravi River, splitting the stream into two branches, one on either side of the Dead; and the watchers of the Dead, who were soldiers, stood about It, moving no more than the still flame of the candles. Their heads were bowed; their hands were clasped; their eyes were cast upon the ground – thus. They were not men, but images, and the multitude went past them in fours by day, and, except for a little while, by night also.

'No, there was no order that the people should come to pay respect. It was a free-will pilgrimage. Eight kings had been commanded to come – who obeyed – but upon his own Sahibs the new King laid no commandment. Of themselves they came.

'I made pilgrimage twice: once for my Salt's sake,[11] and once again for wonder and terror and worship. But my mouth cannot declare one thing of a hundred thousand things in this matter. There were *lakhs* of *lakhs*, *crores* of *crores*[12] of people. I saw them.'

'More than at our great pilgrimages?' the Regimental Chaplain demanded.

'Yes. Those are only cities and districts coming out to pray. This was the world walking in grief. And now, hear you! It is the King's custom that four swords of Our Armies in Hind should stand always before the Presence in case of need.'

'The King's custom, our right,' said the Subadar-Major curtly.

'Also our right. These honoured ones are changed after certain months or years, that the honour may be fairly spread. Now it chanced that when the old King – the Queen's son – completed his days, the four that stood in the Presence were Goorkhas. Neither Sikhs alas, nor Pathans, Rajputs, nor Jats. Goorkhas, my father.'

'Idolaters,' said the Chaplain.

'But soldiers; for I remember in the Tirah[13] –' the Havildar-Major began.

'*But* soldiers, for I remember fifteen campaigns. Go on,' said the Subadar-Major.

'And it was their honour and right to furnish one who should stand in the Presence by day and by night till It went out to burial. There were no more than four all told – four old men to furnish that guard.'

'Old? Old? What talk is this of old men?' said the Subadar-Major.

'Nay. My fault! Your pardon!' The Havildar-Major spread a deprecating hand. 'They were strong, hot, valiant men, and the youngest was a lad of forty-five.'

'That is better,' the Subadar-Major laughed.

'But for all their strength and heat they could not eat strange food from the Sahibs' hands. There was no cooking place in the Temple; but a certain Colonel Forsyth Sahib, who had understanding, made arrangement whereby they should receive at least a little caste-clean parched grain; also cold rice maybe, and water which was pure. Yet, at best, this was no more than a hen's mouthful, snatched as each came off his guard. They lived on grain and were thankful, as the saying is.

'One hour's guard in every four was each man's burden, for, as I have shown, they were but four all told; and the honour of Our Armies in Hind was on their heads. The Sahibs could draw upon all the armies in England for the other watchers – thousands upon thousands of fresh men – if they needed; but these four were but four.

'The Sahibs drew upon the Granadeers for the other watchers. Granadeers be very tall men under very tall bearskins, such as Fusilier regiments wear in cold weather. Thus, when a Granadeer bowed his head but a very little over his stock, the bearskin sloped and showed as though he grieved exceedingly. Now the Goorkhas wear flat, green caps –'

'I see, I see,' said the Subadar-Major impatiently.

'They are bull-necked, too; and their stocks are hard, and when they bend deeply – deeply – to match the Granadeers – they come nigh to choking themselves. That was a handicap against them, when it came to the observance of ritual.

'Yet even with their tall, grief-declaring bearskins, the Granadeers could not endure the full hour's guard in the Presence. There was good cause, as I will show, why no man could endure that terrible hour. So for them the hour's guard was cut to one-half. What did it matter to the Sahibs? They could draw on ten thousand Granadeers. Forsyth Sahib, who had comprehension, put this choice also before the four, and they said, "No, ours is the Honour of the Armies of Hind. Whatever the Sahibs do, we will suffer the full hour."

'Forsyth Sahib, seeing that they were – knowing that they could neither sleep long nor eat much, said, "It is great suffering?" They said, "It is great honour. We will endure."

'Forsyth Sahib, who loves us, said then to the eldest, "Ho, father, tell me truly what manner of burden it is; for the full hour's watch breaks up our men like water."

'The eldest answered, "Sahib, the burden is the feet of the multitude that pass us on either side. Our eyes being lowered and fixed, we see those feet only from the knee down – a river of feet, Sahib, that never – never – never stops. It is not the standing without any motion; it is not hunger; nor is it the dead part before the dawn when maybe a single one comes here to weep. It is the burden of the unendurable procession of feet from the knee down, that never – never – never stops!"

'Forsyth Sahib said, "By God, I had not considered that! Now I know why our men come trembling and twitching off that guard. But at least, my father, ease the stock a little beneath the bent chin for that one hour."

'The eldest said, "We are in the Presence. Moreover *He* knew every button and braid and hook of every uniform in all His armies."

'Then Forsyth Sahib said no more, except to speak about their parched grain, but indeed they could not eat much after their hour, nor could they sleep much because of eye-twitchings and the renewed procession of the feet before the eyes. Yet they endured each his full hour – not half an hour – his one full hour in each four hours.'

'Correct! correct!' said the Subadar-Major and the Chaplain together. 'We come well out of this affair.'

'But seeing that they were old men,' said the Subadar-Major reflectively, 'very old men, worn out by lack of food and sleep, could not arrangements have been made, or influence have been secured, or a petition presented, whereby a well-born Sikh might have eased them of some portion of their great burden, even though his substantive rank –'

'Then they would most certainly have slain me,' said the Havildar-Major with a smile.

'And they would have done correctly,' said the Chaplain. 'What befell the honourable ones later?'

'This. The Kings of the earth and all the Armies sent flowers and such-like to the dead King's palace at Wanidza, where the funeral offerings were accepted. There was no order given, but all the world made oblation. So the four took counsel – three at a time – and either they asked Forsyth Sahib to choose flowers, or themselves they went forth and bought flowers – I do not know; but, however it was arranged, the flowers were bought and made in the shape of a great drum-like circle weighing half a maund.[14]

'Forsyth Sahib had said, "Let the flowers be sent to Wanidza with the other flowers which all the world is sending." But they said among themselves, "It is not fit that these flowers, which are the offerings of His Armies in Hind, should come to the Palace of the Presence by the hands of hirelings or messengers, or of any man not in His service."

'Hearing this, Forsyth Sahib, though he was much occupied with office-work, said, "Give me the flowers, and I will steal a time and myself take them to Wanidza."

'The eldest said, "Since when has Forsyth Sahib worn sword?"

'Forsyth Sahib said, "But always. And I wear it in the Presence when I put on uniform. I am a Colonel in the Armies of Hind." The eldest said, "Of what regiment?" And Forsyth Sahib looked on the carpet and pulled the hair of his lip. He saw the trap.'

'Forsyth Sahib's regiment was once the old Forty-sixth Pathans which was called –' the Subadar-Major gave the almost forgotten title, adding that he had met them in such and such campaigns, when Forsyth Sahib was a young captain.

The Havildar-Major took up the tale, saying, 'The eldest knew that also, my father. He laughed, and presently Forsyth Sahib laughed.

'"It is true," said Forsyth Sahib. "I have no regiment. For

twenty years I have been a clerk tied to a thick pen. Therefore I am the more fit to be your orderly and messenger in this business."

'The eldest then said, "If it were a matter of my life or the honour of *any* of my household, it would be easy." And Forsyth Sahib joined his hands together, half laughing, though he was ready to weep, and he said, "Enough! I ask pardon. Which one of you goes with the offering?"

'The eldest said, feigning not to have heard, "Nor must they be delivered by a single sword – as though we were pressed for men in His service," and they saluted and went out.'

'Were these things seen, or were they told thee?' said the Subadar-Major.

'I both saw and heard in the office full of books and papers where my Colonel Sahib consulted Forsyth Sahib upon the business that had brought my Colonel Sahib to England.'

'And what was that business?' the Regimental Chaplain asked of a sudden, looking full at the Havildar-Major, who returned the look without a quiver.

'That was not revealed to me,' said the Havildar-Major.

'I heard it might have been some matter touching the integrity of certain regiments,' the Chaplain insisted.

'The matter was not in any way open to my ears,' said the Havildar-Major.

'Humph!' The Chaplain drew his hard road-worn feet under his robe. 'Let us hear the tale that it is permitted thee to tell,' he said, and the Havildar-Major went on:

'So then the three, having returned to the Temple, called the fourth, who had only forty-five years, when he came off guard, and said, "We go to the Palace at Wanidza with the offerings. Remain thou in the Presence, and take all our guards, one after the other, till we return."

'Within that next hour they hired a large and strong *mota-kahar* for the journey from the Temple to Wanidza, which is twenty *koss* or more, and they promised expedition. But he who took their guards said, "It is not seemly that we should for any cause appear to be in haste. There are eighteen medals with eleven clasps and three Orders to consider. Go at leisure. I can endure."

'So the three with the offerings were absent three hours and a half, and having delivered the offering at Wanidza in the correct manner they returned and found the lad on guard, and they did not break his guard till his full hour was ended. So *he* endured four hours in the Presence, not stirring one hair, his eyes abased, and the river of feet, from the knee down, passing continually before his eyes. When he was relieved, it was seen that his eyeballs worked like weavers' shuttles.

'And so it was done – not in hot blood, not for a little while, nor yet with the smell of slaughter and the noise of shouting to sustain, but in silence, for a very long time, rooted to one place before the Presence among the most terrible feet of the multitude.'

'Correct!' the Chaplain chuckled.

'But the Goorkhas had the honour,' said the Subadar-Major sadly.

'Theirs was the Honour of His Armies in Hind, and that was Our Honour,' the nephew replied.

'Yet I would one Sikh had been concerned in it – even one low-caste Sikh. And after?'

'They endured the burden until the end – until It went out of the Temple to be laid among the older kings at Wanidza. When all was accomplished and It was withdrawn under the earth, Forsyth Sahib said to the four, "The King gives command that you be fed here on meat cooked by your own cooks. Eat and take ease, my fathers."

'So they loosed their belts and ate. They had not eaten food except by snatches for some long time; and when the meat had given them strength they slept for very many hours; and it was told me that the procession of the unendurable feet ceased to pass before their eyes any more.'

He threw out one hand palm upward to show that the tale was ended.

'We came well and cleanly out of it,' said the Subadar-Major.

'Correct! Correct! Correct!' said the Regimental Chaplain. 'In an evil age it is good to hear such things, and there is certainly no doubt that this is a very evil age.'

Jobson's Amen

'Blessed be the English and all their ways and works.
Cursed be the Infidels, Hereticks, and Turks!'
'Amen,' quo' Jobson, 'but where I used to lie
Was neither Candle, Bell nor Book to curse my brethren by:

'But a palm-tree in full bearing, bowing down, bowing down,
To a surf that drove unsparing at the brown-walled town –
Conches in a temple, oil-lamps in a dome –
And a low moon out of Africa said: "This way home!"'

'Blessed be the English and all that they profess.
Cursed be the Savages that prance in nakedness!'
'Amen,' quo' Jobson, 'but where I used to lie
Was neither shirt nor pantaloons to catch my brethren by:

'But a well-wheel slowly creaking, going round, going round,
By a water-channel leaking over drowned, warm ground –
Parrots very busy in the trellised pepper-vine –
And a high sun over Asia shouting: "Rise and shine!"'

'Blessed be the English and everything they own.
Cursed be the Infidels that bow to wood and stone!'
'Amen,' quo' Jobson, 'but where I used to lie
Was neither pew nor Gospelleer to save my brethren by:

'But a desert stretched and stricken, left and right, left and right,
Where the piled mirages thicken under white-hot light –
A skull beneath a sand-hill and a viper coiled inside –
And a red wind out of Libya roaring: "Run and hide!"'

'Blessed be the English and all they make or do.
Cursed be the Hereticks who doubt that this is true!'
'Amen,' quo' Jobson, 'but where I mean to die
Is neither rule nor calliper to judge the matter by:

In the Presence

'But Himalaya heavenward-heading, sheer and vast, sheer and vast,
In a million summits bedding on the last world's past;
A certain sacred mountain where the scented cedars climb,
And – the feet of my Beloved hurrying back through Time!'

REGULUS

❴ Regulus[1] ❵

(1908)

Regulus, a Roman general, defeated the Carthaginians 256 BC, but was next year defeated and taken prisoner by the Carthaginians, who sent him to Rome with an embassy to ask for peace or an exchange of prisoners. Regulus strongly advised the Roman Senate to make no terms with the enemy. He then returned to Carthage and was put to death.

The Fifth Form had been dragged several times in its collective life, from one end of the school Horace to the other. Those were the years when Army examiners gave thousands of marks for Latin, and it was Mr King's hated business to defeat them.

Hear him, then, on a raw November morning at second lesson.

'Aha!' he began, rubbing his hands. '*Cras ingens iterabimus aequor.* Our portion today is the Fifth Ode of the Third Book, I believe – concerning one Regulus, a gentleman. And how often have we been through it?'

'Twice, sir,' said Malpass, head of the Form.

Mr King shuddered. 'Yes, twice, quite literally,' he said. 'Today, with an eye to your Army *viva-voce* examinations – ugh! – I shall exact somewhat freer and more florid renditions. With feeling and comprehension if that be possible. I except' – here his eye swept the back benches – 'our friend and companion Beetle, from whom, now as always, I demand an absolutely literal translation.' The form laughed subserviently.

'Spare his blushes! Beetle charms us first.'

Beetle stood up, confident in the possession of a guaranteed construe, left behind by M'Turk, who had that day gone into the sick-house with a cold. Yet he was too wary a hand to show confidence.

'*Credidimus*, we – believe – we have believed,' he opened in

205

hesitating slow time, '*tonantem Jovem*, thundering Jove – *regnare*, to reign – *caelo*, in heaven. *Augustus*, Augustus – *habebitur*, will be held or considered – *praesens divus*, a present God – *adjectis Britannis*, the Britons being added – *imperio*, to the Empire – *gravibusque Persis*, with the heavy – er, stern Persians.'

'What?'

'The grave or stern Persians.' Beetle pulled up with the 'Thank-God-I-have-done-my-duty' air of Nelson in the cockpit.

'I am quite aware,' said King, 'that the first stanza is about the extent of your knowledge, but continue, sweet one, continue. *Gravibus*, by the way, is usually translated as "troublesome".'

Beetle drew a long and tortured breath. The second stanza (which carries over to the third) of that Ode is what is technically called a 'stinker'. But M'Turk had done him handsomely.

'*Milesne Crassi*, had – has the soldier of Crassus – *vixit*, lived – *turpis maritus*, a disgraceful husband –'

'You slurred the quantity of the word after *turpis*,' said King. 'Let's hear it.'

Beetle guessed again, and for a wonder hit the correct quantity. 'Er – a disgraceful husband – *conjuge barbara*, with a barbarous spouse.'

'Why do you select *that* disgustful equivalent out of all the dictionary?' King snapped. 'Isn't "wife" good enough for you?'

'Yes, sir. But what do I do about this bracket, sir? Shall I take it now?'

'Confine yourself at present to the soldier of Crassus.'

'Yes, sir. *Et*, and – *consenuit*, has he grown old – *in armis*, in the – er – arms – *hostium socerorum*, of his father-in-law's enemies.'

'Who? How? Which?'

'Arms of his enemies' fathers-in-law, sir.'

'Tha-anks. By the way, what meaning might you attach to *in armis*?'

'Oh, weapons – weapons of war, sir.' There was a virginal note in Beetle's voice as though he had been falsely accused of uttering indecencies. 'Shall I take the bracket now, sir?'

'Since it seems to be troubling you.'

'*Pro Curia*, O for the Senate House – *inversique mores*, and manners upset – upside down.'

'Ve-ry like your translation. Meantime, the soldier of Crassus?'

'*Sub rege Medo*, under a Median King – *Marsus et Apulus*, he being a Marsian and an Apulian.'

'Who? The Median King?'

'No, sir. The soldier of Crassus. *Oblittus* agrees with *milesne Crassi*, sir,' volunteered too hasty Beetle.

'Does it? It doesn't with *me*.'

'*Oh-blight-us*,' Beetle corrected hastily, 'forgetful – *anciliorum*, of the shields, or trophies – *et nominis*, and the – his name – *et togae*, and the toga – *eternaeque Vestae*, and eternal Vesta – *incolumi Jove*, Jove being safe – *et urbe Roma*, and the Roman city.' With an air of hardly restrained zeal – 'Shall I go on, sir?'

Mr King winced. 'No, thank you. You have indeed given us a translation! May I ask if it conveys any meaning whatever to your so-called mind?'

'Oh, I think so, sir.' This with gentle toleration for Horace and all his works.

'We envy you. Sit down.'

Beetle sat down relieved, well knowing that a reef of uncharted genitives stretched ahead of him, on which in spite of M'Turk's sailing-directions he would infallibly have been wrecked.

Rattray, who took up the task, steered neatly through them and came unscathed to port.

'Here we require drama,' said King. 'Regulus himself is speaking now. Who shall represent the provident-minded Regulus? Winton, will you kindly oblige?'

Winton of King's House, a long, heavy, tow-headed Second Fifteen forward, overdue for his First Fifteen colours, and in aspect like an earnest elderly horse, rose up, and announced, among other things, that he had seen 'signs affixed to Punic deluges'. Half the Form shouted for joy, and the other half for joy that there was something to shout about.

Mr King opened and shut his eyes with great swiftness, '*Signa adfixa delubris*,' he gasped. 'So *delubris* is "deluges" is it?

Winton, in all our dealings, have I ever suspected you of a jest?'

'No, sir,' said the rigid and angular Winton, while the Form rocked about him.

'And yet you assert *delubris* means "deluges". Whether I am a fit subject for such a jape is, of course, a matter of opinion, but . . . Winton, you are normally conscientious. May we assume you looked out *delubris*?'

'No, sir.' Winton was privileged to speak that truth dangerous to all who stand before Kings.

''Made a shot at it then?'

Every line of Winton's body showed he had done nothing of the sort. Indeed, the very idea that 'Pater' Winton (and a boy is not called 'Pater' by companions for his frivolity) would make a shot at anything was beyond belief. But he replied, 'Yes,' and all the while worked with his right heel as though he were heeling a ball at punt-about.

Though none dared to boast of being a favourite with King, the taciturn, three-cornered Winton stood high in his House-Master's opinion. It seemed to save him neither rebuke nor punishment, but the two were in some fashion sympathetic.

'Hm!' said King drily. 'I was going to say – *Flagitio additis damnum*, but I think – I think I see the process. Beetle, the translation of *delubris*, please.'

Beetle raised his head from his shaking arm long enough to answer: 'Ruins, sir.'

There was an impressive pause while King checked off crimes on his fingers. Then to Beetle the much-enduring man addressed winged words:

'Guessing,' said he. 'Guessing, Beetle, as usual, from the look of *delubris* that it bore some relation to *diluvium* or deluge, you imparted the result of your half-baked lucu-brations to Winton who seems to have been lost enough to have accepted it. Observing next, your companion's fall, from the presumed security of your undistinguished position in the rear-guard, you took another pot-shot. The turbid chaos of your mind threw up some memory of the word "dilapida-tions" which you have pitifully attempted to disguise under the synonym of "ruins".'

As this was precisely what Beetle had done he looked hurt

but forgiving. 'We will attend to this later,' said King. 'Go on, Winton, and retrieve yourself.'

Delubris happened to be the one word which Winton had not looked out and had asked Beetle for, when they were settling into their places. He forged ahead with no further trouble. Only when he rendered *scilicet* as 'forsooth', King erupted.

'Regulus,' he said, 'was not a leader-writer for the penny press, nor, for that matter, was Horace. Regulus says: "The soldier ransomed by gold will come keener for the fight – will he by – by gum!" *That's* the meaning of *scilicet*. It indicates contempt – bitter contempt. "Forsooth", forsooth! You'll be talking about "speckled beauties" and "eventually transpire" next. Howell, what do you make of that doubled "Vidi ego – ego vidi"? It wasn't put in to fill up the metre, you know.'

'Isn't it intensive, sir?' said Howell, afflicted by a genuine interest in what he read. 'Regulus was a bit in earnest about Rome making no terms with Carthage – and he wanted to let the Romans understand it, didn't he, sir?'

'Less than your usual grace, but the fact. Regulus *was* in earnest. He was also engaged at the same time in cutting his own throat with every word he uttered. He knew Carthage which (your examiners won't ask you this so you needn't take notes) was a sort of God-forsaken nigger Manchester. Regulus was not thinking about his own life. He was telling Rome the truth. He was playing for his side. Those lines from the eighteenth to the fortieth ought to be written in blood. Yet there are things in human garments which will tell you that Horace was a flaneur – a man about town. Avoid such beings. Horace knew a very great deal. *He* knew! *Erit ille fortis* – "will he be brave who once to faithless foes has knelt?" And again (stop pawing with your hooves, Thornton!) *hic unde vitam sumeret inscius.* That means roughly – but I perceive I am ahead of my translators. Begin at *hic unde*, Vernon, and let us see if you have the spirit of Regulus.'

Now no one expected fireworks from gentle Paddy Vernon, sub-prefect of Hartopp's House, but, as must often be the case with growing boys, his mind was in abeyance for the time being, and he said, all in a rush, on behalf of Regulus: '*O* magna Carthago probrosis altior Italiae ruinis, O Carthage, thou wilt stand forth higher than the ruins of Italy.'

Even Beetle, most lenient of critics, was interested at this point, though he did not join the half-groan of reprobation from the wiser heads of the Form.

'*Please* don't mind me,' said King, and Vernon very kindly did not. He ploughed on thus: 'He (Regulus) is related to have removed from himself the kiss of the shameful wife and of his small children as less by the head, and, being stern, to have placed his virile visage on the ground.'

Since King loved 'virile' about as much as he did 'spouse' or 'forsooth' the Form looked up hopefully. But Jove thundered not.

'Until,' Vernon continued, 'he should have confirmed the sliding fathers as being the author of counsel never given under an alias.'

He stopped, conscious of stillness round him like the dread calm of the typhoon's centre. King's opening voice was sweeter than honey.

'I am painfully aware by bitter experience that I cannot give you any idea of the passion, the power, the – the essential guts of the lines which you have so foully outraged in our presence. But –' the note changed, 'so far as in me lies, I will strive to bring home to you, Vernon, the fact that there exist in Latin a few pitiful rules of grammar, of syntax, nay, even of declension, which were not created for your incult sport – your Bœotian diversion. You will, therefore, Vernon, write out and bring to me tomorrow a word-for-word English–Latin translation of the Ode, together with a full list of all adjectives – an adjective is not a verb, Vernon, as the Lower Third will tell you – all adjectives, their number, case, and gender. Even now I haven't begun to deal with you faithfully.'

'I – I'm very sorry, sir,' Vernon stammered.

'You mistake the symptoms, Vernon. You are possibly dis-comfited by the imposition, but sorrow postulates some sort of mind, intellect, *nous*. Your rendering of *probrosis* alone stamps you as lower than the beasts of the field. Will some one take the taste out of our mouths? And – talking of tastes –' He coughed. There was a distinct flavour of chlorine gas in the air. Up went an eyebrow, though King knew perfectly well what it meant.

'Mr Hartopp's st – science class next door,' said Malpass.

'Oh yes. I had forgotten. Our newly established Modern Side, of course. Perowne, open the windows; and Winton, go on once more from *interque maerentes.*'

'And hastened away,' said Winton, 'surrounded by his mourning friends, into – into illustrious banishment. But I got that out of Conington, sir,' he added in one conscientious breath.

'I am aware. The master generally knows his ass's crib, though I acquit *you* of any intention that way. Can you suggest anything for *egregius exul*? Only "egregious exile"? I fear "egregious" is a good word ruined. No! You can't in this case improve on Conington. Now then for *atqui sciebat quae sibi barbarus tortor pararet*. The whole force of it lies in the *atqui.*'

'Although he knew,' Winton suggested.

'Stronger than that, I think.'

'He who knew well,' Malpass interpolated.

'Ye-es. "Well though he knew." I don't like Conington's "well-witting". It's Wardour Street.'

'Well though he knew what the savage torturer was – was getting ready for him,' said Winton.

'Ye-es. Had in store for him.'

'Yet he brushed aside his kinsmen and the people delaying his return.'

'Ye-es; but then how do you render *obstantes*?'

'If it's a free translation mightn't *obstantes* and *morantem* come to about the same thing, sir?'

'Nothing comes to "about the same thing" with Horace, Winton. As I have said, Horace was not a journalist. No, I take it that his kinsmen bodily withstood his departure, whereas the crowd – *populumque* – the democracy stood about futilely pitying him and getting in the way. Now for that noblest of endings – *quam si clientum*,' and King ran off into the quotation:

> 'As though some tedious business o'er
> Of clients' court, his journey lay
> Towards Venafrum's grassy floor
> Or Sparta-built Tarentum's bay.

'All right, Winton. Beetle, when you've quite finished dodging the fresh air yonder, give me the meaning of *tendens* –and turn down your collar.'

'Me, sir? *Tendens*, sir? Oh! Stretching away in the direction of, sir.'

'Idiot! Regulus was not a feature of the landscape. He was a man, self-doomed to death by torture. *Atqui sciebat* – knowing it – having achieved it for his country's sake – can't you hear that *atqui* cut like a knife? – he moved off with some dignity. That is why Horace out of the whole golden Latin tongue chose the one word "tendens" – which is utterly untranslatable.'

The gross injustice of being asked to translate it, converted Beetle into a young Christian martyr, till King buried his nose in his handkerchief again.

'I think they've broken another gas-bottle next door, sir,' said Howell. 'They're always doing it.' The Form coughed as more chlorine came in.

'Well, I suppose we must be patient with the Modern Side,' said King. 'But it is almost insupportable for this Side. Vernon, what are you grinning at?'

Vernon's mind had returned to him glowing and inspired. He chuckled as he underlined his Horace.

'It appears to amuse you,' said King. 'Let us participate. What is it?'

'The last two lines of the Tenth Ode, in this book, sir,' was Vernon's amazing reply.

'What? Oh, I see. *Non hoc semper erit liminis aut aquae caelestis patiens latus.*'[2] King's mouth twitched to hide a grin. 'Was that done with intention?'

'I – I thought it fitted, sir.'

'It does. It's distinctly happy. What put it into your thick head, Paddy?'

'I don't know, sir, except we did the Ode last term.'

'And you remembered? The same head that minted *probrosis* as a verb! Vernon, you are an enigma. No! This Side will *not* always be patient of unheavenly gases and waters. I will make representations to our so-called Moderns. Meantime (who shall say I am not just?) I remit you your accrued pains and penalties in regard to *probrosim*, *probrosis*, *probrosit* and other enormities.

I oughtn't to do it, but this Side is occasionally human. By no means bad, Paddy.'

'Thank you, sir,' said Vernon, wondering how inspiration had visited him.

Then King, with a few brisk remarks about Science, headed them back to Regulus, of whom and of Horace and Rome and evil-minded commercial Carthage and of the democracy eternally futile, he explained, in all ages and climes, he spoke for ten minutes; passing thence to the next Ode – *Delicta majorum* – where he fetched up, full-voiced, upon – '*Dis te minorem quod geris imperas*' (Thou rulest because thou bearest thyself as lower than the Gods) – making it a text for a discourse on manner, morals, and respect for authority as distinct from bottled gases, which lasted till the bell rang. Then Beetle, concertinaing his books, observed to Winton, 'When King's really on tap he's an interestin' dog. Hartopp's chlorine uncorked him.'

'Yes; but why did you tell me *delubris* was "deluges", you silly ass?' said Winton.

'Well, that uncorked him too. Look out, you hoof-handed old owl!' Winton had cleared for action as the Form poured out like puppies at play and was scragging Beetle. Stalky from behind collared Winton low. The three fell in confusion.

'*Dis te minorem quod geris imperas*,' quoth Stalky, ruffling Winton's lint-white locks. ''Mustn't jape with Number Five study. Don't be too virtuous. Don't brood over it. 'Twon't count against you in your future caree-ah. Cheer up, Pater.'

'Pull him off my – er – essential guts, will you?' said Beetle from beneath. 'He's squashin' 'em.'

They dispersed to their studies.

No one, the owner least of all, can explain what is in a growing boy's mind. It might have been the blind ferment of adolescence, Stalky's random remarks about virtue might have stirred him; like his betters he might have sought popularity by way of clowning; or, as the Head asserted years later, the only known jest of his serious life might have worked on him, as a sobersided man's one love colours and dislocates all his after days. But, at the next lesson, mechanical drawing with Mr Lidgett who as drawing-master had very limited powers of punishment, Winton fell suddenly from grace and let loose a live mouse in the form-room. The whole form, shrieking and leaping high, threw at it all the plaster cones, pyramids, and fruit in high relief – not to mention ink-pots – that they could lay hands on. Mr Lidgett reported at once to the Head; Winton owned up to his crime, which, venial in the Upper Third, pardonable at a price in the Lower Fourth, was, of course, rank ruffianism on the part of a Fifth Form boy; and so, by graduated stages, he arrived at the Head's study just before lunch, penitent, perturbed, annoyed with himself and – as the Head said to King in the corridor after the meal – more human than he had known him in seven years.

'You see,' the Head drawled on, 'Winton's only fault is a certain costive and unaccommodating virtue. So this comes very happily.'

'I've never noticed any sign of it,' said King. Winton was in King's House, and though King as pro-consul might, and did, infernally oppress his own Province, once a black and yellow cap was in trouble at the hands of the Imperial authority King fought for him to the very last steps of Caesar's throne.

'Well, you yourself admitted just now that a mouse was beneath the occasion,' the Head answered.

'It was.' Mr King did not love Mr Lidgett. 'It should have been a rat. But – but – I hate to plead it – it's the lad's first offence.'

'Could you have damned him more completely, King?'

'Hm. What is the penalty?' said King, in retreat, but keeping up a rear-guard action.

'Only my usual few lines of Virgil to be shown up by tea-time.'

The Head's eyes turned slightly to that end of the corridor where Mullins, Captain of the Games ('Pot', 'old Pot', or 'Potiphar' Mullins), was pinning up the usual Wednesday notice –'Big, Middle, and Little Side Football – A to K, L to Z, 3 to 4.45 p.m.'

You cannot write out the Head's usual few (which means five hundred) Latin lines and play football for one hour and three-quarters between the hours of 1.30 and 5 p.m. Winton had evidently no intention of trying to do so, for he hung about the corridor with a set face and an uneasy foot. Yet it was law in the school, compared with which that of the Medes and Persians was no more than a non-committal resolution, that any boy, outside the First Fifteen, who missed his football for any reason whatever, and had not a written excuse, duly signed by competent authority to explain his absence, would receive not less than three strokes with a ground-ash from the Captain of the Games, generally a youth between seventeen and eighteen years, rarely under eleven stone ('Pot' was nearer thirteen), and always in hard condition.

King knew without inquiry that the Head had given Winton no such excuse.

'But he is practically a member of the First Fifteen. He has played for it all this term,' said King. 'I believe his Cap should have arrived last week.'

'His Cap has not been given him. Officially, therefore, he is naught. I rely on old Pot.'

'But Mullins is Winton's study-mate,' King persisted.

Pot Mullins and Pater Winton were cousins and rather close friends.

'That will make no difference to Mullins – or Winton, if I know 'em,' said the Head.

'But – but,' King played his last card desperately, 'I was going to recommend Winton for extra sub-prefect in my House, now Carton has gone.'

'Certainly,' said the Head. 'Why not? He will be excellent by tea-time, I hope.'

At that moment they saw Mr Lidgett, tripping down the corridor, waylaid by Winton.

'It's about that mouse-business at mechanical drawing,' Winton opened, swinging across his path.

'Yes, yes, highly disgraceful,' Mr Lidgett panted.

'I know it was,' said Winton. 'It – it was a cad's trick because –'

'Because you knew I couldn't give you more than fifty lines,' said Mr Lidgett.

'Well, anyhow I've come to apologize for it.'

'Certainly,' said Mr Lidgett, and added, for he was a kindly man, 'I think that shows quite right feeling. I'll tell the Head at once I'm satisfied.'

'No – no!' The boy's still unmended voice jumped from the growl to the squeak. 'I didn't mean *that*! I – I did it on principle. Please don't – er – do anything of that kind.'

Mr Lidgett looked him up and down and, being an artist, understood.

'Thank you, Winton,' he said. 'This shall be between ourselves.'

'You heard?' said King, indecent pride in his voice.

'Of course. You thought he was going to get Lidgett to beg him off the impot.'

King denied this with so much warmth that the Head laughed and King went away in a huff.

'By the way,' said the Head, 'I've told Winton to do his lines in your form-room – not in his study.'

'Thanks,' said King over his shoulder, for the Head's orders had saved Winton and Mullins, who was doing extra Army work in the study, from an embarrassing afternoon together.

An hour later, King wandered into his still form-room as though by accident. Winton was hard at work.

'Aha!' said King, rubbing his hands. 'This does not look like games, Winton. Don't let me arrest your facile pen. Whence this sudden love for Virgil?'

'Impot from the Head, sir, for that mouse-business this morning.'

'Rumours thereof have reached us. That was a lapse on your part into Lower Thirdery which I don't quite understand.'

The 'tump-tump' of the puntabouts before the sides settled to games came through the open window. Winton, like his Housemaster, loved fresh air. Then they heard Paddy Vernon, subprefect on duty, calling the roll in the field and marking defaulters. Winton wrote steadily. King curled himself up on a desk, hands round knees. One would have said that the man was gloating over the boy's misfortune, but the boy understood.

'*Dis te minorem quod geris imperas*,' King quoted presently. 'It is necessary to bear oneself as lower than the local gods – even than drawing-masters who are precluded from effective retaliation. I *do* wish you'd tried that mouse-game with me, Pater.'

Winton grinned; then sobered. 'It was a cad's trick, sir, to play on Mr Lidgett.' He peered forward at the page he was copying.

'Well, "the sin *I* impute to each frustrate ghost" ' King stopped himself. 'Why do you goggle like an owl? Hand me the Mantuan and I'll dictate. No matter. Any rich Virgilian measures will serve. I may peradventure recall a few.' He began:

> 'Tu regere imperio populos Romane memento
> Hae tibi erunt artes pacisque imponere morem,
> Parcere subjectis et debellare superbos.[3]

'There you have it all, Winton. Write that out twice and yet once again.'

For the next forty minutes, with never a glance at the book, King paid out the glorious hexameters (and King could read Latin as though it were alive), Winton hauling them in and coiling them away behind him as trimmers in a telegraph-ship's hold coil away deep-sea cable. King broke from the Aeneid to the Georgics and back again, pausing now and then to translate some specially loved line or to dwell on the treble-shot texture of the ancient fabric. He did not allude to the coming interview with Mullins except at the last, when he said, 'I think at this juncture, Pater, I need not ask you for the precise significance of *atqui sciebat quae sibi barbarus tortor*.'[4]

The ungrateful Winton flushed angrily, and King loafed out to take five o'clock call-over, after which he invited little Hartopp to tea and a talk on chlorine-gas. Hartopp accepted the challenge like a bantam, and the two went up to King's study about the same time as Winton returned to the form-room beneath it to finish his lines.

Then half a dozen of the Second Fifteen who should have been washing strolled in to condole with 'Pater' Winton, whose misfortune and its consequences were common talk. No one was more sincere than the long, red-headed, knotty-knuckled 'Paddy' Vernon, but, being a careless animal, he joggled Winton's desk.

'Curse you for a silly ass!' said Winton. 'Don't do that.'

No one is expected to be polite while under punishment, so Vernon, sinking his sub-prefectship, replied peacefully enough:

'Well, don't be wrathy, Pater.'

'I'm not,' said Winton. 'Get out! This ain't your House form-room.'

''Form-room don't belong to you. Why don't you go to your own study?' Vernon replied.

'Because Mullins is there waitin' for the victim,' said Stalky delicately, and they all laughed. 'You ought to have shaken that mouse out of your trouser-leg, Pater. That's the way *I* did in my youth. Pater's revertin' to his second childhood. Never mind, Pater, we all respect you and your future caree-ah.'

Winton, still writhing, growled. Vernon leaning on the desk somehow shook it again. Then he laughed.

'What are you grinning at?' Winton asked.

'I was only thinkin' of *you* being sent up to take a lickin' from Pot. I swear I don't think it's fair. You've never shirked a game in your life, and you're as good as in the First Fifteen already. Your Cap ought to have been delivered last week, oughtn't it?'

It was law in the school that no man could by any means enjoy the privileges and immunities of the First Fifteen till the black velvet cap with the gold tassel, made by dilatory Exeter outfitters, had been actually set on his head. Ages ago, a large-built and unruly Second Fifteen had attempted to change this law, but the prefects of that age were still larger, and the lively experiment had never been repeated.

'Will you,' said Winton very slowly, 'kindly mind your own damned business, you cursed, clumsy, fat-headed fool?'

The form-room was as silent as the empty field in the darkness outside. Vernon shifted his feet uneasily.

'Well, *I* shouldn't like to take a lickin' from Pot,' he said.

'Wouldn't you?' Winton asked as he paged the sheets of lines with hands that shook.

'No, I shouldn't,' said Vernon, his freckles growing more distinct on the bridge of his white nose.

'Well, I'm going to take it' — Winton moved clear of the desk as he spoke. 'But *you*'re going to take a lickin' from me first.' Before any one realized it, he had flung himself neighing against Vernon. No decencies were observed on either side, and the rest looked on amazed. The two met confusedly, Vernon trying to do what he could with his longer reach; Winton, insensible to blows, only concerned to drive his enemy into a corner and batter him to pulp. This he managed over against the fireplace, where Vernon dropped half-stunned. 'Now I'm going to give you your lickin',' said Winton. 'Lie there till I get a ground-ash and I'll cut you to pieces. If you move, I'll chuck you out of the window.' He wound his hands into the boy's collar and waistband, and had actually heaved him half off the ground before the others with one accord dropped on his head, shoulders, and legs. He fought them crazily in an awful hissing silence. Stalky's sensitive nose was rubbed along the floor; Beetle received a jolt in the wind that sent him whistling and crowing against the wall; Perowne's forehead was cut, and Malpass came out with an eye that explained itself like a dying rainbow through a whole week.

'Mad! Quite mad!' said Stalky, and for the third time wriggled back to Winton's throat. The door opened and King came in, Hartopp's little figure just behind him. The mound on the floor panted and heaved but did not rise, for Winton still squirmed vengefully. 'Only a little play, sir,' said Perowne. ''Only hit my head against a form.' This was quite true.

'Oh,' said King. '*Dimovit obstantes propinquos*. You, I presume, are the *populus* delaying Winton's return to – Mullins, eh?'

'No, sir,' said Stalky behind his claret-coloured handkerchief. 'We're the *maerentes amicos*.' [5]

'Not bad! You see, some of it sticks after all,' King chuckled to Hartopp, and the two masters left without further inquiries.

The boys sat still on the now passive Winton.

'Well,' said Stalky at last, 'of all the putrid he-asses, Pater, you are *the* –'

'I'm sorry. I'm awfully sorry,' Winton began, and they let him rise. He held out his hand to the bruised and bewildered Vernon. 'Sorry, Paddy. I – I must have lost my temper. I – I don't know what's the matter with me.'

''Fat lot of good that'll do my face at tea,' Vernon grunted. 'Why couldn't you say there was something wrong with you instead of lamming out like a lunatic? Is my lip puffy?'

'Just a trifle. Look at my beak! Well, we got all these pretty marks at footer – owin' to the zeal with which we played the game,' said Stalky, dusting himself. 'But d'you think you're fit to be let loose again, Pater? 'Sure you don't want to kill another sub-prefect? I wish *I* was Pot. I'd cut your sprightly young soul out.'

'I s'pose I ought to go to Pot now,' said Winton.

'And let all the other asses see you lookin' like this! Not much. We'll all come up to Number Five Study and wash off in hot water. Beetle, you aren't damaged. Go along and light the gas-stove.'

'There's a tin of cocoa in my study somewhere,' Perowne shouted after him. 'Rootle round till you find it, and take it up.'

Separately, by different roads, Vernon's jersey pulled half over his head, the boys repaired to Number Five Study. Little Hartopp and King, I am sorry to say, leaned over the banisters of King's landing and watched.

'Ve-ry human,' said little Hartopp. 'Your virtuous Winton, having got himself into trouble, takes it out of my poor old Paddy. I wonder what precise lie Paddy will tell about his face.'

'But surely you aren't going to embarrass him by asking?' said King.

'*Your* boy won,' said Hartopp.

'To go back to what we were discussing,' said King quickly, 'do you pretend that your modern system of inculcating unrelated facts about chlorine, for instance, all of which may be proved fallacies by the time the boys grow up, can have any real bearing on education – even the low type of it that examiners expect?'

'I maintain nothing. But is it any worse than your Chinese reiteration of uncomprehended syllables in a dead tongue?'

'Dead, forsooth!' King fairly danced. 'The only living tongue on earth! Chinese! On my word, Hartopp!'

'And at the end of seven years – how often have I said it?' Hartopp went on – 'seven years of two hundred and twenty days of six hours each, your victims go away with nothing, absolutely nothing, except, perhaps, if they've been very attentive, a dozen – no, I'll grant you twenty – one score of totally unrelated Latin tags which any child of twelve could have absorbed in two terms.'

'But – but can't you realize that if our system brings later – at any rate – at a pinch – a simple understanding – grammar and Latinity apart – a mere glimpse of the significance (foul word!) of, we'll say, one Ode of Horace, one twenty lines of Virgil, we've got what we poor devils of ushers are striving after?'

'And what might that be?' said Hartopp.

'Balance, proportion, perspective – life. Your scientific man is the unrelated animal – the beast without background. Haven't you ever realized *that* in your atmosphere of stinks?'

'Meantime you make them lose life for the sake of living, eh?'

'Blind again, Hartopp! I told you about Paddy's quotation this morning. (But he made *probrosis* a verb, he did!) You yourself heard young Corkran's reference to *maerentes amicos*. It sticks – a little of it sticks among the barbarians.'

'Absolutely and essentially Chinese,' said little Hartopp, who, alone of the common-room, refused to be outfaced by King. 'But I don't yet understand how Paddy came to be licked by Winton. Paddy's supposed to be something of a boxer.'

'Beware of vinegar made from honey,' King replied. 'Pater, like some other people, is patient and long-suffering, but he has his limits. The Head is oppressing him damnably, too. As I pointed out, the boy has practically been in the First Fifteen since term began.'

'But, my dear fellow, I've known you give a boy an impot and refuse him leave off games, again and again.'

'Ah, but that was when there was real need to get at some oaf who couldn't be sensitized in any other way. Now, in our esteemed Head's action I see nothing but –'

The conversation from this point does not concern us.

Meantime Winton, very penitent and especially polite towards Vernon, was being cheered with cocoa in Number Five Study. They had some difficulty in stemming the flood of his apologies. He himself pointed out to Vernon that he had attacked a sub-prefect for no reason whatever, and, therefore, deserved official punishment.

'I can't think what was the matter with me today,' he mourned. 'Ever since that blasted mouse business –'

'Well, then, don't think,' said Stalky. 'Or do you want Paddy to make a row about it before all the school?'

Here Vernon was understood to say that he would see Winton and all the school somewhere else.

'And if you imagine Perowne and Malpass and me are goin' to give evidence at a prefects' meeting just to soothe your beastly conscience, you jolly well err,' said Beetle. 'I know what you did.'

'What?' croaked Pater, out of the valley of his humiliation.

'You went Berserk. I've read all about it in *Hypatia*.' [6]

'What's "going Berserk"?' Winton asked.

'Never you mind,' was the reply. 'Now, don't you feel awfully weak and seedy?'

'I *am* rather tired,' said Winton, sighing.

'That's what you ought to be. You've gone Berserk and pretty soon you'll go to sleep. But you'll probably be liable to fits of it all your life,' Beetle concluded. ''Shouldn't wonder if you murdered someone some day.'

'Shut up – you and your Berserks!' said Stalky. 'Go to Mullins now and get it over, Pater.'

'I call it filthy unjust of the Head,' said Vernon. 'Anyhow, you've give me my lickin', old man. I hope Pot'll give you yours.'

'I'm awfully sorry – awfully sorry,' was Winton's last word.

It was the custom in that consulship to deal with games' defaulters between five o'clock call-over and tea. Mullins, who was old enough to pity, did not believe in letting boys wait through the night till the chill of the next morning for their punishments. He was finishing off the last of the small fry and their excuses when Winton arrived.

'But, please, Mullins' – this was Babcock tertius, a dear little twelve-year-old mother's darling – 'I had an awful hack on the knee. I've been to the Matron about it and she gave me some iodine. I've been rubbing it in all day. I thought that would be an excuse off.'

'Let's have a look at it,' said the impassive Mullins. 'That's a shin-bruise – about a week old. Touch your toes. I'll give you the iodine.'

Babcock yelled loudly as he had many times before. The face of Jevons, aged eleven, a new boy that dark wet term, low in the

House, low in the Lower School, and lowest of all in his home-sick little mind, turned white at the horror of the sight. They could hear his working lips part stickily as Babcock wailed his way out of hearing.

'Hullo, Jevons! What brings you here?' said Mullins.

'Pl-ease, sir, I went for a walk with Babcock tertius.'

'Did you? Then I bet you went to the tuck-shop – and you paid, didn't you?'

A nod. Jevons was too terrified to speak.

'Of course, and I bet Babcock told you that old Pot 'ud let you off because it was the first time.'

Another nod with a ghost of a smile in it.

'All right.' Mullins picked Jevons up before he could guess what was coming, laid him on the table with one hand, with the other gave him three emphatic spanks, then held him high in air.

'Now you tell Babcock tertius that he's got you a licking from me, and see you jolly well pay it back to him. And when you're prefect of games don't you let any one shirk his footer without a written excuse. Where d'you play in your game?'

'Forward, sir.'

'You can do better than that. I've seen you run like a young buck-rabbit. Ask Dickson from me to try you as three-quarter next game, will you? Get along.'

Jevons left, warm for the first time that day, enormously set up in his own esteem, and very hot against the deceitful Babcock.

Mullins turned to Winton. 'Your name's on the list, Pater.' Winton nodded.

'I know it. The Head landed me with an impot for that mouse-business at mechanical drawing. No excuse.'

'He meant it then?' Mullins jerked his head delicately towards the ground-ash on the table. 'I heard something about it.'

Winton nodded. 'A rotten thing to do,' he said. 'Can't think what I was doing ever to do it. It counts against a fellow so; and there's some more too –'

'All right, Pater. Just stand clear of our photo-bracket, will you?'

The little formality over, there was a pause. Winton swung

round, yawned in Pot's astonished face and staggered towards the window-seat.

'What's the matter with you, Dick? Ill?'

'No. Perfectly all right, thanks. Only – only a little sleepy.' Winton stretched himself out, and then and there fell deeply and placidly asleep.

'It isn't a faint,' said the experienced Mullins, 'or his pulse wouldn't act. 'Tisn't a fit or he'd snort and twitch. It can't be sunstroke, this term, and he hasn't been over-training for anything.' He opened Winton's collar, packed a cushion under his head, threw a rug over him and sat down to listen to the regular breathing. Before long Stalky arrived, on pretence of borrowing a book. He looked at the window-seat.

''Noticed anything wrong with Winton lately?' said Mullins.

''Notice anything wrong with my beak?' Stalky replied. 'Pater went Berserk after call-over, and fell on a lot of us for jesting with him about his impot. You ought to see Malpass's eye.'

'You mean that Pater fought?' said Mullins.

'Like a devil. Then he nearly went to sleep in our study just now. I expect he'll be all right when he wakes up. Rummy business! Conscientious old bargee.[7] You ought to have heard his apologies.'

'But Pater can't fight one little bit,' Mullins repeated.

''Twasn't fighting. He just tried to murder everyone.' Stalky described the affair, and when he left Mullins went off to take counsel with the Head, who, out of a cloud of blue smoke, told him that all would yet be well.

'Winton,' said he, 'is a little stiff in his moral joints. He'll get over that. If he asks you whether today's doings will count against him in his –'

'But you know it's important to him, sir. His people aren't – very well off,' said Mullins.

'That's why I'm taking all this trouble. You must reassure him, Pot. I have overcrowded him with new experiences. Oh, by the way, has his Cap come?'

'It came at dinner, sir.' Mullins laughed.

Sure enough, when he waked at tea-time, Winton proposed to take Mullins all through every one of his day's lapses from grace, and 'Do you think it will count against me?' said he.

'Don't you fuss so much about yourself and your silly career,' said Mullins. 'You're all right. And oh – here's your First Cap at last. Shove it up on the bracket and come on to tea.'

They met King on their way, stepping statelily and rubbing his hands. 'I have applied,' said he, 'for the services of an additional sub-prefect in Carton's unlamented absence. Your name, Winton, seems to have found favour with the powers that be, and – and all things considered – I am disposed to give my support to the nomination. You are therefore a quasi-lictor.'[8]

'Then it didn't count against me,' Winton gasped as soon as they were out of hearing.

A Captain of Games can jest with a sub-prefect publicly.

'You utter ass!' said Mullins, and caught him by the back of his stiff neck and ran him down to the hall where the sub-prefects, who sit below the salt, made him welcome with the economical bloater-paste[9] of mid-term.

King and little Hartopp were sparring in the Reverend John Gillett's study at 10 p.m. – classical *versus* modern as usual.

'Character – proportion – background,' snarled King. 'That is the essence of the Humanities.'

'Analects of Confucius,'[10] little Hartopp answered.

'Time,' said the Reverend John behind the soda-water. 'You men oppress me. Hartopp, what did you say to Paddy in your dormitories tonight? Even *you* couldn't have overlooked his face.'

'But I did,' said Hartopp calmly. 'I wasn't even humorous about it, as some clerics might have been. I went straight through and said naught.'

'Poor Paddy! Now, for my part,' said King, 'and you know I am not lavish in my praises, I consider Winton a first-class type; absolutely first-class.'

'Ha-ardly,' said the Reverend John. 'First-class of the second class, I admit. The very best type of second class but' – he shook his head – 'it should have been a rat. Pater'll never be anything more than a Colonel of Engineers.'

'What do you base that verdict on?' said King stiffly.

'He came to me after prayers – with all his conscience.'

'Poor old Pater. Was it the mouse?' said little Hartopp.

'That, and what he called his uncontrollable temper, and his responsibilities as sub-prefect.'

'And you?'

'If we had had what is vulgarly called a pi-jaw he'd have had hysterics. So I recommended a dose of Epsom salts. He'll take it, too – conscientiously. Don't eat me, King. Perhaps he'll be a K.C.B.'

Ten o'clock struck and the Army class boys in the further studies coming to their houses after an hour's extra work passed along the gravel path below. Some one was chanting, to the tune of 'White sand and grey sand', *Dis te minorem quod geris imperas*. He stopped outside Mullins' study. They heard Mullins' window slide up and then Stalky's voice:

'Ah! Good-evening, Mullins, my *barbarus tortor*. We're the waits. We have come to inquire after the local Berserk. Is he doin' as well as can be expected in his new caree-ah?'

'Better than you will, in a sec, Stalky,' Mullins grunted.

''Glad of that. We thought he'd like to know that Paddy has been carried to the sick-house in ravin' delirium. They think it's concussion of the brain.'

'Why, he was all right at prayers,' Winton began earnestly, and they heard a laugh in the background as Mullins slammed down the window.

' 'Night, Regulus,' Stalky sang out, and the light footsteps went on.

'You see. It sticks. A little of it sticks, among the barbarians,' said King.

'Amen,' said the Reverend John. 'Go to bed.'

A Translation
Horace, Bk. V. Ode 3

There are whose study is of smells,
   And to attentive schools rehearse
How something mixed with something else
   Makes something worse

Some cultivate in broths impure
   The clients of our body – these,
Increasing without Venus, cure,
   Or cause, disease.

Others the heated wheel extol,
   And all its offspring, whose concern
Is how to make it farthest roll
   And fastest turn.

Me, much incurious if the hour
   Present, or to be paid for, brings
Me to Brundusium by the power
   Of wheels or wings;

Me, in whose breast no flame hath burned
   Life-long, save that by Pindar lit,
Such lore leaves cold: I am not turned
   Aside to it

More than when, sunk in thought profound
   Of what the unaltering Gods require,
My steward (friend but slave) brings round
   Logs for my fire.

THE EDGE OF THE EVENING

{ The Edge of the Evening }

(1913)

Ah! What avails the classic bent,
  And what the chosen word,
Against the undoctored incident
  That actually occurred?

And what is Art whereto we press
  Through paint and prose and rhyme —
When Nature in her nakedness
  Defeats us every time?

'Hi! Hi! Hold your horses! Stop! . . . Well! Well!' A lean man in a sable-lined overcoat leaped from a private car and barred my way up Pall Mall. 'You don't know me? You're excusable. I wasn't wearing much of anything last time we met — in South Africa.'

The scales fell from my eyes, and I saw him once more in a sky-blue army shirt, behind barbed wire, among Dutch prisoners bathing at Simonstown, more than a dozen years ago.[1] 'Why, it's Zigler — Laughton O. Zigler!' I cried. 'Well, I *am* glad to see you.'

'Oh no! You don't work any of your English on me. "So glad to see you, doncher know — an' ta-ta!" Do you reside in this village?'

'No. I'm up here buying stores.'

'Then you take my automobile. Where to? . . . Oh, I know *them*! My Lord Marshalton is one of the Directors. Pigott, drive to the Army and Navy, Co-operative Supply Association Limited, Victoria Street, Westminster.'

He settled himself on the deep dove-colour pneumatic cushions, and his smile was like the turning on of all the electrics. His teeth were whiter than the ivory fittings. He smelt of rare soap and cigarettes – such cigarettes as he handed me from a golden box with an automatic lighter. On my side of the car was a gold-mounted mirror, card and toilette case. I looked at him inquiringly.

'Yes,' he nodded, 'two years after I quit the Cape. She's not an Ohio girl, though. She's in the country now. Is that right? She's at our little place in the country. We'll go there as soon as you're through with your grocery-list. Engagements? The only engagement you've got is to grab your grip – get your bag from your hotel, I mean – and come right along and meet her. You are the captive of *my* bow and spear now.'

'I surrender,' I said meekly. 'Did the Zigler automatic gun do all this?' I pointed to the car fittings.

'Psha! Think of your rememberin' that! Well, no. The Zigler is a great gun – the greatest ever – but life's too short, an' too interestin', to squander on pushing her in military society. I've leased my rights in her to a Pennsylvanian-Transylvanian citizen full of mentality and moral uplift. If those things weigh with the Chancelleries of Europe, he will make good and – I shall be surprised. Excuse me!'

He bared his head as we passed the statue of the Great Queen outside Buckingham Palace.

'A very great lady!' said he. 'I have enjoyed her hospitality. She represents one of the most wonderful institutions in the world. The next is the one we are going to. Mrs Zigler uses 'em, and they break her up every week on returned empties.'

'Oh, you mean the Stores?' I said.

'Mrs Zigler means it more. They are quite ambassadorial in their outlook. I guess I'll wait outside and pray while you wrestle with 'em.'

My business at the Stores finished, and my bag retrieved from the hotel, his moving palace slid us into the country.

'I owe it to you,' Zigler began as smoothly as the car, 'to tell you what I am now. I represent the business end of the American Invasion. Not the blame cars themselves – I wouldn't be found dead in one – but the tools that make 'em. I am the Zigler Higher-Speed Tool and Lathe Trust. The Trust, sir, is entirely my own – in my own inventions. I am the Renzalaer ten-cylinder aerial – the lightest aeroplane-engine on the market

– one price, one power, one guarantee. I am the Orlebar Paperwelt, Pulp-panel Company for aeroplane bodies; and I am the Rush Silencer for military aeroplanes – absolutely silent – which the Continent leases under royalty. With three exceptions, the British aren't wise to it yet. That's all I represent at present. You saw me take off my hat to your late Queen? I owe every cent I have to that great an' good Lady. Yes, sir, I came out of Africa, after my eighteen months' rest-cure and open-air treatment and sea-bathing, as her prisoner of war, like a giant refreshed. There wasn't anything could hold me, when I'd got my hooks into it, after that experience. And to you as a representative British citizen, I say here and now that I regard you as the founder of the family fortune – Tommy's and mine.'

'But I only gave you some papers and tobacco.'

'What more does any citizen need? The Cullinan diamond[2] wouldn't have helped me as much then; an' – talking about South Africa, tell me –'

We talked about South Africa till the car stopped at the Georgian lodge of a great park.

'We'll get out here. I want to show you a rather sightly view,' said Zigler.

We walked, perhaps, half a mile, across timber-dotted turf, past a lake, entered a dark rhododendron-planted wood, ticking with the noise of pheasants' feet, and came out suddenly, where five rides met, at a small classic temple between lichened stucco statues which faced a circle of turf, several acres in extent. Irish yews, of a size that I had never seen before, walled the sunless circle like cliffs of riven obsidian, except at the lower end, where it gave on to a stretch of undulating bare ground ending in a timbered slope half-a-mile away.

'That's where the old Marshalton race-course used to be,' said Zigler. 'That ice-house is called Flora's Temple. Nell Gwynne and Mrs Siddons an' Taglioni[3] an' all that crowd used to act plays here for King George the Third. Wasn't it? Well, George is the only king I play. Let it go at that. This circle was the stage, I guess. The kings an' the nobility sat in Flora's Temple. I forget who sculped these statues at the door. They're the Comic and Tragic Muse. But it's a sightly view, ain't it?'

The sunlight was leaving the park. I caught a glint of silver to the southward beyond the wooden ridge.

'That's the ocean – the Channel, I mean,' said Zigler. 'It's twenty-three miles as a man flies. A sightly view, ain't it?'

I looked at the severe yews, the dumb yelling mouths of the two statues, at the blue-green shadows on the unsunned grass, and at the still bright plain in front where some deer were feeding.

'It's a most dramatic contrast, but I think it would be better on a summer's day,' I said, and we went on, up one of the noiseless rides, a quarter of a mile at least, till we came to the porticoed front of an enormous Georgian pile. Four footmen revealed themselves in a hall hung with pictures.

'I hired this off of my Lord Marshalton,' Zigler explained, while they helped us out of our coats under the severe eyes of ruffed and periwigged ancestors. 'Ya-as. They always look at *me* too, as if I'd blown in from the gutter. Which, of course, I have. That's Mary, Lady Marshalton. Old man Joshua [4] painted her. Do you see any likeness to my Lord Marshalton? Why, haven't you ever met up with him? He was Captain Mankeltow – my Royal British Artillery captain that blew up my gun in the war, an' then tried to bury me against my religious principles. Ya-as. His father died and he got the lordship. That was about all he got by the time that your British death-duties were through with him. So he said I'd oblige him by hiring his ranch. It's a hell an' a half of a proposition to handle, but Tommy – Mrs Laughton – understands it. Come right in to the parlour and be very welcome.'

He guided me, hand on shoulder, into a babble of high-pitched talk and laughter that filled a vast drawing-room. He introduced me as the founder of the family fortunes to a little, lithe, dark-eyed woman whose speech and greeting were of the soft-lipped South. She in turn presented me to her mother, a black-browed, snowy-haired old lady with a cap of priceless Venetian point [5] hands that must have held many hearts in their time, and a dignity as unquestioned and unquestioning as an empress. She was, indeed, a Burton of Savannah, who, on their own ground, out-rank the Lees of Virginia. The rest of the company came from Buffalo, Cincinnati, Cleveland and Chicago, with here and there a softening southern strain. A party of young folk popped corn beneath a mantelpiece surmounted by a Gainsborough. Two portly men, half hidden by a cased harp, discussed, over sheaves of type-written documents, the terms of some contract. A knot of matrons talked servants – Irish *versus* German – across the grand piano. A youth ravaged an old bookcase, while beside him a tall girl stared at the portrait of a woman of many loves, dead three hundred years, but now leaping to life and warning under the shaded frame-light. In a corner half-a-dozen girls examined the glazed tables that held the decorations – English and foreign – of the late Lord Marshalton.

'See heah! Would this be the Ordeh of the Gyartah?' one said, pointing.

'I presoom likely. No! The Garter has "*Honey swore*" [6] –I know that much. This is "*Tria juncta*" [7] something.'

'Oh, what's that cunning little copper cross [8] with "For Valurr"?' a third cried.

'Say! Look at here!' said the young man at the bookcase. 'Here's a first edition of *Handley Cross* [9] and a Beewick's *Birds* [10] right next to it – just like so many best sellers. Look, Maidie!'

The girl beneath the picture half turned her body but not her eyes.

'You don't tell *me*!' she said slowly. 'Their women amounted to something after all.'

'But Woman's scope and outlook was vurry limmutted in those days,' one of the matrons put in, from the piano.

'Limutted? For *her*? If they whurr, I guess she was the limmut. Who was she? Peters, whurr's the cat'log?'

A thin butler, in charge of two footmen removing the tea-batteries, slid to a table and handed her a blue-and-gilt book. He was buttonholed by one of the men behind the harp, who wished to get a telephone call through to Edinburgh.

'The local office shuts at six,' said Peters. 'But I can get through to' – he named some town – 'in ten minutes, sir.'

'That suits me. You'll find me here when you've hitched up. Oh, say, Peters! We – Mister Olpherts an' me – ain't goin' by that early morning train tomorrow – but the other one – on the other line – whatever they call it.'

'The nine twenty-seven, sir. Yes, sir. Early breakfast will be at half-past eight and the car will be at the door at nine.'

'Peters!' an imperious young voice called. 'What's the matteh with Lord Marshalton's Ordeh of the Gyartah? We cyan't find it anywheah.'

'Well, miss, I *have* heard that that Order is usually returned to His Majesty on the death of the holder. Yes, miss.' Then in a whisper to a footman, 'More butter for the pop-corn in King Charles's Corner.' He stopped behind my chair. 'Your room is Number Eleven, sir. May I trouble you for your keys?'

He left the room with a six-year-old maiden called Alice who had announced she would not go to bed. ''less Peter, Peter, Punkin-eater takes me – so there!'

He very kindly looked in on me for a moment as I was dressing for dinner. 'Not at all, sir,' he replied to some compliment I paid him. 'I valeted the late Lord Marshalton for fifteen years. He was very abrupt in his movements, sir. As a rule I never received more than an hour's notice of a journey. We used to go to Syria frequently. I have been twice to Babylon. Mr and Mrs Zigler's requirements are, comparatively speaking, few.'

'But the guests?'

'Very little out of the ordinary as soon as one knows their ordinaries. Extremely simple, if I may say so, sir.'

I had the privilege of taking Mrs Burton in to dinner, and was rewarded with an entirely new, and to me rather shocking, view of Abraham Lincoln, who, she said, had wasted the heritage of his land by blood and fire, and had surrendered the remnant to aliens. 'My brother, suh,' she said, 'fell at Gettysburg in order that Armenians should colonize New England today. If I took any interest in any dam-Yankee outside of my son-in-law Laughton yondah, I should say that my brother's death had been amply avenged.'

The man at her right took up the challenge, and the war spread. Her eyes twinkled over the flames she had lit.

'Don't these folk,' she said a little later, 'remind you of Arabs picnicking under the Pyramids?'

'I've never seen the Pyramids,' I replied.

'Hm! I didn't know you were as English as all that.' And when I laughed, 'Are you?'

'Always. It saves trouble.'

'Now that's just what I find so significant among the English' – this was Alice's mother, I think, with one elbow well forward among the salted almonds. 'Oh, I know how *you* feel, Madam Burton, but a Northerner like myself – I'm Buffalo – even though we come over every year – notices the desire for comfort in England. There's so little conflict or uplift in British society.'

'But we like being comfortable,' I said.

'I know it. It's very characteristic. But ain't it a little, just a little, lacking in adaptability an' imagination?'

'They haven't any need for adaptability,' Madam Burton struck in. 'They haven't any Ellis Island [11] standards to live up to.'

'But we can assimilate,' the Buffalo woman charged on.

'Now you *have* done it!' I whispered to the old lady as the blessed word 'assimilation' woke up all the old arguments for and against.

There was not a dull moment in that dinner for me – nor afterwards when the boys and girls at the piano played the rag-time tunes of their own land, while their elders, inexhaustibly interested, replunged into the discussion of that land's future, till there was talk of coon-can. [12] When all the company had been set to tables Zigler led me into his book-lined study, where I noticed he kept his golf-clubs, and spoke simply as a child, gravely as a bishop, of the years that were past since our last meeting . . .

'That's about all, I guess – up to date,' he said when he had unrolled the bright map of his fortunes across three continents. 'Bein' rich suits me. So does your country, sir. My own country? You heard what that Detroit man said at dinner. "A Government of the alien, by the alien, for the alien." [13] Mother's right, too. Lincoln killed us. From the highest motives – but he killed us. Oh, say, that reminds me. 'J'ever kill a man from the highest motives?'

'Not from any motive – as far as I remember.'

'Well, I have. It don't weigh on my mind any, but it was interesting. Life *is* interesting for a rich – for any – man in England. Ya-as! Life in England is like settin' in the front row at the theatre and never knowin' when the whole blame drama won't spill itself into your lap. I didn't always know that. I lie abed now, and I blush to think of some of the breaks I made in South Africa. About the British. Not your official method of doin' business. But the Spirit. I was 'way, 'way off on the Spirit. Are you acquainted with any other country where you'd have to kill a man or two to get at the National Spirit?'

'Well,' I answered, 'next to marrying one of its women, killing one of its men makes for pretty close intimacy with any country. I take it you killed a British citizen.'

'Why, no. Our syndicate confined its operations to aliens – damn-fool aliens ... 'J'ever know an English lord called Lundie?[14] Looks like a frame-food and soap advertisement. I imagine he was in your Supreme Court before he came into his lordship.'

'He is a lawyer – what we call a Law Lord – a Judge of Appeal – not a real hereditary lord.'

'That's as much beyond me as *this*!' Zigler slapped a fat Debrett[15] on the table. 'But I presoom this unreal Law Lord Lundie is kind o' real in his decisions? I judged so. And – one more question. 'Ever meet a man called Walen?'

'D'you mean Burton-Walen, the editor of —' I mentioned the journal.

'That's him. 'Looks like a tough, talks like a Maxim, and trains with kings.'

'He does,' I said. 'Burton-Walen knows all the crowned heads of Europe intimately. It's his hobby.'

'Well, there's the whole outfit for you – exceptin' my Lord Marshalton, *né* Mankeltow, an' me. All active murderers – specially the Law Lords – or accessories after the fact. And what do they hand you out for *that*, in this country?'

'Twenty years, I believe,' was my reply.

He reflected a moment.

'No-o-o,' he said, and followed it with a smoke-ring. 'Twenty months at the Cape is my limit. Say, murder ain't the soul-shatterin' event those nature-fakers in the magazines make out. It develops naturally like any other proposition ... Say, 'j'ever play this golf game? It's come up in the States from Maine to California, an' we're prodoocin' all the champions in sight. Not a business man's play, but interestin'. I've got a golf-links in the park there that they tell me is the finest inland course ever. I had to pay extra for that when I hired the ranche – last year. It was just before I signed the papers that our murder eventuated. My Lord Marshalton he asked me down for the weekend to fix up something or other – about Peters and the linen, I think 'twas. Mrs Zigler took a holt of the proposition. She understood Peters from the word "go". There wasn't any house-party; only fifteen or twenty folk. A full house is thirty-two, Tommy tells me. 'Guess we must be near on that tonight. In the smoking-room here, my Lord Marshalton – Mankeltow that was – introduces me to this Walen man with the nose. He'd been in the War too, from start to finish. He knew all the columns and generals that I'd battled with in the days of my Zigler gun. We kinder fell into each other's arms an' let the harsh world go by for a while.

'Walen he introduces me to your Lord Lundie. *He* was a new proposition to me. If he hadn't been a lawyer he'd have made a lovely cattle-king. I thought I had played poker some. Another of my breaks. Ya-as! It cost me eleven hundred dollars besides what Tommy said when I retired. I have no fault to find with your hereditary aristocracy, or your judiciary, or your press.

'Sunday we all went to Church across the Park here . . . Psha! Think o' your rememberin' my religion! I've become an Episcopalian since I married. Ya-as . . . After lunch Walen did his crowned-heads-of-Europe stunt in the smokin'-room here. He was long on Kings. And Continental crises. I do not pretend to follow British domestic politics, but in the aeroplane business a man has to know something of international possibilities. At present, you British are settin' in kimonoes on dynamite kegs. Walen's talk put me wise on the location and size of some of the kegs. Ya-as!

'After that, we four went out to look at those golf-links I was hirin'. We each took a club. Mine' – he glanced at a great tan bag by the fire-place – 'was the beginner's friend – the cleek.[16] Well, sir, this golf proposition took a holt of me as quick as – quick as death. They had to prise me off the greens when it got too dark to see, and then we went back to the house. I was walkin' ahead with my Lord Marshalton talkin' beginners' golf.

(*I* was the man who ought to have been killed by rights.) We cut 'cross lots through the woods to Flora's Temple — that place I showed you this afternoon. Lundie and Walen were, maybe, twenty or thirty rod [17] behind us in the dark. Marshalton and I stopped at the theatre to admire at the ancestral yew-trees. He took me right under the biggest — King Somebody's Yew — and while I was spannin' it with my handkerchief, he says, "Look heah!" just as if it was a rabbit — and down comes a bi-plane into the theatre with no more noise than the dead. My Rush Silencer is the only one on the market that allows that sort of gumshoe work . . . What? A bi-plane — with two men in it. Both men jump out and start fussin' with the engines. I was starting to tell Mankeltow — I can't remember to call him Marshalton any more — that it looked as if the Royal British Flying Corps had got on to my Rush Silencer at last; but he steps out from under the yew to these two Stealthy Steves and says, "What's the trouble? Can I be of any service?" He thought — so did I — 'twas some of the boys from Aldershot or Salisbury. Well, sir, from there on, the situation developed like a motion-picture in Hell. The man on the nigh side of the machine whirls round, pulls his gun and fires into Mankeltow's face. I laid him out with my cleek automatically. Any one who shoots a friend of mine gets what's comin' to him if I'm within reach. He drops. Mankeltow rubs his neck with his handkerchief. The man the far side of the machine starts to run. Lundie down the ride, or it might have been Walen, shouts, "What's happened?" Mankeltow says, "Collar that chap."

'The second man runs ring-a-ring-o'-roses round the machine, one hand reachin' behind him. Mankeltow heads him off to me. He breaks blind for Walen and Lundie, who are runnin' up the ride. There's some sort of mix-up among 'em, which it's too dark to see, and a thud. Walen says, "Oh, well collared!" Lundie says, "That's the only thing I never learned at Harrow!" . . . Mankeltow runs up to 'em, still rubbin' his neck, and says, "*He* didn't fire at me. It was the other chap. Where is he?"

'"I've stretched him alongside his machine," I says.

'"Are they poachers?" says Lundie.

'"No. Airmen. I can't make it out," says Mankeltow.

'"Look at here," says Walen, kind of brusque. "This man ain't breathin' at all. Didn't you hear somethin' crack when he lit, Lundie?"

'"My God!" says Lundie. "Did I? I thought it was my suspenders" – no, he said "braces".

'Right there I left them and sort o' tip-toed back to my man, hopin' he'd revived and quit. But he hadn't. That darned cleek had hit him on the back of the neck just where his helmet stopped. He'd got *his*. I knew it by the way the head rolled in my hands. Then the others came up the ride totin' *their* load. No mistakin' that shuffle on grass. D'you remember it – in South Africa? Ya-as.

'"Hsh!" says Lundie. "Do you know I've broken this man's neck?"

'"Same here," I says.

'"What? Both?" says Mankeltow.

'"Nonsense!" says Lord Lundie. "Who'd have thought he was that out of training? A man oughtn't to fly if he ain't fit."

'"What did they want here, anyway?" said Walen; and Mankeltow says, "We can't leave them in the open. Someone'll come. Carry 'em to Flora's Temple."

'We toted 'em again and laid 'em out on a stone bench. They was still dead in spite of our best attentions. We knew it, but we went through the motions till it was quite dark. 'Wonder if all murderers do that? "We want a light on this," says Walen after a spell. "There ought to be one in the machine. Why didn't they light it?"

'We come out of Flora's Temple, and shut the doors behind us. Some stars were showing then – same as when Cain did his little act, I guess. I climbed up and searched the machine. She was very well equipped. I found two electric torches in clips alongside her barometers by the rear seat.

'"What make is she?" says Mankeltow.

'"Continental Renzalaer," I says. "My engines and my Rush Silencer."

'Walen whistles. "Here – let me look," he says, and grabs the other torch. She was sure well equipped. We gathered up an armful of cameras an' maps an' note-books an' an album of mounted photographs which we took to Flora's Temple and spread on a marble-topped table (I'll show you tomorrow) which the King of Naples had presented to grandfather Marshalton. Walen starts to go through 'em. We wanted to know why our friends had been so prejudiced against our society.

'"Wait a minute," says Lord Lundie. "Lend me a hand-kerchief."

'He pulls out his own, and Walen contributes his green-and-red bandanna, and Lundie covers their faces. "Now," he says, "we'll go into the evidence."

'There wasn't any flaw in that evidence. Walen read out their last observations, and Mankeltow asked questions, and Lord Lundie sort o' summarized, and I looked at the photos in the album. 'J'ever see a bird's-eye telephoto-survey of England for military purposes? It's interestin' but indecent – like turnin' a man upside down. None of those close-range panoramas of forts could have been taken without my Rush Silencer.

'"I wish *we* was as thorough as they are," says Mankeltow, when Walen stopped translatin'.

'"We've been thorough enough," says Lord Lundie. "The evidence against both accused is conclusive. Any other country would give 'em seven years in a fortress. We should probably give 'em eighteen months as first-class misdemeanants. But their case," he says, "is out of our hands. We must review our own. Mr Zigler," he said, "will you tell us what steps you took to bring about the death of the first accused?" I told him. He wanted to know specially whether I'd stretched first accused before or after he had fired at Mankeltow. Mankeltow testified he'd been shot at, and exhibited his neck as evidence. It was scorched.

'"Now, Mr Walen," says Lord Lundie. "Will you kindly tell us what steps you took with regard to the second accused?"

'"The man ran directly at me, me lord," says Walen. "I said, 'Oh no, you don't,' and hit him in the face."

'Lord Lundie lifts one hand and uncovers second accused's face. There was a bruise on one cheek and the chin was all greened with grass. He was a heavy-built man.

'"What happened after that?" says Lord Lundie.

'"To the best of my remembrance he turned from me towards your lordship."

'Then Lundie goes ahead. "I stooped, and caught the man round the ankles," he says. "The sudden check threw him partially over my left shoulder. I jerked him off that shoulder, still holding his ankles, and he fell heavily on, it would appear, the point of his chin, death being instantaneous."

'"Death being instantaneous," says Walen.

'Lord Lundie takes off his gown and wig — you could see him do it — and becomes our fellow-murderer. "That's our case," he says. "I know how *I* should direct the jury, but it's an undignified business for a Lord of Appeal to lift his hand to, and some of my learned brothers," he says, "might be disposed to be facetious."

'I guess I can't be properly sensitized. Any one who steered me out of that trouble might have had the laugh on me for generations. But I'm only a millionaire. I said we'd better search second accused in case he'd been carryin' concealed weapons.

'"That certainly is a point," says Lord Lundie. "But the question for the jury would be whether I exercised more force than was necessary to prevent him from usin' them." *I* didn't say anything. He wasn't talkin' my language. Second accused had his gun on him sure enough, but it had jammed in his hip-pocket. He was too fleshy to reach behind for business purposes, and he didn't look a gun-man anyway. Both of 'em carried wads of private letters. By the time Walen had translated, we knew how many children the fat one had at home and when the thin one reckoned to be married. Too bad! Ya-as.

'Says Walen to me while we was rebuttonin' their jackets (they was not in uniform): "Ever read a book called *The Wreckers*,[18] Mr Zigler?"

'"Not that I recall at the present moment," I says.

'"Well, do," he says. "You'd appreciate it. You'd appreciate it now, I assure you."

'"I'll remember," I says. "But I don't see how this song and dance helps us any. Here's our corpses, here's their machine, and daylight's bound to come."

'"Heavens! That reminds me," says Lundie. "What time's dinner?"

'"Half-past eight," says Mankeltow "It's half-past five now. We knocked off golf at twenty to, and if they hadn't been such silly asses, firin' pistols like civilians, we'd have had them to dinner. Why, they might be sitting with us in the smoking-room this very minute," he says. Then he said that no man had a right to take his profession so seriously as these two mounte-banks.

'"How interestin'!" says Lundie. "I've noticed this impatient attitude toward their victim in a good many murderers. I never understood it before. Of course, it's the disposal of the body that annoys 'em. Now, I wonder," he says, "who our case will come up before? Let's run through it again."

'Then Walen whirls in. He'd been bitin' his nails in a corner. We was all nerved up by now . . . Me? The worst of the bunch. I had to think for Tommy as well.

'"We *can't* be tried," says Walen. "We *mustn't* be tried! It'll make an infernal international stink. What did I tell you in the smoking-room after lunch? The tension's at breaking-point already. This 'ud snap it. Can't you see that?"

'"I was thinking of the legal aspect of the case," says Lundie. "With a good jury we'd likely be acquitted."

'"Acquitted!" says Walen. "Who'd dare acquit us in the face of what 'ud be demanded by – the other party? Did you ever hear of the War of Jenkins' ear?[19] 'Ever hear of Mason and Slidell?[20] 'Ever hear of an ultimatum? You know who *these* two idiots are; you know who *we* are – a Lord of Appeal, a Viscount of the English peerage, and me – *me* knowing all I know, which the men who know dam' well know that I *do* know! It's our necks or Armageddon. Which do you think this Government would choose? We *can't* be tried!" he says.

'"Then I expect I'll have to resign me club," Lundie goes on. "I don't think that's ever been done before by an *ex-officio* member. I must ask the secretary." I guess he was kinder bunkered for the minute, or maybe 'twas the lordship comin' out on him.

'"Rot!" says Mankeltow. "Walen's right. We can't afford to be tried. We'll have to bury them; but my head-gardener locks up all the tools at five o'clock."

'"Not on your life!" says Lundie. He was on deck again – as the high-class lawyer. "Right or wrong, if we attempt con-cealment of the bodies we're done for."

'"I'm glad of that," says Mankeltow, "because, after all, it ain't cricket to bury 'em."

'Somehow – but I know I ain't English – that consideration didn't worry me as it ought. An' besides, I was thinkin' – I had to – an' I'd begun to see a light 'way off – a little glimmerin' light o' salvation.

'"Then what *are* we to do?" says Walen. "Zigler, what do you advise? Your neck's in it too."

'"Gentlemen," I says, "something Lord Lundie let fall a while back gives me an idea. I move that this committee empowers Big Claus and Little Claus, who have elected to commit suicide in our midst, to leave the premises *as* they came. I'm asking you to take big chances," I says, "but they're all we've got," and then I broke for the bi-plane.

'Don't tell me the English can't think as quick as the next man when it's up to them! They lifted 'em out o' Flora's Temple – reverent, but not wastin' time – whilst I found out what had brought her down. One cylinder was misfirin'. I didn't stop to fix it. My Renzalaer will hold up on six. We've proved that. If her crew had relied on my guarantees, they'd had been halfway home by then, instead of takin' their seats with hangin' heads like they was ashamed. They ought to have been ashamed too, playin' gun-men in a British peer's park! I took big chances startin' her without controls, but 'twas a dead still night an' a clear run – you saw it – across the Theatre into the park, and I prayed she'd rise before she hit high timber. I set her all I dared for a quick lift. I told Mankeltow that if I gave her too much nose she'd be liable to up-end and flop. He didn't want another inquest on his estate. No, sir! So I had to fix her up in the dark. Ya-as!

'I took big chances, too, while those other three held on to her and I worked her up to full power. My Renzalaer's no ventilation-fan to pull against. But I climbed out just in time. I'd hitched the signallin' lamp to her tail so's we could track her. Otherwise, with my Rush Silencer, we might's well have shooed an owl out of a barn. She left just that way when we let her go. No sound except the propellers – *Whoo-oo-oo! Whoo-oo-oo!* There was a dip in the ground ahead. It hid her lamp for a second – but there's no such thing as time in real life. Then that lamp travelled up the far slope slow – too slow. Then it kinder lifted, we judged. Then it sure was liftin'. Then it lifted good. D'you know why? Our four naked perspirin' souls was out there underneath her, hikin' her heavens high. Yes, sir. *We* did it! . . . And that lamp kept liftin' and liftin'. Then she side-slipped! My God, she side-slipped twice, which was what I'd been afraid of all along! Then she straightened up, and went away climbin' to glory, for that blessed star of our hope got smaller and smaller till we couldn't track it any more. Then we breathed. We hadn't breathed any since their arrival, but we didn't know it till we breathed that time – all together. Then we dug our finger-nails out of our palms an' came alive again – in instalments.

'Lundie spoke first. "We therefore commit their bodies to the air," he says, an' puts his cap on.

'"The deep – the deep," says Walen. "It's just twenty-three miles to the Channel."

'"Poor chaps! Poor chaps!" says Mankeltow. "We'd have had 'em to dinner if they hadn't lost their heads. I can't tell you how this distresses me, Laughton."

'"Well, look at here, Arthur," I says. "It's only God's Own Mercy you an' me ain't lyin' in Flora's Temple now, and if that fat man had known enough to fetch his gun around while he was runnin', Lord Lundie and Walen would have been alongside us."

'"I see that," he says. "But we're alive and they're dead, don't ye know."

'"I know it," I says. "That's where the dead are always so damned unfair on the survivors."

'"I see that too," he says. "But I'd have given a good deal if it hadn't happened, poor chaps!"

'"Amen!" says Lundie. Then? Oh, then we sorter walked back two an' two to Flora's Temple an' lit matches to see we hadn't left anything behind. Walen, he had confiscated the note-books before they left. There was the first man's pistol, which we'd forgot to return him, lyin' on the stone bench. Mankeltow puts his hand on it – he never touched the trigger – an', bein' an automatic, of course the blame thing jarred off – spiteful as a rattler!

'"Look out! They'll have one of us yet," says Walen in the dark. But they didn't – the Lord hadn't quit being our shepherd – and we heard the bullet zip across the veldt – quite like old times. Ya-as!

'"Swine!" says Mankeltow.

'After that I didn't hear any more "Poor chap" talk . . . Me? I never worried about killing *my* man. I was too busy figurin' how a British jury might regard the proposition. I guess Lundie felt that way too.

'Oh, but say! We had an interestin' time at dinner. Folks was expected whose auto had hung up on the road. They hadn't wired, and Peters had laid two extra places. We noticed 'em as soon as we sat down. I'd hate to say how noticeable they were. Mankeltow with his neck bandaged (he'd caught a relaxed throat golfin') sent for Peters and told him to take those empty places away – *if you please*. It takes something to rattle Peters. He was rattled that time. Nobody else noticed anything. And now . . .'

'Where did they come down?' I asked, as he rose.

'In the Channel, I guess. There was nothing in the papers about 'em. Shall we go into the drawin'-room, and see what these boys and girls are doin'? But say, ain't life in England inter*e*stin'?'

Rebirth

If any God should say
    'I will restore
The world her yesterday
    Whole as before
My Judgment blasted it' – who would not lift
Heart, eye, and hand in passion o'er the gift?

If any God should will
    To wipe from mind
The memory of this ill
    Which is mankind
In soul and substance now – who would not bless
Even to tears His loving-tenderness?

If any God should give
    Us leave to fly
These present deaths we live,
    And safely die
In those lost lives we lived ere we were born –
What man but would not laugh the excuse to scorn?

For we are what we are –
    So broke to blood
And the strict works of war –
    So long subdued
To sacrifice, that threadbare Death commands
Hardly observance at our busier hands.

Yet we were what we were,
    And, fashioned so,
It pleases us to stare
    At the far show
Of unbelievable years and shapes that flit,
In our own likeness, on the edge of it.

THE HORSE MARINES

The Horse Marines

(1911)

The Rt. Hon. R. B. Haldane, Secretary of State for War, was questioned in the House of Commons on April 8th about the rocking-horses which the War Office is using for the purpose of teaching recruits to ride. Lord Ronaldshay asked the War Secretary if rocking-horses were to be supplied to all the cavalry regiments for teaching recruits to ride. 'The noble Lord,' replied Mr Haldane, 'is doubtless alluding to certain dummy horses on rockers which have been tested with very satisfactory results' . . . The mechanical steed is a wooden horse with an astonishing tail. It is painted brown and mounted on swinging rails. The recruit leaps into the saddle and pulls at the reins while the riding-instructor rocks the animal to and fro with his foot. The rocking-horses are being made at Woolwich. They are quite cheap.

Daily Paper

My instructions to Mr Leggatt, my engineer, had been accurately obeyed. He was to bring my car on completion of annual overhaul, from Coventry *via* London, to Southampton Docks to await my arrival; and very pretty she looked, under the steamer's side among the railway lines, at six in the morning. Next to her new paint and varnish I was most impressed by her four brand-new tyres.

'But I didn't order new tyres,' I said as we moved away. 'These are Irresilients, too.'

'Treble-ribbed,' said Leggatt. 'Diamond-stud sheathing.'

'Then there has been a mistake.'

'Oh no, sir; they're gratis.'

The number of motor manufacturers who give away complete sets of treble-ribbed Irresilient tyres is so limited that I believe I asked Leggatt for an explanation.

'I don't know that I could very well explain, sir,' was the answer. 'It 'ud come better from Mr Pyecroft.[1] He's on leaf at

251

Portsmouth – staying with his uncle. His uncle 'ad the body all night. I'd defy you to find a scratch on her even with a microscope.'

'Then we will go home by the Portsmouth road,' I said.

And we went at those speeds which are allowed before the working-day begins or the police are thawed out. We were blocked near Portsmouth by a battalion of Regulars on the move.

'Whitsuntide manoeuvres just ending,' said Leggatt. 'They've had a fortnight in the Downs.'

He said no more until we were in a narrow street somewhere behind Portsmouth Town Railway Station, where he slowed at a green-grocery shop. The door was open, and a small old man sat on three potato-baskets swinging his feet over a stooping blue back.

'You call that shinin' 'em?' he piped. 'Can you see your face in 'em yet? No! Then shine 'em, or I'll give you a beltin' you'll remember!'

'If you stop kickin' me in the mouth perhaps I'd do better,' said Pyecroft's voice meekly.

We blew the horn.

Pyecroft arose, put away the brushes, and received us not otherwise than as a king in his own country.

'Are you going to leave me up here all day?' said the old man.

Pyecroft lifted him down and he hobbled into the back room.

'It's his corns,' Pyecroft explained. 'You can't shine corny feet – and he hasn't had his breakfast.'

'I haven't had mine either,' I said.

'Breakfast for two more, uncle,' Pyecroft sang out.

'Go out an' buy it then,' was the answer, 'or else it's half-rations.'

Pyecroft turned to Leggatt, gave him his marketing orders, and dispatched him with the coppers.

'I have got four new tyres on my car,' I began impressively.

'Yes,' said Mr Pyecroft. 'You have, and I *will* say' – he patted my car's bonnet – 'you earned 'em.'

'I want to know why –' I went on.

'Quite justifiable. You haven't noticed anything in the papers, have you?'

'I've only just landed. I haven't seen a paper for weeks.'

'Then you can lend me a virgin ear. There's been a scandal in the Junior Service – the Army, I believe they call 'em.'

A bag of coffee-beans pitched on the counter. 'Roast that,' said the uncle from within.

Pyecroft rigged a small coffee-roaster, while I took down the shutters, and sold a young lady in curl-papers two bunches of mixed greens and one soft orange.

'Sickly stuff to handle on an empty stomach, ain't it?' said Pyecroft.

'What about my new tyres?' I insisted.

'Oh, any amount. But the question is' – he looked at me steadily – 'is this what you might call a court-martial or a post-mortem inquiry?'

'Strictly a post-mortem,' said I.

'That being so,' said Pyecroft, 'we can rapidly arrive at facts. Last Thursday – the shutters go behind those baskets – last Thursday at five bells in the forenoon watch, otherwise ten-thirty a.m., your Mr Leggatt was discovered on Westminster Bridge laying his course for the Old Kent Road.'

'But that doesn't lead to Southampton,' I interrupted.

'Then perhaps he was swinging the car for compasses. Be that as it may, we found him in that latitude, simultaneous as Jules and me was *ong route*[2] for Waterloo to rejoin our respective ships – or Navies I should say. Jules was a *permissionaire*,[3] which meant being on leave, same as me, from a French cassowary-cruiser[4] at Portsmouth. A party of her trusty and well-beloved petty officers 'ad been seeing London, chaperoned by the RC chaplain. Jules 'ad detached himself from the squadron and was cruisin' on his own when I joined him, in company of copious lady-friends. *But*, mark you, your Mr Leggatt drew the line at the girls. Loud and long he drew it.'

'I'm glad of that,' I said.

'You may be. He adopted the puristical formation from the first. "Yes," he said, when we was annealing him at – but you wouldn't know the pub – "I *am* going to Southampton," he says, "and I'll stretch a point to go *via* Portsmouth; *but*," says he, "seeing what sort of one hell of a time invariably trarnspires when we cruise together, Mr Pyecroft, I do *not* feel myself

253

justified towards my generous and long-suffering employer in takin' on that kind of ballast as well." I assure you he considered your interests.'

'And the girls?' I asked.

'Oh, I left that to Jules. I'm a monogomite by nature. So we embarked strictly *ong garçong*.[5] But I should tell you, in case he didn't, that your Mr Leggatt's care for your interests 'ad extended to sheathing the car in matting and gunny-bags to preserve her paint-work. She was all swathed up like an Italian baby.'

'He *is* careful about his paint-work,' I said.

'For a man with no Service experience I should say he was fair homicidal on the subject. If we'd been Marines he couldn't have been more pointed in his allusions to our hob-nailed socks. However, we reduced him to a malleable condition, and embarked for Portsmouth. I'd seldom rejoined my *vaisseau ong automobile, avec*[6] a fur coat and goggles. Nor 'ad Jules.'

'Did Jules say much?' I asked, helplessly turning the handle of the coffee-roaster.

'That's where I pitied the pore beggar. He 'adn't the language, so to speak. He was confined to heavings and shruggin's and copious *Mong Jews*![7] The French are very badly fitted with relief-valves. And then our Mr Leggatt drove. He drove.'

'Was he in a very malleable condition?'

'Not him! We recognized the value of his cargo from the outset. He hadn't a chance to get more than moist at the edges. After which we went to sleep; and now we'll go to breakfast.'

We entered the back room where everything was in order, and a screeching canary made us welcome. The uncle had added sausages and piles of buttered toast to the kippers. The coffee, cleared with a piece of fish-skin, was a revelation.

Leggatt, who seemed to know the premises, had run the car into the tiny backyard where her mirror-like back almost blocked up the windows. He minded shop while we ate. Pyecroft passed him his rations through a flap in the door. The uncle ordered him in, after breakfast, to wash up, and he jumped in his gaiters at the old man's commands as he has never jumped to mine.

'To resoom the post-mortem,' said Pyecroft, lighting his

pipe. 'My slumbers were broken by the propeller ceasing to revolve, and by vile language from your Mr Leggatt.'

'I – I –' Leggatt began, a blue-checked duster in one hand and a cup in the other.

'When you're wanted aft you'll be sent for, Mr Leggatt,' said Pyecroft amiably. 'It's clean mess decks for you now. Resooming once more, we was on a lonely and desolate ocean near Portsdown, surrounded by gorse bushes, and a Boy Scout was stirring my stomach with his little copper-stick.'

'"You count ten," he says.

'"Very good, Boy Jones," I says, "count 'em," and I hauled him in over the gunnel, and ten I gave him with my large flat hand. The remarks he passed, lying face down tryin' to bite my leg, would have reflected credit on any Service. Having finished I dropped him overboard again, which was my gross political error. I ought to 'ave killed him; because he began signalling – rapid and accurate – in a sou' westerly direction. Few equatorial calms are to be apprehended when BP's little pets [8] take to signallin'. Make a note o' that! Three minutes later we were stopped and boarded by Scouts up our backs, down our necks, and in our boots! The last I heard from your Mr Leggatt as he went under, brushin' 'em off his cap, was thanking Heaven he'd covered up the new paint-work with mats. An 'eroic soul!'

'Not a scratch on her body,' said Leggatt, pouring out the coffee-grounds.

'And Jules?' said I.

'Oh, Jules thought the much advertised Social Revolution had begun, but his mackintosh hampered him.'

'You told me to bring the mackintosh,' Leggatt whispered to me.

'And when I 'ad 'em half convinced he was a French vicomte coming down to visit the Commander-in-Chief at Portsmouth, he tried to take it off. Seeing his uniform underneath, some sucking Sherlock Holmes of the Pink Eye Patrol (they called him Eddy) deduced that I wasn't speaking the truth. Eddy said I was tryin' to sneak into Portsmouth unobserved – unobserved mark you! – and join hands with the enemy. It trarnspired that the Scouts was conducting a field-day against opposin' forces, ably assisted by all branches of the Service, and they was so afraid the car wouldn't count ten points to them in the fray, that they'd have scalped us, but for the intervention of an umpire – also in short under-drawers. A fleshy sight!'

Here Mr Pyecroft shut his eyes and nodded. 'That umpire,' he said suddenly, 'was our Mr Morshed – a gentleman whose acquaintance you have already made *and* profited by, if I mistake not.'[9]

'Oh, was the Navy in it too?' I said; for I had read of wild doings occasionally among the Boy Scouts on the Portsmouth Road, in which Navy, Army, and the world at large seemed to have taken part.

'The Navy *was* in it. I was the only one out of it – for several seconds. Our Mr Morshed failed to recognize me in my fur boa, and my appealin' winks at 'im behind your goggles didn't arrive. But when Eddy darling had told his story, I saluted, which is difficult in furs, and I stated I was bringin' him dispatches from the North. My Mr Morshed cohered on the instant. I've never known his ethergram installations out of order yet. "Go and guard your blessed road," he says to the Fratton Orphan Asylum standing at attention all round him, and, when they was removed – "Pyecroft," he says, still *sotte voce*, "what in Hong-Kong are you doing with this dun-coloured *sampan*?"[10]

'It was your Mr Leggatt's paint-protective matting which caught his eye. She *did* resemble a *sampan*, especially about the stern-works. At these remarks I naturally threw myself on 'is bosom, so far as Service conditions permitted, and revealed him all, mentioning that the car was yours. You know his way of working his lips like a rabbit? Yes, he was quite pleased. "*His* car!" he kept murmuring, working his lips like a rabbit. "I owe 'im more than a trifle for things he wrote about me. I'll keep the car."

'Your Mr Leggatt now injected some semi-mutinous remarks to the effect that he was your chauffeur in charge of your car, and, as such, capable of so acting. Mr Morshed threw him a glarnce. It sufficed. Didn't it suffice, Mr Leggatt?'

'I knew if something didn't happen, something worse would,' said Leggatt. 'It never fails when you're aboard.'

'And Jules?' I demanded.

'Jules was, so to speak, panicking in a water-tight flat through his unfortunate lack of language. I had to introduce him as part of the *entente cordiale*, and he was put under arrest, too. Then we sat on the grass and smoked, while Eddy and Co. violently annoyed the traffic on the Portsmouth Road, till the umpires, all in short panties, conferred on the valuable lessons of the field–day and added up points, same as at target-practice. I didn't hear their conclusions, but our Mr Morshed delivered a farewell address to Eddy and Co., tellin' 'em they ought to have deduced from a hundred signs about me, that I was a friendly bringin' in dispatches from the North. We left 'em tryin' to find those signs in the Scout book, and we reached Mr Morshed's hotel at Portsmouth at 6.27 p.m. *ong automobile.* Here endeth the first chapter.'

'Begin the second,' I said.

The uncle and Leggatt had finished washing up and were seated, smoking, while the damp duster dried at the fire.

'About what time was it,' said Pyecroft to Leggatt, 'when our Mr Morshed began to talk about uncles?'

'When he came back to the bar, after he'd changed into those rat–catcher clothes,' said Leggatt.

'That's right. "Pye," said he, "have you an uncle?" "I have," I says. "Here's santy [11] to him," and I finished my sherry and bitters to *you*, uncle.'

'That's right,' said Pyecroft's uncle sternly. 'If you hadn't I'd have belted you worth rememberin', Emmanuel. I had the body all night.'

Pyecroft smiled affectionately. 'So you 'ad, uncle,' an' beautifully you looked after her. But as I was saying, "I have an uncle, too," says Mr Morshed, dark and lowering. "Yet somehow I can't love him. I want to mortify the beggar. Volunteers to mortify my uncle, one pace to the front."

'I took Jules with me the regulation distance. Jules was getting interested. Your Mr Leggatt preserved a strictly nootral attitude.

'"You're a pressed man," says our Mr Morshed. "I owe your late employer much, so to say. The car will manoeuvre all night, as requisite."

'Mr Leggatt come out noble as your employee, and, by

'Eaven's divine grace, instead of arguing, he pleaded his new paint and varnish which was Mr Morshed's one vital spot (he's lootenant on one of the new catch-'em-alive-o's now). "True," says he, "paint's an 'oly thing. I'll give you one hour to arrange a *modus vivendi*. Full bunkers and steam ready by 9 p.m. tonight, *if* you please."

'Even so, Mr Leggatt was far from content. *I* 'ad to arrange the details. We run her into the yard here.' Pyecroft nodded through the window at my car's glossy back-panels. 'We took off the body with its mats and put it in the stable, substitooting (and that yard's a tight fit for extensive repairs) the body of uncle's blue delivery cart. It overhung a trifle, but after I'd lashed it I knew it wouldn't fetch loose. Thus, in our composite cruiser, we repaired once more to the hotel, and was immediately dispatched to the toy-shop in the High Street where we took aboard one rocking-horse which was waiting for us.'

'Took aboard *what?*' I cried.

'One fourteen-hand dapple-grey rocking-horse, with pure green rockers and detachable tail, pair gashly glass eyes, complete set 'orrible grinnin' teeth, and two bloody-red nostrils which, protruding from the brown papers, produced the *tout ensemble* of a Ju-ju sacrifice in the Benin campaign. Do I make myself comprehensible?'

'Perfectly. Did you say anything?' I asked.

'Only to Jules. To him, I says, wishing to try him, "*Allez à votre bateau. Je say mon Lootenong. Eel voo donneray porkwor.*" To me, says he, "*Vous ong ate hurro! Jamay de la vee!*" [12] and I saw by his eye he'd taken on for the full term of the war. Jules was a blue-eyed, brindle-haired beggar of a useful make and inquirin' habits. Your Mr Leggatt he only groaned.'

Leggatt nodded. 'It was like nightmares,' he said. 'It was like nightmares.'

'Once more, then,' Pyecroft swept on, 'we returned to the hotel and partook of a sumptuous repast, under the able and genial chairmanship of our Mr Morshed, who laid his projecks unreservedly before us. "In the first place," he says, opening out bicycle-maps, "my uncle, who, I regret to say, is a brigadier-general, has sold his alleged soul to Dicky Bridoon for a feathery hat and a pair o' gilt spurs. Jules, *conspuez l'oncle;*" [13] So Jules, you'll be glad to hear –'

'One minute, Pye,' I said. 'Who is Dicky Bridoon?'

'I don't usually mingle myself up with the bickerings of the Junior Service, but it trarnspired that he was Secretary o' State for Civil War, an' he'd been issuing mechanical leather-belly gee-gees which doctors recommend for tumour – to the British cavalry in loo of real meat horses, to learn to ride on. Don't you remember there was quite a stir in the papers owing to the cavalry not appreciatin' 'em? But that's a minor item. The main point was that our uncle, in his capacity of brigadier-general, mark you, had wrote to the papers highly approvin' o' Dicky Bridoon's mechanical substitutes an 'ad thus obtained promotion – all same as a agnosticle stoker psalm-singin' 'imself up the Service under a pious captain. At that point of the narrative we caught a phosphorescent glimmer why the rocking-horse might have been issued; but none the less the navigation was intricate. Omitting the fact it was dark and cloudy, our brigadier-uncle lay somewhere in the South Downs with his brigade, which was manoeuvrin' at Whitsun manoeuvres on a large scale – Red Army *versus* Blue, et cetera; an' all we 'ad to go by was those flapping bicycle-maps and your Mr Leggatt's groans.'

'I was thinking what the Downs mean after dark,' said Leggatt angrily.

'They was worth thinkin' of,' said Pyecroft. 'When we had studied the map till it fair spun, we decided to sally forth and creep for uncle by hand in the dark, dark night, an' present 'im with the rocking-horse. So we embarked at 8.57 p.m.'

'One minute again, please. How much did Jules understand by that time?' I asked.

'Sufficient unto the day – or night, perhaps I should say. He told our Mr Morshed he'd follow him *more sang frays*, which is French for dead, drunk or damned. Barrin' 'is paucity o' language, there wasn't a blemish on Jules. But what I wished to imply was, when we climbed into the back parts of the car, our Lootenant Morshed says to me, "I doubt if I'd flick my cigar-ends about too lavish, Mr Pyecroft. We ought to be sitting on five pounds' worth of selected fireworks, and I think the rockets are your end." Not being able to smoke with my 'ead over the side I threw it away; and then your Mr Leggatt, 'aving been as nearly mutinous as it pays to be with my Mr Morshed, arched his back and drove.'

'Where did he drive to, please?' said I.

'Primerrily, in search of any or either or both armies; seconderrily, of course, in search of our brigadier-uncle. Not finding him on the road, we ran about the grass looking for him. This took us to a great many places in a short time. 'Ow 'eavenly that lilac did smell on top of that first Down – stinkin' its blossomin' little heart out!'

'I 'adn't leesure to notice,' said Mr Leggatt. 'The Downs were full o' chalk-pits, and we'd no lights.'

'We 'ad the bicycle-lamp to look at the map by. Didn't you notice the old lady at the window where we saw the man in the night-gown? I thought night-gowns as sleepin' rig was extinck, so to speak.'

'I tell you I 'adn't leesure to notice,' Leggatt repeated.

'That's odd. Then what might 'ave made you tell the sentry at the first camp we found that you was the *Daily Express* delivery-waggon?'

'You can't touch pitch without being defiled,' Leggatt answered. ''Oo told the officer in the bath we were umpires?'

'Well, he asked us. That was when we found the Territorial battalion undressin' in slow time. It lay on the left flank o' the Blue Army, and it cackled as it lay, too. But it gave us our position as regards the respective armies. We wandered a little more, and at 11.7 p.m., not having had a road under us for twenty minutes, we scaled the heights of something or other – which are about six hundred feet high. Here we 'alted to tighten the lashings of the superstructure, and we smelt leather and horses three counties deep all round. We was, as you might say, in the thick of it.'

'"Ah!" says my Mr Morshed. "My 'orizon has indeed broadened. What a little thing is an uncle, Mr Pyecroft, in the presence o' these glitterin' constellations! Simply ludicrous!" he says, "to waste a rocking-horse on an individual. We must socialize it. But we must get their 'eads up first. Touch off one rocket, if you please."

'I touched off a green three-pounder which rose several thousand metres, and burst into gorgeous stars. "Reproduce the manoeuvre," he says, "at the other end o' this ridge – if it don't end in another cliff." So we steamed down the ridge a mile and a half east, and then I let Jules touch off a pink rocket, or he'd ha' kissed me. That was his only way to express his emotions, so to speak. Their heads come up then all around us to the extent o' thousands. We hears bugles like cocks crowing below, and on the top of it a most impressive sound which I'd never enjoyed before because 'itherto I'd always been an inteegral part of it, so to say – the noise of 'ole armies gettin' under arms. They must 'ave anticipated a night attack, I imagine. Most impressive. Then we 'eard a threshin'-machine. "Tutt! Tutt! This is childish!" says Lootenant Morshed. "We can't wait till they've finished cutting chaff for their horses. We must make 'em understand we're not to be trifled with. Expedite 'em with another rocket, Mr Pyecroft."

'"It's barely possible, sir," I remarks, "that that's a searchlight churnin' up," and by the time we backed into a providential chalk cutting (which was where our first tyre went pungo) she broke out to the northward, and began searching the ridge. A smart bit o' work.'

''Twasn't a puncture. The inner tube had nipped because we skidded so,' Leggatt interrupted.

'While your Mr Leggatt was effectin' repairs, another searchlight broke out to the southward, and the two of 'em swept our ridge on both sides. Right at the west end of it they showed us the ground rising into a hill, so to speak, crowned with what looked like a little fort. Morshed saw it before the beams shut off. "That's the key of the position!" he says. "Occupy it at all hazards."

'"I haven't half got occupation for the next twenty minutes," says your Mr Leggatt, rootin' and blasphemin' in the dark. Mark, now, 'ow Morshed changed his tactics to suit 'is environment. "Right!" says he. "I'll stand by the ship. Mr Pyecroft and Jules, oblige me by doubling along the ridge to the east with all the maroons and crackers you can carry without spilling. Read the directions careful for the maroons, Mr Pyecroft, and touch them off at half-minute intervals. Jules represents musketry an' maxim fire under your command. Remember, it's death or Salisbury Gaol! Prob'ly both!"

'By these means and some moderately 'ard runnin', we distracted 'em to the eastward. Maroons, you may not be aware, are same as bombs, with the anarchism left out. In confined spots like chalk-pits, they knock a four-point-seven silly. But you should read the directions before'and. In the intervals of the slow but well-directed fire of my cow-guns, Jules, who had found a sheep-pond in the dark a little lower down, gave what you might call a cinematograph reproduction o' sporadic musketry. They was large size crackers, and he concluded with the dull, sicken' thud o' blind shells burstin' on soft ground.'

'How did he manage that?' I said.

'You throw a lighted squib into water and you'll see,' said Pyecroft. 'Thus, then, we improvised till supplies was exhausted and the surrounding landscapes fair 'owled and 'ummed at us. The Junior Service might 'ave 'ad their doubts about the rockets, but they couldn't overlook our gunfire. Both sides tumbled out full of initiative. I told Jules no two flat-feet 'ad any right to be as happy as us, and we went back along the ridge to the derelict, and there was our Mr Morshed apostrophin' his 'andiwork over fifty square mile o' country with "Attend, all ye who list to hear!" out of the Fifth Reader. He'd got as far as "And roused the shepherds o' Stonehenge, the rangers o' Beaulieu" when we come up, and he drew our attention to its truth as well as its beauty. That's rare in poetry, I'm told. He went right on to — "The red glare on Skiddaw roused those beggars at Carlisle" — which he pointed out was poetic licence for Leith Hill. This allowed your Mr Leggatt time to finish pumpin' up his tyres. I 'eard the sweat 'op off his nose.'

'You know what it is, sir,' said poor Leggatt to me.

'It warfted across my mind, as I listened to what was trarnspirin', that it might be easier to make the mess than to wipe it up, but such considerations weighed not with our valiant leader.'

'"Mr Pyecroft," he says, "it can't have escaped your notice that we 'ave one angry and 'ighly intelligent army in front of us, an' another 'ighly angry and equally intelligent army in our rear. What 'ud you recommend?"

'Most men would have besought 'im to do a lateral glide while there was yet time, but all I said was: "The rocking-horse isn't expended yet, sir."

'He laid his hand on my shoulder. "Pye," says he, "there's worse men than you in loftier places. They shall 'ave it. None the less," he remarks, "the ice is undeniably packing."

'I may 'ave omitted to point out that at this juncture two large armies, both deprived of their night's sleep, was awake, as you might say, and hurryin' into each other's arms. Here endeth the second chapter.'

He filled his pipe slowly. The uncle had fallen asleep. Leggatt lit another cigarette.

'We then proceeded *ong automobile* along the ridge in a westerly direction towards the miniature fort which had been so kindly revealed by the searchlight, but which on inspection (your Mr Leggatt bumped into an outlyin' reef of it) proved to be a wurzel-clump; *c'est-à-dire*,[14] a parallelogrammatic pile of about three million mangold-wurzels, brought up there for the sheep, I suppose. On all sides, excep' the one we'd come by, the ground fell away moderately quick, and down at the bottom there was a large camp lit up an' full of harsh words of command.

'"I said it was the key to the position," Lootenant Morshed remarks. "Trot out Persimmon!" which we rightly took to read, "Un-wrap the rocking-horse."

'"Houp la!" sayd Jules in a insubordinate tone, an' slaps Persimmon on the flank.

'"Silence!" says the Lootenant. "This is the Royal Navy, not Newmarket"; and we carried Persimmon to the top of the mangel-wurzel clump as directed.

'Owing to the inequalities of the terrain (I *do* think your Mr Leggatt might have had a spirit-level in his kit) he wouldn't rock free on the bed-plate, and while adjustin' him, his detachable tail fetched adrift. Our Lootenant was quick to seize the advantage.

'"Remove that transformation," he says. "Substitute one Roman candle. Gas-power is superior to manual propulsion."

'So we substituted. He arranged the *pièce de resistarnce* in the shape of large drums — not saucers, mark you — drums of coloured fire, with printed instructions, at proper distances round Persimmon. There was a brief interregnum while we dug ourselves in among the wurzels by hands. Then he touched off the fires, *not* omitting the Roman candle, and, you may take it from me, all was visible. Persimmon shone out in his naked splendour, red to port, green to starboard, and one white light at his bows, as per Board o' Trade regulations. Only he didn't so much rock, you might say, as shrug himself, in a manner of speaking every time the candle went off. One can't have everything. But the rest surpassed our highest expectations. I think Persimmon was noblest on the starboard or green side – more like when a man thinks he's seeing mackerel in hell, don't you know? And yet I'd be the last to deprecate the effect of the port light on his teeth, or that bloodshot look in his left eye. He knew there was something going on he didn't approve of. He looked worried.'

'Did you laugh?' I said.

'I'm not much of a wag myself; nor it wasn't as if we 'ad time to allow the spectacle to sink in. The coloured fires was supposed to burn ten minutes, whereas it was obvious to the meanest capacity that the Junior Service would arrive by forced marches in about two and a half. They grarsped our topical allusion as soon as it was across the foot-lights, so to speak. They were quite chafed at it. Of course, 'ad we reflected, we might have known that exposin' illuminated rockin' horses to an army that was learnin' to ride on 'em partook of the nature of a *double entender*, as the French say – same as waggling the tiller lines at a man who's had a hanging in the family. I knew the cox of the *Archimandrite*'s galley 'arf killed for a similar *plaisanteree*.[15] But we never anticipated lobsters being so sensitive. That was why we shifted. We could 'ardly tear our commandin' officer away. He put his head on one side, and kept cooin'. The only thing he' ad neglected to provide was a line of retreat; but your Mr Leggatt – an 'eroic soul in the last stage of wet prostration – here took command of the van, or, rather, the rear-guard. We walked downhill beside him, holding on to the superstructure to prevent her capsizing. These technical details, 'owever, are beyond me.' He waved his pipe towards Leggatt.

'I saw there was two deepish ruts leadin' down'ill somewhere,' said Leggatt. 'That was when the soldiers stopped laughin', and begun to run uphill.'

'Stroll, lovey, stroll!' Pyecroft corrected. 'The Dervish rush took place later.'

'So I laid her in these ruts. That was where she must 'ave scraped her silencer a bit. Then they turned sharp right – the ruts did – and then she stopped bonnet-high in a manure-heap, sir; but I'll swear it was all of a one in three gradient. I think it was a barnyard. We waited there,' said Leggatt.

'But not for long,' said Pyecroft. 'The lights were towering out of the drums on the position we 'ad so valiantly abandoned; and the Junior Service was escaladin' it *en masse*. When numerous bodies of 'ighly trained men arrive simultaneous in the same latitude from opposite directions, each remarking briskly, "What the 'ell did you do *that* for?" detonation, as you might say, is practically assured. They didn't ask for extraneous aids. If we'd come out with sworn affidavits of what we'd done they wouldn't 'ave believed us. They wanted each other's company exclusive. Such was the effect of Persimmon on their clarss feelings. Idol'try, *I* call it! Events transpired with the utmost velocity and rapidly increasing pressures. There was a few remarks about Dicky Bridoon and mechanical horses, and then some one was smacked – hard by the sound – in the middle of a remark.'

'That was the man who kept calling for the Forty-fifth Dragoons,' said Leggatt. 'He got as far as Drag . . .'

'Was it?' said Pyecroft dreamily. 'Well, he couldn't say they didn't come. They all came, and they all fell to arguin' whether the Infantry should 'ave Persimmon for a regimental pet or the Cavalry should keep him for stud purposes. Hence the issue was soon clouded with mangold-wurzels. Our commander said we 'ad sowed the good seed, and it was bearing abundant fruit. (They weigh between four and seven pounds apiece.) Seein' the children 'ad got over their shyness, and 'ad really begun to play games, we backed out o' the pit and went down, by steps, to the camp below, no man, as you might say, making us afraid. Here we enjoyed a front view of the battle, which rolled with renewed impetus, owing to both sides receiving strong reinforcements every minute. All arms were freely represented; Cavalry, on this occasion only, acting in concert with Artillery. They argued the relative merits of horses *versus* feet, so to say, but they didn't neglect Persimmon. The wounded rolling downhill with the wurzels informed us that he had long ago been socialized, and the smallest souvenirs were worth a man's life. Speaking broadly, the Junior Service appeared to be a shade out of 'and, if I may venture so far. They did *not* pay prompt and unhesitating obedience to the "Retires" or the "Cease Fires" or the "For 'Eaven's sake come to bed, ducky" of their officers, who, I regret to say, were 'otly embroiled at the heads of their respective units.'

'How did you find that out?' I asked.

'On account of Lootenant Morshed going to the Mess tent to call on his uncle and raise a drink; but all hands had gone to the front. We thought we 'eard somebody bathing behind the tent, and we found an oldish gentleman tryin' to drown a boy in knickerbockers in a horse-trough. He kept him under with a bicycle, so to speak. He 'ad nearly accomplished his fell design, when we frustrated him. He was in a highly malleable condition and full o' *juice de spree*.¹⁶ "Arsk not what I am," he says. "My wife'll tell me that quite soon enough. Arsk rather what I've been," he says. "I've been dinin' here," he says. "I commanded 'em in the Eighties," he says, "and, Gawd forgive me," he says, sobbin' 'eavily, "I've spent this holy evening telling their Colonel they was a set of educated inefficients. Hark to 'em!" We could, without strainin' ourselves; but how *he* picked up the gentle murmur of his own corps in that on-the-knee party up the hill I don't know. "They've marched and fought thirty miles today," he shouts, "and now they're tearin' the intes*tines* out of the Cavalry up yonder! They won't stop this side the gates o' Delhi," he says. "I commanded their ancestors. There's nothing wrong with the Service," he says, wringing out his trousers on his lap. " 'Eaven pardon me for doubtin' 'em! Same old game – same young beggars."

'The boy in the knickerbockers, languishing on a chair, puts in a claim for one drink. "Let him go dry," says our friend in shirt-tails. "He's a reporter. He run into me on his filthy bicycle and he asked me if I could furnish 'im with particulars about the mutiny in the Army. You false-'earted proletarian publicist," he says, shakin' his finger at 'im – for he was reelly annoyed – "I'll teach you to defile what you can't comprehend! When my regiment's in a state o' mutiny, I'll do myself the honour of informing you personally. You particularly ignorant and very narsty little man," he says, "you're no better than a dhobi's [17] donkey! If there wasn't dirty linen to wash, you'd starve," he says, "and why I haven't drowned you will be the lastin' regret of my life."

'Well, we sat with 'em and 'ad drinks for about half-an-hour in front of the Mess tent. He'd ha' killed the reporter if there hadn't been witnesses, and the reporter might have taken notes of the battle; so we acted as two-way buffers, in a sense. I don't hold with the Press mingling up with Service matters. They draw false conclusions. Now, mark you, at a moderate estimate, there were seven thousand men in the fighting line, half of 'em hurt in their professional feelings, an' the other half rubbin' in the liniment, as you might say. All due to Persimmon! If you 'adn't seen it you wouldn't 'ave believed it. And yet, mark you, not one single unit of 'em even resorted to his belt. They confined themselves to natural producks – hands and the wurzels. I thought Jules was havin' fits, till it trarnspired the same thought had impressed him in the French language. He called it *incroyable*,[18] I believe. Seven thousand men, with seven thousand rifles, belts, and bayonets, in a violently agitated condition, and not a ungenteel blow struck from first to last. The old gentleman drew our attention to it as well. It was quite noticeable.

'Lack of ammunition was the primerry cause of the battle ceasin'. A Brigade-Major came in, wipin' his nose on both cuffs, and sayin' he 'ad 'ad snuff. The brigadier-uncle followed. He was, so to speak, sneezin'. We thought it best to shift our moorings without attractin' attention; so we shifted. They 'ad called the cows 'ome by then. The Junior Service was going to bye-bye all round us, as happy as the ship's monkey when he's been playin' with the paints, and Lootenant Morshed and Jules kept bowin' to port and starboard of the superstructure, acknowledgin' the unstinted applause which the multitude would 'ave give 'em if they'd known the facts. On the other 'and, as your Mr Leggatt observed, they might 'ave killed us.

'That would have been about five bells in the middle watch, say half-past two. A well-spent evening. There was but little to be gained by entering Portsmouth at that hour, so we turned off on the grass (this was after we had found a road under us), and we cast anchors out at the stern and prayed for the day.

'But your Mr Leggatt he had to make and mend tyres all our watch below. It trarnspired she had been running on the rim o' two or three wheels, which, very properly, he hadn't reported till the close of the action. And that's the reason of your four new tyres. Mr Morshed was of opinion you'd earned 'em. Do you dissent?'

I stretched out my hand, which Pyecroft crushed to pulp. 'No, Pye,' I said, deeply moved, 'I agree entirely. But what happened to Jules?'

'We returned him to his own Navy after breakfast. He wouldn't have kept much longer without some one in his own language to tell it to. I don't know any man I ever took more compassion on than Jules. 'Is sufferings swelled him up centimetres, and all he could do on the Hard was to kiss Lootenant Morshed and me, *and* your Mr Leggatt. He deserved that much. A cordial beggar.'

Pyecroft looked at the washed cups on the table, and the low sunshine on my car's back in the yard.

''Too early to drink to him,' he said. 'But I feel it just the same.'

The uncle, sunk in his chair, snored a little; the canary answered with a shrill lullaby. Pyecroft picked up the duster, thew it over the cage, put his finger to his lips, and we tiptoed out into the shop, while Leggatt brought the car round.

'I'll look out for the news in the papers,' I said, as I got in.

'Oh, we short-circuited that! Nothing trarnspired excep' a statement to the effect that some Territorial battalions had played about with turnips at the conclusion of the manoeuvres. The taxpayer don't know all he gets for his money. Farewell!'

We moved off just in time to be blocked by a regiment coming towards the station to entrain for London.

'Beg your pardon, sir,' said a sergeant in charge of the baggage, 'but would you mind backin' a bit till we get the waggons past?'

'Certainly,' I said. 'You don't happen to have a rocking-horse among your kit, do you?'

The rattle of our reverse drowned his answer, but I saw his eyes. One of them was blackish-green, about four days old.

The Legend of Mirth

The Four Archangels, so the legends tell,
Raphael, Gabriel, Michael, Azrael,
Being first of those to whom the Power was shown,
Stood first of all the Host before The Throne,
And when the Charges were allotted burst
Tumultuous-winged from out the assembly first.
Zeal was their spur [1] that bade them strictly heed
Their own high judgment on their lightest deed.
Zeal was their spur that, when relief was given,
Urged them unwearied to fresh toil in Heaven;
For Honour's sake perfecting every task
Beyond what e'en Perfection's self could ask . . .
And Allah, Who created Zeal and Pride,
Knows how the train are perilous-near allied.

It chanced on one of Heaven's long-lighted days,
The Four and all the Host having gone their ways
Each to his Charge, the shining Courts were void
Save for one Seraph whom no charge employed,
With folden wings and slumber-threatened brow.
To whom The Word: 'Beloved, what dost thou?'
'By the Permission,' came the answer soft,
'Little I do nor do that little oft.
As is The Will in Heaven so on Earth
Where by The Will I strive to make men mirth.'
He ceased and sped, hearing The Word once more:
'Beloved, go thy way and greet the Four.'

Systems and Universes overpast,
The Seraph came upon the Four, at last,
Guiding and guarding with devoted mind
The tedious generations of mankind
Who lent at most unwilling ear and eye
When they could not escape the ministry . . .
Yet, patient, faithful, firm, persistent, just
Toward all that gross, indifferent, facile dust,
The Archangels laboured to discharge their trust
By precept and example, prayer and law,
Advice, reproof, and rule, but, labouring, saw

270

Each in his fellow's countenance confessed,
The Doubt that sickens: 'Have I done my best?'

Even as they sighed and turned to toil anew,
The Seraph hailed them with observance due;
And after some fit talk of higher things
Touched tentative on mundane happenings.
This they permitting, he, emboldened thus,
Prolused [2] of humankind promiscuous.
And, since the large contention less avails
Than instances observed, he told them tales –
Tales of the shop, the bed, the court, the street,
Intimate, elemental, indiscreet:
Occasions where Confusion smiting swift
Piles jest on jest as snow-slides pile the drift
Whence, one by one, beneath derisive skies,
The victims bare, bewildered heads arise:
Tales of the passing of the spirit, graced
With humour blinding as the doom it faced:
Stark tales of ribaldry that broke aside
To tears, by laughter swallowed ere they dried:
Tales to which neither grace nor grain accrue,
But only (Allah be exalted!) true,
And only, as the Seraph showed that night,
Delighting to the limits of delight.

These he rehearsed with artful pause and halt,
And such pretence of memory at fault,
That soon the Four – so well the bait was thrown –
Came to his aid with memories of their own –
Matters dismissed long since as small or vain,
Whereof the high significance had lain
Hid, till the ungirt glosses made it plain.
Then, as enlightenment came broad and fast,
Each marvelled at his own oblivious past
Until – the Gates of Laughter opened wide –
The Four, with that bland Seraph at their side,
While they recalled, compared, and amplified,
In utter mirth forgot both zeal and pride.

High over Heaven the lamps of midnight burned
Ere, weak with merriment, the Four returned,
Not in that order they were wont to keep –

Pinion to pinion answering, sweep for sweep,
In awful diapason heard afar,
But shoutingly adrift 'twixt star and star.
Reeling a planet's orbit left or right
As laughter took them in the abysmal Night;
Or, by the point of some remembered jest,
Winged and brought helpless down through gulfs unguessed,
Where the blank worlds that gather to the birth
Leaped in the womb of Darkness at their mirth,
And e'en Gehenna's bondsmen understood.
They were not damned from human brotherhood.

Not first nor last of Heaven's high Host, the Four
That night took place beneath The Throne once more.
O lovelier than their morning majesty,
The understanding light behind the eye!
O more compelling than their old command,
The new-learned friendly gesture of the hand!
O sweeter than their zealous fellowship,
The wise half-smile that passed from lip to lip!
O well and roundly, when Command was given,
They told their tale against themselves to Heaven,
And in the silence, waiting on The Word,
Received the Peace and Pardon of The Lord!

'MY SON'S WIFE'

'My Son's Wife"

(1913)

He had suffered from the disease of the century since his early youth, and before he was thirty he was heavily marked with it. He and a few friends had rearranged Heaven very comfortably, but the reorganization of Earth, which they called Society, was even greater fun. It demanded Work in the shape of many taxi-rides daily; hours of brilliant talk with brilliant talkers; some sparkling correspondence; a few silences (but on the understanding that their own turn should come soon) while other people expounded philosophies; and a fair number of picture-galleries, tea-fights, concerts, theatres, music-halls, and cinema shows; the whole trimmed with love-making to women whose hair smelt of cigarette-smoke. Such strong days sent Frankwell Midmore back to his flat assured that he and his friends had helped the World a step nearer the Truth, the Dawn, and the New Order.

His temperament, he said, led him more towards concrete data than abstract ideas. People who investigate detail are apt to be tired at the day's end. The same temperament, or it may have been a woman, made him early attach himself to the Immoderate Left of his Cause in the capacity of an experimenter in Social Relations. And since the Immoderate Left contains plenty of women anxious to help earnest inquirers with large independent incomes to arrive at evaluations of essentials, Frankwell Midmore's lot was far from contemptible.

At that hour Fate chose to play with him. A widowed aunt, widely separated by nature, and more widely by marriage, from all that Midmore's mother had ever been or desired to be, died and left him possessions. Mrs Midmore, having that summer embraced a creed which denied the existence of death, naturally could not stoop to burial; but Midmore had to leave London

275

for the dank country at a season when Social Regeneration works best through long, cushioned conferences, two by two, after tea. There he faced the bracing ritual of the British funeral, and was wept at across the raw grave by an elderly coffin-shaped female with a long nose, who called him 'Master Frankie'; and there he was congratulated behind an echoing top-hat by a man he mistook for a mute, who turned out to be his aunt's lawyer. He wrote his mother next day, after a bright account of the funeral:

'So far as I can understand, she has left me between four and five hundred a year. It all comes from Ther Land, as they call it down there. The unspeakable attorney, Sperrit, and a green-eyed daughter, who hums to herself as she tramps but is silent on all subjects except "huntin'"', insisted on taking me to see it. Ther Land is brown and green in alternate slabs like chocolate and pistachio cakes, speckled with occasional peasants who do not utter. In case it should not be wet enough there is a wet brook in the middle of it. Ther House is by the brook. I shall look into it later. If there should be any little memento of Jenny that you care for, let me know. Didn't you tell me that mid-Victorian furniture is coming into the market again? Jenny's old maid – it is called Rhoda Dolbie – tells me that Jenny promised it thirty pounds a year. The will does not. Hence, I suppose, the tears at the funeral. But that is close on ten per cent of the income. I fancy Jenny has destroyed all her private papers and records of her *vie intime*, if, indeed, life be possible in such a place. The Sperrit man told me that if I had means of my own I might come and live on Ther Land. I didn't tell him how much I would pay not to! I cannot think it right that any human being should exercise mastery over others in the merciless fashion our tom-fool social system permits; so, as it is all mine, I intend to sell it whenever the unholy Sperrit can find a purchaser.'

And he went to Mr Sperrit with the idea next day, just before returning to town.

'Quite so,' said the lawyer. 'I see your point, of course. But the house itself is rather old-fashioned – hardly the type purchasers demand nowadays. There's no park, of course, and the bulk of the land is left to a life-tenant, a Mr Sidney. As long as he pays his rent, he can't be turned out, and even if he didn't' – Mr Sperrit's face relaxed a shade – 'you might have a difficulty.'

'The property brings four hundred a year, I understand,' said Midmore.

'Well, hardly – ha-ardly. Deducting land and income tax, tithes, fire insurance, cost of collection and repairs of course, it returned two hundred and eighty-four pounds last year. The repairs are rather a large item – owing to the brook. I call it Liris [1] – out of Horace, you know.'

Midmore looked at his watch impatiently.

'I suppose you can find somebody to buy it?' he repeated.

'We will do our best, of course, if those are your instructions. Then, that is all except' – here Midmore half rose, but Mr Sperrit's little grey eyes held his large brown ones firmly – 'except about Rhoda Dolbie, Mrs Werf's maid. I may tell you that we did not draw up your aunt's last will. She grew secretive towards the last – elderly people often do – and had it done in London. I expect her memory failed her, or she mislaid her notes. She used to put them in her spectacle-case . . . My motor only takes eight minutes to get to the station, Mr Midmore . . . but, as I was saying, whenever she made her will with *us*, Mrs Werf always left Rhoda thirty pounds per annum. Charlie, the wills!' A clerk with a baldish head and a long nose dealt documents on to the table like cards, and breathed heavily behind Midmore. 'It's in no sense a legal obligation, of course,' said Mr Sperrit. 'Ah, that one is dated January the 11th, eighteen eighty-nine.'

Midmore looked at his watch again and found himself saying with no good grace: 'Well, I suppose she'd better have it – for the present at any rate.'

He escaped with an uneasy feeling that two hundred and fifty-four pounds a year was not exactly four hundred, and that Charlie's long nose annoyed him. Then he returned, first-class, to his own affairs.

Of the two, perhaps three, experiments in Social Relations which he had then in hand, one interested him acutely. It had run for some months and promised most variegated and interesting developments, on which he dwelt luxuriously all the way to town. When he reached his flat he was not well prepared for a twelve-page letter explaining, in the diction of the Immoderate Left which rubricates its I's and illuminates its T's, that the lady had realized greater attractions in another Soul. She re-stated, rather than pleaded, the gospel of the Immoderate Left as her justification, and ended in an impassioned demand for her right to express herself in and on her own life, through which, she pointed out, she could pass but once. She added that if, later, she should discover Midmore was 'essentially com-plementary to her needs', she would tell him so. That Midmore had himself written much the same sort of epistle – barring the hint of return – to a woman of whom his needs for self-expression had caused him to weary three years before, did not assist him in the least. He expressed himself to the gas-fire in terms essential but not complimentary. Then he reflected on the detached criticism of his best friends and her best friends, male and female, with whom he and she and others had talked so openly while their gay adventure was in flower. He recalled, too – this must have been about midnight – her analysis from every angle, remote and most intimate, of the mate to whom she had been adjudged under the base convention which is styled marriage. Later, at that bad hour when the cattle wake for a little, he remembered her in other aspects and went down into the hell appointed; desolate, desiring, with no God to call upon. About eleven o'clock next morning Eliphaz the Temanite. Bildad the Shuhite, and Zophar the Naamathite [2] called upon him 'for they had made appointment together' to see how he took it; but the janitor told them that Job had gone – into the country, he believed.

Midmore's relief when he found his story was not written across his aching temples for Mr Sperrit to read – the defeated lover, like the successful one, believes all earth privy to his soul – was put down by Mr Sperrit to quite different causes. He led him into a morning-room. The rest of the house seemed to be full of people, singing to a loud piano idiotic songs about cows, and the hall smelt of damp cloaks.

'It's our evening to take the winter cantata,' Mr Sperrit explained. 'It's "High Tide on the Coast of Lincolnshire".[3] I hoped you'd come back. There are scores of little things to settle. As for the house, of course, it stands ready for you at any time. I couldn't get Rhoda out of it – nor could Charlie for that matter. She's the sister, isn't she, of the nurse who brought you down here when you were four, she says, to recover from measles?'

'Is she? Was I?' said Midmore through the bad tastes in his mouth. 'D'you suppose I could stay there the night?'

Thirty joyous young voices shouted appeal to some one to leave their 'pipes of parsley 'ollow – 'ollow – 'ollow!' Mr Sperrit had to raise his voice above the din.

'Well, if I asked you to stay *here*, I should never hear the last of it from Rhoda. She's a little cracked, of course, but the soul of devotion and capable of anything. *Ne sit ancellae*,[4] you know.'

'Thank you. Then I'll go. I'll walk.' He stumbled out dazed and sick into the winter twilight, and sought the square house by the brook.

It was not a dignified entry, because when the door was unchained and Rhoda exclaimed, he took two valiant steps into the hall and then fainted – as men sometimes will after twenty-two hours of strong emotion and little food.

'I'm sorry,' he said when he could speak. He was lying at the foot of the stairs, his head on Rhoda's lap.

'Your 'ome is your castle, sir,' was the reply in his hair. 'I smelt it wasn't drink. You lay on the sofa till I get your supper.'

She settled him in a drawing-room hung with yellow silk, heavy with the smell of dead leaves and oil lamp. Something murmured soothingly in the background and overcame the noises in his head. He thought he heard horses' feet on wet gravel and a voice singing about ships and flocks and grass. It passed close to the shuttered bay-window.

> But each will mourn his own, she saith,
> And sweeter woman ne'er drew breath
> Than my son's wife, Elizabeth ...
> Cusha – cusha – cusha – calling.[5]

The hoofs broke into a canter as Rhoda entered with the tray. 'And then I'll put you to bed,' she said. 'Sidney's coming in the morning.' Midmore asked no questions. He dragged his poor bruised soul to bed and would have pitied it all over again, but the food and warm sherry and water drugged him to instant sleep.

Rhoda's voice wakened him, asking whether he would have "'ip, foot, or sitz,' which he understood were the baths of the establishment. 'Suppose you try all three,' she suggested. 'They're all yours, you know, sir.'

He would have renewed his sorrows with the daylight, but her words struck him pleasantly. Everything his eyes opened upon was his very own to keep for ever. The carved four-post Chippendale bed, obviously worth hundreds; the wavy walnut William and Mary chairs – he had seen worse ones labelled twenty guineas apiece; the oval medallion mirror; the delicate eighteenth-century wire fireguard; the heavy brocaded curtains were his – all his. So, too, a great garden full of birds that faced him when he shaved; a mulberry tree, a sun-dial, and a dull, steel-coloured brook that murmured level with the edge of a lawn a hundred yards away. Peculiarly and privately his own was the smell of sausages and coffee that he sniffed at the head of the wide square landing, all set round with mysterious doors and Bartolozzi prints. He spent two hours after breakfast in exploring his new possessions. His heart leaped up at such things as sewing-machines, a rubber-tyred bath-chair in a tiled passage, a malachite-headed Malacca cane, boxes and boxes of unopened stationery, seal-rings, bunches of keys, and at the bottom of a steel-net reticule a little leather purse with seven pounds ten shillings in gold and eleven shillings in silver.

'You used to play with that when my sister brought you down here after your measles,' said Rhoda as he slipped the money into his pocket. 'Now, this was your pore dear auntie's business-room.' She opened a low door. 'Oh, I forgot about Mr Sidney! There he is.' An enormous old man with rheumy red eyes that blinked under downy white eyebrows sat in an Empire chair, his cap in his hands. Rhoda withdrew sniffing. The man looked Midmore over in silence, then jerked a thumb towards the door. 'I reckon she told you who I be,' he began. 'I'm the only farmer you've got. Nothin' goes off my place 'thout it walks on its own feet. What about my pig-pound?'

'Well, what about it?' said Midmore.

'That's just what I be come about. The County Councils are

getting more particular. Did ye know there was swine fever at Pashell's? There *be*. It'll 'ave to be in brick.'

'Yes,' said Midmore politely.

'I've bin at your aunt that was, plenty times about it. I don't say she wasn't a just woman, but she didn't read the lease same way I did. I be used to bein' put upon, but there's no doing any longer 'thout that pig-pound.'

'When would you like it?' Midmore asked. It seemed the easiest road to take.

'Any time or other suits me, I reckon. He ain't thrivin' where he is, an' I paid eighteen shillin' for him.' He crossed his hands on his stick and gave no further sign of life.

'Is that all?' Midmore stammered.

'All now – excep'' – he glanced fretfully at the table beside him – 'excep' my usuals. Where's that Rhoda?'

Midmore rang the bell. Rhoda came in with a bottle and a glass. The old man helped himself to four stiff fingers, rose in one piece, and stumped out. At the door he cried ferociously: 'Don't suppose it's any odds to you whether I'm drowned or not, but them flood-gates want a wheel and winch, they do. I be too old for liftin' 'em with the bar – my time o' life.'

'Good riddance if 'e was drowned,' said Rhoda. 'But don't you mind him. He's only amusin' himself. Your pore dear auntie used to give 'im 'is usual – 'tisn't the whisky *you* drink – an' send 'im about 'is business.'

'I see. Now, is a pig-pound the same thing as a pig-sty?'

Rhoda nodded. ''E needs one, too, but 'e ain't entitled to it. You look at 'is lease – third drawer on the left in the Bombay cabinet – an' next time 'e comes you ask 'im to read it. That'll choke 'im off, because 'e can't!'

There was nothing in Midmore's past to teach him the message and significance of a hand-written lease of the late 'eighties, but Rhoda interpreted.

'It don't mean anything reelly,' was her cheerful conclusion, 'excep' you mustn't get rid of him anyhow, an' 'e can do what 'e likes always. Lucky for us 'e *do* farm; and if it wasn't for 'is woman –'

'Oh, there's a Mrs Sidney, is there?'

'Lor, *no!*' The Sidneys don't marry. They keep. That's his

fourth since – to my knowledge. He was a takin' man from the first.'

'Any families?'

'They'd be grown up by now if there was, wouldn't they? But you can't spend all your days considerin' 'is interests. That's what gave your pore aunt 'er indigestion. 'Ave you seen the gun-room?'

Midmore held strong views on the immorality of taking life for pleasure. But there was no denying that the late Colonel Werf's seventy-guinea breechloaders were good at their filthy job. He loaded one, took it out and pointed – merely pointed – it at a cock-pheasant which rose out of a shrubbery behind the kitchen, and the flaming bird came down in a long slant on the lawn, stone dead. Rhoda from the scullery said it was a lovely shot, and told him lunch was ready.

He spent the afternoon gun in one hand, a map in the other, beating the bounds of his lands. They lay altogether in a shallow, uninteresting valley, flanked with woods and bisected by a brook. Up stream was his own house; down stream, less than half a mile, a low red farm-house squatted in an old orchard, beside what looked like small lock-gates on the Thames. There was no doubt as to ownership. Mr Sidney saw him while yet far off, and bellowed at him about pig-pounds and flood-gates. These last were two great sliding shutters of weedy oak across the brook, which were prised up inch by inch with a crowbar along a notched strip of iron, and when Sidney opened them they at once let out half the water. Midmore watched it shrink between its aldered banks like some conjuring trick. This, too, was his very own.

'I see,' he said. 'How interesting! Now, what's that bell for?' he went on, pointing to an old ship's bell in a rude belfry at the end of an outhouse. 'Was that a chapel once?' The red-eyed giant seemed to have difficulty in expressing himself for the moment and blinked savagely.

'Yes,' he said at last. 'My chapel. When you 'ear that bell ring you'll 'ear something. Nobody but me ud put up with it – but I reckon it don't make any odds to you.' He slammed the gates down again, and the brook rose behind them with a suck and a grunt.

Midmore moved off, conscious that he might be safer with Rhoda to hold his conversational hand. As he passed the front of the farm-house a smooth fat woman, with neatly parted grey hair under a widow's cap, curtsied to him deferentially through the window. By every teaching of the Immoderate Left she had a perfect right to express herself in any way she pleased, but the curtsey revolted him. And on his way home he was hailed from behind a hedge by a manifest idiot with no roof to his mouth, who hallooed and danced round him.

'What did that beast want?' he demanded of Rhoda at tea.

'Jimmy? He only wanted to know if you 'ad any telegrams to send. 'E'll go anywhere so long as 'tisn't across running water. That gives 'im 'is seizures. Even talkin' about it for fun like makes 'im shake.'

'But why isn't he where he can be properly looked after?'

'What 'arm's 'e doing? 'E's a love-child, but 'is family can pay for 'im. If 'e was locked up 'e'd die all off at once, like a wild rabbit. Won't you, please, look at the drive, sir?'

Midmore looked in the fading light. The neat gravel was pitted with large roundish holes, and there was a punch or two of the same sort on the lawn.

'That's the 'unt comin' 'ome,' Rhoda explained. 'Your pore dear auntie always let 'em use our drive for a short cut after the Colonel died. The Colonel wouldn't so much because he preserved; but your auntie was always an 'orsewoman till 'er sciatica.'

'Isn't there someone who can rake it over or — or something?' said Midmore vaguely.

'Oh yes. You'll never see it in the morning, but — you was out when they came 'ome an' Mister Fisher — he's the Master — told me to tell you with 'is compliments that if you wasn't preservin' and cared to 'old to the old understandin', 'is gravel-pit is at your service same as before. 'E thought, perhaps, you mightn't know, and it 'ad slipped my mind to tell you. It's good gravel, Mister Fisher's, and it binds beautiful on the drive. We 'ave to draw it, o' course, from the pit, but —'

Midmore looked at her helplessly.

'Rhoda,' said he, 'what am I supposed to do?'

'Oh, let 'em come through,' she replied. 'You never know. You may want to 'unt yourself some day.'

That evening it rained and his misery returned on him, the worse for having been diverted. At last he was driven to paw over a few score books in a panelled room called the library, and realized with horror what the late Colonel Werf's mind must have been in its prime. The volumes smelt of a dead world as strongly as they did of mildew. He opened and thrust them back, one after another, till crude coloured illustrations of men on horses held his eye. He began at random and read a little, moved into the drawing-room with the volume, and settled down by the fire still reading.[6] It was a foul world into which he peeped for the first time – a heavy-eating, hard-drinking hell of horse-copers, swindlers, matchmaking mothers, economically dependent virgins selling themselves blushingly for cash and lands: Jews, tradesmen, and an ill-considered spawn of Dickens-and-horsedung characters (I give Midmore's own criticism), but he read on, fascinated, and behold, from the pages leaped, as it were, the brother to the red-eyed man of the brook, bellowing at a landlord (here Midmore realized that *he* was that very animal) for new barns; and another man who, like himself again, objected to hoof-marks on gravel. Outrageous as thought and conception were, the stuff seemed to have the rudiments of observation. He dug out other volumes by the same author, till Rhoda came in with a silver candlestick.

'Rhoda,' said he, 'did you ever hear about a character called James Pigg – and Batsey?'

'Why, o' course,' said she. 'The Colonel used to come into the kitchen in 'is dressin'-gown an' read us all those Jorrockses.'

'Oh, Lord!' said Midmore, and went to bed with a book called *Handley Cross* under his arm, and a lonelier Columbus into a stranger world the wet-ringed moon never looked upon.

Here we omit much. But Midmore never denied that for the epicure in sensation the urgent needs of an ancient house, as interpreted by Rhoda pointing to daylight through attic-tiles held in place by moss, gives an edge to the pleasure of Social Research elsewhere. Equally he found that the reaction following prolonged research loses much of its grey terror if one knows one can at will bathe the soul in the society of plumbers (all the water-pipes had chronic appendicitis), village idiots

(Jimmy had taken Midmore under his weak wing and camped daily at the drive-gates), and a giant with red eyelids whose every action is an unpredictable outrage.

Towards spring Midmore filled his house with a few friends of the Immoderate Left. It happened to be the day when, all things and Rhoda working together, a cartload of bricks, another of sand, and some bags of lime had been dispatched to build Sidney his almost daily-demanded pig-pound. Midmore took his friends across the flat fields with some idea of showing them Sidney as a type of 'the peasantry'. They hit the minute when Sidney, hoarse with rage, was ordering brick-layer, mate, carts and all off his premises. The visitors disposed themselves to listen.

'You never give me no notice about changin' the pig,' Sidney shouted. The pig – at least eighteen inches long – reared on end in the old sty and smiled at the company.

'But, my good man –' Midmore opened.

'I ain't! For aught you know I be a dam' sight worse than you be. You can't come and be'ave arbit'ry with me. You *are* be'avin' arbit'ry! All you men go clean away an' don't set foot on my land till I bid ye.'

'But you asked' – Midmore felt his voice jump up – 'to have the pig-pound built.'

''Spose I did. That's no reason you shouldn't send me notice to change the pig. 'Comin' down on me like this 'thout warnin'! That pig's got to be got into the cowshed an' all.'

'Then open the door and let him run in,' said Midmore.

'Don't you be'ave arbit'ry with *me*! Take all your dam' men 'ome off my land. I won't be treated arbit'ry.'

The carts moved off without a word, and Sidney went into the house and slammed the door.

'Now, I hold that is enormously significant,' said a visitor. 'Here you have the logical outcome of centuries of feudal op-pression – the frenzy of fear.' The company looked at Midmore with grave pain.

'But he *did* worry my life out about his pig-sty,' was all Midmore found to say.

Others took up the parable and proved to him if he only held true to the gospels of the Immoderate Left the earth would soon be covered with 'jolly little' pig-sties, built in the intervals of morris-dancing by 'the peasant' himself.

Midmore felt grateful when the door opened again and Mr Sidney invited them all to retire to the road which, he pointed out, was public. As they turned the corner of the house, a smooth-faced woman in a widow's cap curtsied to each of them through the window.

Instantly they drew pictures of that woman's lot, deprived of all vehicle for self-expression – 'the set grey life and apathetic end',[7] one quoted – and they discussed the tremendous significance of village theatricals. Even a month ago Midmore would have told them all that he knew and Rhoda had dropped about Sidney's forms of self-expression. Now, for some strange reason, he was content to let the talk run on from village to metropolitan and world drama.

Rhoda advised him after the visitors left that 'if he wanted to do that again' he had better go up to town.

'But we only sat on cushions on the floor,' said her master.

'They're too old for romps,' she retorted, 'an' it's only the beginning of things. I've seen what *I've* seen. Besides, they talked and laughed in the passage going to their baths – such as took 'em.'

'Don't be a fool, Rhoda,' said Midmore. No man – unless he has loved her – will casually dismiss a woman on whose lap he has laid his head.

'Very good,' she snorted, 'but that cuts both ways. An' now, you go down to Sidney's this evenin' and put him where he ought to be. He was in his right about you givin' 'im notice about changin' the pig, but he 'adn't any right to turn it up before your company. No manners, no pig-pound. He'll understand.'

Midmore did his best to make him. He found himself reviling the old man in speech and with a joy quite new in all his experience. He wound up – it was a plagiarism from a plumber – by telling Mr Sidney that he looked like a turkey-cock, had the morals of a parish bull, and need never hope for a new pig-pound as long as he or Midmore lived.

'Very good,' said the giant. 'I reckon you thought you 'ad something against me, and now you've come down an' told it me like man to man. Quite right. I don't bear malice. Now, you send along those bricks an' sand, an' I'll make a do to build the pig-pound myself. If you look at my lease you'll find out you're bound to provide me materials for the repairs. Only – only I thought there'd be no 'arm in my askin' you to do it throughout like.'

Midmore fairly gasped. 'Then, why the devil did you turn my carts back when – when I sent them up here to do it throughout for you?'

Mr Sidney sat down on the flood-gates, his eyebrows knitted in thought.

'I'll tell you,' he said slowly. ''Twas too dam' like cheatin' a suckin' baby. My woman, she said so too.'

For a few seconds the teachings of the Immoderate Left, whose humour is all their own, wrestled with those of Mother Earth, who has her own humours. Then Midmore laughed till he could scarcely stand. In due time Mr Sidney laughed too – crowing and wheezing crescendo till it broke from him in roars. They shook hands, and Midmore went home grateful that he had held his tongue among his companions.

When he reached his house he met three or four men and women on horseback, very muddy indeed, coming down the drive. Feeling hungry himself, he asked them if they were hungry. They said they were, and he bade them enter. Jimmy took their horses, who seemed to know him. Rhoda took their battered hats, led the women upstairs for hairpins, and presently fed them all with tea-cakes, poached eggs, anchovy toast, and drinks from a coromandel-wood liqueur case which Midmore had never known that he possessed.

'And I *will* say,' said Miss Connie Sperrit, her spurred foot on the fender and a smoking muffin in her whip hand, 'Rhoda does one top-hole. She always did since I was eight.'

'Seven, Miss, was when you began to 'unt,' said Rhoda, setting down more buttered toast.

'And so,' the M. F. H. was saying to Midmore, 'when he got to your brute Sidney's land, we had to whip 'em off. It's a regular Alsatia for 'em. They know it. Why' – he dropped his voice – 'I don't want to say anything against Sidney as your tenant, of course, but I do believe the old scoundrel's perfectly capable of putting down poison.'

'Sidney's capable of anything,' said Midmore with immense feeling; but once again he held his tongue. They were a queer community; yet when they had stamped and jingled out to their horses again, the house felt hugely big and disconcerting.

This may be reckoned the conscious beginning of his double life. It ran in odd channels that summer – a riding school, for instance, near Hayes Common and a shooting ground near Wormwood Scrubs. A man who has been saddle-galled or shoulder-bruised for half the day is not at his London best of evenings; and when the bills for his amusements come in he curtails his expenses in other directions. So a cloud settled on Midmore's name. His London world talked of a hardening of heart and a tightening of purse-strings which signified disloyalty to the Cause. One man, a confidant of the old expressive days, attacked him robustiously and demanded account of his soul's progress. It was not furnished, for Midmore was calculating how much it would cost to repave stables so dilapidated that even the village idiot apologized for putting visitors' horses into them. The man went away, and served up what he had heard of the pig-pound episode as a little newspaper sketch, calculated to annoy. Midmore read it with an eye as practical as a woman's, and since most of his experiences had been among women, at once sought out a woman to whom he might tell his sorrow at the disloyalty of his own familiar friend. She was so sympathetic that he went on to confide how his bruised heart – she knew all about it – had found so-lace, with a long O, in another quarter which he indicated rather carefully in case it might be betrayed to other loyal friends. As his hints pointed directly towards facile Hampstead, and as his urgent business was the purchase of a horse from a dealer, Beckenham way, he felt he had done good work. Later, when his friend, the scribe, talked to him alluringly of 'secret gardens' and those so-laces to which every man who follows the Wider Morality is entitled, Midmore lent him a five-pound note which he had got back on the price of a ninety-guinea bay gelding. So true it is, as he read in one of the late Colonel Werf's books, that 'the young man of the present day would sooner lie under an imputation against his morals than against his knowledge of horse-flesh'.[8]

Midmore desired more than he desired anything else at that

moment to ride and, above all, to jump on a ninety-guinea bay gelding with black points and a slovenly habit of hitting his fences. He did not wish many people except Mr Sidney, who very kindly lent his soft meadow behind the flood-gates, to be privy to the matter, which he rightly foresaw would take him to the autumn. So he told such friends as hinted at country week-end visits that he had practically let his newly inherited house. The rent, he said, was an object to him, for he had lately lost large sums through ill-considered benevolences. He would name no names, but they could guess. And they guessed loyally all round the circle of his acquaintance as they spread the news that explained so much.

There remained only one couple of his once intimate associates to pacify. They were deeply sympathetic and utterly loyal, of course, but as curious as any of the apes whose diet they had adopted. Midmore met them in a suburban train, coming up to town, not twenty minutes after he had come off two hours' advanced tuition (one guinea an hour) over hurdles in a hall. He had, of course, changed his kit, but his too heavy bridle-hand shook a little among the newspapers. On the inspiration of the moment, which is your natural liar's best hold, he told them that he was condemned to a rest-cure. He would lie in semi-darkness drinking milk, for weeks and weeks, cut off even from letters. He was astonished and delighted at the ease with which the usual lie confounds the unusual intellect. They swallowed it as swiftly as they recommended him to live on nuts and fruit; but he saw in the woman's eyes the exact reason she would set forth for his retirement. After all, she had as much right to express herself as he purposed to take for himself; and Midmore believed strongly in the fullest equality of the sexes.

That retirement made one small ripple in the strenuous world. The lady who had written the twelve-page letter ten months before sent him another of eight pages, analysing all the motives that were leading her back to him – should she come? – now that he was ill and alone. Much might yet be retrieved, she said, out of the waste of jarring lives and piteous misunderstandings. It needed only a hand.

But Midmore needed two, next morning very early, for a devil's diversion, among wet coppices, called 'cubbing'.

'You haven't a bad seat,' said Miss Sperrit through the morning-mists. 'But you're worrying him.'

'He pulls so,' Midmore grunted.

'Let him alone, then. Look out for the branches,' she shouted, as they whirled up a splashy ride. Cubs were plentiful. Most of the hounds attached themselves to a straight-necked youngster of education who scuttled out of the woods into the open fields below.

'Hold on!' some one shouted. 'Turn 'em, Midmore. That's your brute Sidney's land. It's all wire.'

'Oh, Connie, stop!' Mrs Sperrit shrieked as her daughter charged at a boundary-hedge.

'Wire be damned! I had it all out a fortnight ago. Come on!' This was Midmore, buffeting into it a little lower down.

'*I* knew that!' Connie cried over her shoulder, and she flitted across the open pasture, humming to herself.

'Oh, of course! If some people have private information, they can afford to thrust.' This was a snuff-coloured habit into which Miss Sperrit had cannoned down the ride.

'What! 'Midmore got Sidney to heel? *You* never did that, Sperrit.' This was Mr Fisher, M.F.H., enlarging the breach Midmore had made.

'No, confound him!' said the father testily. 'Go on, sir! *Injecto ter pulvere* [9] – you've kicked half the ditch into my eye already.'

They killed that cub a little short of the haven his mother had told him to make for – a two-acre Alsatia of a gorse-patch to which the M.F.H. had been denied access for the last fifteen seasons. He expressed his gratitude before all the field and Mr Sidney, at Mr Sidney's farmhouse door.

'And if there should be any poultry claims –' he went on.

'There won't be,' said Midmore. 'It's too like cheating a sucking child, isn't it, Mr Sidney?'

'You've got me!' was all the reply. 'I be used to bein' put upon, but you've got me, Mus' Midmore.'

Midmore pointed to a new brick pig-pound built in strict disregard of the terms of the life-tenant's lease. The gesture told the tale to the few who did not know, and they shouted.

Such pagan delights as these were followed by pagan sloth of evenings when men and women elsewhere are at their brightest.

But Midmore preferred to lie out on a yellow silk couch, reading works of a debasing vulgarity; or, by invitation, to dine with the Sperrits and savages of their kidney. These did not expect flights of fancy or phrasing. They lied, except about horses, grudgingly and of necessity, not for art's sake; and, men and women alike, they expressed themselves along their chosen lines with the serene indifference of the larger animals. Then Midmore would go home and identify them, one by one, out of the natural-history books by Mr Surtees, on the table beside the sofa. At first they looked upon him coolly, but when the tale of the removed wire and the recaptured gorse had gone the rounds, they accepted him for a person willing to play their games. True, a faction suspended judgment for a while, because they shot, and hoped that Midmore would serve the glorious mammon of pheasant-raising rather than the unkempt god of fox-hunting. But after he had shown his choice, they did not ask by what intellectual process he had arrived at it. He hunted three, sometimes four, times a week, which necessitated not only one bay gelding (£94:10s.), but a mannerly white-stockinged chestnut (£114), and a black mare, rather long in the back but with a mouth of silk (£150), who so evidently preferred to carry a lady that it would have been cruel to have baulked her. Besides, with that handling she could be sold at a profit. And besides, the hunt was a quiet, intimate, kindly little hunt, not anxious for strangers, of good report in the *Field*, the servant of one M.F.H., given to hospitality, riding well its own horses, and, with the exception of Midmore, not novices. But as Miss Sperrit observed, after the M.F.H. had said some things to him at a gate: 'It *is* a pity you don't know as much as your horse, but you will in time. It takes years and yee-ars. I've been at it for fifteen and I'm only just learning. But you've made a decent kick-off.'

So he kicked off in wind and wet and mud, wondering quite sincerely why the bubbling ditches and sucking pastures held him from day to day, or what so-lace he could find on off days in chasing grooms and bricklayers round outhouses.

To make sure he up-rooted himself one week-end of heavy mid-winter rain, and re-entered his lost world in the character of Galahad[10] fresh from a rest-cure. They all agreed, with an eye over his shoulder for the next comer, that he was a different man; but when they asked him for the symptoms of nervous strain, and led him all through their own, he realized he had lost much of his old skill in lying. His three months' absence, too, had put him hopelessly behind the London field. The movements, the allusions, the slang of the game had changed. The couples had rearranged themselves or were re-crystallizing in fresh triangles, whereby he put his foot in it badly. Only one great soul (he who had written the account of the pig-pound episode) stood untouched by the vast flux of time, and Midmore lent him another fiver for his integrity. A woman took him, in the wet forenoon, to a pronouncement on the Oneness of Impulse in Humanity, which struck him as a polysyllabic *résumé* of Mr Sidney's domestic arrangements, plus a clarion call to 'shock civilization into common-sense.'

'And you'll come to tea with me tomorrow?' she asked, after lunch, nibbling cashew nuts from a saucer. Midmore replied that there were great arrears of work to overtake when a man had been put away for so long.

'But you've come back like a giant refreshed . . . I hope that Daphne' – this was the lady of the twelve and the eight-page letter – 'will be with us too. She has misunderstood herself, like so many of us,' the woman murmured, 'but I think eventually . . .' she flung out her thin little hands. 'However, these are things that each lonely soul must adjust for itself.'

'Indeed, yes,' said Midmore with a deep sigh. The old tricks were sprouting in the old atmosphere like mushrooms in a dung-pit. He passed into an abrupt reverie, shook his head, as though stung by tumultuous memories, and departed without any ceremony of farewell to – catch a midafternoon express where a man meets associates who talk horse, and weather as it affects the horse, all the way down. What worried him most was that he had missed a day with the hounds.

He met Rhoda's keen old eyes without flinching; and the drawing-room looked very comfortable that wet evening at tea. After all, his visit to town had not been wholly a failure. He had burned quite a bushel of letters at his flat. A flat – here he reached mechanically toward the worn volumes near the sofa – a flat was a consuming animal. As for Daphne . . . he opened at random on the words: 'His lordship then did as desired and disclosed a *tableau* of considerable strength and variety.'[11] Midmore reflected: 'And I used to think . . . But she wasn't . . . We were all babblers and skirters together . . . I didn't babble much – thank goodness – but I skirted.' He turned the pages backward for more *Sortes Surteesianae*, and read: 'When at length they rose to go to bed it struck each man as he followed his neighbour upstairs, that the man before him walked very crookedly.' He laughed aloud at the fire.

'What about tomorrow?' Rhoda asked, entering with garments over her shoulder. 'It's never stopped raining since you left. You'll be plastered out of sight an' all in five minutes. You'd better wear your next best, 'adn't you? I'm afraid they've shrank. 'Adn't you best try 'em on?'

'Here?' said Midmore.

''Suit yourself. I bathed you when you wasn't larger than a leg o' lamb,' said the ex-ladies'-maid.

'Rhoda, one of these days I shall get a valet, and a married butler.'

'There's many a true word spoke in jest. But nobody's huntin' tomorrow.'

'Why? Have they cancelled the meet?'

'They say it only means slipping and over-reaching in the mud, and they all 'ad enough of that today. Charlie told me so just now.'

'Oh!' It seemed that the word of Mr Sperrit's confidential clerk had weight.

'Charlie came down to help Mr Sidney lift the gates,' Rhoda continued.

'The flood-gates? They are perfectly easy to handle now. I've put in a wheel and a winch.'

'When the brook's really up they must be took clean out on account of the rubbish blockin' 'em. That's why Charlie came down.'

Midmore grunted impatiently. 'Everybody has talked to me about that brook ever since I came here. It's never done anything yet.'

'This 'as been a dry summer. If you care to look now, sir, I'll get you a lantern.'

She paddled out with him into a large wet night. Half-way

down the lawn her light was reflected on shallow brown water, pricked through with grass blades at the edges. Beyond that light, the brook was strangling and kicking among hedges and tree-trunks.

'What on earth will happen to the big rose-bed?' was Midmore's first word.

'It generally 'as to be restocked after a flood. Ah!' she raised her lantern. 'There's two garden-seats knockin' against the sundial. Now, that won't do the roses any good.'

'This is too absurd. There ought to be some decently thought-out system – for – for dealing with this sort of thing.' He peered into the rushing gloom. There seemed to be no end to the moisture and the racket. In town he had noticed nothing.

'It can't be 'elped,' said Rhoda. 'It's just what it does do once in just so often. We'd better go back.'

All earth under foot was sliding in a thousand liquid noises towards the hoarse brook. Somebody wailed from the house: ''Fraid o' the water! Come 'ere! 'Fraid o' the water!'

'That's Jimmy. Wet always takes 'im that way,' she explained. The idiot charged into them, shaking with terror.

'Brave Jimmy! How brave of Jimmy! Come into the hall. What Jimmy got now?' she crooned. It was a sodden note which ran: 'Dear Rhoda – Mr Lotten, with whom I rode home this afternoon, told me that if this wet keeps up, he's afraid the fish-pond he built last year, where Coxen's old mill-dam was, will go, as the dam did once before, he says. If it does it's bound to come down the brook. It may be all right, but perhaps you had better look out. C.S.'

'If Coxen's dam goes, that means . . . I'll 'ave the drawing-room carpet up at once to be on the safe side. The claw-'ammer is in the libery.'

'Wait a minute. Sidney's gates are out, you said?'

'Both. He'll need it if Coxen's pond goes . . . I've seen it once.'

'I'll just slip down and have a look at Sidney. Light the lantern again, please, Rhoda.'

'You won't get *him* to stir. He's been there since he was born. But *she* don't know anything. I'll fetch your waterproof and some top-boots.'

''Fraid o' the water! 'Fraid o' the water!' Jimmy sobbed, pressed against a corner of the hall, his hands to his eyes.

'All right, Jimmy. Jimmy can help play with the carpet,' Rhoda answered, as Midmore went forth into the darkness and the roarings all round. He had never seen such an utterly unregulated state of affairs. There was another lantern reflected on the streaming drive.

'Hi! Rhoda! Did you get my note? I came down to make sure. I thought, afterwards, Jimmy might funk the water!'

'It's me – Miss Sperrit,' Midmore cried. 'Yes, we got it, thanks.'

'You're back, then. Oh, good! . . . Is it bad down with you?'

'I'm going to Sidney's to have a look.'

'You won't get *him* out. 'Lucky I met Bob Lotten. I told him he hadn't any business impounding water for his idiotic trout without rebuilding the dam.'

'How far up is it? I've only been there once.'

'Not more than four miles as the water will come. He says he's opened all the sluices.'

She had turned and fallen into step beside him, her hooded head bowed against the thinning rain. As usual she was humming to herself.

'Why on earth did you come out in this weather?' Midmore asked.

'It was worse when you were in town. The rain's taking off now. If it wasn't for that pond, I wouldn't worry so much. There's Sidney's bell. Come on!' She broke into a run. A cracked bell was jangling feebly down the valley.

'Keep on the road!' Midmore shouted. The ditches were snorting bank-full on either side, and towards the brook-side the fields were afloat and beginning to move in the darkness.

'Catch me going off it! There's his light burning all right.' She halted undistressed at a little rise. 'But the flood's in the orchard. Look!' She swung her lantern to show a front rank of old apple-trees reflected in still, out-lying waters beyond the half-drowned hedge. They could hear above the thud-thud of the gorged flood-gates, shrieks in two keys as monotonous as a steam-organ.

'The high one's the pig.' Miss Sperrit laughed.

'All right! I'll get *her* out. You stay where you are, and I'll see you home afterwards.'

'But the water's only just over the road,' she objected.

'Never mind. Don't you move. Promise?'

'All right. You take my stick, then, and feel for holes in case anything's washed out anywhere. This *is* a lark!'

Midmore took it, and stepped into the water that moved sluggishly as yet across the farm road which ran to Sidney's front door from the raised and metalled public road. It was half way up to his knees when he knocked. As he looked back Miss Sperrit's lantern seemed to float in mid-ocean.

'You can't come in or the water 'll come with you. I've bunged up all the cracks,' Mr Sidney shouted from within. 'Who be ye?'

'Take me out! Take me out!' the woman shrieked, and the pig from his sty behind the house urgently seconded the motion.

'I'm Midmore! Coxen's old mill-dam is likely to go, they say. Come out!'

'I told 'em it would when they made a fish-pond of it. 'Twasn't ever puddled proper. But it's a middlin' wide valley. She's got room to spread . . . Keep still, or I'll take and duck you in the cellar! . . . You go 'ome, Mus' Midmore, an' take the law o' Mus' Lotten soon 's you've changed your socks.'

'Confound you, aren't you coming out?'

'To catch my death o' cold? I'm all right where I be. I've seen it before. But you can take *her*. She's no sort o' use or sense . . . Climb out through the window. Didn't I tell you I'd plugged the door-cracks, you fool's daughter?' The parlour window opened, and the woman flung herself into Midmore's arms, nearly knocking him down. Mr Sidney leaned out of the window, pipe in mouth.

'Take her 'ome,' he said, and added oracularly:

> 'Two women in one house,
> Two cats an' one mouse,
> Two dogs an' one bone –
> Which I will leave alone.[12]

'I've seen it before.' Then he shut and fastened the window.

'A trap! A trap! You had ought to have brought a trap for

me. I'll be drowned in this wet,' the woman cried.

'Hold up! You can't be any wetter than you are. Come along!' Midmore did not at all like the feel of the water over his boot-tops.

'Hooray! Come along!' Miss Sperrit's lantern, not fifty yards away, waved cheerily.

The woman threshed towards it like a panic-stricken goose, fell on her knees, was jerked up again by Midmore, and pushed on till she collapsed at Miss Sperrit's feet.

'But you won't get bronchitis if you go straight to Mr Midmore's house,' said the unsympathetic maiden.

'O Gawd! O Gawd! I wish our 'eavenly Father 'ud forgive me my sins an' call me 'ome,' the woman sobbed. 'But I won't go to '*is* 'ouse! I won't.'

'All right, then. Stay here. Now, if we run,' Miss Sperrit whispered to Midmore, 'she'll follow us. Not too fast!'

They set off at a considerate trot, and the woman lumbered behind them, bellowing, till they met a third lantern – Rhoda holding Jimmy's hand. She had got the carpet up, she said, and was escorting Jimmy past the water that he dreaded.

'That's all right,' Miss Sperrit pronounced. 'Take Mrs Sidney back with you, Rhoda, and put her to bed. I'll take Jimmy with me. You aren't afraid of the water now, are you, Jimmy?'

'Not afraid of anything now.' Jimmy reached for her hand. 'But get away from the water quick.'

'I'm coming with you,' Midmore interrupted.

'You most certainly are not. You're drenched. She threw you twice. Go home and change. You may have to be out again all night. It's only half-past seven now. I'm perfectly safe.' She flung herself lightly over a stile, and hurried uphill by the footpath, out of reach of all but the boasts of the flood below.

Rhoda, dead silent, herded Mrs Sidney to the house.

'You'll find your things laid out on the bed,' she said to Midmore as he came up. 'I'll attend to – to this. *She's* got nothing to cry for.'

Midmore raced into dry kit, and raced uphill to be rewarded by the sight of the lantern just turning into the Sperrit's gate. He came back by way of Sidney's farm, where he saw the light twinkling across three acres of shining water, for the rain had ceased and the clouds were stripping overhead, though the brook was noisier than ever. Now there was only that doubtful mill-pond to look after – that and his swirling world abandoned to himself alone.

'We shall have to sit up for it,' said Rhoda after dinner. And as the drawing-room commanded the best view of the rising flood, they watched it from there for a long time, while all the clocks of the house bore them company.

''Tisn't the water, it's the mud on the skirting-board after it goes down that I mind,' Rhoda whispered. 'The last time Coxen's mill broke, I remember it came up to the second – no, third – step o' Mr Sidney's stairs.'

'What did Sidney do about it?'

'He made a notch on the step. 'E said it was a record. Just like 'im.'

'It's up to the drive now,' said Midmore after another long wait. 'And the rain stopped before eight, you know.'

'Then Coxen's dam 'as broke, and that's the first of the flood-water.' She stared out beside him. The water was rising in sudden pulses – an inch or two at a time, with great sweeps and lagoons and a sudden increase of the brook's proper thunder.

'You can't stand all the time. Take a chair,' Midmore said presently.

Rhoda looked back into the bare room. 'The carpet bein' up *does* make a difference. Thank you, sir, I *will* 'ave a set-down.'

''Right over the drive now,' said Midmore. He opened the window and leaned out. 'Is that wind up the valley, Rhoda?'

'No, that's *it*! But I've seen it before.'

There was not so much a roar as the purposeful drive of a tide across a jagged reef, which put down every other sound for twenty minutes. A wide sheet of water hurried up to the little terrace on which the house stood, pushed round either corner, rose again and stretched, as it were, yawning beneath the moon-light, joined other sheets waiting for them in unsuspected hollows, and lay out all in one. A puff of wind followed.

'It's right up to the wall now. I can touch it with my finger.' Midmore bent over the window-sill.

'I can 'ear it in the cellars,' said Rhoda dolefully. 'Well, we've done what we can! I think I'll 'ave a look.' She left the room and was absent half an hour or more, during which time he saw a full-grown tree hauling itself across the lawn by its naked roots. Then a hurdle knocked against the wall, caught on an iron foot-scraper just outside, and made a square-headed ripple. The cascade through the cellar-windows diminished.

'It's dropping,' Rhoda cried, as she returned. 'It's only tricklin' into my cellars now.'

'Wait a minute. I believe – I believe I can see the scraper on the edge of the drive just showing!'

In another ten minutes the drive itself roughened and became gravel again, tilting all its water towards the shrubbery.

'The pond's gone past,' Rhoda announced. 'We shall only 'ave the common flood to contend with now. You'd better go to bed.'

'I ought to go down and have another look at Sidney before daylight.'

'No need. You can see 'is light burnin' from all the upstairs windows.'

'By the way. I forgot about *her*. Where've you put her?'

'In my bed.' Rhoda's tone was ice. 'I wasn't going to undo a room for *that* stuff.'

'But it – it couldn't be helped,' said Midmore. 'She was half drowned. One mustn't be narrow-minded, Rhoda, even if her position isn't quite – er – regular.'

'Pfff! I wasn't worryin' about that.' She leaned forward to the window. 'There's the edge of the lawn showin' now. It falls as fast as it rises. Dearie' – the change of tone made Midmore jump – 'didn't you know that I was 'is first? *That*'s what makes it so hard to bear.' Midmore looked at the long lizard-like back and had no words.

She went on, still talking through the black window-pane:

'Your pore dear auntie was very kind about it. She said she'd make all allowances for one, but no more. Never any more . . . Then, you didn't know 'oo Charlie was all this time?'

'Your nephew, I always thought.'

'Well, well,' she spoke pityingly. 'Everybody's business being nobody's business, I suppose no one thought to tell you. But

Charlie made 'is own way for 'imself from the beginnin'! . . .
But *her* upstairs, she never produced anything. Just an 'ouse-
keeper, as you might say. 'Turned over an' went to sleep
straight off. She 'ad the impudence to ask me for 'ot sherry-
gruel.'

'Did you give it to her,' said Midmore.

'Me? Your sherry? No!'

The memory of Sidney's outrageous rhyme at the window,
and Charlie's long nose (he thought it looked interested at the
time) as he passed the copies of Mrs Werf's last four wills,
overcame Midmore without warning.

'This damp is givin' you a cold,' said Rhoda, rising. 'There
you go again! Sneezin's a sure sign of it. Better go to bed. You
can't do anythin' excep'' – she stood rigid, with crossed arms –
'about me.'

'Well. What about you?' Midmore stuffed the handkerchief
into his pocket.

'Now you know about it, what are you goin' to do – sir?'

She had the answer on her lean cheek, before the sentence
was finished.

'Go and see if you can get us something to eat, Rhoda. And
beer.'

'I expec' the larder 'll be in a swim,' she replied, 'but old
bottled stuff don't take any harm from wet.' She returned with
a tray, all in order, and they ate and drank together, and took
observations of the falling flood till dawn opened its bleared
eyes on the wreck of what had been a fair garden. Midmore,
cold and annoyed, found himself humming:

> 'That flood strewed wrecks upon the grass,
>   That ebb swept out the flocks to sea.

'There isn't a rose left, Rhoda!

> 'An awesome ebb and flow it was
>   To many more than mine and me.
>   But each will mourn his . . .[13]

'It'll cost me a hundred.'

'Now we know the worst,' said Rhoda, 'we can go to bed. I'll
lay on the kitchen sofa. His light's burnin' still.'

'And *she*?'

'Dirty old cat! You ought to 'ear 'er snore!'

At ten o'clock in the morning, after a maddening hour in his own garden on the edge of the retreating brook, Midmore went off to confront more damage at Sidney's. The first thing that met him was the pig, snowy white, for the water had washed him out of his new sty, calling on high heaven for breakfast. The front door had been forced open, and the flood had registered its own height in a brown dado on the walls. Midmore chased the pig out and called up the stairs.

'I be abed o' course. Which step 'as she rose to?' Sidney cried from above. 'The fourth? Then it's beat all records. Come up.'

'Are you ill?' Midmore asked as he entered the room. The red eyelids blinked cheerfully. Mr Sidney, beneath a sumptuous patch-work quilt, was smoking.

'Nah! I'm only thankin' God I ain't my own landlord. Take that cheer. What's she done?'

'It hasn't gone down enough for me to make sure.'

'Them flood-gates o' yourn 'll be middlin' far down the brook by now; an' your rose-garden have gone after 'em. I saved my chickens, though. You'd better get Mus' Sperrit to take the law o' Lotten an' is fish-pond.'

'No, thanks. I've trouble enough without that.'

'Hev ye?' Mr Sidney grinned. 'How did ye make out with those two women o' mine last night? I lay they fought.'

'You infernal old scoundrel!' Midmore laughed.

'I be – an' then again I bain't,' was the placid answer. 'But, Rhoda, *she* wouldn't ha' left me last night. Fire or flood, she wouldn't.'

'Why didn't you ever marry her?' Midmore asked.

'Waste of good money. She was willin' without.'

There was a step on the gritty mud below, and a voice humming. Midmore rose quickly saying: 'Well, I suppose you're all right now.'

'I be. I ain't a landlord, nor I ain't young – nor anxious. Oh, Mus' Midmore! Would it make any odds about her thirty pounds comin' regular if I married her? Charlie said maybe 'twould.'

'Did he?' Midmore turned at the door. 'And what did Jimmy say about it?'

'Jimmy?' Mr Sidney chuckled as the joke took him. 'Oh, *he*'s none o' mine. He's Charlie's look-out.'

Midmore slammed the door and ran downstairs.

'Well, this is a – sweet – mess,' said Miss Sperrit in shortest skirts and heaviest riding-boots. 'I had to come down and have a look at it. "The old mayor climbed the belfry tower."'[14] Been up all night nursing your family?'

'Nearly that! Isn't it cheerful?' He pointed through the door to the stairs with small twig-drift on the last three treads.

'It's a record, though,' said she, and hummed to herself:

> 'That flood strewed wrecks upon the grass,
>   That ebb swept out the flocks to sea.'[15]

'You're always singing that, aren't you?' Midmore said suddenly as she passed into the parlour where slimy chairs had been stranded at all angles.

'Am I? Now I come to think of it I believe I do. They say I always hum when I ride. Have you noticed it?'

'Of course I have. I notice every –'

'Oh,' she went on hurriedly. 'We had it for the village cantata last winter – "The Brides of Enderby".'

'No! "High Tide on the Coast of Lincolnshire".' For some reason Midmore spoke sharply.

'Just like that.' She pointed to the befouled walls. 'I say . . . Let's get this furniture a little straight . . . You know it too?'

'Every word, since you sang it, of course.'

'When?'

'The first night I ever came down. You rode past the drawing-room window in the dark singing it – "And sweeter woman –"'[16]

'I thought the house was empty then. Your aunt always let us use that short cut. Ha-hadn't we better get this out into the passage? It'll all have to come out anyhow. You take the other side.' They began to lift a heavyish table. Their words came jerkily between gasps and their faces were as white as – a newly washed and very hungry pig.

'Look out!' Midmore shouted. His legs were whirled from

under him, as the table, grunting madly, careened and knocked the girl out of sight.

The wild boar of Asia could not have cut down a couple more scientifically, but this little pig lacked his ancestor's nerve and fled shrieking over their bodies.

'Are you hurt, darling?' was Midmore's first word, and 'No – I'm only winded – dear,' was Miss Sperrit's, as he lifted her out of her corner, her hat over one eye and her right cheek a smear of mud.

They fed him a little later on some chicken-feed that they found in Sidney's quiet barn, a pail of buttermilk out of the dairy, and a quantity of onions from a shelf in the back-kitchen.

'Seed-onions, most likely,' said Connie. 'You'll hear about this.'

'What does it matter? They ought to have been gilded. We must buy him.'

'And keep him as long as he lives,' she agreed. 'But I think I ought to go home now. You see, when I came out I didn't expect . . . Did you?'

'No! Yes . . . It had to come . . . But if any one had told me an hour ago! . . . Sidney's unspeakable parlour – and the mud on the carpet.'

'Oh I say! Is my cheek clean now?'

'Not quite. Lend me your hanky again a minute, darling . . . What a purler you came!'

'You can't talk. 'Remember when your chin hit that table and you said "blast"! I was just going to laugh.'

'You didn't laugh when I picked you up. You were going "oo–oo–oo" like a little owl.'

'My dear child –'

'Say that again!'

'My dear child (Do you really like it? I keep it for my best friends.) My *dee-ar* child, I thought I was going to be sick there and then. He knocked every ounce of wind out of me – the angel! But I must really go.'

They set off together, very careful not to join hands or take arms.

'Not across the fields,' said Midmore at the stile. 'Come round by — by your own place.'

She flushed indignantly.

'It will be yours in a little time,' he went on, shaken with his own audacity.

'Not so much of your little times, if you please!' She shied like a colt across the road; then instantly, like a colt, her eyes lit with new curiosity as she came in sight of the drive-gates.

'And not quite so much of your airs and graces, Madam,' Midmore returned, 'or I won't let you use our drive as a short cut any more.'

'Oh, I'll be good. I'll be good.' Her voice changed suddenly. 'I swear I'll try to be good, dear. I'm not much of a thing at the best. What made *you* . . .'

'I'm worse — worse! Miles and oceans worse. But what does it matter now?'

They halted beside the gate-pillars.

'I see!' she said, looking up the sodden carriage sweep to the front door porch where Rhoda was slapping a wet mat to and fro. '*I* see . . . Now, I really must go home. No! Don't you come. I must speak to Mother first all by myself.'

He watched her up the hill till she was out of sight.

The Floods

The rain it rains without a stay
   In the hills above us, in the hills;
And presently the floods break way
   Whose strength is in the hills.
The trees they suck from every cloud,
The valley brooks they roar aloud —
Bank-high for the lowlands, lowlands,
   Lowlands under the hills!

The first wood down is sere and small,
   From the hills, the brishings [1] off the hills;
And then come by the bats and all
   We cut last year in the hills;
And then the roots we tried to cleave
But found too tough and had to leave —
Polting [2] through the lowlands, lowlands,
   Lowlands under the hills!

The eye shall look, the ear shall hark
   To the hills, the doings in the hills,
And rivers mating in the dark
   With tokens from the hills.
Now what is weak will surely go,
And what is strong must prove it so.
Stand fast in the lowlands, lowlands,
   Lowlands under the hills!

The floods they shall not be afraid —
   Nor the hills above 'em, nor the hills —
Of any fence which man has made
   Betwixt him and the hills.
The waters shall not reckon twice
For any work of man's device,
But bid it down to the lowlands, lowlands,
   Lowlands under the hills!

The floods shall sweep corruption clean —
   By the hills, the blessing of the hills —

A Diversity of Creatures

That more the meadows may be green
　New-mended from the hills.
The crops and cattle shall increase,
Nor little children shall not cease —
Go — plough the lowlands, lowlands,
　Lowlands under the hills!

The Fabulists

When all the world would have a matter hid,
   Since Truth is seldom friend to any crowd,
Men write in fable, as old Æsop did,
   Jesting at that which none will name aloud.
And this they needs must do, or it will fall
Unless they please they are not heard at all.

When desperate Folly daily laboureth
   To work confusion upon all we have,
When diligent Sloth demandeth Freedom's death,
   And banded Fear commandeth Honour's grave —
Even in that certain hour before the fall
Unless men please they are not heard at all.

Needs must all please, yet some not all for need
   Needs must all toil, yet some not all for gain,
But that men taking pleasure may take heed,
   Whom present toil shall snatch from later pain.
Thus some have toiled but their reward was small
Since, though they pleased, they were not heard at all.

This was the lock that lay upon our lips,
   This was the yoke that we have undergone,
Denying us all pleasant fellowships
   As in our time and generation.
Our pleasures unpursued age past recall.
And for our pains — we are not heard at all.

What man hears aught except the groaning guns?
   What man heeds aught save what each instant brings?
When each man's life all imaged life outruns,
   What man shall pleasure in imaginings?
So it hath fallen, as it was bound to fall,
We are not, nor we were not, heard at all.

THE VORTEX

{ The Vortex }

(August 1914)

'Thy Lord spoke by inspiration to the Bee.'
Al Koran

I have, to my grief and loss, suppressed several notable stories of my friend, the Hon. A. M. Penfentenyou,[1] once Minister of Woods and Waysides in De Thouar's first administration; later, Premier in all but name of one of Our great and growing Dominions;[2] and now, as always, the idol of his own Province, which is two and one-half the size of England.

For this reason I hold myself at liberty to deal with some portion of the truth concerning Penfentenyou's latest visit to Our shores. He arrived at my house by car, on a hot summer day, in a white waistcoat and spats, sweeping black frock-coat and glistening top-hat – a little rounded, perhaps, at the edges, but agile as ever in mind and body.

'What is the trouble now?' I asked, for the last time we had met, Penfentenyou was floating a three-million pound loan for his beloved but unscrupulous Province, and I did not wish to entertain any more of his financial friends.

'We,' Penfentenyou replied ambassadorially, 'have come to have a Voice in Your Councils. By the way, the Voice is coming down on the evening train with my Agent-General. I thought you wouldn't mind if I invited 'em. You know We're going to share Your burdens henceforward. You'd better get into training.'

'Certainly,' I replied. 'What's the Voice like?'

'He's in earnest,' said Penfentenyou. 'He's got It, and he's got It bad. He'll give It to you,' he said.

'What's his name?'

'We call him all sorts of names, but I think you'd better call him Mr Lingnam. You won't have to do it more than once.'

'What's he suffering from?'

'The Empire. He's pretty nearly cured us all of Imperialism at home. P'raps he'll cure you.'

'Very good. What am I to do with him?'

'Don't you worry,' said Penfentenyou. 'He'll do it.'

And when Mr Lingnam appeared half-an-hour later with the Agent-General for Penfentenyou's Dominion, he did just that.

He advanced across the lawn eloquent as all the tides. He said he had been observing to the Agent-General that it was both politically immoral and strategically unsound that forty-four million people should bear the entire weight of the defences of Our mighty Empire, but, as he had observed (here the Agent-General evaporated), we stood now upon the threshold of a new era in which the self-governing *and* self-respecting (bis) Dominions would rightly and righteously, as co-partners in Empery, shoulder their share of any burden which the Pan-Imperial Council of the Future should allot. The Agent-General was already arranging for drinks with Penfentenyou at the other end of the garden. Mr Lingnam swept me on to the most remote bench and settled to his theme.

We dined at eight. At nine Mr Lingnam was only drawing abreast of things Imperial. At ten the Agent-General, who earns his salary, was shamelessly dozing on the sofa. At eleven he and Penfentenyou went to bed. At midnight Mr Lingnam brought down his big-bellied dispatch box with the newspaper clippings and set to federating the Empire in earnest. I remember that he had three alternative plans. As a dealer in words, I plumped for the resonant third – 'Reciprocally co-ordinated Senatorial Hegemony' – which he then elaborated in detail for three-quarters of an hour. At half-past one he urged me to have faith and to remember that nothing mattered except the Idea. Then he retired to his room, accompanied by one glass of cold water, and I went into the dawn-lit garden and prayed to any Power that might be off duty for the blood of Mr Lingnam, Penfentenyou, and the Agent-General.

To me, as I have often observed elsewhere, the hour of earliest dawn is fortunate, and the wind that runs before it has ever been my most comfortable counsellor.

'Wait!' it said, all among the night's expectant rosebuds. 'Tomorrow is also a day. Wait upon the Event!'

I went to bed so at peace with God and Man and Guest that when I waked I visited Mr Lingnam in pyjamas, and he talked to me Pan-Imperially for half-an-hour before his bath. Later, the Agent-General said he had letters to write, and Penfentenyou invented a Cabinet crisis in his adored Dominion which would keep him busy with codes and cables all the forenoon. But I said firmly, 'Mr Lingnam wishes to see a little of the country round here. You are coming with us in your own car.'

'It's a hired one,' Penfentenyou objected.

'Yes. Paid for by me as a taxpayer,' I replied.

'And yours has a top, and the weather looks thundery,' said the Agent-General. 'Ours hasn't a wind-screen. Even our goggles were hired.'

'I'll lend you goggles,' I said. 'My car is under repairs.'

The hireling who had looked to be returned to London spat and growled on the drive. She was an open car, capable of some eighteen miles on the flat, with tetanic³ gears and a perpetual palsy.

'It won't make the least difference,' sighed the Agent-General. 'He'll only raise his voice. He did it all the way coming down.'

'I say,' said Penfentenyou suspiciously, 'what are you doing all this *for*?'

'Love of the Empire,' I answered, as Mr Lingnam tripped up in dust-coat and binoculars. 'Now, Mr Lingnam will tell us exactly what he wants to see. He probably knows more about England than the rest of us put together.'

'I read it up yesterday,' said Mr Lingnam simply. While we stowed the lunch-basket (one can never make too sure with a hired car) he outlined a very pretty and instructive little day's run.

'You'll drive, of course?' said Penfentenyou to him. 'It's the only thing you know anything about.'

This astonished me, for your greater Federationists are rarely mechanicians, but Mr Lingnam said he would prefer to be inside for the present and enjoy our conversation.

Well settled on the back seat, he did not once lift his eyes to the mellow landscape around him, or throw a word at the life of the English road which to me is one renewed and unreasoned orgy of delight. The mustard-coloured scouts of the Automobile Association; their natural enemies, the unjust police; our natural enemies, the deliberate market-day cattle, broadside-on at all corners, the bicycling butcher-boy a furlong behind; road-engines that pulled giddy-go-rounds, rifle galleries, and swings, and sucked snortingly from wayside ponds in defiance of the notice-board; traction-engines, their trailers piled high with road metal; uniformed village nurses, one per seven statute miles, flitting by on their wheels; governess-carts full of pink children jogging unconcernedly past roaring, brazen touring-cars; the wayside rector with virgins in attendance, their faces screwed up against our dust; motor-bicycles of every shape charging down at every angle; red flags of rifle-ranges; detachments of dusty-putteed Territorials; coveys of flagrant children playing in mid-street, and the wise, educated English dog safe and quite silent on the pavement if his fool-mistress would but cease from trying to save him, passed and repassed us in sunlit or shaded settings. But Mr Lingnam only talked. He talked — we all sat together behind so that we could not escape him — and he talked above the worn gears and a certain maddening swish of one badly patched tyre — *and* he talked of the Federation of the Empire against all conceivable dangers except himself. Yet I was neither brutally rude like Penfentenyou, nor swooningly bored like the Agent-General. I remembered a certain Joseph Finsbury who delighted the Tregonwell Arms on the borders of the New Forest with 'nine' — it should have been ten — 'versions of a single income of two hundred pounds' placing the imaginary person in — but I could not recall the list of towns further than 'London, Paris, Bagdad, and Spitzbergen'. This last I must have murmured aloud, for the Agent-General suddenly became human and went on: 'Bussoran, Heligoland, and the Scilly Islands —'

'What?' growled Penfentenyou.

'Nothing,' said the Agent-General, squeezing my hand affectionately. 'Only we have just found out that we are brothers.'

'Exactly,' said Mr Lingnam. 'That's what I've been trying to lead up to. We're *all* brothers. D'you realize that fifteen years ago such a conversation as we're having would have been unthinkable? The Empire wouldn't have been ripe for it. To go back, even ten years –'

'I've got it,' cried the Agent-General. '"Brighton, Cincinnati, and Nijni-Novgorod!" God bless R. L. S.! Go on, Uncle Joseph. I can endure much now.'

Mr Lingnam went on like our shandrydan,[4] slowly and loudly. He admitted that a man obsessed with a Central Idea – and, after all, the only thing that mattered was the Idea – might become a bore, but the World's Work, he pointed out, had been done by bores. So he laid his bones down to that work till we abandoned ourselves to the passage of time and the Mercy of Allah, Who Alone closes the Mouths of His Prophets. And we wasted more than fifty miles of summer's vivid own England upon him the while.

About two o'clock we topped Sumtner Rising and looked down on the village of Sumtner Barton, which lies just across a single railway line, spanned by a red brick bridge. The thick, thunderous June airs brought us gusts of melody from a giddy-go-round steam-organ in full blast near the pond on the village green. Drums, too, thumped and banners waved and regalia flashed at the far end of the broad village street. Mr Lingnam asked why.

'Nothing Imperial, I'm afraid. It looks like a Foresters' Fête – one of our big Mutual Benefit Societies,' I explained.

'The Idea only needs to be co-ordinated to Imperial scale –' he began.

'But it means that the pub. will be crowded,' I went on.

'What's the matter with lunching by the roadside here?' said Penfentenyou. 'We've got the lunch-basket.'

'Haven't you ever heard of Sumtner Barton ales?' I demanded, and he became the administrator at once, saying, '*I* see! Lingnam can drive us in and we'll get some, while Holford' – this was the hireling chauffeur, whose views on beer we knew not – 'lays out lunch here. That'll be better than eating at the pub. We can take in the Foresters' Fête as well, and perhaps I can buy some newspapers at the station.'

'True,' I answered. 'The railway station is just under that bridge, and we'll come back and lunch here.'

I indicated a terrace of cool clean shade beneath kindly beeches at the head of Sumtner Rise. As Holford got out the lunch-basket, a detachment of Regular troops on manoeuvres swung down the baking road.

'Ah!' said Mr Lingnam, the monthly-magazine roll in his voice. 'All Europe is an armed camp, groaning, as I remember I once wrote, under the weight of its accoutrements.'

'Oh, hop in and drive,' cried Penfentenyou. 'We want that beer!'

It made no difference. Mr Lingnam could have federated the Empire from a tight rope. He continued his oration at the wheel as we trundled.

'The danger to the Younger Nations is of being drawn into this vortex of Militarism,' he went on, dodging the rear of the soldiery.

'Slow past troops,' I hinted. 'It saves 'em dust. And we overtake on the right as a rule in England.'

'Thanks!' Mr Lingnam slued over. 'That's another detail which needs to be co-ordinated throughout the Empire. But to go back to what I was saying. My idea has always been that the component parts of the Empire should take counsel among themselves on the approach of war, so that, after we have decided on the merits of the *casus belli*, we can co-ordinate what part each Dominion shall play whenever war is, unfortunately, a possibility.'

We neared the hog-back railway bridge, and the hireling knocked piteously at the grade. Mr Lingnam changed gears, and she hoisted herself up to a joyous *Youp-i-addy-i-ay!* from the steam-organ. As we topped the arch we saw a Foresters' band with banners marching down the street.

'That's all very fine,' said the Agent-General, 'but in real life things have a knack of happening without approaching –'

(Some schools of Thought hold that Time is not; and that when we attain complete enlightenment we shall behold past, present, and future as One Awful Whole. I myself have nearly achieved this.)

*

We dipped over the bridge into the village. A boy on a bicycle, loaded with four paper bonnet-boxes, pedalled towards us, out of an alley on our right. He bowed his head the better to overcome the ascent, and naturally took his left. Mr Lingnam swerved frantically to the right. Penfentenyou shouted. The boy looked up, saw the car was like to squeeze him against the bridge wall, flung himself off his machine and across the narrow pavement into the nearest house. He slammed the door at the precise moment when the car, all brakes set, bunted [5] the abandoned bicycle, shattering three of the bonnet-boxes and jerking the fourth over the unscreened dashboard into Mr Lingnam's arms.

There was a dead stillness, then a hiss like that of escaping steam, and a man who had been running towards us ran the other way.

'Why! I think that those must be bees,' said Mr Lingnam.

They were – four full swarms – and the first living objects which he had remarked upon all day.

Some one said, 'Oh, God!' The Agent-General went out over the back of the car, crying resolutely: 'Stop the traffic! Stop the traffic, there!' Penfentenyou was already on the pavement ringing a door-bell, so I had both their rugs, which – for I am an apiarist – I threw over my head. While I was tucking my trousers into my socks – for I am an apiarist of experience – Mr Lingnam picked up the unexploded bonnet-box and with a single magnificent gesture (he told us afterwards he thought there was a river beneath) hurled it over the parapet of the bridge, ere he ran across the road toward the village green. Now, the station platform immediately below was crowded with Foresters and their friends waiting to welcome a delegation from a sister Court. I saw the box burst on the flint edging of the station garden and the contents sweep forward cone-wise like shrapnel. But the result was stimulating rather than sedative. All those well-dressed people below shouted like Sodom and Gomorrah. Then they moved as a unit into the booking-office, the waiting-rooms, and other places, shut doors and windows and declaimed aloud, while the incoming train whistled far down the line.

I pivoted round cross-legged on the back seat, like a Circassian [6] beauty beneath her veil, and saw Penfentenyou, his coat-collar over his ears, dancing before a shut door and holding up handfuls of currency to a silver-haired woman at an upper window, who only mouthed and shook her head. A little child, carrying a kitten, came smiling round a corner. Suddenly (but these things moved me no more than so many yards of three-penny cinematograph-film) the kitten leaped spitting from her arms, the child burst into tears, Penfentenyou, still dancing, snatched her up and tucked her under his coat, the woman's countenance blanched, the front door opened, Penfentenyou and the child pressed through, and I was alone in an inhospitable world where every one was shutting windows and calling children home.

A voice cried: 'You've frowtened 'em! You've frowtened 'em! Throw dust on 'em and they'll settle!'

I did not desire to throw dust on any created thing. I needed both hands for my draperies and two more for my stockings. Besides, the bees were doing me no hurt. They recognized me as a member of the County Bee-keepers' Association who had paid his annual subscription and was entitled to a free seat at all apicultural exhibitions. The quiver and the churn of the hireling car, or it might have been the lurching banners and the arrogant big drum, inclined many of them to go up street, and pay court to the advancing Foresters' band. So they went, such as had not followed Mr Lingnam in his flight toward the green, and I looked out of two goggled eyes instead of half a one at the approaching musicians, while I listened with both ears to the delayed train's second whistle down the line beneath me.

The Foresters' band no more knew what was coming than do troops under sudden fire. Indeed, there were the same extravagant gestures and contortions as attend wounds and deaths in war; the very same uncanny cessations of speech – for the trombone was cut off at midslide, even as a man drops with a syllable on his tongue. They clawed, they slapped, they fled, leaving behind them a trophy of banners and brasses crudely arranged round the big drum. Then that end of the street also shut its windows, and the village, stripped of life, lay round me like a reef at low tide. Though I am, as I have said, an apiarist in good standing, I never realized that there were so many bees in the world. When they had woven a flashing haze from one end of the deserted street to the other, there remained reserves enough to form knops and pendules on all window-sills and gutter-ends, without diminishing the multitudes in the three oozing bonnet-boxes, or drawing on the Fourth (Railway) Battalion in charge of the station below. The prisoners in the waiting-rooms and other places there cried out a great deal (I argued that they were dying of the heat), and at regular intervals the stationmaster called and called to a signalman who was not on duty, and the train whistled as it drew nearer.

Then Penfentenyou, venal and adaptable politician of the type that survives at the price of all the higher emotions, appeared at the window of the house on my right, broken and congested with mirth, the woman beside him, and the child in his arms. I saw his mouth open and shut, he hollowed his hands round it, but the churr of the motor and the bees drowned his words. He pointed dramatically across the street many times and fell back, tears running down his face. I turned like a hooded barbette in a heavy seaway (not knowing when my trousers would come out of my socks again) through one hundred and eighty degrees, and in due time bore on the village green. There was a salmon in the pond, rising short at a cloud of midges to the tune of *Yip-i-addy*; but there was none to gaff him. The swing-boats were empty, cocoanuts sat still on their red sticks before white screens, and the gay-painted horses of the giddy-go-rounds revolved riderless. All was melody, green turf, bright water, and this greedy gambolling fish. When I had identified it by its grey gills and binoculars as Lingnam, I prostrated myself before Allah in that mirth which is more truly labour than any prayer. Then I turned to the purple Penfentenyou at the window, and wiped my eyes on the rug edge.

He raised the window half one cautious inch and bellowed through the crack: 'Did you see *him*? Have they got *you*? I can see lots of things from here. It's like a three-ring circus!'

'Can you see the station?' I replied, nodding toward the right rear mudguard.

He twisted and craned sideways, but could not command that beautiful view.

'No! What's it like?' he cried.

'Hell!' I shouted. The silvery-haired woman frowned; so did Penfentenyou, and, I think, apologized to her for my language.

'You're always so extreme,' he fluted reproachfully. 'You forget that nothing matters except the Idea. Besides, they are this lady's bees.'

He closed the window, and introduced us through it in dumb show; but he contrived to give the impression that *I* was the specimen under glass.

A spurt of damp steam saved me from apoplexy. The train had lost patience at last, and was coming into the station directly beneath me to see what was the matter. Happy voices sang and heads were thrust out all along the compartments, but none answered their songs or greetings. She halted, and the people began to get out. Then they began to get in again, as their friends in the waiting-rooms advised. All did not catch the warning, so there was congestion at the doors, but those whom the bees caught got in first.

Still the bees, more bent on their own business than wanton torture, kept to the south end of the platform by the bookstall, and that was why the completely exposed engine-driver at the north end of the train did not at first understand the hermetically sealed stationmaster when the latter shouted to him many times to 'get on out o' this'.

'Where are you?' was the reply. 'And what for?'

'It don't matter where I am, an' you'll get what for in a minute if you don't shift,' said the stationmaster. 'Drop 'em at Parson's Meadow and they can walk up over the fields.'

That bare-armed, thin-shirted idiot, leaning out of the cab, took the stationmaster's orders as an insult to his dignity, and roared at the shut offices: 'You'll give me what for, will you? Look 'ere, I'm not in the 'abit of –' His outstretched hand flew to his neck . . . Do you know that if you sting an engine-driver it is the same as stinging his train? She starts with a jerk that nearly smashes the couplings, and runs, barking like a dog, till she is out of sight. Nor does she think about spilled people and parted families on the platform behind her. I had to do all that. There was a man called Fred, and his wife Harriet – a cheery, full-blooded couple – who interested me immensely before

320

they battered their way into a small detached building, already densely occupied. There was also a nameless bachelor who sat under a half-opened umbrella and twirled it dizzily, which was so new a game that I applauded aloud.

When they had thoroughly cleared the ground, the bees set about making comb for publication at the bookstall counter. Presently some bold hearts tiptoed out of the waiting-rooms over the loud gravel with the consciously modest air of men leaving church, climbed the wooden staircase to the bridge, and so reached my level, where the inexhaustible bonnet-boxes were still vomiting squadrons and platoons. There was little need to bid them descend. They had wrapped their heads in hand-kerchiefs, so that they looked like the disappointed dead scuttling back to Purgatory. Only one old gentleman, pon-tifically draped in a banner embroidered 'Temperance and Fortitude', ran the gauntlet up-street, shouting as he passed me, 'It's night or Blücher,[7] Mister.' They let him in at the White Hart, the pub. where I should have bought the beer.

After this the day sagged. I fell to reckoning how long a man in a Turkish bath, weakened by excessive laughter, could live without food, and specially drink; and how long a dis-enfranchised bee could hold out under the same conditions.

Obviously, since her one practical joke costs her her life, the bee can have but small sense of humour; but her fundamentally dismal and ungracious outlook on life impressed me beyond words. She had paralysed locomotion, wiped out trade, social intercourse, mutual trust, love, friendship, sport, music (the lonely steam-organ had run down at last), all that gives sub-stance, colour or savour to life, and yet, in the barren desert she had created, was not one whit more near to the evolution of a saner order of things. The Heavens were darkened with the swarms' divided counsels; the street shimmered with their purposeless sallies. They clotted on tiles and gutter-pipes, and began frenziedly to build a cell or two of comb ere they dis-covered that their queen was not with them; then flung off to seek her, or whirled, dishevelled and insane, into another hissing nebula on the false rumour that she was there. I scowled upon them with disfavour, and a massy, blue thunder-head rose majestically from behind the elm-trees of Sumtner Barton

Rectory, arched over and scowled with me. Then I realized that it was not bees nor locusts that had darkened the skies, but the oncoming of the malignant English thunderstorm – the one thing before which even Deborah the bee cannot express her silly little self.

'Aha! *Now* you'll catch it,' I said, as the herald gusts set the big drum rolling down the street like a box-kite. Up and up yearned the dark cloud, till the first lightning quivered and cut. Deborah cowered. Where she flew, there she fled; where she was, there she sat still; and the solid rain closed in on her as a book that is closed when the chapter is finished. By the time it had soaked to my second rug, Penfentenyou appeared at the window, wiping his false mouth on a napkin.

'Are you all right?' he inquired. 'Then *that*'s all right! Mrs Bellamy says that her bees don't sting in the wet. You'd better fetch Lingnam over. He's got to pay for them and the bicycle.'

I had no words which the silver-haired lady could listen to, but paddled across the flooded street between flashes to the pond on the green. Mr Lingnam, scarcely visible through the sheeting downpour, trotted round the edge. He bore himself nobly, and lied at the mere sight of me.

'Isn't this wet?' he cried. 'It has drenched me to the skin. I shall need a change.'

'Come along,' I said. 'I don't know what you'll get, but you deserve more.'

Penfentenyou, dry, fed, and in command, let us in. 'You,' he whispered to me, 'are to wait in the scullery. Mrs Bellamy didn't like the way you talked about her bees. Hsh! Hsh! She's a kind-hearted lady. She's a widow, Lingnam, but she's kept *his* clothes, and as soon as you've paid for the damage she'll rent you a suit. I've arranged it all!'

'Then tell him he mustn't undress in my hall,' said a voice from the stair-head.

'Tell *her* –' Lingnam began.

'Come and look at the pretty suit I've chosen,' Penfentenyou cooed, as one cajoling a maniac.

I staggered out-of-doors again, and fell into the car, whose ever-running machinery masked my yelps and hiccups. When I raised my forehead from the wheel, I saw that traffic through the village had been resumed, after, as my watch showed, one and one-half hour's suspension. There were two limousines, one landau, one doctor's car, three touring-cars, one patent steam-laundry van, three tricars, one traction-engine, some motor-cycles, one with a side-car, and one brewery lorry. It was the allegory of my own imperturbable country, delayed for a short time by unforeseen external events but now going about her business, and I blessed Her with tears in my eyes, even though I knew She looked upon me as drunk and incapable.

Then troops came over the bridge behind me – a company of dripping wet Regulars without any expression. In their rear, carrying the lunch-basket, marched the Agent-General and Holford the hired chauffeur.

'I say,' said the Agent-General, nodding at the darkened khaki backs. 'If *that*'s what we've got to depend on in event of war they're a broken reed. They ran like hares – ran like hares, I tell you.'

'And you?' I asked.

'Oh, I just sauntered back over the bridge and stopped the traffic that end. Then I had lunch. 'Pity about the beer, though. I say – these cushions are sopping wet!'

'I'm sorry,' I said. 'I haven't had time to turn 'em.'

'Nor there wasn't any need to 'ave kept the engine runnin' all this time,' said Holford sternly. 'I'll 'ave to account for the expenditure of petrol. It exceeds the mileage indicated, you see.'

'I'm sorry,' I repeated. After all, that is the way that taxpayers regard most crises.

The house-door opened and Penfentenyou and another came out into the now thinning rain.

'Ah! There you both are! Here's Lingnam,' he cried. 'He's got a little wet. He's had to change.'

We saw that. I was too sore and weak to begin another laugh, but the Agent-General crumpled up where he stood. The late Mr Bellamy must have been a man of tremendous personality, which he had impressed on every angle of his garments. I was told later that he had died in delirium tremens, which at once explained the pattern, and the reason why Mr Lingnam, writhing inside it, swore so inspiredly. Of the deliberate and diffuse Federationist there remained no trace, save the binoculars and two damp whiskers. We stood on the pavement, before Elemental Man calling on Elemental Powers to condemn and incinerate Creation.

'Well, hadn't we better be getting back?' said the Agent-General.

'Look out!' I remarked casually. 'Those bonnet-boxes are full of bees still!'

'Are they?' said the livid Mr Lingnam, and tilted them over with the late Mr Bellamy's large boots. Deborah rolled out in drenched lumps into the swilling gutter. There was a muffled shriek at the window where Mrs Bellamy gesticulated.

'It's all right. I've paid for them,' said Mr Lingnam. He dumped out the last dregs like mould from a pot-bound flower-pot.

'What? Are you going to take 'em home with you?' said the Agent-General.

'No!' He passed a wet hand over his streaky forehead. 'Wasn't there a bicycle that was the beginning of this trouble?' said he.

'It's under the fore-axle, sir,' said Holford promptly. 'I can fish it out from 'ere.'

'Not till I've done with it, please.' Before we could stop him, he had jumped into the car and taken charge. The hireling leaped into her collar, surged, shrieked (less loudly than Mrs Bellamy at the window), and swept on. That which came out behind her was, as Holford truly observed, no joy-wheel. Mr Lingnam swung round the big drum in the market-place and thundered back, shouting: 'Leave it alone. It's my meat!'

'Mince-meat, 'e means,' said Holford after this second trituration.[8] 'You couldn't say now it 'ad ever *been* one, could you?'

Mrs Bellamy opened the window and spoke. It appears she had only charged for damage to the bicycle, not for the entire machine which Mr Lingnam was ruthlessly gleaning, spoke by spoke, from the highway and cramming into the slack of the hood. At last he answered, and I have never seen a man foam at the mouth before. 'If you don't stop, I shall come into your house – in this car – and drive upstairs and – kill you!'

She stopped; he stopped. Holford took the wheel, and we got

away. It was time, for the sun shone after the storm, and Deborah beneath the tiles and the eaves already felt its reviving influence compel her to her interrupted labours of federation. We warned the village policeman at the far end of the street that he might have to suspend traffic again. The proprietor of the giddy-go-round, swings, and cocoanut-shies wanted to know from whom, in this world or another, he could recover damages. Mr Lingnam referred him most directly to Mrs Bellamy ... Then we went home.

After dinner that evening Mr Lingnam rose stiffly in his place to make a few remarks on the Federation of the Empire on the lines of Co-ordinated, Offensive Operations, backed by the Entire Effective Forces, Moral, Military and Fiscal, of Permanently Mobilized Communities, the whole brought to bear, without any respect to the merits of any *casus belli*, instantaneously, automatically, and remorselessly at the first faint buzz of war.

'The trouble with Us,' said he, 'is that We take such an infernally long time making sure that We are right that We don't go ahead when things happen. For instance, *I* ought to have gone ahead instead of pulling up when I hit that bicycle.'

'But you were in the wrong, Lingnam, when you turned to the right,' I put in.

'I don't want to hear any more of your damned, detached, mugwumping⁹ excuses for the other fellow,' he snapped.

'Now you're beginning to see things,' said Penfentenyou. 'I hope you won't backslide when the swellings go down.'

The Song of Seven Cities

I was Lord of Cities very sumptuously builded.
Seven roaring Cities paid me tribute from afar.
Ivory their outposts were – the guardrooms of them gilded,
And garrisoned with Amazons invincible in war.

All the world went softly when it walked before my Cities –
Neither King nor Army vexed my peoples at their toil.
Never horse nor chariot irked or overbore my Cities,
Never Mob nor Ruler questioned whence they drew their spoil.

Banded, mailed and arrogant from sunrise unto sunset,
Singing while they sacked it, they possessed the land at large.
Yet when men would rob them, they resisted, they made onset
And pierced the smoke of battle with a thousand-sabred charge!

So they warred and trafficked only yesterday, my Cities.
Today there is no mark or mound of where my Cities stood.
For the River rose at midnight and it washed away my Cities.
They are evened with Atlantis and the towns before the Flood.

Rain on rain-gorged channels raised the water-levels round them,
Freshet backed on freshet swelled and swept their world from
                                  sight,
Till the emboldened floods linked arms and flashing forward
                                  drowned them –
Drowned my Seven Cities and their peoples in one night!

Low among the alders lie their derelict foundations,
The beams wherein they trusted and the plinths whereon they
                                  built –
My rulers and their treasure and their unborn populations,
Dead, destroyed, aborted, and defiled with mud and silt!

The Daughters of the Palace whom they cherished in my Cities,
My silver-tongued Princesses, and the promise of their May –
Their bridegrooms of the June-tide – all have perished in my Cities,
With the harsh envenomed virgins that can neither love nor play.

I was Lord of Cities – I will build anew my Cities,
Seven, set on rocks, above the wrath of any flood.

The Vortex

Nor will I rest from search till I have filled anew my Cities
With peoples undefeated of the dark, enduring blood.

To the sound of trumpets shall their seed restore my Cities
Wealthy and well-weaponed, that once more may I behold
All the world go softly when it walks before my Cities,
And the horses and the chariots fleeing from them as of old!

'SWEPT AND GARNISHED'

{ 'Swept and Garnished' [1] }

(January 1915)

When the first waves of feverish cold stole over Frau Ebermann she very wisely telephoned for the doctor and went to bed. He diagnosed the attack as mild influenza, prescribed the appropriate remedies, and left her to the care of her one servant, in her comfortable Berlin flat. Frau Ebermann, beneath the thick coverlet, curled up with what patience she could until the aspirin should begin to act, and Anna should come back from the chemist with the formamint, the ammoniated quinine, the eucalyptus, and the little tin steam-inhaler. Meantime, every bone in her body ached; her head throbbed; her hot, dry hands would not stay the same size for a minute together; and her body, tucked into the smallest possible compass, shrank from the chill of the well-warmed sheets.

Of a sudden she noticed that an imitation-lace cover which should have lain mathematically square with the imitation-marble top of the radiator behind the green plush sofa had slipped away so that one corner hung over the bronze-painted steam pipes. She recalled that she must have rested her poor head against the radiator-top while she was taking off her boots. She tried to get up and set the thing straight, but the radiator at once receded toward the horizon, which, unlike true horizons, slanted diagonally, exactly parallel with the dropped lace edge of the cover. Frau Ebermann groaned through sticky lips and lay still.

'Certainly, I have a temperature,' she said. 'Certainly, I have a grave temperature. I should have been warned by that chill after dinner.'

She resolved to shut her hot-lidded eyes, but opened them in a little while to torture herself with the knowledge of that ungeometrical thing against the far wall. Then she saw a child — an untidy, thin-faced little girl of about ten, who must have

331

strayed in from the adjoining flat. This proved — Frau Ebermann groaned again at the way the world falls to bits when one is sick — proved that Anna had forgotten to shut the outer door of the flat when she went to the chemist. Frau Ebermann had had children of her own, but they were all grown up now, and she had never been a child-lover in any sense. Yet the intruder might be made to serve her scheme of things.

'Make — put,' she muttered thickly, 'that white thing straight on the top of that yellow thing.'

The child paid no attention, but moved about the room, investigating everything that came in her way — the yellow cut-glass handles of the chest of drawers, the stamped bronze hook to hold back the heavy puce curtains, and the mauve enamel, New Art finger-plates on the door. Frau Ebermann watched indignantly.

'Aie! That is bad and rude. Go away!' she cried, though it hurt her to raise her voice. 'Go away by the road you came!' The child passed behind the bed-foot, where she could not see her. 'Shut the door as you go. I will speak to Anna, but — first, put that white thing straight.'

She closed her eyes in misery of body and soul. The outer door clicked, and Anna entered, very penitent that she had stayed so long at the chemist's. But it had been difficult to find the proper type of inhaler, and —

'Where did the child go?' moaned Frau Ebermann — 'the child that was here?'

'There was no child,' said startled Anna. 'How should any child come in when I shut the door behind me after I go out? All the keys of the flats are different.'

'No, no! You forgot this time. But my back is aching, and up my legs also. Besides, who knows what it may have fingered and upset? Look and see.'

'Nothing is fingered, nothing is upset,' Anna replied, as she took the inhaler from its paper box.

'Yes, there is. Now I remember all about it. Put — put that white thing, with the open edge — the lace, I mean — quite straight on that —' she pointed. Anna, accustomed to her ways, understood and went to it.

'Now, is it quite straight?' Frau Ebermann demanded.

'Perfectly,' said Anna. 'In fact, in the very centre of the radiator.' Anna measured the equal margins with her knuckle, as she had been told to do when she first took service.

'And my tortoise-shell hair-brushes?' Frau Ebermann could not command her dressing-table from where she lay.

'Perfectly straight, side by side in the big tray, and the comb laid across them. Your watch also in the coralline watch-holder. Everything' – she moved round the room to make sure – 'everything is as you have it when you are well.' Frau Ebermann sighed with relief. It seemed to her that the room and her head had suddenly grown cooler.

'Good!' said she. 'Now warm my nightgown in the kitchen, so it will be ready when I have perspired. And the towels also. Make the inhaler steam, and put in the eucalyptus; that is good for the larynx. Then sit you in the kitchen, and come when I ring. But, first, my hot-water bottle.'

It was brought and scientifically tucked in.

'What news?' said Frau Ebermann drowsily. She had not been out that day.

'Another victory,'[2] said Anna. 'Many more prisoners and guns.'

Frau Ebermann purred, one might almost say grunted, contentedly.

'That is good too,' she said; and Anna, after lighting the inhaler-lamp, went out.

Frau Ebermann reflected that in an hour or so the aspirin would begin to work, and all would be well. Tomorrow – no, the day after – she would take up life with something to talk over with her friends at coffee. It was rare – everyone knew it – that she should be overcome by any ailment. Yet in all her distresses she had not allowed the minutest deviation from daily routine and ritual. She would tell her friends – she ran over their names one by one – exactly what measures she had taken against the lace cover on the radiator-top and in regard to her two tortoise-shell hair-brushes and the comb at right angles. How she had set everything in order – everything in order. She roved further afield as she wriggled her toes luxuriously on the hot-water bottle. If it pleased our dear God to take her to Himself, and she was not so young as she had been – there was that plate of the four lower ones in the blue tooth-glass, for instance – He should find all her belongings fit to meet His eye. 'Swept and garnished' were the words that shaped themselves in her intent brain. 'Swept and garnished for –'

No, it was certainly not for the dear Lord that she had swept; she would have her room swept out tomorrow or the day after, and garnished. Her hands began to swell again into huge pillows of nothingness. Then they shrank, and so did her head, to minute dots. It occurred to her that she was waiting for some event, some tremendously important event, to come to pass. She lay with shut eyes for a long time till her head and hands should return to their proper size.

She opened her eyes with a jerk.

'How stupid of me,' she said aloud, 'to set the room in order for a parcel of dirty little children!'

They were there – five of them, three little boys and two girls – headed by the anxious-eyed ten-year-old whom she had seen before. They must have entered by the outer door, which Anna had neglected to shut behind her when she returned with the inhaler. She counted them backward and forward as one counts scales – one, two, three, four, five.

They took no notice of her, but hung about, first on one foot then on the other, like strayed chickens, the smaller ones holding by the larger. They had the air of utterly wearied passengers in a railway waiting-room, and their clothes were disgracefully dirty.

'Go away!' cried Frau Ebermann at last, after she had struggled, it seemed to her, for years to shape the words.

'You called?' said Anna at the living-room door.

'No,' said her mistress. 'Did you shut the flat door when you came in?'

'Assuredly,' said Anna. 'Besides, it is made to catch shut of itself.'

'Then go away,' said she, very little above a whisper. If Anna pretended not to see the children, she would speak to Anna later on.

'And now,' she said, turning toward them as soon as the door closed. The smallest of the crowd smiled at her, and shook his head before he buried it in his sister's skirts.

'Why – don't – you – go – away?' she whispered earnestly.

Again they took no notice, but, guided by the elder girl, set themselves to climb, boots and all, on to the green plush sofa in front of the radiator. The little boys had to be pushed, as they could not compass the stretch unaided. They settled themselves in a row, with small gasps of relief, and pawed the plush approvingly.

'I ask you – I ask you why do you not go away – why do you not go away?' Frau Ebermann found herself repeating the question twenty times. It seemed to her that everything in the world hung on the answer. 'You know you should not come into houses and rooms unless you are invited. Not houses and bedrooms, you know.'

'No,' a solemn little six-year-old repeated, 'not houses nor bedrooms, nor dining-rooms, nor churches, nor all those places. Shouldn't come in. It's rude.'

'Yes, he said so,' the younger girl put in proudly. 'He said it. He told them only pigs would do that.' The line nodded and dimpled one to another with little explosive giggles, such as children use when they tell deeds of great daring against their elders.

'If you know it is wrong, that makes it much worse,' said Frau Ebermann.

'Oh yes; much worse,' they assented cheerfully, till the smallest boy changed his smile to a baby wail of weariness.

'When will they come for us?' he asked, and the girl at the head of the row hauled him bodily into her square little capable lap.

'He's tired,' she explained. 'He is only four. He only had his first breeches this spring.' They came almost under his armpits, and were held up by broad linen braces, which, his sorrow diverted for the moment, he patted proudly.

'Yes, beautiful, dear,' said both girls.

'Go away!' said Frau Ebermann. 'Go home to your father and mother!'

Their faces grew grave at once.

'H'sh! We *can't*,' whispered the eldest. 'There isn't anything left.'

'All gone,' a boy echoed, and he puffed through pursed lips. 'Like *that*, uncle told me. Both cows too.'

'And my own three ducks,' the boy on the girl's lap said sleepily.

'So, you see, we came here.' The elder girl leaned forward a little, caressing the child she rocked.

'I – I don't understand,' said Frau Ebermann. 'Are you lost, then? You must tell our police.'

'Oh no; we are only waiting.'

'But what are you waiting *for*?'

'We are waiting for our people to come for us. They told us to come here and wait for them. So we are waiting till they come,' the eldest girl replied.

'Yes. We are are waiting till our people come for us,' said all the others in chorus.

'But,' said Frau Ebermann very patiently – 'but now tell me, for I tell you that I am not in the least angry, where do you come from? Where do you come from?'

The five gave the names of two villages of which she had read in the papers.

'That is silly,' said Frau Ebermann. 'The people fired on us, and they were punished. Those places are wiped out, stamped flat.'

'Yes, yes, wiped out, stamped flat. That is why and – I have lost the ribbon off my pigtail,' said the younger girl. She looked behind her over the sofa-back.

'It is not here,' said the elder. 'It was lost before. Don't you remember?'

'Now, if you are lost, you must go and tell our police. They will take care of you and give you food,' said Frau Ebermann. 'Anna will show you the way there.'

'No,' – this was the six-year-old with the smile – 'we must wait here till our people come for us. Mustn't we, sister?'

'Of course. We wait here till our people come for us. All the world knows that,' said the eldest girl.

'Yes.' The boy in her lap had waked again. 'Little children, too – as little as Henri, and *he* doesn't wear trousers yet. As little as all that.'

'I don't understand,' said Frau Ebermann, shivering. In spite of the heat of the room and the damp breath of the steam-inhaler, the aspirin was not doing its duty.

The girl raised her blue eyes and looked at the woman for an instant.

'You see,' she said, emphasizing her statements with her fingers, '*they* told *us* to wait *here* till *our* people came for us. So we came. We wait till our people come for us.'

'That is silly again,' said Frau Ebermann. 'It is no good for you to wait here. Do you know what this place is? You have been to school? It is Berlin, the capital of Germany.'

'Yes, yes,' they all cried; 'Berlin, capital of Germany. We know that. That is why we came.'

'So, you see, it is no good,' she said triumphantly, 'because your people can never come for you here.'

'They told us to come here and wait till our people came for us.' They delivered this as if it were a lesson in school. Then they sat still, their hands orderly folded on their laps, smiling as sweetly as ever.

'Go away! Go away!' Frau Ebermann shrieked.

'You called?' said Anna, entering.

'No. Go away! Go away!'

'Very good, old cat,' said the maid under her breath. 'Next time you *may* call,' and she returned to her friend in the kitchen.

'I ask you – ask you, *please* to go away,' Frau Ebermann pleaded. 'Go to my Anna through that door, and she will give you cakes and sweeties. It is not kind of you to come into my room and behave so badly.'

'Where else shall we go now?' the elder girl demanded, turning to her little company. They fell into discussion. One preferred the broad street with trees, another the railway station; but when she suggested an Emperor's palace, they agreed with her.

'We will go then,' she said, and added half apologetically to Frau Ebermann, 'You see, they are so little they like to meet all the others.'

'What others?' said Frau Ebermann.

'The others – hundreds and hundreds and thousands and thousands of the others.'

'That is a lie. There cannot be a hundred even, much less a thousand,' cried Frau Ebermann.

'So?' said the girl politely.

'Yes. *I* tell you; and I have very good information. I know how it happened. You should have been more careful. You should not have run out to see the horses and guns passing.

That is how it is done when our troops pass through My son has written me so.'

They had clambered down from the sofa, and gathered round the bed with eager, interested eyes.

'Horses and guns going by – how fine!' some one whispered.

'Yes, yes; believe me, *that* is how the accidents to the children happen. You must know yourself that it is true. One runs out to look –'

'But I never saw any at all,' a boy cried sorrowfully. 'Only one noise I heard. That was when Aunt Emmeline's house fell down.'

'But listen to me. *I* am telling you! One runs out to look, because one is little and cannot see well. So one peeps between the man's legs, and then – you know how close those big horses and guns turn the corners – then one's foot slips and one gets run over. That's how it happens. Several times it had happened, but not many times; certainly not a hundred, perhaps not twenty. So, you see, you *must* be all. Tell me now that you are all that there are, and Anna shall give you the cakes.'

'Thousands,' a boy repeated monotonously. 'Then we all come here to wait till our people come for us.'

'But now we will go away from here. The poor lady is tired,' said the elder girl, plucking his sleeve.

'Oh, you hurt, you hurt!' he cried, and burst into tears.

'What is that for?' said Frau Ebermann. 'To cry in a room where a poor lady is sick is very inconsiderate.'

'Oh, but look, lady!' said the elder girl.

Frau Ebermann looked and saw.

'*Au revoir*, lady.' They made their little smiling bows and curtseys undisturbed by her loud cries. '*Au revoir*, lady. We will wait till our people come for us.'

When Anna at last ran in, she found her mistress on her knees, busily cleaning the floor with the lace cover from the radiator, because, she explained, it was all spotted with the blood of five children – she was perfectly certain there could not be more than five in the whole world – who had gone away for the moment, but were now waiting round the corner, and Anna was to find them and give them cakes to stop the bleeding, while her mistress swept and garnished that Our dear Lord when He came might find everything as it should be.

MARY POSTGATE

{ Mary Postgate }

(1915)

Of Miss Mary Postgate, Lady McCausland wrote that she was 'thoroughly conscientious, tidy, companionable, and ladylike. I am very sorry to part with her, and shall always be interested in her welfare.'

Miss Fowler engaged her on this recommendation, and to her surprise, for she had had experience of companions, found that it was true. Miss Fowler was nearer sixty than fifty at the time, but though she needed care she did not exhaust her attendant's vitality. On the contrary, she gave out, stimulatingly and with reminiscences. Her father had been a minor Court official in the days when the Great Exhibition of 1851 had just set its seal on Civilization made perfect. Some of Miss Fowler's tales, none the less, were not always for the young. Mary was not young, and though her speech was as colourless as her eyes or her hair, she was never shocked. She listened unflinchingly to every one; said at the end, 'How interesting!' or 'How shocking!' as the case might be, and never again referred to it, for she prided herself on a trained mind, which 'did not dwell on these things'. She was, too, a treasure at domestic accounts, for which the village tradesmen, with their weekly books, loved her not. Otherwise she had no enemies; provoked no jealousy even among the plainest; neither gossip nor slander had ever been traced to her; she supplied the odd place at the Rector's or the Doctor's table at half an hour's notice; she was a sort of public aunt to very many small children of the village street, whose parents, while accepting everything, would have been swift to resent what they called 'patronage'; she served on the Village Nursing Committee as Miss Fowler's nominee when Miss Fowler was crippled by rheumatoid arthritis, and came out of six months' fortnightly meetings equally respected by all the cliques.

341

And when Fate threw Miss Fowler's nephew, an unlovely orphan of eleven, on Miss Fowler's hands, Mary Postgate stood to her share of the business of education as practised in private and public schools. She checked printed clothes-lists, and un-itemized bills of extras; wrote to Head and House masters, matrons, nurses and doctors, and grieved or rejoiced over half-term reports. Young Wyndham Fowler repaid her in his holidays by calling her 'Gatepost', 'Postey', or 'Packthread', by thumping her between her narrow shoulders, or by chasing her bleating, round the garden, her large mouth open, her large nose high in air, at a stiff-necked shamble very like a camel's. Later on he filled the house with clamour, argument, and harangues as to his personal needs, likes and dislikes, and the limitations of 'you women', reducing Mary to tears of physical fatigue, or, when he chose to be humorous, of helpless laughter. At crises, which multiplied as he grew older, she was his ambassadress and his interpretress to Miss Fowler, who had no large sympathy with the young; a vote in his interest at the councils on his future; his sewing-woman, strictly account-able for mislaid boots and garments; always his butt and his slave.

And when he decided to become a solicitor, and had entered an office in London; when his greeting had changed from 'Hullo, Postey, you old beast,' to 'Mornin', Packthread,' there came a war which, unlike all wars that Mary could remember, did not stay decently outside England and in the newspapers, but intruded on the lives of people whom she knew. As she said to Miss Fowler, it was 'most vexatious'. It took the Rector's son who was going into business with his elder brother; it took the Colonel's nephew on the eve of fruit-farming in Canada; it took Mrs Grant's son who, his mother said, was devoted to the ministry; and, very early indeed, it took Wynn Fowler, who announced on a postcard that he had joined the Flying Corps and wanted a cardigan waistcoat.

'He must go, and he must have the waistcoat,' said Miss Fowler. So Mary got the proper-sized needles and wool, while Miss Fowler told the men of her establishment – two gardeners and an odd man, aged sixty – that those who could join the Army had better do so. The gardeners left. Cheape, the odd man, stayed on, and was promoted to the gardener's cottage. The cook, scorning to be limited in luxuries, also left, after a spirited scene with Miss Fower, and took the housemaid with her. Miss Fowler gazetted Nellie, Cheape's seventeen-year-old daughter, to the vacant post; Mrs Cheape to the rank of cook, with occasional cleaning bouts; and the reduced establishment moved forward smoothly.

Wynn demanded an increase in his allowance. Miss Fowler, who always looked facts in the face, said, 'He must have it. The chances are he won't live long to draw it, and if three hundred makes him happy –'

Wynn was grateful, and came over, in his tight-buttoned uniform, to say so. His training centre was not thirty miles away, and his talk was so technical that it had to be explained by charts of the various types of machines. He gave Mary such a chart.

'And you'd better study it, Postey,' he said. 'You'll be seeing a lot of 'em soon.' So Mary studied the chart, but when Wynn next arrived to swell and exalt himself before his womenfolk, she failed badly in cross-examination, and he rated her as in the old days.

'You *look* more or less like a human being,' he said in his new Service voice. 'You *must* have had a brain at some time in your past. What have you done with it? Where d'you keep it? A sheep would know more than you do, Postey. You're lamentable. You are less use than an empty tin can, you dowey old cassowary.' [1]

'I suppose that's how your superior officer talks to *you*?' said Miss Fowler from her chair.

'But Postey doesn't mind,' Wynn replied. 'Do you, Packthread?'

'Why? Was Wynn saying anything? I shall get this right next time you come,' she muttered, and knitted her pale brows again over the diagrams of Taubes, Farmans, and Zeppelins. [2]

In a few weeks the mere land and sea battles which she read to Miss Fowler after breakfast passed her like idle breath. Her heart and her interest were high in the air with Wynn, who had finished 'rolling' (whatever that might be) and had gone on from a 'taxi' to a machine more or less his own. One morning it circled over their very chimneys, alighted on Vegg's Heath, almost outside the garden gate, and Wynn came in, blue with cold, shouting for food. He and she drew Miss Fowler's bath-chair, as they had often done, along the Heath foot-path to look at the biplane. Mary observed that 'it smelt very badly'.

'Postey, I believe you think with your nose,' said Wynn. 'I know you don't with your mind. Now, what type's that?'

'I'll go and get the chart,' said Mary.

'You're hopeless! You haven't the mental capacity of a white mouse,' he cried, and explained the dials and the sockets for bomb-dropping till it was time to mount and ride the wet clouds once more.

'Ah!' said Mary, as the stinking thing flared upward. 'Wait till our Flying Corps gets to work! Wynn says it's much safer than in the trenches.'

'I wonder,' said Miss Fowler. 'Tell Cheape to come and tow me home again.'

'It's all downhill. I can do it,' said Mary, 'if you put the brake on.' She laid her lean self against the pushing-bar and home they trundled.

'Now, be careful you aren't heated and catch a chill,' said overdressed Miss Fowler.

'Nothing makes me perspire,' said Mary. As she bumped the chair under the porch she straightened her long back. The exertion had given her a colour, and the wind had loosened a wisp of hair across her forehead. Miss Fowler glanced at her.

'What do you ever think of, Mary?' she demanded suddenly.

'Oh, Wynn says he wants another three pairs of stockings — as thick as we can make them.'

'Yes. But I mean the things that women think about. Here you are, more than forty —'

'Forty-four,' said truthful Mary.

'Well?'

'Well?' Mary offered Miss Fowler her shoulder as usual.

'And you've been with me ten years now.'

'Let's see,' said Mary. 'Wynn was eleven when he came. He's twenty now, and I came two years before that. It must be eleven.'

'Eleven! And you've never told me anything that matters in

344

all that while. Looking back, it seems to me that *I*'ve done all the talking.'

'I'm afraid I'm not much of a conversationalist. As Wynn says, I haven't the mind. Let me take your hat.'

Miss Fowler, moving stiffly from the hip, stamped her rubber-tipped stick on the tiled hall floor. 'Mary, aren't you *anything* except a companion? Would you *ever* have been anything except a companion?'

Mary hung up the garden hat on its proper peg. 'No,' she said after consideration. 'I don't imagine I ever should. But I've no imagination, I'm afraid.'

She fetched Miss Fowler her eleven-o'clock glass of Contrexeville.[3]

That was the wet December when it rained six inches to the month, and the women went abroad as little as might be. Wynn's flying chariot visited them several times, and for two mornings (he had warned her by postcard) Mary heard the thresh of his propellers[4] at dawn. The second time she ran to the window, and stared at the whitening sky. A little blur passed overhead. She lifted her lean arms towards it.

That evening at six o'clock there came an announcement in an official envelope that Second Lieutenant W. Fowler had been killed during a trial flight. Death was instantaneous. She read it and carried it to Miss Fowler.

'I never expected anything else,' said Miss Fowler; 'but I'm sorry it happened before he had done anything.'

The room was whirling round Mary Postgate, but she found herself quite steady in the midst of it.

'Yes,' she said. 'It's a great pity he didn't die in action after he had killed somebody.'

'He was killed instantly. That's one comfort,' Miss Fowler went on.

'But Wynn says the shock of a fall kills a man at once — whatever happens to the tanks,' quoted Mary.

The room was coming to rest now. She heard Miss Fowler say impatiently, 'But why can't we cry, Mary?' and herself replying, 'There's nothing to cry for. He has done his duty as much as Mrs Grant's son did.'

'And when he died, *she* came and cried all the morning,' said

Miss Fowler. 'This only makes me feel tired – terribly tired. Will you help me to bed, please, Mary? – And I think I'd like the hot-water bottle.'

So Mary helped her and sat beside, talking of Wynn in his riotous youth.

'I believe,' said Miss Fowler suddenly, 'that old people and young people slip from under a stroke like this. The middle-aged feel it most.'

'I expect that's true,' said Mary, rising. 'I'm going to put away the things in his room now. Shall we wear mourning?'

'Certainly not,' said Miss Fowler. 'Except, of course, at the funeral. I can't go. You will. I want you to arrange about his being buried here. What a blessing it didn't happen at Salisbury!'

Every one, from the Authorities of the Flying Corps to the Rector, was most kind and sympathetic. Mary found herself for the moment in a world where bodies were in the habit of being dispatched by all sorts of conveyances to all sorts of places. And at the funeral two young men in buttoned-up uniforms stood beside the grave and spoke to her afterwards.

'You're Miss Postgate, aren't you?' said one. 'Fowler told me about you. He was a good chap – a first-class fellow – a great loss.'

'Great loss!' growled his companion. 'We're all awfully sorry.'

'How high did he fall from?' Mary whispered.

'Pretty nearly four thousand feet, I should think, didn't he? You were up that day, Monkey?'

'All of that,' the other child replied. 'My bar made three thousand, and I wasn't as high as him by a lot.'

'Then *that*'s all right,' said Mary. 'Thank you very much.'

They moved away as Mrs Grant flung herself weeping on Mary's flat chest, under the lych-gate, and cried, '*I* know how it feels! *I* know how it feels!'

'But both his parents are dead,' Mary returned, as she fended her off. 'Perhaps they've all met by now,' she added vaguely as she escaped towards the coach.

'I've thought of that too,' wailed Mrs Grant; 'but then he'll be practically a stranger to them. Quite embarrassing!'

Mary faithfully reported every detail of the ceremony to Miss Fowler, who, when she described Mrs Grant's outburst, laughed aloud.

'Oh, how Wynn would have enjoyed it! He was always utterly unreliable at funerals. D'you remember —' And they talked of him again, each piecing out the other's gaps. 'And now,' said Miss Fowler, 'we'll pull up the blinds and we'll have a general tidy. That always does us good. Have you seen to Wynn's things?'

'Everything — since he first came,' said Mary. 'He was never destructive — even with his toys.'

They faced that neat room.

'It can't be natural not to cry,' Mary said at last. 'I'm *so* afraid you'll have a reaction.'

'As I told you, we old people slip from under the stroke. It's you I'm afraid for. Have you cried yet?'

'I can't. It only makes me angry with the Germans.'

'That's sheer waste of vitality,' said Miss Fowler. 'We must live till the war's finished.' She opened a full wardrobe. 'Now, I've been thinking things over. This is my plan. All his civilian clothes can be given away — Belgian refugees, and so on.'

Mary nodded. 'Boots, collars, and gloves?'

'Yes. We don't need to keep anything except his cap and belt.'

'They came back yesterday with his Flying Corps clothes' — Mary pointed to a roll on the little iron bed.

'Ah, but keep his Service things. Someone may be glad of them later. Do you remember his sizes?'

'Five feet eight and a half; thirty-six inches round the chest. But he told me he's just put on an inch and a half. I'll mark it on a label and tie it on his sleeping-bag.'

'So that disposes of *that*,' said Miss Fowler, tapping the palm of one hand with the ringed third finger of the other. 'What waste it all is! We'll get his old school trunk tomorrow and pack his civilian clothes.'

'And the rest?' said Mary. 'His books and pictures and the games and the toys — and — and the rest?'

'My plan is to burn every single thing,' said Miss Fowler. 'Then we shall know where they are and no one can handle them afterwards. What do you think?'

'I think that would be much the best,' said Mary. 'But there's such a lot of them.'

'We'll burn them in the destructor,' said Miss Fowler.

This was an open-air furnace for the consumption of refuse; a little circular four-foot tower of pierced brick over an iron grating. Miss Fowler had noticed the design in a gardening journal years ago, and had had it built at the bottom of the garden. It suited her tidy soul, for it saved unsightly rubbish-heaps, and the ashes lightened the stiff clay soil.

Mary considered for a moment, saw her way clear, and nodded again. They spent the evening putting away well-remembered civilian suits, underclothes that Mary had marked, and the regiments of very gaudy socks and ties. A second trunk was needed, and, after that, a little packing-case, and it was late next day when Cheape and the local carrier lifted them to the cart. The Rector luckily knew of a friend's son, about five feet eight and a half inches high, to whom a complete Flying Corps outfit would be most acceptable, and sent his gardener's son down with a barrow to take delivery of it. The cap was hung up in Miss Fowler's bedroom, the belt in Miss Postgate's; for, as Miss Fowler said, they had no desire to make tea-party talk of them.

'That disposes of *that*,' said Miss Fowler. 'I'll leave the rest to you, Mary. I can't run up and down the garden. You'd better take the big clothes-basket and get Nellie to help you.'

'I shall take the wheelbarrow and do it myself,' said Mary, and for once in her life closed her mouth.

Miss Fowler, in moments of irritation, had called Mary deadly methodical. She put on her oldest waterproof and gardening-hat and her ever-slipping goloshes, for the weather was on the edge of more rain. She gathered fire-lighters from the kitchen, a half-scuttle of coals, and a faggot of brushwood. These she wheeled in the barrow down the mossed paths to the dank little laurel shrubbery where the destructor stood under the drip of three oaks. She climbed the wire fence into the Rector's glebe[5] just behind, and from his tenant's rick pulled two large armfuls of good hay, which she spread neatly on the fire-bars. Next, journey by journey, passing Miss Fowler's white face at the morning-room window each time, she brought down in the towel-covered clothes-basket, on the wheelbarrow, thumbed and used Hentys, Marryats, Levers, Stevensons, Baroness Orczys, Garvices, schoolbooks, and atlases, unrelated piles of the *Motor Cyclist*, the *Light Car*, and catalogues of Olympia Exhibitions; the remnants of a fleet of sailing-ships from nine-penny cutters to a three-guinea yacht; a prep-school dressing-gown; bats from three-and-sixpence to twenty-four shillings; cricket and tennis balls; disintegrated steam and clockwork loco-motives with their twisted rails; a grey and red tin model of a submarine; a dumb gramophone and cracked records; golf-clubs that had to be broken across the knee, like his walking-sticks, and an assegai; [6] photographs of private and public school cricket and football elevens, and his O.T.C. [7] on the line of march; kodaks, and film-rolls; some pewters, and one real silver cup, for boxing competitions and Junior Hurdles; sheaves of school photographs; Miss Fowler's photograph; her own which he had borne off in fun and (good care she took not to ask!) had never returned; a playbox with a secret drawer; a load of flannels, belts, and jerseys, and a pair of spiked shoes unearthed in the attic; a packet of all the letters that Miss Fowler and she had ever written to him, kept for some absurd reason through all these years; a five-day attempt at a diary; framed pictures of racing motors in full Brooklands [8] career, and load upon load of undistinguishable wreckage of tool-boxes, rabbit-hutches, electric batteries, tin soldiers, fret-saw outfits, and jig-saw puzzles.

Miss Fowler at the window watched her come and go, and said to herself, 'Mary's an old woman. I never realized it before.'

After lunch she recommended her to rest.

'I'm not in the least tired,' said Mary. 'I've got it all arranged. I'm going to the village at two o'clock for some paraffin. Nellie hasn't enough, and the walk will do me good.'

She made one last quest round the house before she started, and found that she had overlooked nothing. It began to mist as soon as she had skirted Vegg's Heath, where Wynn used to descend – it seemed to her that she could almost hear the beat of his propellers overhead, but there was nothing to see. She hoisted her umbrella and lunged into the blind wet till she had reached the shelter of the empty village. As she came out of Mr Kidd's shop with a bottle full of paraffin in her string shopping-bag, she met Nurse Eden, the village nurse, and fell into talk with her, as usual, about the village children. They were just parting opposite the 'Royal Oak', when a gun, they fancied, was fired immediately behind the house. It was followed by a child's shriek dying into a wail.

'Accident!' said Nurse Eden promptly, and dashed through the empty bar, followed by Mary. They found Mrs Gerritt, the publican's wife, who could only gasp and point to the yard, where a little cart-lodge was sliding sideways amid a clatter of tiles. Nurse Eden snatched up a sheet drying before the fire, ran out, lifted something from the ground, and flung the sheet round it. The sheet turned scarlet and half her uniform too, as she bore the load into the kitchen. It was little Edna Gerritt, aged nine, whom Mary had known since her perambulator days.

'Am I hurted bad?' Edna asked, and died between Nurse Eden's dripping hands. The sheet fell aside and for an instant, before she could shut her eyes, Mary saw the ripped and shredded body.

'It's a wonder she spoke at all,' said Nurse Eden. 'What in God's name was it?'

'A bomb,' said Mary.

'One o' the Zeppelins?'

'No. An aeroplane. I thought I heard it on the Heath, but I fancied it was one of ours. It must have shut off its engines as it came down. That's why we didn't notice it.'

'The filthy pigs!' said Nurse Eden, all white and shaken. 'See the pickle I'm in! Go and tell Dr Hennis, Miss Postgate.' Nurse looked at the mother, who had dropped face down on the floor. 'She's only in a fit. Turn her over.'

Mary heaved Mrs Gerritt right side up, and hurried off for the doctor. When she told her tale, he asked her to sit down in the surgery till he got her something.

'But I don't need it, I assure you,' said she. 'I don't think it would be wise to tell Miss Fowler about it, do you? Her heart is so irritable in this weather.'

Dr Hennis looked at her admiringly as he packed up his bag.

'No. Don't tell anybody till we're sure,' he said, and hastened to the 'Royal Oak', while Mary went on with the paraffin. The village behind her was as quiet as usual, for the news had not yet spread. She frowned a little to herself, her large nostrils expanded uglily, and from time to time she muttered a phrase which Wynn, who never restrained himself before his women-folk, had applied to the enemy. 'Bloody pagans! They *are* bloody pagans. But,' she continued, falling back on the teaching that had made her what she was, 'one mustn't let one's mind dwell on these things.'

Before she reached the house Dr Hennis, who was also a special constable, overtook her in his car.

'Oh, Miss Postgate,' he said, 'I wanted to tell you that that accident at the "Royal Oak" was due to Gerritt's stable tumbling down. It's been dangerous for a long time. It ought to have been condemned.'

'I thought I heard an explosion too,' said Mary.

'You might have been misled by the beams snapping. I've been looking at 'em. They were dry-rotted through and through. Of course, as they broke, they would make a noise just like a gun.'

'Yes?' said Mary politely.

'Poor little Edna was playing underneath it,' he went on, still holding her with his eyes, 'and that and the tiles cut her to pieces, you see?'

'I saw it,' said Mary, shaking her head. 'I heard it too.'

'Well, we cannot be sure.' Dr Hennis changed his tone completely. 'I know both you and Nurse Eden (I've been speaking to her) are perfectly trustworthy, and I can rely on you not to say anything – yet at least. It is no good to stir up people unless –'

'Oh, I never do – anyhow,' said Mary, and Dr Hennis went on to the county town.

After all, she told herself, it might, just possibly, have been the collapse of the old stable that had done all those things to poor little Edna. She was sorry she had even hinted at other things, but Nurse Eden was discretion itself. By the time she reached home the affair seemed increasingly remote by its very monstrosity. As she came in, Miss Fowler told her that a couple of aeroplanes had passed half an hour ago.

'I thought I heard them,' she replied, 'I'm going down to the garden now. I've got the paraffin.'

'Yes, but – what *have* you got on your boots? They're soaking wet. Change them at once.'

Not only did Mary obey but she wrapped the boots in a newspaper, and put them into the string bag with the bottle. So, armed with the longest kitchen poker, she left.

'It's raining again,' was Miss Fowler's last word, 'but – I know you won't be happy till that's disposed of.'

'It won't take long. I've got everything down there, and I've put the lid on the destructor to keep the wet out.'

The shrubbery was filling with twilight by the time she had completed her arrangements and sprinkled the sacrificial oil. As she lit the match that would burn her heart to ashes, she heard a groan or a grunt behind the dense Portugal laurels.

'Cheape?' she called impatiently, but Cheape, with his ancient lumbago, in his comfortable cottage would be the last man to profane the sanctuary. 'Sheep,' she concluded, and threw in the fusee. The pyre went up in a roar, and the immediate flame hastened night around her.

'How Wynn would have loved this!' she thought, stepping back from the blaze.

By its light she saw, half hidden behind a laurel not five paces away, a bareheaded man sitting very stiffly at the foot of one of the oaks. A broken branch lay across his lap – one booted leg protruding from beneath it. His head moved ceaselessly from side to side, but his body was as still as the tree's trunk. He was dressed – she moved sideways to look more closely – in a uniform something like Wynn's, with a flap buttoned across the chest. For an instant, she had some idea that it might be one of the young flying men she had met at the funeral. But their heads were dark and glossy. This man's was as pale as a baby's, and so closely cropped that she could see the disgusting pinky skin beneath. His lips moved.

'What do you say?' Mary moved towards him and stooped.

'Laty! [9] Laty! Laty!' he muttered, while his hands picked at the dead wet leaves. There was no doubt as to his nationality. It made her so angry that she strode back to the destructor, though it was still too hot to use the poker there. Wynn's books seemed to be catching well. She looked up at the oak behind the man; several of the light upper and two or three rotten lower branches

352

had broken and scattered their rubbish on the shrubbery path. On the lowest fork a helmet with dependent strings, showed like a bird's-nest in the light of a long-tongued flame. Evidently this person had fallen through the tree. Wynn had told her that it was quite possible for people to fall out of aeroplanes. Wynn told her too, that trees were useful things to break an aviator's fall, but in this case the aviator must have been broken or he would have moved from his queer position. He seemed helpless except for his horrible rolling head. On the other hand, she could see a pistol case at his belt – and Mary loathed pistols. Months ago, after reading certain Belgian reports together, she and Miss Fowler had had dealings with one – a huge revolver with flat-nosed bullets, which latter, Wynn said, were forbidden by the rules of war to be used against civilized enemies. 'They're good enough for us,' Miss Fowler had replied. 'Show Mary how it works.' And Wynn, laughing at the mere possibility of any such need, had led the craven winking Mary into the Rector's disused quarry, and had shown her how to fire the terrible machine. It lay now in the top-left-hand drawer of her toilet-table – a memento not included in the burning. Wynn would be pleased to see how she was not afraid.

She slipped up to the house to get it. When she came through the rain, the eyes in the head were alive with expectation. The mouth even tried to smile. But at sight of the revolver its corners went down just like Edna Gerritt's. A tear trickled from one eye, and the head rolled from shoulder to shoulder as though trying to point out something.

'Cassée. Tout cassée,'[10] it whimpered.

'What do you say?' said Mary disgustedly, keeping well to one side, though only the head moved.

'Cassée,' it repeated. 'Che me rends. Le médicin![11] Toctor!'

'Nein!' said she, bringing all her small German to bear with the big pistol. 'Ich haben der todt Kinder gesehn.'[12]

The head was still. Mary's hand dropped. She had been careful to keep her finger off the trigger for fear of accidents. After a few moments' waiting, she returned to the destructor, where the flames were falling, and churned up Wynn's charring books with the poker. Again the head groaned for the doctor.

'Stop that!' said Mary, and stamped her foot. 'Stop that, you bloody pagan!'

The words came quite smoothly and naturally. They were Wynn's own words, and Wynn was a gentleman who for no consideration on earth would have torn little Edna into those vividly coloured strips and strings. But this thing hunched under the oak-tree had done that thing. It was no question of reading horrors out of newspapers to Miss Fowler. Mary had seen it with her own eyes on the 'Royal Oak' kitchen table. She must not allow her mind to dwell upon it. Now Wynn was dead, and everything connected with him was lumping and rustling and tinkling under her busy poker into red black dust and grey leaves of ash. The thing beneath the oak would die too. Mary had seen death more than once. She came of a family that had a knack of dying under, as she told Miss Fowler, 'most distressing circumstances'. She would stay where she was till she was entirely satisfied that It was dead – dead as dear papa in the late 'eighties; aunt Mary in 'eighty-nine; mamma in 'ninety-one; cousin Dick in 'ninety-five; Lady McCausland's housemaid in 'ninety-nine; Lady McCausland's sister in nineteen hundred and one; Wynn buried five days ago; and Edna Gerritt still waiting for decent earth to hide her. As she thought – her underlip caught up by one faded canine, brows knit and nostrils wide – she wielded the poker with lunges that jarred the grating at the bottom, and careful scrapes round the brickwork above. She looked at her wrist-watch. It was getting on to half-past four, and the rain was coming down in earnest. Tea would be at five. If It did not die before that time, she would be soaked and would have to change. Meantime, and this occupied her, Wynn's things were burning well in spite of the hissing wet, though now and again a book-back with a quite distinguishable title would be heaved up out of the mass. The exercise of stoking had given her a glow which seemed to reach to the marrow of her bones. She hummed – Mary never had a voice – to herself. She had never believed in all those advanced views – though Miss Fowler herself leaned a little that way – of woman's work in the world; but now she saw there was much to be said for them. This, for instance, was *her* work – work which no man, least of all Dr Hennis, would ever have done. A man, at such a crisis, would be what Wynn called a 'sportsman'; would leave everything to fetch help, and would certainly bring It into the house. Now a woman's business was to make a happy home for – for a husband and children. Failing these – it was not a thing one should allow one's mind to dwell upon – but –

'Stop it!' Mary cried once more across the shadows. 'Nein, I tell you! Ich haben der todt Kinder gesehn.'

But it was a fact. A woman who had missed these things could still be useful – more useful than a man in certain respects. She thumped like a pavior [13] through the settling ashes at the secret thrill of it. The rain was damping the fire, but she could feel – it was too dark to see – that her work was done. There was a dull red glow at the bottom of the destructor, not enough to char the wooden lid if she slipped it half over against the driving wet. This arranged, she leaned on the poker and waited, while an increasing rapture laid hold on her. She ceased to think. She gave herself up to feel. Her long pleasure was broken by a sound that she had waited for in agony several times in her life. She leaned forward and listened, smiling. There could be no mistake. She closed her eyes and drank it in. Once it ceased abruptly.

'Go on,' she murmured, half aloud. 'That isn't the end.'

Then the end came very distinctly in a lull between two rain-gusts. Mary Postgate drew her breath short between her teeth and shivered from head to foot. '*That's* all right,' said she contentedly, and went up to the house, where she scandalized the whole routine by taking a luxurious hot bath before tea, and came down looking, as Miss Fowler said when she saw her lying all relaxed on the other sofa, 'quite handsome!'

The Beginnings

It was not part of their blood,
　　It came to them very late
With long arrears to make good,
　　When the English began to hate.

They were not easily moved,
　　They were icy willing to wait
Till every count should be proved,
　　Ere the English began to hate.

Their voices were even and low,
　　Their eyes were level and straight.
There was neither sign nor show,
　　When the English began to hate.

It was not preached to the crowd,
　　It was not taught by the State.
No man spoke it aloud,
　　When the English began to hate.

It was not suddenly bred,
　　It will not swiftly abate,
Through the chill years ahead,
　　When Time shall count from the date
　　That the English began to hate.

Notes

As Easy as A.B.C.

1. *With the Night Mail*: Kipling's *Actions and Reactions* (1909).
2. *Foggia*: A town north-east of Naples.
3. *Gothaven*: A town in northern Greenland, now known as Godthaab.
4. *Bureau Creek*: In Bureau County, Illinois.
5. *When a Woman . . . sicken*: This is probably Kipling's own couplet.
6. *bilge-doors*: The bilge is the nearly horizontal part of a ship's bottom, on the inside or out.
7. *Oh, cruel lamps . . . London Town*: Four lines from 'The Lamps of London' by George R. Sims (1847–1922).
8. *The Little Village*: A pet name for London.

Friendly Brook

1. *two rod thick*: A rod is five and a half yards.
2. *handbill*: A light bill-hook.
3. *witness-board*: A line to guide them along the hedge.
4. *cord an' a half*: A cord is usually 8 × 4 × 4 feet (so called because it is measured with a rope or cord).
5. *sowed it abed*: Stayed in bed.
6. *'Cardenly*: Accordingly.
7. *chance-born*: Illegitimate.
8. *muck-grubber*: A miser.
9. *farden in the mire*: A farden is a farthing – Jim's mother is a muck-grubber.
10. *scadderin'*: Scattering, chancy.
11. *hem*: A portmanteau dialect word – [a] hell of a damn [sight worse].
12. *a little concerned in liquor*: A nice understatement.
13. *mask*: Completely covered with mud.
14. *backwent*: Backward.
15. *naun*: Nothing.
16. *beazled*: Tired out, puzzled.

17. *in his usuals*: Drunken.
18. *chestnut-bats*: Staffs from a chestnut tree.
19. *elber*: Elbow-bend in the stream.
20. *sallies*: Small, light willows.
21. *our pieces*: Our lunch.
22. *cried dunghill an' run*: Given up and quit.
23. *poltin'*: Striking a hard, drawing blow.
24. *bee-skep*: Bee-hive.
25. *hobbed*: Reared.

The Land

1. *Hobden*: Cf. Kipling's *Puck of Pook's Hill* (1906) and *Rewards and Fairies* (1910).

In the Same Boat

1. *A fox to every Spartan*: Spartan training led boys who may have stolen and secreted a fox to prefer to be bitten in the vitals than to admit the theft (cf. Plutarch's *Lives*, 'Lycurgus').
2. *Abernethy*: John Abernethy (1764–1831), a famous London surgeon at St Bartholomew's Hospital and Professor at the Royal College of Surgeons.
3. *Post hoc, propter hoc*: 'After it, therefore due to it.'
4. *ipso facto*: 'By that very fact.'
5. *nux vomica*: Homeopathic medicine.
6. *Necropolis*: The location of the headquarters and cemetery of the Necropolis (funeral arrangement) Company.
7. *wry-neck*: A bird of genus Jynx, which writhes its neck and head.
8. *All dorn*: All gone.
9. *Methody*: Nonconformist.
10. *Toots . . . Dr Blimber*: Characters from Dickens's *Dombey and Son*. Toots is an innocent, warm-hearted young man, deeply in love. Being very nervous he never appears to advantage, but 'there are few better fellows in the world'. He is famous for saying, 'It is of no consequence.' Dr Blimber is the kind-hearted head of a school for sons of gentlemen.
11. *Sir Pandarus of Troy become*: Cf. Shakespeare's *Merry Wives of Windsor*, I.iii. Pandarus was an ally of Priam in the Trojan war. Shakespeare depicts him as procuring for Troilus the good graces of Cressida, in *Troilus and Cressida*.

12. *fettle up*: North of England dialect for getting ready, putting in order, planning out.
13. *The Cloister and the Hearth*: A novel written in 1861 by Charles Reade (1814–84), which Kipling greatly admired.
14. *pikelets*: Crumpets.
15. *Naaman and Gehazi*: Cf. II Kings V. Naaman was cured of leprosy by Elisha; Gehazi, Elisha's servant, extracted money on false pretences from Naaman, and was struck down with leprosy by Elisha.
16. *Mola or Molo*: The leper settlement at Molokai, a Hawaiian island in the mid-north Pacific Ocean.
17. *Jarrow*: In County Durham, England.
18. *Bradshaw*: The famous railway guide first published in 1839 by George Bradshaw (1801–53).
19. *eighty-five*: This makes Conroy about twenty-five years old when the story was written in 1911.

The Honours of War

1. *Clausewitz*: General Karl von Clausewitz (1780–1831); a Prussian strategist who revolutionized the theory of war.
2. *Blue Fairy Book*: Andrew Lang's collection of fairy tales, published in 1889.
3. *pendente lite*: 'While the lawsuit is pending'.
4. *ekka*: A tonga or trap.
5. *Heidsieck*: A brand of champagne.
6. *nosque mutamur in illis*: A proverb (in full, *Tempora mutantur, nos et mutamur in illis*): 'The times change and we change with them.'
7. *'Put Me Among the Girls'*: A music-hall song.

The Dog Hervey

1. *Malachi*: *vide* note 11, below.
2. *chorea – St Vitus's dance*: A convulsive disorder, characterized by irregular, involuntary contractions of the muscles, especially of the face and neck.
3. *as queer as Dick's hatband*: Dick is Richard Cromwell (1626–1712), Second Protector of England (1658–9) who succeeded his father Oliver Cromwell. The hatband is the crown, and the saying suggests that nothing could have been more absurd than the exaltation of the Protector's son.

4. *Little Bingo*: Cf. *The Ingoldsby Legends* by Rev. Richard Harris Barham (1788–1845). The Preface to *A Lay of St Gengulphus* quotes a spelling ballad whose first stanza runs:

> A Franklyn's dogge leped over a style
> And hys name was Littel Byngo.
> B with a Y – Y with an N –
> N with a G – G with an O –
> They call'd hym Littel Byngo!

5. *Jean Ingelow*: (1820–97). The eight quoted (some misquoted) lines are from her poem 'Sailing Beyond Seas'.

6. *loud pedal*: An error; there is no such pedal on the piano. Kipling means the sustaining pedal, whose effects are associated with loudness.

7. *Zvengali*: Svengali was a character in the novel *Trilby*, who had hypnotic powers which he used on the eponymous heroine. George du Maurier (1834–96) had an immense success with this novel when it was published in 1894 and the characters' names passed into common speech.

8. *'It's good for me to be here'*: Cf. St Mark's Gospel IX:5 and St Luke's Gospel IX:33.

9. *'Thou art the man'*: Cf. II Samuel XII:7.

10. *Drummond Castle*: A liner wrecked off Ushant in 1910.

11. *collar of gold*: Cf. 'Let Erin Remember' from *Irish Melodies* by Thomas Moore (1779–1852):

> Let Erin remember the days of old,
>   Ere her faithless sons betray'd her,
>   When Malachi wore the collar of gold ...

12. *Demosthenes*: Athenian orator, *c.* 383–322 BC.

13. *'If you call a dog Hervey, I shall love him'*: Samuel Johnson (1709–84) said of his friend Cornet Harry Hervey, a young rake, that he was 'a vicious man, but very kind to me. If you call a dog Hervey, I shall love him.'

The Village that Voted the Earth was Flat

1. *home address at Jerusalem*: A touch of anti-Semitism.

2. *dub*: Literally, a muddy or stagnant pool. Also, eighteenth-century slang for a jailer.

3. *Brasenose*: An Oxford college, one of whose fellows, Walter Pater, personified exquisite English.

4. *eheu ab angulo!*: 'Alas for that rustic nook!'

5. *Spec.*: The *Spectator*, a weekly review.

6. *Non nobis gloria!*: 'Not unto us the glory!'

7. *boskage*: A thicket.

8. *polled Angus*: Hornless beef-breed of cattle.

9. *King-Emperor*: Edward VII, King of England and Emperor of India.

10. *some nuts*: Around 1910 the word 'nut' colloquially came to mean a debonair young-man-about-town, who usually wore yellow chamois gloves.

11. *By the grace of God, Master Ridley*: Words (continuing, 'we have lit such a candle in England this day as shall never be put out') spoken by Hugh Latimer (*c.* 1485–1555), sometime Bishop of Worcester, to Nicholas Ridley (*c.* 1500–55), sometime Bishop of London, as they were being taken to be burnt alive in Oxford during Marian persecutions.

12. *Hone's 'Every-Day Book'*: Or 'Everlasting Calendar of Popular Amusements, Sports, Pastimes, Ceremonies, Manners, Customs and Events', issued between January 1825 and December 1827.

13. *Nellie Farren*: Ellen Farren (1848–1904) was a popular Cockney actress, famous as a comedienne and principal boy.

14. *Peter's vision at Joppa*: Cf. Acts of the Apostles X:9–16.

15. *'By God, what a genius I was yesterday!'*: In imitation of Swift's remark about *A Tale of a Tub* –'Good God, what a genius I had when I wrote that book!'

16. *'The Holy City'*: A drawing-room ballad composed by Stephen Adams, to words by Frederic E. Weatherley (1848–1929), the author of 'Danny Boy'. The refrain begins: 'Jerusalem! Jerusalem! Lift up your voice and sing!'

17. *'Ta-ra-ra-boom-de-ay'*: The title and refrain of a song by Henry J. Sayers (1858–1934).

18. *'Everybody's doing it'*: One of the first ragtime songs.

19. *key-bugles*: There are no such things – bugles are keyless and valveless.

20. *a grateful South Kensington*: The Victoria and Albert Museum is located in this part of London.

21. *'Margaritas ante Porcos'*: 'Pearls before swine': cf. St Matthew's Gospel VII:6 (in the Vulgate).

22. *'Village Hausmania'*: A reference to Baron Georges Haussmann, who, when Prefect of the Seine (1853–70) under Napoleon III, remodelled Paris.

23. *triple-dubs*: Dubs is slang for fees or salary.

24. *'Like that strange song ... rose into towers'*: From Tennyson's *Tithonus*, a dramatic monologue.

25. *Gehazi*: *Vide* 'In the Same Boat', note 15.
26. *Antaeus*: He was the son of Poseidon, in Greek mythology; whenever he touched the ground his strength was renewed.
27. *vain was the help of man*: Cf. Psalm 108.

In the Presence

1. *district*: Near Lahore.
2. *Naik*: Corporal.
3. *Sri wah guru . . . ki futteh!*: Urdu greetings used by one orthodox Sikh to another.
4. *cartouches*: Cartridges, bullets.
5. *nautches*: Indian dancing-girls.
6. *King*: Edward VII (b. 1842), reigned 1901–10.
7. *in a certain Temple*: St George's Hall, Westminster.
8. *Durbar Sahib*: The Golden Temple of the Sikhs in Amritsar.
9. *Wanidza*: Windsor.
10. *koss*: About two miles.
11. *Salt's sake*: I.e., as a professional soldier.
12. *lakhs of lakhs, crores of crores*: A lakh is 100,000, a crore one hundred lakhs.
13. *Tirah*: An area near the Khyber Pass.
14. *maund*: About eighty-two pounds (avoirdupois), but this varies in different parts of India.

Regulus

1. 'Regulus': This story was written nine years after the *Stalky & Co.* stories (1899) to which it belongs. The Latin quotes are mostly translated within – indeed as part of – the story itself.
2. *Non hoc semper . . . patiens latus*: 'This side will not always be patient of rain and waiting on the threshold.'
3. *Tu regere imperio . . . debellare superbos*: Virgil, *Aeneid*, vi line 851–3.
4. *atqui sciebat . . . barbarus tortor*: Cf. the thirteenth stanza of the Horace ode (Book 3, no. 5):

> atqui sciebat quae sibi barbarus
> tortor pararet; non aliter tamen
> dimovit obstantis propinquos
> et populum reditus morantem.

James Michie's translation:

And yet he knew what the barbarian torturer
Had ready for him. Kinsmen blocked his passage,
  The people held him back,
But he returned as unconcernedly . . .

5. *maerentes amicos*: 'Grieving friends.'
6. *'Hypatia'*: A historical novel set in fifth-century Alexandria, written in 1851 by Charles Kingsley (1819–75).
7. *bargee*: Literally, a person working on a barge.
8. *quasi-lictor*: A lictor was a Roman officer bearing fasces (ensigns of authority) and executing sentences on offenders.
9. *bloater-paste*: A bloater is a herring cured by bloating or inflation.
10. *Analects of Confucius*: Analects are literary gleanings. Confucius's *Analects* contain poetry, ethics, history, and works on ritual and divination.

The Edge of the Evening

1. *a dozen years ago*: Cf. 'The Captive' from Kipling's *Traffics and Discoveries* (1904).
2. *Cullinan diamond*: A large diamond discovered in South Africa in 1905, the mainstones of which were incorporated into the Crown Jewels in 1908.
3. *Nell Gwynne and Mrs Siddons an' Taglioni*: Nell Gwynne (or Gwyn) (*c.* 1650–87) was an orange-girl, actress and mistress to King Charles II; Mrs (Sarah) Siddons (1755–1831) was one of the greatest of tragediennes; (Marie) Taglioni (1804–84) was a famous Italian ballet-dancer.
4. *Old man Joshua*: Sir Joshua Reynolds (1723–92), an English portrait painter, and the first president of the Royal Academy.
5. *Venetian point*: Point lace from Venice: thread lace made wholly with the needle.
6. *Honey swore*: The Order of the Garter bears the motto, *Honi soit qui mal y pense.*
7. *Tria juncta*: *Tria juncta in uno* is the motto of the Order of the Bath.
8. *cunning little copper cross*: The Victoria Cross.
9. *Handley Cross*: A comic, sporting novel by Robert Smith Surtees (1805–64) which details the adventures of Mr Jorrocks, a sporting Cockney grocer, and deals with the characteristic aspects of British fox-hunting society.
10. *Beewick's Birds*: *A History of British Birds* (published 1797–1804)

was illustrated by Thomas Bewick (1753–1828), a wood-engraver famous for his vignettes of country life, as well as his close observation of the natural world.

11. *Ellis Island*: An island in Upper New York Bay, which served as the United States's major immigration station from 1892 to 1943, and as a detention centre for aliens and deportees until 1954.

12. *coon-can*: A card-game from Mexico.

13. *A Government of the alien . . . for the alien*: A reference to President Lincoln's Gettysburg Address (19 November 1863), which spoke of a 'government of the people, by the people, for the people'.

14. *An English lord called Lundie*: Cf. 'The Puzzler' from Kipling's *Actions and Reactions* (1909).

15. *Debrett*: *Debrett's Peerage, Baronetage, Knightage and Companionage*, a guide to the titled families of Great Britain and Ireland, first published in 1802.

16. *cleek*: An iron-headed golf-club with a straight, narrow face and a long shaft.

17. *rod*: A rod is five and a half yards.

18. *'The Wreckers'*: Probably *The Wrecker* (1892) by Robert Louis Stevenson and his stepson, Lloyd Osbourne.

19. *War of Jenkins' ear*: This is a reference to an incident in 1731 which precipitated a war between Great Britain and Spain in 1739. Robert Jenkins, an English merchant captain, alleged that his sloop had been boarded by the Spanish, and that he had been tortured and his ear torn off. He presented this ear to the House of Commons in 1738, thus starting the 'War of Jenkins' Ear', which eventually merged with the War of the Austrian Succession (1740–8).

20. *Mason and Slidell*: James Murray Mason and John Slidell joined the Confederacy at the outbreak of the American Civil War in 1861. They were sent to England as Commissioners of the Confederacy, but en route their ship, a British vessel, the *Trent*, was seized by a Federal man-of-war, and the two men taken prisoner. War with Britain was only averted when President Lincoln publicly acknowledged that their capture was a violation of British neutrality.

The Horse Marines

1. *Mr Pyecroft*: Mr Pyecroft appears in several other stories by Kipling, including '"Their Lawful Occasions"' and 'Steam Tactics' in *Traffics and Discoveries* (1904).

2. *ong route*: En route.
3. *permissionaire*: A soldier or sailor on furlough.
4. *cassowary-cruiser*: Derisory reference to (wooden) ship. (Cf. 'Mary Postgate', note 1.)
5. *ong garçong*: 'As a bachelor'.
6. *. . . vaisseau ong automobile, avec . . .*: 'Vessel in an automobile, with'.
7. *Mong Jews!*: Mon Dieu!, 'My God!'
8. *B.P.'s little pets*: The Boy Scouts; a reference to Robert Baden-Powell (1857–1941), the founder of the movement.
9. *if I mistake not*: Cf. '"Their Lawful Occasions"'.
10. *sampan*: A small Chinese boat.
11. *santy*: Santé. 'Your health', the French equivalent of 'Cheers!'
12. *Allez à votre bateau . . . Jamay de la vee!*: 'Go to your ship. I know my lieutenant. He'll give you what for.' 'That would make you happy! Not on your life!'
13. *conspuez l'oncle*: 'Spit upon uncles!'
14. *c'est-à-dire*: 'That is to say'.
15. *plaisanteree*: 'A joke'.
16. *juice de spree*: Jeux d'esprit, 'witticisms, witty trifles'.
17. *dhobi*: An Indian washerman.
18. *incroyable*: 'Unbelievable'.

The Legend of Mirth

1. *Zeal was their spur*: Cf. Milton's *Lycidas*, l. 70: 'Fame is the spur that the clear spirit doth raise/ (The last infirmity of noble mind)'.
2. *Prolused*: Prolusion, a preliminary essay or attempt.

My Son's Wife

1. *Liris*: Horace's 'peaceful river silently undermining its banks'.
2. *Eliphaz the Temanite . . . Naamathite*: Job's comforters, cf. Job II:11.
3. *winter cantata . . . Lincolnshire*: 'High Tide on the Coast of Lincolnshire', set to music by Eric Thinman, and published in 1900.
4. *Ne sit ancillae*: Part of the first line of the Fourth Ode in Horace's Second Book; it continues, 'tibi amor puderi': 'Let not love for thy handmaid shame thee.'
5. *But each . . . calling*: More verses from 'High Tide'.
6. *still reading*: The author in question is Robert Smith Surtees, *vide* 'The Edge of Evening', note 9.

7. *the set grey life and apathetic end*: A line from Tennyson's *Love and Duty*.

8. *horse-flesh*: A misquotation from *Handley Cross* (cf. 'The Edge of Evening', note 9). It should read: 'no man wot would not rather have a himputation on his morality than on his 'ossmanship' (chapter XVI).

9. *Injecto ter pulvere*: 'I cast in dust three times.'

10. *Galahad*: Cf. Tennyson's *Idylls of the King*. Galahad is the purest and noblest knight of the Round Table.

11. *variety*: A quotation from Surtees.

12. *Two women . . . alone*: An old English proverb.

13. *That flood . . . mourn his*: More verses from 'High Tide'.

14. *The old mayor . . . tower*: Another line from 'High Tide'.

15. *That flood . . . to sea*: More verses from 'High Tide'.

16. *And sweeter woman*: Another line from 'High Tide'.

The Floods

1. *brishings*: Brish is an obsolete form of brush: brushwood or underwood.

2. *Polting*: *Vide* 'Friendly Brook', note 23.

The Vortex

1. *A. M. Penfentenyou*: Cf. 'The Puzzler' from Kipling's *Actions and Reactions* (1909).

2. *Dominions*: Canada is referred to here.

3. *tetanic*: As in tetanus: gears with 'lockjaw'.

4. *shandrydan*: A kind of chaise with a hood, later a jocular name for a rickety, dilapidated vehicle.

5. *bunted*: Butted.

6. *Circassian*: The country north of the Caucasus, in southern Russia.

7. *It's night or Blücher*: A phrase attributed to Wellington at Waterloo: unless General Blücher's troops arrived soon, all that could save the battle for the Allies would be early darkness.

8. *trituration*: Grinding to a fine powder.

9. *mugwumping*: Sitting on the fence; American slang, first used in 1832.

'Swept and Garnished'

1. *'Swept and Garnished'*: Cf. St Luke's Gospel XI:25.
2. *Another victory*: This refers to the German invasion of Belgium in 1914.

Mary Postgate

1. *cassowary*: A large, flightless bird, related to the emu.
2. *Taubes*: Early German planes. *Farmans*: Early French planes (also used by the British Services from 1912). *Zeppelins*: German airships.
3. *Contrexeville*: French medicinal water.
4. *propellers*: This should more properly be singular.
5. *glebe*: Land included as part of a clergyman's living.
6. *assegai*: An Arab or Zulu lance or spear.
7. *OTC*: Officers' Training Corps, at a public or grammar school.
8. *Brooklands*: The first motor racing track in Britain; near Woking, Surrey.
9. *Laty*: Lady.
10. *Cassée. Tout cassée*: 'Broken. All broken.'
11. *Che me rends. Le médecin!*: 'I surrender. Doctor!'
12. *Nein . . . Ich haben . . . gesehn*: 'No . . . I have seen the dead child.'
13. *pavior*: One who lays paving stones.

READ MORE IN PENGUIN

In every corner of the world, on every subject under the sun, Penguin represents quality and variety – the very best in publishing today.

For complete information about books available from Penguin – including Puffins, Penguin Classics and Arkana – and how to order them, write to us at the appropriate address below. Please note that for copyright reasons the selection of books varies from country to country.

In the United Kingdom: Please write to *Dept. JC, Penguin Books Ltd, FREEPOST, West Drayton, Middlesex UB7 0BR*

If you have any difficulty in obtaining a title, please send your order with the correct money, plus ten per cent for postage and packaging, to *PO Box No. 11, West Drayton, Middlesex UB7 0BR*

In the United States: Please write to *Penguin USA Inc., 375 Hudson Street, New York, NY 10014*

In Canada: Please write to *Penguin Books Canada Ltd, 10 Alcorn Avenue, Suite 300, Toronto, Ontario M4V 3B2*

In Australia: Please write to *Penguin Books Australia Ltd, 487 Maroondah Highway, Ringwood, Victoria 3134*

In New Zealand: Please write to *Penguin Books (NZ) Ltd,182–190 Wairau Road, Private Bag, Takapuna, Auckland 9*

In India: Please write to *Penguin Books India Pvt Ltd, 706 Eros Apartments, 56 Nehru Place, New Delhi 110 019*

In the Netherlands: Please write to *Penguin Books Netherlands B.V., Keizersgracht 231 NL–1016 DV Amsterdam*

In Germany: Please write to *Penguin Books Deutschland GmbH, Friedrichstrasse 10–12, W–6000 Frankfurt/Main 1*

In Spain: Please write to *Penguin Books S. A., C. San Bernardo 117–6^{0} E–28015 Madrid*

In Italy: Please write to *Penguin Italia s.r.l., Via Felice Casati 20, I–20124 Milano*

In France: Please write to *Penguin France S. A., 17 rue Lejeune, F–31000 Toulouse*

In Japan: Please write to *Penguin Books Japan, Ishikiribashi Building, 2–5–4, Suido, Tokyo 112*

In Greece: Please write to *Penguin Hellas Ltd, Dimocritou 3, GR–106 71 Athens*

In South Africa: Please write to *Longman Penguin Southern Africa (Pty) Ltd, Private Bag X08, Bertsham 2013*